The Fractured

The Fractured Continent

Bryson Mine

Published by Bryson Mine, 2024.

THE FRACTURED CONTINENT

First edition. October 21, 2024.

Copyright © 2024 Bryson Mine.

ISBN: 979-8227786159

Written by Bryson Mine.

Prologue: The Warning

In the early years of the 21st century, Europe was a continent in flux. It had been less than a generation since the European Union had expanded its borders eastward, welcoming new member states and cementing itself as a beacon of political and economic unity. Borders had softened, trade flourished, and with each passing year, the continent was on a steady march toward an era of unparalleled prosperity and peace.

But beneath the surface, tensions simmered.

In the halls of government, there were whispers of unease. The global economy was teetering, populations were aging, and political fragmentation was starting to erode the foundations of liberal democracies. Extremist movements—once fringe voices relegated to the outskirts of political discourse—began to find new life, feeding off the discontent of those who felt left behind in the rush toward globalization.

The first tremors of what was to come were easy to ignore, obscured by the noise of everyday politics. Wars in the Middle East and North Africa displaced millions, sending waves of migrants across the Mediterranean toward Europe's shores. These people—desperate, hungry, and war-weary—fled conflict zones with nothing but the hope of a better life in Europe. In the beginning, they were met with compassion. In 2015, when the images of small children washed ashore on the beaches of Greece went viral, the world was outraged. Europe opened its arms, with countries like Germany, France, and Sweden accepting hundreds of thousands of refugees. Angela Merkel, the Chancellor of Germany, famously declared, *"Wir schaffen das"*—*"We can do this."*

But compassion had its limits. As the flow of migrants grew, so did the resistance. Governments, unprepared for the scale of the crisis, struggled to provide housing, jobs, and services for the newcomers. Integration proved difficult, especially as the cultural and religious differences between the Muslim-majority migrants and the Christian European populations became more pronounced. The cracks in the social fabric widened.

Far-right movements, once marginal, began to gain traction. Political leaders like Marine Le Pen in France and Viktor Orbán in Hungary seized on fears of immigration, calling for tighter borders and an end to multiculturalism. They warned of an impending cultural conflict, a "clash of civilizations," where European values and identities would be consumed by a rising tide of Muslim migrants. Their rhetoric, once dismissed as alarmist, began to resonate with a growing number of Europeans.

In town squares and public squares across Europe, there were quiet debates that masked a growing unease. Was Europe's open-door policy a mistake? Could the continent absorb so many people from war-torn, culturally distinct regions without tearing apart its social fabric?

Warnings came from many corners. Sociologists, historians, and political analysts all issued forecasts of unrest. Some warned that the inability to integrate such large numbers of refugees—mostly young men, separated from their families—could lead to parallel societies, enclaves within cities where European laws and norms would hold little sway. Others feared that the rise of far-right nationalism would bring back the ghosts of Europe's darkest times, with the potential for renewed ethnic conflict on a scale unseen since the Balkan Wars.

But the most chilling warnings came from those few who foresaw a religious war, something not seen in Europe since the 17th century. A conflict born not of politics or borders, but of deeply held beliefs. The Specter of Islam and Christianity locked in violent opposition once again was a prediction dismissed by many as fearmongering, but the signs were there for those willing to see them.

The refugee crisis was merely the spark. The fuel for the fire had been building for decades. Uneven economic growth, political disenfranchisement, and the erosion of national identities were all ingredients in a volatile mix. In countries like Germany, the UK, and France, some regions were growing more polarized—ethnic enclaves formed, often left isolated from the rest of society. Radicalization festered in the shadows, both among the immigrant communities, who felt unwelcome and disenfranchised, and among the far-right, who believed their way of life was under siege.

By 2020, the atmosphere across Europe had shifted dramatically. The economic fallout from the COVID-19 pandemic had exacerbated existing tensions, with governments struggling to cope with the demands of both their native populations and the growing migrant communities. The far-right, emboldened by a growing base of support, began to win seats in parliaments across Europe. In some countries, they were no longer fringe movements; they were legitimate contenders for power.

Yet, still, the warnings went unheeded.

The turning point came in 2025, when small-scale clashes in French suburbs, German industrial towns, and British cities evolved into something much darker. Isolated incidents of violence between far-right groups and Muslim migrants escalated into full-blown riots, and the media, always eager for sensationalism, framed these conflicts as the harbinger of a larger, inevitable clash. Each skirmish inflamed the other side, each tragedy hardening the hearts of those involved.

In hindsight, the path to war was clear. The migrant crisis had merely accelerated processes that were already in motion. Demographic shifts, economic stagnation, and political fragmentation created the perfect storm.

By the summer of 2027, the warnings had become reality.

Europe was on fire.

The prologue is not just a reflection on how it all began, but a reminder that Europe's descent into chaos was not inevitable. There were moments where things could have been different choices that could have been made to alter the course of history. But those moments had passed.

The warning signs had been there all along, and yet, the world had watched as the continent marched steadily toward its darkest hour.

And now, in the aftermath, it was too late to turn back.

Chapter 1: A Changing Europe

Berlin, Germany – 2010-2015

Malik had learned to navigate the complexities of his existence in Berlin, but by 2010, the slow, simmering tension in the city had reached a boiling point. The migrant workers he laboured alongside were no longer talking just about their homes or how much money they had managed to send back to their families. The conversation had shifted. It was now about survival in a Europe that seemed increasingly hostile. In 2010, a fire erupted in a Neukölln apartment building that housed predominantly migrant families. Though officially ruled as an accident, rumours spread that it had been arson, with the far-right having targeted the area to send a message. Malik hadn't known anyone personally from the building, but the news hit close to home. He had walked by that very block almost daily on his way to work. As the rumours swirled, Malik found himself unable to sleep, replaying the images of the charred remains on the news over and over.

It wasn't just the fear of violence that was unsettling him—it was the steady drumbeat of anti-immigrant rhetoric that seemed to fill the airwaves. Germany was in the midst of an economic downturn, and it didn't take long for some to start blaming migrants like Malik for the country's woes. Merkel's government, which had previously been seen as a model of stability in Europe, began to feel the pressure from the growing right-wing populist movements.

By 2012, the rise of the Alternative für Deutschland (AfD) party was impossible to ignore. What had once been dismissed as a fringe movement was now gaining serious political traction. Their message was clear: Germany was being "Islamized," and unless something was done, the very identity of the nation would be at risk. Malik saw the posters plastered around the city: "Germany for the Germans!" They felt like a direct attack, a call to push people like him out of the country. The mosque where Malik found solace was now filled with whispers of worry. The sermons became more urgent, pleading with the congregation to stay strong, to hold on to their faith, and not to give in to the rising tide of hate. But even within the mosque, there were divisions. Some of the younger men had become more radicalized by the violence and racism they faced. They spoke in hushed tones about standing up, about resisting. Malik wasn't sure what they meant by resistance, but he could see the anger in their eyes.

Then, in 2015, everything changed. The Syrian refugee crisis had reached its peak, and Chancellor Angela Merkel made the decision that would come to define her career: she opened Germany's borders to over a million refugees. The influx of migrants, fleeing war and persecution in Syria, Afghanistan, and beyond, further deepened the divisions in the country. Malik was torn—on the one hand, he sympathized with the refugees. They were fleeing unimaginable horrors, just like his father's generation had once done when they migrated to Europe. But on the other hand, he knew that the arrival of so many people would only make his life harder. The competition for jobs would increase, the already tense social fabric would be stretched even thinner, and the resentment toward Muslims would only grow. He wasn't wrong. The AfD surged in the polls, capitalizing on the fear that had gripped large parts of the German population. They framed the refugee crisis as a direct threat to Germany's security and identity, claiming that Merkel had betrayed the nation. By the end of 2015, Germany felt like a different place. The streets of Berlin, once vibrant and diverse, now felt hostile. Malik could see it in the way people looked at him on the train, the way they avoided eye contact, the way they muttered under their breath when he passed by.

At work, things were no better. The factory where he laboured had started laying people off, and Malik feared his turn would come soon. The German workers were the first to complain, saying that the refugees were taking their jobs, and that the government cared more about foreigners than its own citizens. Malik's manager, a stout man named Karl, had always treated Malik fairly, but even he was starting to change. The other day, Karl had pulled Malik aside and said, "I don't have anything against you, but you should be careful. People are getting angry." Malik knew what that meant. It meant that his time in Berlin might be coming to an end.

Paris, France – 2012-2015

For Yasmine, the years between 2012 and 2015 were a time of profound disillusionment. By the time she completed her degree at the Sorbonne, she had become fully immersed in the struggle for Muslim rights in France. The burqa ban had set off a chain of events that escalated tensions between Muslim communities and the French state. Yasmine had thrown herself into activism, joining marches, writing op-eds, and speaking at rallies. Yet, despite her best efforts, it felt like she was fighting an uphill battle.

The rise of terror attacks in Europe—starting with the shooting at the Charlie Hebdo offices in January 2015—changed everything. The attackers, who claimed to be acting in the name of Islam, unleashed a wave of fear and paranoia that swept across France. The Muslim community, already under scrutiny, found itself on the defensive. Yasmine, who had always argued that the actions of a few extremists did not represent Islam, now felt like her voice was being drowned out by a cacophony of fearmongering. The aftermath of Charlie Hebdo was immediate and brutal. Muslims were attacked in the streets, mosques were vandalized, and anti-Muslim hate crimes surged. The French government responded by increasing surveillance of Muslim communities, closing down mosques they deemed "radical," and passing new laws that further restricted religious expression. For Yasmine, it was a nightmare come true. Everything she had feared about France's trajectory was happening before her eyes.

She had once believed that through education and dialogue, things could change. That France's secular ideals could coexist with the religious diversity of its people. But now, she wasn't so sure. Her activism had taken a toll on her. She was exhausted, worn down by the constant need to defend her identity, her faith, her very existence in a country that seemed determined to erase her. The media was relentless, painting Muslims as either victims or villains, with no room for nuance. Yasmine no longer felt like a student of the Sorbonne; she felt like a target.

In the banlieues—the impoverished suburbs of Paris where many Muslim immigrants lived—the situation was dire. Riots had broken out in several areas, sparked by police violence and the growing sense that the state had abandoned these communities. Yasmine visited the banlieues often as part of her activism, meeting with young Muslim men and women who were grappling with the same identity crises she had once faced. But their anger was different. It was raw, more explosive. Many of the young men she spoke to no longer believed in the possibility of change through peaceful means. One night, Yasmine found herself in a heated argument with a group of young men in a café in Aubervilliers. They were furious about the way Muslims were being treated in France, and they didn't hide their contempt for the French state. "The time for talking is over," one of them said, slamming his fist on the table. "We've tried playing by their rules and look where it's gotten us. They don't want us here. They'll never see us as French. It's time we stand up for ourselves."

Yasmine recoiled at the anger in his voice. She understood his frustration—she felt it too—but she was terrified of what it might lead to. "Violence won't solve anything," she argued. "It'll only make things worse." But the young man wasn't convinced. "Worse for who?" he shot back. "For them? They're already winning. What have we got to lose?"

Yasmine left the café shaken. She had always believed in peaceful resistance, in the power of words and ideas to change minds. But she could see that belief eroding in others, and, if she was honest with herself, even within her own heart. France was at a breaking point, and she wasn't sure which way it would tip.

London, United Kingdom – 2015-2016

By 2015, Amir Farouk's world was unravelling. The butcher shop in Whitechapel, which had been the cornerstone of his family's livelihood, was on the verge of closing. The rising rents, combined with the slow erosion of the neighbourhood's immigrant community, had made it impossible for the business to survive. His father, now in his late sixties, refused to accept it. "We've been here for over 30 years," he would say. "This is our home. We can't just leave." But Amir knew the truth. Whitechapel wasn't their home anymore. The gentrification that had begun years earlier had transformed the area into something unrecognizable. The local mosque, once a hub of community life, was now surrounded by artisan bakeries and boutique yoga studios. The working-class families that had made the neighbourhood their own were being pushed out, replaced by young professionals with no ties to the area's history.

Then came Brexit.

The referendum was the culmination of years of anti-immigrant sentiment that had been building in the UK. The Leave campaign, driven by figures like Nigel Farage, had made immigration the central issue, painting a picture of a country overrun by foreigners. The result was shocking, even to those who had voted for it. By a narrow margin, the UK had decided to leave the European Union. For Amir, Brexit was a punch to the gut. He had grown up in London, born to parents who had emigrated from Egypt in the 1970s. He had always considered himself British. But in the aftermath of the referendum, it became clear that not everyone saw him that way. The day after the vote, Amir was walking through Whitechapel when a man shouted at him from across the street, "Go back to where you came from!"

It wasn't the first time Amir had heard something like that, but it was the first time in a long while. And it wasn't just the isolated incident. Across the UK, reports of hate crimes surged. Immigrants, particularly those from Muslim backgrounds, were being targeted. The veneer of tolerance that Amir had always taken for granted was crumbling. His father was devastated by the result of the referendum. "This isn't the country I came to," he said one evening, shaking his head in disbelief. "We built our lives here. We worked hard. And now they're telling us we don't belong?"

Amir didn't have any answers. He had always believed in the idea of a multicultural Britain, a place where people from all backgrounds could coexist. But Brexit had revealed a different reality—one where people like him were seen as outsiders, even after generations of living in the country.

Chapter 2: Shadows of Unrest

Berlin, Germany – 2016-2018

Malik had seen Berlin change before his eyes, but by 2016, the transformations were undeniable. The neighbourhoods that once bustled with life had started to fracture along lines of identity, religion, and nationality. Neukölln, which was once his haven, felt like it was teetering on the brink of chaos.

The far-right rallies became more frequent, their chants echoing down the streets, calling for deportations and an end to "Merkel's madness." By now, Malik had found a small community of men like him—immigrants trying to eke out a living while their sense of belonging slowly eroded. They gathered at a café owned by Tariq, a Syrian man who had arrived just before the refugee wave. Tariq's café was more than a place for food and drink; it was a sanctuary.

"I hear the AfD is gaining more seats in the Bundestag," Malik said one evening as the café buzzed with quiet conversations. Tariq grimaced, shaking his head. "The AfD, PEGIDA marches... it's like they don't even see us as human anymore. Everything is our fault—crime, unemployment. Even though most of us work harder than some of them ever will. That night, Malik couldn't shake a growing sense of dread. As Europe lurched further to the right, what hope did people like him have for the future? He thought about his children, who were still back in Syria with his wife. Would there ever be a safe place for them here?

But there were deeper, more troubling conversations happening in the shadows of their community. One night, after most of the café's customers had left, a group of young men Malik barely recognized stayed behind. They spoke in low, urgent voices. One of them, a tall man with a scar on his cheek named Karim, caught Malik's eye. "You should join us," Karim said bluntly. "The time for sitting and waiting is over. We need to stand up for ourselves."

Malik felt a cold shiver crawl down his spine. He knew what that meant. It wasn't just talk. Karim had been organizing men—angry, frustrated men—who had decided that the only way to be heard in Europe was through violence. Malik stood, shaking his head. "That's not the way. "Karim's eyes hardened. "What other way is there?"

Paris, France – 2016-2018

Yasmine had long stopped believing in France's promises of égalité and liberté. Since the attacks on Charlie Hebdo and Bataclan, it felt like the whole country had turned its back on people like her. As the far-right National Front surged in popularity, led by Marine Le Pen, the streets of Paris became battlegrounds of identity and belonging.

In 2017, Le Pen made it to the second round of the presidential election, and though she was ultimately defeated by Emmanuel Macron, the narrowness of her loss sent a chilling message. France was no longer a country where immigrants and their descendants were seen as equals.

Yasmine threw herself even deeper into her activism, now joined by a growing movement of young Muslim women who were tired of defending their right to exist. Among them was Amina, a fiery 19-year-old who had been expelled from her school for refusing to remove her hijab. Amina's story resonated deeply with Yasmine, who saw in her the same defiance she had once felt as a student. "We need to do more," Amina insisted one evening after a protest. "Writing articles and holding signs isn't going to change anything."

Yasmine was torn. She had always believed in peaceful protest, in finding common ground. But as police brutality against Muslim youths in the banlieues escalated, she wasn't so sure anymore. Amina's impatience was becoming more common, and Yasmine saw a worrying trend. The younger generation wasn't interested in dialogue—they wanted change, and fast. In the midst of all this, Yasmine was approached by a man named Driss, a charismatic organizer who had been working within the French political system to gain more representation for Muslims. Driss was sharp, articulate, and strategic. He argued that the only way to protect their community was to have a political voice.

"The next election cycle is crucial," Driss said during one of their meetings. "If we don't have our own candidates, our own policies, we'll be crushed under the weight of this growing hate. We need to be in the room where the decisions are made. Yasmine was hesitant but intrigued. Was this the solution they needed? Or was it too late for politics to heal the growing rift?

London, United Kingdom – 2016-2018

Amir's world had crumbled after Brexit. The referendum had torn through the immigrant communities of East London like a wrecking ball, sowing division and suspicion. People who had lived side by side for decades now looked at each other through a lens of distrust.

In 2017, the Conservative government, emboldened by their victory on Brexit, pushed through increasingly harsh immigration policies. It wasn't just about who could come to the UK—it was about who could stay. Amir's father, who had lived in London since the 1970s, now feared he might be deported due to a technicality. The so-called "Windrush scandal" exposed the fragility of their status in a country they had helped to build. In Whitechapel, the gentrification Amir had feared became a full-blown displacement. Many of the older Muslim families were being forced out, unable to afford the rising rents. The mosque, once a thriving center of the community, was losing its congregants.

Amir's sense of helplessness grew as the butcher shop finally closed its doors in early 2018. His father, a proud man, had taken the loss hard, retreating into silence. But Amir had no time to grieve. He had started driving for a rideshare service to make ends meet. London's streets had become an endless blur of passengers and complaints, the city a disjointed mess of anger and apathy.

One evening, after a long shift, Amir found himself at a meeting of young activists in East London. Among them was Zayn, a former university student who had dropped out after facing repeated racist abuse. Zayn spoke passionately about the need for the Muslim community to unite and push back against the wave of hate they faced. "We can't just sit around and watch as they take everything from us," Zayn said. "They want us out. They've made that clear. We need to take matters into our own hands."

Amir wasn't sure what Zayn meant, but the anger in the room was palpable. People were tired, scared, and fed up. The political environment had shifted dramatically, and there was no longer any pretence of unity in the country. But what worried Amir most was the direction this anger was heading in.

Broader Political Developments

By 2018, Europe was gripped by a wave of nationalism that spread across borders like wildfire. In Italy, Matteo Salvini's hard-right coalition had taken power, while Viktor Orbán's Hungary became the face of Europe's anti-immigrant sentiment. Each country, from Austria to Poland, seemed to be turning inward, embracing policies that sought to protect "national identity" at the expense of migrants and refugees.

The European Union itself was in crisis. Brexit was the first crack in the union's foundation, but other fractures were becoming visible. Talk of other countries leaving—Frexit, Italexit—became more than just fringe ideas. The refugee crisis had turned Europe against itself, with nations fighting over who should bear the responsibility of hosting the millions fleeing war and poverty.

In Germany, Chancellor Merkel announced in late 2018 that she would not seek re-election, a decision seen by many as a response to the growing pressure from the right-wing AfD. The political landscape in Germany shifted dramatically as Merkel's departure loomed, raising fears about what kind of leadership would follow.

France, under Macron, was embroiled in protests from all sides. The yellow vests movement—initially about economic inequality—had evolved into something more complex, with elements of anti-immigrant sentiment surfacing in its ranks. The country was a powder keg, and the 2022 elections loomed ominously.

Meanwhile, in the UK, Theresa May's government was consumed by the chaos of Brexit negotiations, with every step toward leaving the EU only exacerbating the divisions within the country. The UK was no longer the beacon of stability it once was, and for immigrants like Amir, the future looked bleaker by the day.

In the midst of these broader developments, Malik, Yasmine, and Amir continued to navigate their increasingly hostile worlds. They faced personal and political crossroads that would define not only their futures but also the future of Europe itself.

Chapter 3: Winds of Change

Berlin, Germany – 2018-2020

Malik found himself standing on the fringes of a political storm as 2018 turned into 2020. Germany was no longer the safe haven he once thought it could be, and with Merkel's political era coming to an end, the atmosphere was thick with uncertainty. The AfD continued to grow, stoking the flames of resentment toward immigrants, Muslims in particular. For Malik and the men at Tariq's café, it felt as if they were bracing for an inevitable confrontation.

"What are we going to do?" Tariq asked one evening as they watched the news coverage of yet another AfD rally in Dresden. "It's getting worse. People don't even try to hide their hate anymore. Malik had no answers. There was a time when he believed things would settle, that Germany's institutions were strong enough to push back against extremism. But now, he wasn't sure.

Then, in late 2019, riots broke out in Chemnitz after a German man was killed, allegedly by two asylum seekers. The far-right descended on the city, staging violent protests that quickly spread across the country. The police struggled to maintain control, and the chaos spilled over into Berlin, where clashes between far-right groups and counter-protesters turned violent. Malik and Tariq watched helplessly as Neukölln's streets became the battleground.

Malik wasn't sure how long they could hold out. More young men like Karim had been radicalized, drawn to a dangerous ideology that promised retribution. Malik could see the pull it had on them—many were angry, disillusioned, and felt betrayed by the country they had worked so hard to integrate into. He thought of his children, still in Syria, and wondered if he would ever see them again. Berlin was his home, but the city felt less and less like it belonged to him. Every day, the stares, the muttered insults, the suspicion weighed him down.

Amid this growing tension, a new face appeared in Malik's life. A woman named Sabine, a German activist who had been working with migrant communities, reached out to him after hearing of his struggles. Sabine was different—she didn't see migrants as a problem to be solved, but as people to be empowered. We need to mobilize politically," she told him during one of their first meetings. "The AfD can only rise because we let them. You and the others have a voice, but we need to make it heard."

Sabine introduced Malik to a network of activists, human rights lawyers, and sympathetic politicians who were working to create a counter-narrative. She pushed him to get involved, to tell his story. Reluctantly, Malik agreed to speak at a community forum. His story, about fleeing Syria, starting a life in Berlin, and trying to build a future for his children, resonated with many. It was a moment of solidarity, but it didn't erase the undercurrent of fear that gripped the city.

Paris, France – 2018-2020

In Paris, Yasmine's disillusionment had reached new depths. Macron's presidency, which she had once believed would restore France's values of unity, had done little to bridge the growing divide between the state and its Muslim population. Anti-Muslim rhetoric wasn't just limited to far-right groups anymore—it had crept into mainstream politics.

The year 2019 saw the passing of new laws that restricted religious symbols in public spaces, particularly targeting Muslim women wearing hijabs. The legislation sparked protests across the country, but the French government doubled down, citing concerns over "secularism." To Yasmine, it felt like a deliberate erasure of Muslim identity. Aren't we part of France?" she asked rhetorically during one of her speeches at a protest in Place de la République. "Or are we only French when it's convenient for them?"

The crowd cheered, but Yasmine wasn't sure it mattered. The government seemed deaf to their pleas. Among the protestors, Amina's voice had become louder, more defiant. The younger generation wasn't just angry—they were on the verge of breaking. In 2020, the murder of a Muslim schoolgirl by a right-wing extremist triggered a wave of violence in the banlieues. Riots erupted in cities across France, and the tension between Muslim communities and the French state boiled over.

Yasmine watched in horror as neighbourhoods burned, as the police cracked down with brutal force. She had spent her whole life fighting for dialogue, for mutual understanding, but now she saw that hope slipping away. Amina and others like her no longer believed in peaceful resistance—they wanted action, and they were willing to do whatever it took to defend themselves.

In the midst of this turmoil, Driss continued to push his political agenda. He had gained some traction in local elections, managing to get several Muslim representatives elected to municipal councils. But even this success came with a price—those representatives were constantly under scrutiny, their every move dissected by a hostile media.

Yasmine found herself pulled in two directions. On the one hand, she believed in Driss's vision of gaining political power. On the other, she couldn't ignore the growing radicalization of the youth, who saw no place for themselves in a system they felt was rigged against them. One night, after another exhausting day of protests, Yasmine sat down with Driss. Maybe it's time for a different approach," he said, his voice quiet but firm. "The political route isn't enough on its own. We need to organize, to build networks outside the traditional system. The youth aren't going to wait for us to fix things."

Yasmine nodded, though she wasn't sure what he meant. A new approach? What did that look like in a country that seemed determined to strip them of their identity?

London, United Kingdom – 2018-2020

By 2018, London was a city in flux. The post-Brexit fallout had left the country deeply divided, and for Amir, the cracks in his community had only grown wider. The butcher shop was gone, his father's health was failing, and Amir was barely holding things together with his rideshare work.

But Brexit wasn't just about economics—it had ignited a cultural war. The rise of Islamophobia had become more overt, with attacks on Muslim women and men becoming disturbingly common. Amir had witnessed it firsthand passengers in his car would sometimes make offhand remarks about Muslims, assuming he would agree. Other times, he'd be the target of their anger.

One evening in early 2020, Amir found himself driving a young man named Zayn, who he hadn't seen since that activist meeting years ago. Zayn had changed—he was sharper now, more focused, but there was a coldness in his eyes that Amir hadn't noticed before. You heard what happened in Paris? Zayn asked as they drove through the rain-soaked streets of East London. Yeah. It's all over the news. Zayn shook his head. "It's not just Paris. It's going to happen here too. It's just a matter of time." Amir glanced at him, concerned. "What are you talking about?"

"The riots, the attacks—it's going to spread. People like us—we're not safe. And if we don't do something, we're going to end up like those kids in Paris."

Amir felt a knot tighten in his stomach. Zayn was talking about violence, about retaliation. It was the same rhetoric he'd heard from Karim back in Berlin, the same anger that had been simmering in the cafés and mosques across Europe. We need to be smart about this, Amir said carefully. "Violence isn't going to help."

Zayn's eyes flicked to Amir, dark and unreadable. "Maybe not. But what other choice do we have?"

As they drove in silence, Amir couldn't shake the feeling that London was teetering on the edge. The city was a pressure cooker, and it wouldn't take much to set it off. But what worried him more was the realization that people like Zayn weren't waiting for permission to act.

Broader Political Developments

Across Europe, the winds of change had turned into a storm. In 2020, the political landscape had become almost unrecognizable. Nationalist parties had taken power in Italy, Hungary, Poland, and Austria, each pushing a vision of Europe that excluded immigrants and refugees. The European Union itself was fracturing under the weight of these pressures. While Brussels tried to maintain a semblance of unity, the truth was that Europe was divided. Countries like Germany and France, once the pillars of the EU, were struggling to manage their own internal crises.

In France, the 2022 elections loomed large. Marine Le Pen, buoyed by the growing unrest and disillusionment, announced her candidacy once more. This time, her chances of victory seemed more likely than ever. In the UK, Boris Johnson's government faced increasing pressure to deliver on the promises of Brexit, all while dealing with rising tensions over immigration and security.

The refugee crisis had never truly ended, and the Mediterranean continued to be a deathtrap for those fleeing conflict in the Middle East and Africa. Italy, Greece, and Spain were overwhelmed by the constant arrival of boats filled with desperate people, and the EU's asylum system had all but collapsed. As the 2020s began, it was clear that Europe was on the verge of something unprecedented. Malik, Yasmine, and Amir, along with millions of others, stood at the intersection of personal survival and political upheaval. The fight between identity and survival was no longer just a battle of ideologies—it had become a fight for the future of Europe itself.

Chapter 4: The Fault Lines Deepen

Berlin, Germany – 2020-2022

By the beginning of 2020, Berlin's simmering tensions had begun to boil over. For Malik, the reality of living as a migrant in Germany had shifted dramatically. The AfD, now a significant political force, wasn't just a fringe group anymore—they held power in several regional governments. Anti-immigrant sentiment wasn't confined to angry mobs; it was policy. The rise of nationalists across Europe empowered their base, and Malik could feel the consequences in everyday life.

One cold January morning, Malik sat with Sabine in a café near Alexanderplatz, their conversation hushed as they discussed the upcoming elections in Berlin. The stakes couldn't have been higher. With Merkel stepping down, the question of who would lead Germany next loomed large. The leading candidates were either bending to nationalist pressures or outright embracing them. We need to do more than just resist," Sabine said, her voice determined. "We need to mobilize, to push back in ways they won't expect. Malik nodded, though doubt tugged at him. Mobilizing sounded like a solution, but the constant weight of survival had drained him. His thoughts drifted back to his family, still stuck in Syria, living in limbo. They had applied for reunification under Germany's laws, but the process was slow, and the rhetoric around migrants was making it harder for cases like his to get approved.

He had attended meetings organized by Sabine's network, where they discussed ways to counteract the far-right's influence. But the meetings often felt like echo chambers—people preaching to the converted, while outside, Germany was moving in the opposite direction. Karim had reappeared, too, increasingly vocal in the immigrant community. The group of young men around him had grown, and their rhetoric had shifted to something more dangerous. Malik was aware of the anger, the frustration that came from feeling marginalized, but Karim's approach felt wrong. There were rumours of connections to groups outside Germany—radicalized cells from Belgium and France—who were encouraging more violent methods to "defend" Muslim communities.

One night in early 2021, Malik found Karim waiting for him outside the café. We can't wait any longer, Karim said, his eyes gleaming with urgency. "Look around, Malik. It's not just words anymore. They're attacking us. This country will never accept us unless we force them to." Malik clenched his fists, torn between rage and fear. He had seen too much violence in Syria. He didn't want that here. But Karim's words echoed the sentiments Malik heard in every corner of Neukölln. More and more, people were asking themselves if it was time to fight back.

That year, Germany saw its most contentious election in decades. The AfD gained even more ground, fuelled by a narrative of protecting German culture from the "Islamization" of Europe. Malik could only watch as the country he had worked so hard to integrate into began to view people like him as a threat.

Paris, France – 2020-2022

Yasmine's fight had changed since the riots of 2020. In the aftermath, Paris was a city under siege—by both its government and its people. The French state, terrified of more violence, passed new legislation that expanded police powers, targeted Muslim organizations, and cracked down on so-called "separatism." For Yasmine, this was more than just a political battle—it was personal. She had spent years advocating for Muslim rights, only to see the very fabric of her identity being criminalized. The new laws made it harder for Muslim charities to operate, and many mosques were closed under the pretence of preventing radicalization.

The streets of Paris were no longer safe for young Muslim women like her. Racist attacks increased, and even wearing the hijab had become a political act. Amina had stopped going to university altogether after being harassed one too many times. Yasmine feared for the younger generation—they were growing up in a country that had rejected them entirely. Driss continued to gain political influence, and by 2021, he had helped form a coalition of Muslim politicians across France. But the victories were bittersweet. For every representative they managed to elect, there was a barrage of media scrutiny, accusations of extremism, and violent threats.

One night, as Yasmine returned home from a rally, she found Amina waiting for her. The girl was shaking with anger. "They shut down our mosque," Amina spat, her eyes blazing. "It wasn't even connected to anything radical. They just don't want us to gather." Yasmine's heart sank. She had heard of this happening in other cities—mosques closed; charities raided. The government was treating every expression of Muslim identity as a potential threat. "We need to be smart about this," Yasmine said, trying to keep calm. "We need to build our own networks, our own institutions. We can't give them an excuse to keep doing this."

But Amina wasn't interested in diplomacy anymore. "You still think there's a peaceful solution? How many more of our spaces need to be destroyed before you see what's happening?" Yasmine didn't have an answer. The truth was, she wasn't sure anymore. Paris felt like a powder keg, ready to explode at any moment. And as the 2022 elections approached, Marine Le Pen's popularity soared once more, riding on a wave of fear and resentment. Yasmine knew that if Le Pen won, everything they had fought for would be wiped away.

London, United Kingdom – 2020-2022

For Amir, life in post-Brexit Britain had become a slow erosion of the world he once knew. The economic uncertainty of Brexit had given rise to nationalism and xenophobia, especially in cities like London. The immigrants who had long been the backbone of the city were now seen as expendable.

In East London, the tension was palpable. The Muslim community felt increasingly isolated, targeted by both the government's anti-terrorism measures and the growing hostility of white nationalist groups emboldened by Brexit. Amir's father's health had declined, and the stress of potential deportation weighed heavily on the family. The Windrush scandal, which had affected thousands of people of Caribbean descent, made Amir realize how easily the British government could turn on its citizens of colour. He feared his father would be next. One evening, after a gruelling shift, Amir joined a meeting at the local community center. The topic was clear: how to protect themselves from the increasing threats. Zayn was there, now a prominent voice in the room. But what Amir heard disturbed him. "We can't rely on the government to protect us," Zayn argued. "They're the ones attacking us. We need to build our own defence."

Some of the younger men nodded in agreement. They were tired of waiting for change. They had seen too many hate crimes, too many raids, and too little action from the authorities. Zayn's message was gaining traction.

After the meeting, Amir pulled Zayn aside. "What are you really planning, Zayn?" Zayn gave him a hard look. "You know what I'm planning. We can't just keep taking this. They're pushing us into a corner." Amir's stomach churned. He had seen this before, in other parts of the world. Once people felt they had nothing left to lose, they became dangerous. As 2022 approached, the UK faced a crossroads. The government, now led by increasingly hardline Tories, had passed draconian immigration laws, making it nearly impossible for families like Amir's to bring over relatives or even stay in the country without constant fear of being deported. The far-right, led by figures like Tommy Robinson, was emboldened, staging massive protests that often turned violent. Amir had watched as the Muslim Community in East London became more insular, more afraid. Mosques were frequently targeted, and the media seemed to amplify every negative story about Muslims. But even more frightening were the whispers—of radicalized youth, of weapons being stockpiled, of plans to strike back.

Broader Political Developments

By the early 2020s, the political landscape of Europe was in turmoil. In Germany, the AfD made its biggest gains yet in the 2021 elections, becoming the second-largest party in the Bundestag. The once unimaginable prospect of a far-right government was now very real, as coalitions began to shift and collapse under the weight of extremism.

France, too, was on the brink. The 2022 elections were a battle for the soul of the country. Marine Le Pen's rhetoric had grown even more divisive, capitalizing on the fear of Muslim communities and promising to protect France from the "foreign threat." Polls showed her neck and neck with Macron, and many feared that if she won, France's already fragile social fabric would tear apart.

In the UK, Brexit had not brought the prosperity that its proponents had promised. Instead, the economy faltered, and the divisions within society deepened. Anti-immigrant sentiment, already rampant during the Brexit campaign, exploded into open hostility. Far-right groups like Britain First and the English Defence League gained followers, and attacks on immigrant communities became more frequent.

The EU itself was at risk of collapse. Hungary and Poland openly defied Brussels' attempts to impose sanctions for their authoritarian moves, and Italy's populist government threatened to follow the UK's example and leave the union. The refugee crisis continued unabated, with thousands of people arriving on Europe's shores every week. The Mediterranean had become a graveyard, and Europe's leaders seemed paralyzed, unable to agree on a coherent response. As 2022 drew near, the winds of change had become a hurricane, sweeping across Europe with a force that threatened to unravel decades of progress. Malik, Yasmine, and Amir found themselves at the heart of this storm, their personal struggles now intertwined with the fate of entire nations.

Chapter 5: Crossroads of Despair and Defiance

Berlin, Germany – 2022-2023

By 2022, Berlin felt like a city standing on the edge of a precipice. The political landscape in Germany had grown darker since the 2021 elections, and the country seemed to be split into two opposing camps. On one side were those who still believed in a multicultural Germany, a nation built on the ideals of tolerance and integration. On the other side were the growing numbers of people who saw immigrants as invaders, a threat to their way of life.

Malik had become more involved with Sabine's activism network, even though he was deeply conflicted about his place in the movement. They organized protests, staged sit-ins, and lobbied politicians to protect the rights of immigrants and refugees. Yet every time they seemed to gain a small victory, the far-right would rally with even more energy, more numbers. The country felt like it was careening toward something Malik had witnessed before: civil strife.

In the Neukölln neighbourhood, the disillusionment among migrants grew palpable. The promises of a better life, of safety and opportunity, had become hollow in the face of increasing police raids, racial profiling, and violent confrontations with nationalist groups. Malik's evenings at Tariq's café were filled with discussions of despair—of the friends who had been deported, of the families still stuck in refugee camps, of the ever-present fear that their futures were hanging by a thread.

Karim had continued his path toward radicalization, and Malik watched helplessly as more young men began to drift into his orbit. The shift was subtle at first—angry conversations, late-night meetings, the presence of strangers who spoke in hushed tones about "preparing" for what was to come. Karim no longer tried to hide his disdain for Malik's cautious approach. "You're wasting your time with those protests," Karim spat one evening, his eyes filled with barely concealed rage. "The Germans don't care about dialogue. They don't want us here. And we'll never belong."

Malik's stomach turned. He had heard this argument before—from men who had once taken up arms in Syria, believing that violence was the only language their oppressors would understand. He had seen the destruction that mentality wrought, and it terrified him to see the same seeds being planted here, in the heart of Europe. "I've seen where this leads," Malik said quietly. "You don't want that. Trust me." Karim's face hardened. "Maybe it's different here. Maybe it's what we need."

Malik couldn't find the words to argue anymore. The anger Karim felt wasn't unique. Across Berlin, across Germany, more young men were being drawn into extremist circles, convinced that the only way to fight back against their exclusion was through violence. Malik had seen it before—too many times. As 2023 began, Berlin's streets saw more frequent clashes between far-right groups and left-wing activists. The city's vibrant immigrant neighbourhoods became targets for violent nationalist attacks, and the police seemed either unable or unwilling to protect them. Malik no longer felt safe walking the streets at night. Sabine warned him to be careful, but even she seemed unsure of how much longer they could hold out.

The turning point came in the spring of 2023. A massive far-right march through Berlin turned violent, with rioters attacking migrant-owned businesses and mosques. Malik's worst fears were realized when Tariq's café was firebombed in the chaos. It was a place that had become a refuge, a small island of peace in an increasingly hostile city. Watching it burn, Malik felt something inside him crack. In the aftermath, Malik knew that his time in Berlin was running out. The city was no longer a place where he could build a future. The dream of reuniting with his family here felt distant, almost absurd. Germany had changed, and Malik had to face the truth: he might never belong in this new, hardened version of the country.

Paris, France – 2022-2023

For Yasmine, the 2022 French presidential election was a devastating blow. When Marine Le Pen won the election, France's Muslim community braced for the worst. The new president wasted no time in implementing her agenda, cracking down on what she called the "Islamist threat" and tightening restrictions on religious freedoms. Yasmine had fought for years to defend the rights of Muslims in France, but now it felt as though all her efforts had been for nothing.

Le Pen's government enacted sweeping laws that made it nearly impossible for Muslim charities and organizations to operate. Mosques were shut down on the flimsiest pretexts, and Muslim women faced even more harassment in public spaces. The sense of fear and isolation that had been growing in France's banlieues reached a fever pitch.

Yasmine's activist work became more dangerous as the government ramped up surveillance on Muslim leaders and organizations. Driss, who had risen to a position of prominence within the Muslim political coalition, found himself constantly under threat—both from the state and from far-right extremists who saw Muslim politicians as traitors to the French nation. "We have to be careful," Driss warned Yasmine during one of their late-night strategy meetings. "They're looking for any excuse to take us down. We have to be smarter than them." Yasmine nodded, but the stress was taking its toll. She had lost count of the number of death threats she received each week, and the police offered no protection. They, too, were increasingly hostile toward the Muslim community, emboldened by Le Pen's rhetoric.

The 2023 summer protests erupted across France, fuelled by a combination of economic despair and the growing alienation of minority communities. In Paris, the protests turned into violent clashes between the police and demonstrators. The banlieues, long neglected by the government, became the epicentre of the unrest. Yasmine found herself in the middle of it, trying to coordinate relief efforts and keep the protests peaceful, but the anger in the air was too thick, too overwhelming.

Amina, once so passionate about peaceful resistance, had taken a different path. She had joined a more radical group, one that believed peaceful protests had achieved nothing and that it was time for direct action. When Yasmine confronted her about it, the young woman's frustration boiled over. "We've been trying it your way for years, Yasmine!" Amina shouted, her voice cracking with emotion. "And what has it gotten us? More oppression, more surveillance, more violence! It's time to fight back!" Yasmine had no words. The fear that had been gnawing at her for years now felt like a tidal wave threatening to sweep her under. France had changed irrevocably, and she was no longer sure how to navigate this new, hostile landscape. The streets of Paris were ablaze, and Yasmine couldn't shake the feeling that they were on the brink of something far worse.

London, United Kingdom – 2022-2023

Amir's world had continued to shrink in post-Brexit Britain. The economic promises of Brexit had evaporated, leaving a country divided and increasingly hostile to immigrants. For Muslims in East London, life had become a balancing act—avoiding the attention of both the government and the far-right groups that had become emboldened by the toxic political climate.

The rise of a new political figure—Nathan Hawke, a charismatic right-wing populist—had thrown fuel on the fire. Hawke positioned himself as the voice of "real Britain," calling for a total shutdown of immigration and the deportation of "undesirables." His rallies attracted thousands, and his message resonated with those who felt betrayed by the economic stagnation and social decay that had followed Brexit. Amir had watched Hawke's rise with a growing sense of dread. Zayn, too, had become increasingly vocal, warning that Hawke was just the beginning. "This is what we've been telling you, Amir," Zayn said one evening after a particularly heated meeting at the community center. "They want us gone. And they're not going to stop until we're either out of the country or dead."

Amir didn't want to believe it, but it was becoming harder to ignore. The attacks on mosques had escalated, with arson and physical assaults becoming common. Zayn's group had started stockpiling weapons, convinced that they would need to defend themselves when the inevitable crackdown came. Amir had tried to distance himself from it, but the lines between survival and radicalization were blurring.

By the summer of 2023, London was a city on the edge. The tension between immigrant communities and the far-right exploded into open violence. A mosque in East London was firebombed, killing several worshippers and sparking riots across the city. The government responded with draconian measures, imposing curfews and increasing police patrols in immigrant neighbourhoods. But instead of quelling the unrest, it only fanned the flames. Amir found himself torn between loyalty to his community and fear of what was coming. His father's health had deteriorated rapidly, and Amir felt trapped, unable to leave the city, unable to protect his family. Zayn's group had become more brazen, talking openly about striking back, about taking the fight to the enemy. Amir knew that if things continued down this path, there would be no turning back.

Broader Political Developments

By 2023, the political situation across Europe had reached a critical juncture. In Germany, the AfD had become the largest opposition party, its influence growing with every election. The far-right's anti-immigrant message resonated with a population increasingly disillusioned with the EU and fearful of the growing Muslim population. The political establishment in Germany was crumbling under the pressure, unable to contain the rising tide of nationalism.

In France, Marine Le Pen's government tightened its grip on power. The country's secular identity was now being weaponized against its Muslim citizens, and the cracks in France's social fabric were becoming unbridgeable. The banlieues, long neglected and marginalized, were seething with anger, and many feared that a full-scale uprising was on the horizon.

The United Kingdom, meanwhile, had retreated further into its nationalist shell. The economic fallout from Brexit had deepened the divide between the country's rich and poor, and immigrants bore the brunt of the anger. Nathan Hawke's rise to prominence signalled a new, darker chapter in British politics, one that sought to undo decades of progress toward multiculturalism.

The European Union itself was on the verge of collapse. Eastern European countries openly defied Brussels, while southern Europe struggled to cope with the never-ending waves of refugees crossing the Mediterranean. As 2023 came to a close, it seemed that Europe was no longer a place of stability and unity, but a continent teetering on the edge of civil conflict. For Malik, Yasmine, and Amir, the world they had fought so hard to survive in was becoming unrecognizable. Their fates were now tied to the broader political currents sweeping through Europe—currents that threatened to drown them all.

Chapter 6: Unravelling Nations

Berlin, Germany – 2023-2024

Malik's life had become a quiet exercise in survival. Berlin, once a city of opportunity, now felt like a fortress closing in around him. The firebombing of Tariq's café had shaken him deeply. It was a brutal reminder that even in the heart of Germany, in one of the world's most progressive cities, the hate he had fled in Syria was taking root. But here, it wasn't just civil war—it was something more insidious, creeping through everyday life, turning neighbours against each other. After the café attack, Malik kept a low profile, attending fewer protests and avoiding public debates. Sabine's network was shrinking, too, as the nationalist rhetoric grew louder and more dangerous. The far-right AfD party's rise to prominence had emboldened extremists across the country, and it seemed the police were either unwilling or unable to contain the violence.

In Neukölln, the atmosphere had become tense. The once-vibrant immigrant community was now on high alert, fearing the next attack. More mosques had been vandalized, and Malik had heard of young men being harassed on the streets simply for looking "foreign." Karim's rhetoric had grown even more dangerous, and now, Malik saw a much younger version of himself in the faces of those who gathered around Karim. Lost, desperate, and angry.

"Malik, we can't wait anymore," Karim said one evening, his voice tinged with frustration. "They're coming for us. You know it, I know it. And you're still standing on the sidelines, hoping this will go away. It won't."

Malik looked at him, feeling the weight of the choices ahead. He didn't want violence, didn't want the streets of Berlin to become like the warzones of Aleppo. But as much as he wanted to resist Karim's logic, the reality of Germany's descent into chaos was becoming harder to ignore. News reports showed escalating riots in other cities—Leipzig, Hamburg, Munich—where immigrant communities clashed with far-right groups in running battles. The government response was increasingly militarized, fuelling the sense that the country was on a dangerous, irreversible path.

One night, Malik sat in his small apartment, staring at his phone. His family was still in Syria, waiting for his help. But he had no idea when—or if—they would ever be allowed to join him. Germany's reunification policies had become stricter, with endless bureaucratic hurdles and growing political pressure to limit Muslim migration. Malik had applied for his family's visas months ago, but with the current government, he knew their chances were dwindling. As he thought about his parents and siblings, stuck in a liminal space between war and refuge, Malik's despair deepened. The promises of Europe as a safe haven had faded, replaced by a harsher reality. The dream of reunification, of building a new life, seemed like a distant memory.

In early 2024, Berlin erupted once again, this time in the aftermath of a far-right rally that turned violent. The streets of the city center were filled with smoke and broken glass, and the news was flooded with images of burning cars and injured protesters. Malik watched the footage on his phone, feeling numb. Each event like this pushed him closer to an impossible decision—stay and try to fight for his place in Germany or leave and hope to find safety elsewhere.

Paris, France – 2023-2024

Yasmine had always been a fighter, but by 2023, even she was beginning to lose hope. The election of Marine Le Pen had opened a Pandora's box of racist, xenophobic, and anti-Muslim policies that were tearing France apart. Yasmine and her fellow activists had spent years pushing back, but the government's authoritarian grip was tightening. Le Pen's administration passed a series of laws aimed squarely at France's Muslim population. The laws banned the wearing of religious symbols in public spaces and made it nearly impossible for Muslim schools, charities, and mosques to function. The banlieues, already isolated and marginalized, were under siege. Police raids became a common occurrence, with officers targeting Muslim families under the guise of preventing terrorism.

Yasmine continued to organize, but each new protest seemed to achieve less than the last. The streets of Paris had become battlegrounds, with riot police cracking down on demonstrators, and far-right mobs targeting Muslim neighbourhoods. The city was divided, and Yasmine could feel the weight of the division in every interaction she had. People were choosing sides—either they were with the government or against it. There was no middle ground anymore.

Amina, once Yasmine's protégé, had become a full-fledged radical. The young woman's frustration had boiled over after years of police harassment, and she had joined a clandestine network that believed in direct action against the government. Yasmine had tried to talk her out of it, but Amina's mind was made up. "They're never going to let us live in peace," Amina said one evening, her voice cold. "We have to take what's ours, by force if necessary."

Yasmine shook her head. "That's exactly what they want, Amina. If we resort to violence, we'll prove them right. We'll give them the justification they need to wipe us out."

But Amina wasn't listening anymore. She had hardened in ways Yasmine feared, and she wasn't alone. Across the country, Muslim youth were losing faith in peaceful resistance. The government's oppressive policies had radicalized an entire generation, and now the fear of jihadist cells rising in France was becoming a self-fulfilling prophecy.

The summer of 2023 saw a wave of bombings across Paris and other major cities. No one claimed responsibility, but the government blamed Islamist extremists, using the attacks as justification for even harsher crackdowns. Yasmine feared for the future of her country—France was no longer a place of liberté, égalité, fraternité. It was a place of division, fear, and violence.

By early 2024, Yasmine's organization was barely functioning. Driss had gone underground, fearing arrest, and many of Yasmine's colleagues had fled the country. The weight of the struggle was crushing her. But she couldn't bring herself to leave Paris, even as the city became more dangerous. She still believed that France could be saved, even if that belief was hanging by a thread.

London, United Kingdom – 2023-2024

London had always been a city of immigrants, a place where people from all over the world could find a home. But by 2023, that image was crumbling. Post-Brexit Britain was unravelling, with the economic fallout from leaving the EU creating deep resentment and anger. Immigrants, especially Muslims, had become the scapegoats for everything wrong with the country.

Amir had watched as the political climate in Britain grew more toxic. Nathan Hawke, now a major figure in British politics, was openly calling for mass deportations and the shutdown of Muslim institutions. His rallies drew thousands, and his message resonated with those who felt left behind by globalization. The country was splitting apart at the seams, and Amir's community in East London was at the center of it.

Hawke's supporters had begun staging attacks on immigrant communities, and the police often turned a blind eye. In East London, mosques were defaced with racist graffiti, and Muslim-owned businesses were firebombed. The violence was escalating, and Amir's family was feeling the pressure. His father's health had deteriorated further, and Amir feared that they would be targeted next.

Zayn had gone further down the path of militancy, convinced that the Muslim community needed to arm itself for the coming conflict. His group had grown larger, and Amir had overheard conversations about stockpiling weapons and preparing for a "final showdown" with the far-right. Amir was torn. He didn't want to see London descend into the kind of violence he had heard about from Malik's experiences in Syria. But he also couldn't stand by as his community was terrorized.

In the winter of 2023, a major riot broke out in East London after a far-right group attacked a mosque during Friday prayers. The resulting violence left several dead and dozens injured. The government responded by imposing martial law in parts of the city, sending in troops to restore order. But the move only deepened the divide, and soon the streets were filled with protesters on both sides, ready to fight.

Amir felt like he was watching his world collapse. The UK had once been a beacon of stability and tolerance, but now it was spiralling into chaos. His father, bedridden and weak, urged Amir to leave London, to take the family and escape the violence. But Amir didn't know where to go. Europe was in turmoil, and there seemed to be no safe place left.

The Broader Collapse of Europe

By 2024, Europe had become a continent divided along religious, ethnic, and political lines. The European Union, once a symbol of unity and cooperation, was unravelling under the weight of its internal conflicts. Nationalism, xenophobia, and fear had taken hold, and the dream of a united Europe was fading.

In Germany, the AfD had become the dominant political force, with the ruling coalition fractured under pressure from the far-right. Germany's immigrant population, especially Muslims, had been pushed to the margins of society, and violence against minorities had become a regular occurrence. The government's attempts to restore order only seemed to exacerbate the tension.

France, under Marine Le Pen's authoritarian rule, was descending into open conflict. The banlieues were in a state of rebellion, with police and military forces engaged in daily battles with residents. The country was teetering on the edge of a civil war, as the Muslim population fought back against the state's repressive measures.

In the UK, Nathan Hawke's populist movement had taken control of Parliament, and his anti-immigrant agenda was being implemented with brutal efficiency. Britain's Muslim population, concentrated in cities like London and Birmingham, was living in fear, as far-right militias roamed the streets with impunity.

The Mediterranean refugee crisis had reached new heights, with thousands of people from Africa and the Middle East attempting to flee the chaos in Europe. But the borders were closing, and nations like Italy, Greece, and Spain were overwhelmed by the influx. Europe, once a refuge for the world's displaced, had become a place of fear and exclusion.

As the conflict escalated, many feared that Europe was heading toward a religious war—one that would pit Christians against Muslims, nationalists against immigrants, in a battle for the soul of the continent. For Malik, Yasmine, and Amir, the future was uncertain. But one thing was clear: the Europe they had come to for safety and opportunity was gone. In its place was a continent on the brink of destruction.

Chapter 7: The Gathering Storm

Berlin, Germany – Early 2025

The winter of 2025 brought with it an eerie silence to the streets of Berlin. Snow blanketed the city, softening the jagged edges of broken storefronts and the charred remains of cars left over from the last wave of riots. It was a temporary reprieve, a brief lull before the next round of unrest that everyone knew was coming. Malik stood by his apartment window, gazing down at the city below, feeling a deep sense of foreboding.

Germany had transformed in ways Malik never thought possible. The far-right had all but taken over the political landscape, and the AfD's rhetoric had evolved from covert racism to an outright call for ethnic cleansing. Immigrants, particularly Muslims, were living in constant fear. Deportations had increased tenfold, and those who weren't deported were harassed, detained, or worse.

Malik had stopped attending protests altogether. The movement had fractured—Sabine's activism had been silenced by the state, and many of her colleagues had been arrested. The few remaining protests were now met with brutal force. Malik felt helpless. His dreams of reunifying his family had long since evaporated. Every visa application had been rejected, with the government citing increasingly absurd reasons.

He hadn't heard from his family in months, and the sporadic reports coming out of Syria spoke of worsening conditions. Malik knew they were still alive—his brother had sent a brief, cryptic message six weeks ago, but it had only deepened Malik's anxiety. He felt trapped between two worlds: a war-torn homeland he couldn't return to and a hostile country that no longer welcomed him.

Karim's influence had grown in Neukölln. His message had become darker, more desperate, and more violent. Where once Karim had preached about organizing and self-defence, now he spoke openly about taking up arms. "We're already in a war," Karim said during a tense meeting in Malik's apartment. "The only difference is we're the ones being slaughtered, and they're doing it quietly. You think the police raids are random? They're testing us. If we don't fight back now, they'll wipe us out."

Malik's gut churned at the thought of following Karim down that path, but he could no longer deny the truth of his words. The attacks on Muslim neighbourhoods had become more coordinated, more brutal. The police seemed indifferent, often arriving too late to stop the violence, if they arrived at all. Malik had already seen several of his neighbours disappear—some detained without charge, others found dead in alleyways.

Karim wasn't alone in his radicalization. A growing number of young men, especially those from war-torn countries like Syria and Iraq, were flocking to him. The European dream had been shattered for them, replaced by a grim reality of survival. Malik couldn't fault them for their anger. He shared it. But he couldn't cross that line, not yet. He still held out hope that something might change, though that hope was dwindling with every passing day.

Paris, France – 2025

Yasmine stood at the edge of the Seine, staring at the water as it rushed beneath the Pont des Arts. Paris was no longer the city of love, art, or beauty that the world knew it to be. In the past year, the streets had become a battleground, with daily clashes between police and protesters. The banlieues were on fire—literally and figuratively.

Marine Le Pen's government had declared a state of emergency in early 2025, claiming that radical Islamist cells were plotting attacks across the country. The declaration had given the police and military free rein to crack down on any dissent, and the result was a constant state of fear and paranoia. Yasmine's apartment in Saint-Denis had been raided twice, and she lived in perpetual uncertainty, never knowing when the next knock on her door might be the last.

Driss had disappeared shortly after the state of emergency was declared. Yasmine had heard rumours that he was arrested, possibly tortured, but there had been no official word. Others in their activist circle had fled the country, while some had gone underground, joining clandestine networks that were organizing what they called the "final resistance."

Yasmine's own resistance had been worn down. She had once been the firebrand, the fearless leader of protests and marches, but now she found herself retreating from the frontlines. She still organized, still fought in her own way, but it felt like she was losing. The government's iron grip on the Muslim population was unrelenting, and more and more young people were turning to radical measures.

Amina had become one of them. Despite Yasmine's best efforts to keep her from falling into extremism, Amina had slipped away. She was now part of an underground network, one that was planning direct attacks on government targets. Yasmine knew that Amina was gone for good—that she was lost to the cause, to the anger, to the desire for vengeance.

In late February 2025, Paris was rocked by a series of coordinated bombings. The attacks targeted government buildings, police stations, and military barracks. Hundreds were killed, and Le Pen's government immediately blamed Islamist extremists. The crackdown that followed was swift and brutal. Entire neighbourhoods were cordoned off, residents arrested en masse, and the military patrolled the streets of Paris as though it were an occupied city.

Yasmine knew that Amina's group was responsible for at least some of the bombings, but she couldn't bring herself to condemn them. She understood their rage. She had felt it, too. But she also knew that these attacks would only make things worse. The government's grip would tighten, and the cycle of violence would continue. Still, Yasmine couldn't help but feel that the tipping point had been reached—that France was no longer simply divided but at war with itself.

London, United Kingdom – 2025

In London, the conflict was escalating. Nathan Hawke's government had embraced authoritarian measures, turning the city into a powder keg. The far-right militias, which had once been fringe movements, were now openly aligned with the government, patrolling immigrant neighbourhoods and instigating violence. Muslim communities, particularly in East London, had formed their own militias in response. The clashes between the two sides were becoming more frequent and more deadly.

Amir had tried to stay out of the conflict, but it was impossible to remain neutral in a city that was tearing itself apart. Zayn's group had grown into a fully armed militia, and Amir had found himself pulled into their orbit. At first, he had helped with logistics—coordinating supplies, transporting food and medical aid to families caught in the crossfire. But as the situation worsened, Zayn had asked for more. "We need to defend ourselves, Amir. You can't just sit on the sidelines forever."

Amir's father had grown weaker, barely able to leave his bed now. The stress of the worsening situation weighed heavily on him. "I don't want this for you, son," he had said one night, his voice frail. "But I understand. You have to protect our family. You have to protect our people."

And so, Amir had reluctantly taken up arms. He wasn't a fighter—he had never wanted to be one—but the world around him had given him no choice. He couldn't stand by while his community was attacked, while people he cared about were hurt or killed. The streets of East London had become a warzone, and survival meant doing things he had never imagined doing.

The government's response was brutal. After a series of violent clashes between far-right militias and Muslim groups in early 2025, Hawke imposed martial law in London, deploying the military to "restore order." The move only escalated the conflict. Both sides saw the military presence as an occupying force, and the fighting intensified.

Amir found himself at the center of it. Zayn's militia had grown bolder, launching counterattacks against far-right strongholds and police outposts. Amir had tried to stay on the periphery, but Zayn kept pulling him in deeper. "We need you, brother. You're one of us. You can't walk away now."

By the spring of 2025, London was a city divided. Whole neighbourhoods had been cordoned off, controlled either by the government or by militias. The economy had collapsed, and food shortages were rampant. Amir's father passed away in April, a victim not of violence but of neglect. The healthcare system had broken down, and there were no doctors or nurses available to care for him in his final days.

Amir felt a hollow emptiness as he buried his father, knowing that the city he had once loved, the city his father had helped build, was gone forever.

The Collapse of Europe – Mid-2025

By the middle of 2025, Europe was no longer a cohesive continent but a patchwork of warzones. The European Union had effectively disintegrated. Nationalist governments in Poland, Hungary, and other Eastern European nations had openly defied Brussels, declaring themselves free from the influence of the EU. Southern Europe had become a humanitarian disaster, with Italy, Greece, and Spain overwhelmed by the refugee crisis and internal unrest.

Germany was on the brink of civil war. The AfD's rule had sparked widespread violence, with immigrant communities organizing their own militias to defend themselves against far-right attacks. The government's attempt to suppress the violence with military force only deepened the divisions, and by mid-2025, large swaths of Berlin and other major cities were effectively no-go zones.

France was a police state, with the military patrolling the streets and Muslim neighbourhoods under siege. The government's harsh policies had radicalized a generation of young Muslims,

Chapter 8: The Seeds of War

Berlin, Germany – Late 2025

By the end of 2025, the streets of Berlin had become unrecognizable. Once known for its culture, diversity, and resilience, the city now stood divided by invisible battle lines. Whole neighbourhoods were cordoned off by makeshift barricades, where police dared not venture, and armed militias patrolled the streets. These zones were now under the control of various factions: far-right extremists, nationalist militias, and increasingly, Muslim self-defence groups like the one led by Karim.

Malik had been dragged deeper into the conflict than he ever intended. Karim's once relatively moderate stance had given way to open calls for armed resistance. The group had grown larger and more organized, and Malik found himself spending his nights in clandestine meetings, helping coordinate supply lines for food, weapons, and information. The conversations were grim, always focusing on survival. Hope, it seemed, had long since left the room.

"We're not fighting for a better life anymore, Malik," Karim had told him during one of those long nights. "We're fighting to exist, to make sure they can't erase us from this country."

Malik didn't disagree, but his heart wasn't in it the way it once had been. Every step toward violent resistance felt like a step toward the destruction of everything he had once hoped for. He couldn't shake the images from Aleppo, the endless cycles of destruction that left only devastation in their wake. Yet, every time he thought about backing out, something would happen—a new attack on a mosque, another family torn apart by the police raids—and Malik would be pulled right back into the fight.

In December, the German government declared an official state of emergency, effectively handing over control of large parts of Berlin to the military. The country was now deeply divided, not just along political lines, but by geography. Urban centers, where immigrant communities were concentrated, had become isolated from rural and suburban areas that were dominated by far-right groups. The economy had tanked, and basic services were crumbling. People like Malik, who had once come to Europe for refuge, now found themselves in a war zone again, only this time the war was in their new homeland.

Sabine, who had once been such a vocal activist, had been silenced. The government had cracked down hard on those who opposed its growing authoritarianism, and many of her colleagues had been arrested or forced into hiding. Malik had lost contact with her months ago. He assumed she had either gone underground or left the country altogether.

With no end in sight, the people of Berlin began to prepare for a new kind of war—one that wasn't fought by soldiers in uniforms but by ordinary people, fighting to survive in a crumbling society.

Paris, France – Late 2025

Paris had become a city under siege. The military presence that had once been focused on controlling the protests had now expanded to full-scale occupation in many parts of the city. Entire districts, especially in the banlieues, were declared "zones of insurgency," and the French government had given the military carte blanche to suppress any form of resistance.

Yasmine, now a seasoned underground activist, moved through these zones with increasing caution. She had always been good at blending in, but the city was becoming more dangerous by the day. Amina's group had claimed responsibility for several high-profile attacks on military targets, and the government's response had been swift and brutal. Anyone suspected of being involved with the insurgency faced immediate arrest, often without trial. Some simply disappeared, taken to secret detention centers where they were never heard from again.

Yasmine knew that her time in Paris was running out. The network of activists she had built was rapidly disintegrating under the weight of the crackdown. Many had already fled the country, seeking refuge in places like Turkey or North Africa. But Yasmine couldn't bring herself to leave. She felt a responsibility to stay and fight for the city she loved, even though that fight was becoming more futile with every passing day.

The Le Pen government had used the insurgency as an excuse to pass even more draconian laws. Religious symbols were banned outright, not just in public buildings but everywhere. Mosques were being systematically shut down, and entire Muslim communities were under constant surveillance. In some areas, it felt like martial law had been imposed solely on Muslims, while other parts of the city continued to function as though nothing had changed.

But things had changed. The divide between France's Muslim population and the rest of the country was now a gaping chasm. Yasmine watched as the city she had grown up in became something she no longer recognized. The Parisian values of liberté, égalité, fraternité had been twisted beyond recognition.

Yasmine spent her days moving from one safe house to another, trying to maintain what little remained of her network. Her contact with Amina was sporadic, but Yasmine knew that Amina's group was preparing something big. They had grown increasingly bold, and there were rumours that they were planning an attack that would dwarf anything they had done before.

One evening, Yasmine received a coded message from Amina: *We're ready. It's happening soon. Be safe.*

Yasmine felt a chill. She knew what that meant. Paris was on the verge of descending into full-blown civil war, and once that line was crossed, there would be no going back.

London, United Kingdom – Late 2025

London had become a fortress. The city that once prided itself on being a global hub of diversity and tolerance was now split into warring factions. Nathan Hawke's government had fully embraced the far-right militias, integrating them into the official security apparatus under the guise of maintaining order. Muslim communities in East London, once vibrant and thriving, had turned into enclaves of resistance, cut off from the rest of the city.

Amir found himself thrust into the middle of this conflict, torn between his desire to protect his family and his growing disillusionment with Zayn's increasingly violent tactics. Zayn's militia had become more brazen, launching attacks not just on far-right strongholds but on government buildings as well. They saw themselves as the last line of defence for the Muslim population, but Amir feared that their actions were only making things worse.

In October 2025, a series of bombings rocked central London. The government blamed Islamist extremists, and the crackdown that followed was swift and unforgiving. Entire neighbourhoods were cordoned off, and anyone suspected of harbouring sympathies for the insurgency was arrested. The government's response only deepened the divide between Muslims and the rest of the population, and London's streets became a battleground.

Amir's family had long since retreated into the safety of their home, rarely venturing outside. His father had passed away earlier in the year, and now Amir felt the full weight of responsibility on his shoulders. His mother was too frail to leave, and his younger siblings looked to him for guidance. But Amir didn't know what to do. The city was falling apart, and it felt like every decision he made carried life-or-death consequences.

Zayn's group had grown reckless, and Amir could see that their anger was consuming them. "This isn't the way," Amir said during a heated argument with Zayn. "We're playing right into their hands. Every attack we launch just gives them more justification to come after us."

Zayn was unmoved. "What choice do we have? You think they'll stop if we just sit back and do nothing? Look around you, Amir. They want us dead. This is the only way we survive."

Amir knew Zayn was right in some ways, but he couldn't bring himself to believe that violence was the solution. Yet, as the fighting intensified and the government's grip tightened, Amir found himself questioning everything he had once believed in. How could he protect his family in a city that no longer had room for them?

By late December, London was a city on the brink. The government had declared martial law, and the military presence in the streets had grown. Far-right militias operated with impunity, and Muslim neighbourhoods were effectively under siege. Amir knew that the city he had once called home was gone. The only question left was how long it would take for everything to collapse completely.

Europe in Crisis – Late 2025

Across Europe, the situation was rapidly deteriorating. The European Union, once a symbol of unity and peace, had all but collapsed under the weight of its internal divisions. Nationalist movements had risen to power in nearly every major European country, and the continent was now fractured along religious, ethnic, and political lines.

Germany was in the grip of a full-blown civil conflict. The AfD government had lost control of large parts of the country, and armed militias—both far-right and immigrant—were battling for dominance in the streets. The military was overstretched, and the country's infrastructure was collapsing. The German economy, once the strongest in Europe, had spiralled into a deep recession, and basic services were becoming scarce.

France was in a similar state of disarray. Marine Le Pen's government had declared war on the Muslim population, and the insurgency that had begun in the banlieues was now spreading to other parts of the country. The military occupation of Paris and other major cities had only fuelled the resistance, and the violence was escalating by the day.

In the United Kingdom, Nathan Hawke's populist regime had transformed the country into an authoritarian state. Muslim communities, especially in London and Birmingham, were living under constant siege, with militias and government forces clashing in the streets. Britain had become a deeply divided nation, with no clear path toward reconciliation.

As the violence spread across the continent, many feared that Europe was on the verge of a new kind of war—one that wasn't fought between nations, but between the people themselves. Christian and Muslim communities were increasingly pitted against each other, and the nationalist movements that had gained power were stoking the flames of hatred and division.

The seeds of war had been planted, and now, it seemed, the harvest was coming.

Europe, once a beacon of stability and prosperity, was teetering on the edge of chaos. And for Malik, Yasmine, Amir, and millions of others caught in the crossfire, there was no longer any clear path forward—only the desperate hope that they might survive what was to come.

Chapter 9: Fault Lines

Berlin, Germany – Early 2026

The new year brought little relief to the beleaguered city of Berlin. By early 2026, the conflict had escalated into what many were now openly calling a civil war. The government's declaration of martial law had done little to quell the violence, and in fact, it only exacerbated tensions. Neighbourhoods had turned into battle zones, and the once diverse and multicultural city was now divided into enclaves controlled by various factions.

Malik found himself living in a state of constant tension. He had abandoned the illusion of normalcy long ago. The once regular routines of work, socializing, and everyday life had been replaced with strategies for survival. For weeks now, he had been helping Karim's group smuggle supplies into their stronghold in Neukölln, where Muslim families had banded together for protection.

But Malik's involvement was deeper now. Karim's group had morphed into something far more organized and militant. What had started as a defensive network had evolved into an armed resistance. They were no longer just defending themselves from far-right militias but launching counterattacks against police and government forces. The escalation of violence was inevitable, and Malik was caught in the middle.

"Malik, we need to make a choice," Karim said one night as they sat around a table in a makeshift war room. Maps of the city, marked with the territories controlled by various factions, lay before them. "We can't just keep reacting. We have to take the fight to them."

Malik shook his head, weary of the conversation that had become all too familiar. "And what happens after that, Karim? What's the endgame here? We take the fight to them, they come back stronger, and we're left with nothing but more bodies in the streets."

Karim's eyes burned with the fire of someone who had long since passed the point of no return. "There's no future for us if we don't fight. The government sees us as an enemy. The far-right wants us dead. What other choice do we have?"

Malik didn't have an answer. The truth was, there were no good options anymore. They were fighting for survival in a war they hadn't started, and the rules of engagement had long since been thrown out the window. But as Malik stared at the map, he felt a growing sense of dread. The city was collapsing, and it wouldn't be long before it fell completely.

Berlin was now a city of checkpoints and barricades. The government had lost control of large swathes of the city, and the military was spread too thin to reclaim them. Far-right militias had taken over entire neighbourhoods, while immigrant communities fortified their own sections of the city. The battle lines were constantly shifting, and Malik knew it was only a matter of time before Berlin became a warzone like the cities he had fled from in Syria.

Paris, France – Early 2026

The Seine was no longer the symbol of Parisian romance and beauty; it had become the dividing line between the haves and the have-nots, between those who still lived in relative comfort and those who were struggling to survive. The government had effectively abandoned the banlieues, leaving them to their own devices. In the eyes of the state, these areas were lost, overrun by insurgents and radicals.

Yasmine watched from the roof of an abandoned building as military trucks rumbled down the streets of central Paris. The government's stranglehold on the city had tightened since the bombings in late 2025. Entire sections of the city were now under martial law, with curfews strictly enforced and anyone caught outside after dark either arrested or shot on sight.

Yasmine had grown used to the constant surveillance, but it didn't make it any easier. Her network of activists had shrunk to a handful of people, most of them too scared or too disillusioned to continue. Amina's group had gone fully underground, their attacks on military and police targets becoming more frequent and more lethal.

It was a bitter winter, both in terms of weather and atmosphere. Paris felt like a city waiting for its inevitable collapse. The divide between the government and the Muslim population had become irreparable. There were no more protests, no more negotiations. It was war now, plain and simple, and the lines had been drawn.

One night, Yasmine received another cryptic message from Amina. *They're planning something big. The final push is coming. Be ready.*

Yasmine stared at the message for a long time. She knew that whatever Amina's group was planning would push the city further into chaos, and while part of her wanted to stop it, she knew she couldn't. The anger, the frustration, the years of marginalization and violence—it had built up to this point. Amina's group wasn't just fighting back; they were seeking retribution.

Yasmine's own resolve was faltering. She had stayed behind, clinging to the belief that there was still something worth fighting for in Paris, that there was still a way to bridge the divide. But now, as the city burned around her and the bodies piled up, she wasn't so sure. The Paris she had loved was gone, and in its place was a battlefield.

London, United Kingdom – Early 2026

The military presence in London had grown overwhelming. Tanks rolled down the streets of East London, and helicopters buzzed overhead, surveilling the neighbourhoods where Muslim communities had barricaded themselves in. The government's lockdown on these areas had reached new levels of repression, with daily raids, curfews, and military checkpoints. Nathan Hawke's regime had made it clear: there would be no negotiation, no compromise. The insurgency, as he called it, would be crushed.

Amir had reluctantly become more involved in Zayn's militia, though it was still something he struggled with. He had never wanted to be part of this conflict, but he had no choice. His family was at risk, and every day, the situation became more desperate.

"Amir, we can't keep waiting," Zayn said during one of their late-night meetings. "Hawke's government is tightening the noose. If we don't act soon, we'll be wiped out."

Amir stared at the map spread out before them, detailing the government's strongholds in East London. Zayn was right. The far-right militias had become de facto arms of the government, and they were operating with impunity. The Muslim communities, meanwhile, had been cut off from the rest of the city. Supplies were running low, and the government had blocked most aid organizations from entering.

"What's the plan?" Amir asked, though his voice was heavy with reluctance.

Zayn's eyes gleamed with intensity. "We're going to hit them where it hurts. We've got intel on a major government supply line. We take it out, and we cripple their operations in the area. It'll give us the breathing room we need."

Amir nodded, though his stomach churned at the thought of what was coming. He knew that every action they took only escalated the violence, and there was no way to know if they would ever come out the other side. But he also knew that Zayn was right about one thing: if they didn't fight back, they would be erased.

As the night stretched on, Amir's thoughts drifted to his father. He remembered the stories his father had told him about their homeland, about the struggles they had endured, and the hope that had once brought them to London. It seemed so long ago now, almost like a different lifetime. His father had believed in this city, in the promise of a better future. But that future had turned into a nightmare.

Amir felt the weight of the decision before him. He wasn't a soldier, and he never wanted to be one. But in this city, in this war, he had no other choice.

The Crumbling Union – Early 2026

Across Europe, the chaos had reached a fever pitch. The European Union had been rendered virtually powerless, unable to intervene in the internal conflicts that were tearing the continent apart. In Brussels, the once formidable political machinery of the EU was now a ghost of its former self, with leaders unable to agree on any unified action.

Germany was in the throes of a civil war. The AfD government had lost control of several major cities, where far-right militias and immigrant groups were locked in a violent struggle for dominance. The German military, stretched too thin to maintain order, was losing ground to both sides. The economy had collapsed, and basic services were breaking down across the country.

In France, the insurgency had spread beyond Paris. The French military was engaged in a brutal campaign to suppress the Muslim population, with entire towns being razed in the process. The government had declared martial law across the country, and the violence was spiralling out of control.

The United Kingdom was barely holding itself together. Nathan Hawke's authoritarian regime was facing increasing resistance not just from Muslim communities but from other marginalized groups who had been swept up in the far-right's purges. London, once the jewel of Europe's diversity, had become a city of fear and repression.

As the conflict escalated, the possibility of reconciliation or peace seemed more distant than ever. The lines had been drawn, and the battles were being fought on multiple fronts—religious, ethnic, and political.

Europe, once a symbol of unity and prosperity, was now a fractured continent on the brink of collapse. And for Malik, Yasmine, Amir, and countless others, the hope of a peaceful future was slipping further and further away.

The seeds of war had been planted years ago, and now, as the new year dawned, those seeds were bearing their bitter fruit

Chapter 10: The Final Sparks

Berlin, Germany – Mid 2026

Berlin had become a shadow of its former self. The once vibrant capital of Europe was now reduced to a grid of military zones and no-go areas, patrolled by government forces and armed militias. The city's infrastructure was in tatters—public transport systems had shut down, and the power grid was unstable. Yet, despite the chaos, the battle for control of Berlin raged on.

Malik stood at the edge of what had once been a bustling marketplace in Neukölln, now reduced to rubble. A thick layer of smoke hung over the area as if the city itself were suffocating. Karim's group had taken control of this territory months ago, but it was becoming harder to defend. Resources were dwindling, and skirmishes with far-right militias were becoming more frequent and violent.

Karim was no longer the cautious leader Malik had known at the start of their resistance. He had fully embraced the role of a warlord, directing operations with an iron fist. The pressure of defending their shrinking enclave and the relentless attacks from rival militias had hardened him. Malik had seen it happen before, in Syria, as leaders who once fought for a just cause became consumed by the violence, their humanity eroded by the demands of war.

As Malik walked through the devastated streets, his thoughts drifted to his family—his wife and two daughters, who had fled to safety in Turkey months earlier. He hadn't heard from them in weeks. He told himself that they were safe, but deep down, he feared the worst. Every day, he considered leaving Berlin to join them, but each time, something pulled him back. Maybe it was loyalty to Karim, or perhaps it was the fact that after all the destruction, Malik didn't know where else he could belong.

His reverie was interrupted by a distant explosion, followed by the crackle of gunfire. It was becoming a regular occurrence now, almost routine. Malik turned and saw a group of Karim's fighters rushing toward the sound. He sighed and followed, knowing that it wouldn't be the last time he would find himself drawn into a battle he didn't want to fight.

When he arrived at the scene, he found a familiar sight: a group of far-right extremists had attempted to breach the perimeter. They had been beaten back, but the fight had left several of Karim's men dead, their bodies lying motionless in the street.

Karim appeared moments later, his face set in a grim mask of anger. "We can't keep doing this, Malik," he said, surveying the carnage. "We need to take the offensive. Hit them where it hurts."

Malik looked at him, exhaustion evident in his eyes. "And then what, Karim? We attack them, they retaliate, and the cycle continues. When does it end?"

Karim's gaze hardened. "It ends when they're gone. When we've taken this city back for ourselves."

Malik didn't reply. He didn't have the energy to argue anymore. He just wanted it all to stop.

Paris, France – Mid 2026

The city of lights had become a city of darkness. Curfews were strictly enforced, and anyone caught in the streets after sundown was risking their life. Paris was now divided into zones controlled by the French military, the far-right militias, and the insurgent Muslim groups that had formed in the banlieues. Yasmine moved cautiously through these areas, knowing that her life depended on her ability to stay invisible.

The final push that Amina had warned her about had come. In early 2026, Amina's group had launched a massive, coordinated attack on military installations across Paris. The violence was brutal and indiscriminate, and the government's response had been even harsher. The French military retaliated with a series of bombings and raids on the Muslim enclaves, killing hundreds and driving the insurgency deeper underground. Paris was now a city under siege, and the government had essentially declared war on its own people.

Yasmine had tried to distance herself from Amina's increasingly violent tactics, but the lines were too blurred now. There was no longer a distinction between activists and insurgents. Anyone who opposed the government's brutal repression was considered an enemy of the state.

Late one night, Yasmine received a message from Amina: *We need you for this one. Meet me at the safe house.*

Yasmine hesitated. She had already seen too much death, too much destruction. Every step she took deeper into the resistance felt like a step away from the person she had once been. But Amina had been there from the start, and Yasmine couldn't abandon her now, not when the stakes were so high.

The safe house was hidden in a nondescript building on the outskirts of the city, far from the government's checkpoints. Inside, Amina and her group were preparing for what would be their most ambitious attack yet—a coordinated strike on government buildings in the heart of Paris. The goal was to send a message, to show the world that the Muslim population of France would not be cowed by oppression.

"This is it, Yasmine," Amina said as she explained the plan. "We've been pushed to the edge. Now it's time to push back."

Yasmine felt a pit forming in her stomach. She understood the anger, the frustration, but she couldn't shake the feeling that this was all leading to something far worse. Still, she had made her choice, and there was no turning back now.

As Yasmine listened to the details of the plan, she realized that Paris, once her beloved city, was no longer the place she had fought for. It had become a battleground, and she was just another soldier in a war she had never wanted to fight.

London, United Kingdom – Mid 2026

In London, the situation had reached a breaking point. The city had been divided into fortified zones, with far-right militias controlling much of the west and Muslim militias holding the east. The government's lockdown of East London had turned the area into a virtual prison, with residents cut off from the rest of the city. Supplies were scarce, and tensions were at an all-time high.

Amir stood at a window overlooking the streets of East London, watching as soldiers and militia fighters patrolled the area. The situation had deteriorated rapidly in the past few months. Zayn's group had grown increasingly bold, launching attacks on government forces and far-right strongholds with a ferocity that Amir hadn't seen before.

Zayn had changed too. The calm, strategic leader that Amir had once admired had given way to someone consumed by rage. The attacks had become more reckless, more violent, and Amir wasn't sure how much longer they could hold out.

One evening, Zayn called a meeting with his core group of fighters. Amir sat quietly in the corner as Zayn outlined his latest plan: an all-out assault on a government supply depot that would cripple the military's operations in East London.

"This is our chance," Zayn said, his voice filled with determination. "If we take this depot, we cut off their supplies. We can force them to negotiate, maybe even push them out of East London."

Amir listened, but his mind was elsewhere. He couldn't shake the feeling that this was a suicide mission. The government forces were too strong, too well-armed, and Zayn's militia was running on fumes. But Zayn was right about one thing—there was no other choice. They were trapped, and the only way out was through.

As the meeting ended, Amir pulled Zayn aside. "Are you sure about this? We've lost so many already. What if this just leads to more bloodshed?"

Zayn's expression was grim. "There's no going back, Amir. We're too deep in now. This is the only way we survive."

Amir nodded, though his heart wasn't in it. He knew that Zayn was right, but he couldn't help but feel that this war was leading them all toward oblivion.

The Collapse of Europe – Mid 2026

Across Europe, the cracks that had been forming for years had finally split wide open. Germany was no longer a functioning state. The AfD government had been driven from Berlin, and what remained of the German military was engaged in a desperate battle to hold onto control of the country's major cities. The far-right militias, emboldened by the chaos, had taken over large parts of the countryside, while immigrant communities fortified themselves in urban enclaves.

France was on the brink of total collapse. The insurgency in the banlieues had spread to other cities, and the French government's efforts to suppress the rebellion had only fuelled the violence. The country was now in the grips of a full-scale civil war, with no end in sight.

The United Kingdom was faring no better. Nathan Hawke's government had doubled down on its authoritarian measures, but the resistance in London and other major cities had grown more organized. Muslim militias had taken control of East London, while far-right groups dominated the west. The country was now effectively divided, and the central government was losing its grip.

As Europe descended further into chaos, the international community watched in horror. What had once been the heart of the Western world was now a battlefield, torn apart by the very forces it had once tried to suppress. The dream of a united Europe had crumbled, leaving in its wake a continent divided by religion, race, and ideology.

For Malik, Yasmine, and Amir, the future was uncertain. They had each made their choices, and now they had to live with the consequences. The seeds of war had been sown, and now the fires were burning out of control. There was no clear path to victory, only survival.

As 2026 dragged on, it became clear that Europe was no longer the Europe they had once known. It was a new world now, one defined by conflict and division. And as the flames of war spread across the continent, there was no telling what the future would hold.

Chapter 11: The Siege

Berlin, Germany – Late 2026

By late 2026, Berlin was unrecognizable. The city had been split into various warring zones, each controlled by rival militias and government forces that were struggling to maintain even a semblance of order. Civilian life had come to a complete halt, and the once-thriving neighbourhoods were now bombed-out shells, marked by street battles, explosions, and the haunting wail of sirens.

Malik had grown numb to the sight of death. The bodies of civilians and fighters alike lay strewn across the streets, casualties of a war that no longer had any clear objectives. Karim's group, which had once been a defensive force aimed at protecting their community, had turned into a full-fledged militia. They were no longer simply defending their territory—they were actively fighting for control of Berlin's crumbling infrastructure.

The escalation had been inevitable. Supplies were running low, and with each passing day, the survival of their enclave seemed more uncertain. Malik spent his days helping organize supply runs and coordinating defensive strategies, but he could feel the hope draining from those around him. The young men who had joined the fight with fire in their eyes were now weary, broken by the endless cycle of violence.

One evening, Malik sat in a makeshift command center with Karim, watching as their few remaining fighters prepared for another skirmish. This time, the target was a far-right stronghold that had been harassing their enclave with sniper attacks and mortar fire. The plan was risky, but Karim was desperate to gain some kind of advantage.

"We can't keep this up much longer," Karim admitted, his voice hoarse from exhaustion. "We're running out of food, out of weapons. If we don't hit them hard now, they'll eventually overrun us."

Malik stared at the map of Berlin, marked with the shifting battle lines that carved the city into fragments. "And what happens after we hit them? We take their territory, then someone else comes along and takes it from us. It's just a cycle, Karim."

Karim's eyes were bloodshot, the toll of the war etched into his face. "There is no after, Malik. This is it. This is the war we've been dragged into, and there's no way out. We fight until we win or we die."

Malik said nothing. He had long stopped believing in the idea of victory. Survival was all that mattered now, and even that seemed like a distant hope.

Paris, France – Late 2026

The Paris that Yasmine had grown up in was gone. The city was now a battlefield, with entire districts sealed off by the French military and insurgents fighting for control of the streets. The Eiffel Tower, once a symbol of France's unity and culture, now stood as a silent witness to the destruction around it, shrouded in smoke and flames.

Amina's group had carried out their most audacious attack yet, striking a series of government buildings in the heart of the city. The assault had been devastating, causing significant damage to the military command center and leaving the French government reeling. In retaliation, the government had unleashed a brutal wave of airstrikes on the banlieues, targeting anyone suspected of harbouring insurgents.

Yasmine had managed to escape the worst of the violence, but barely. She was now living in a safe house on the outskirts of Paris, moving constantly to avoid detection. Her network of activists had been decimated, and most of the people she had worked with were either dead, in hiding, or imprisoned. The dream of peaceful resistance was gone, replaced by the cold reality of war.

One night, Yasmine received word that Amina had been captured during a government raid. The news hit her like a blow to the chest. Amina had been the heart of their resistance, the one who had kept them going even when all seemed lost. Without her, Yasmine felt adrift, unsure of what to do next.

She met with the remaining members of her group in the basement of an abandoned building. The atmosphere was tense, heavy with the weight of their losses.

"They're going to execute her," one of the younger members said, his voice shaking. "We can't let that happen."

Yasmine clenched her fists, her mind racing. Amina had been their leader but rescuing her seemed impossible. The French government had fortified its military presence in the city, and any attempt to free her would be met with overwhelming force.

But doing nothing felt like a betrayal.

"I'll go," Yasmine said finally, her voice steady. "We can't just leave her to die."

The others looked at her in disbelief. "How? It's suicide."

Yasmine didn't have an answer. She just knew that she couldn't stand by and watch her friend, her sister-in-arms, be executed by the same government they had fought so hard against. It was reckless, but Yasmine had lost too much already. If she was going to die, she wanted to die fighting for something, someone, she believed in.

London, United Kingdom – Late 2026

In London, the government's grip on the city had tightened. East London had become a fortress, with Muslim militias like Zayn's holding out against overwhelming odds. The far-right militias had taken control of large sections of West London, and the government forces were caught in between, trying to reclaim territory from both sides.

Amir had become a reluctant commander in Zayn's militia. His once peaceful existence as a university student now seemed like a distant memory, replaced by the brutal reality of urban warfare. He had watched friends die, seen families torn apart by the violence, and yet he had no choice but to continue fighting. To stop now would mean death, either at the hands of the government or the far-right extremists who wanted them all eradicated.

Zayn had grown increasingly fanatical in his determination to win. The attacks on government forces had become more frequent, more deadly, but each victory was short-lived. The government always came back stronger, with more soldiers, more weapons, and more support from the far-right.

Amir, meanwhile, had grown tired of the endless cycle of violence. He had watched as Zayn's once noble cause had been twisted into something darker, something driven more by hatred and revenge than by the desire to protect their people. But he couldn't leave. His family was trapped in East London and leaving them behind was not an option.

One evening, Zayn called another meeting. This time, the plan was to launch a coordinated attack on a major government checkpoint that controlled access to the rest of the city. If they could break through, it would give them a lifeline, a way to bring in supplies and maybe even start evacuating civilians.

"We hit them hard, take the checkpoint, and we open up the route to the rest of London," Zayn explained, his eyes gleaming with determination. "This is our chance to break the siege."

Amir listened, but he couldn't shake the feeling that this was a last-ditch effort, a desperate move that would only lead to more bloodshed. But as much as he wanted to resist, he knew that Zayn was right about one thing—they were running out of time.

The Fragmenting Continent – Late 2026

As 2026 drew to a close, Europe was no longer a unified entity. The European Union had effectively disintegrated, with individual countries descending into civil war. Germany was now divided into territories controlled by far-right militias, immigrant enclaves, and a weakened central government that had lost control of most major cities. The once-powerful economy had collapsed, and millions of people were fleeing the country in search of safety.

France was in a similar state. The insurgency in the banlieues had spread to other regions, and the French government was barely holding on to power. The military's efforts to crush the rebellion had only fuelled more resistance, and the violence had spread to other cities like Marseille and Lyon. The dream of a united France was dead, replaced by a fractured, war-torn country.

The United Kingdom was no better. Nathan Hawke's authoritarian regime had lost control of large parts of London, and other major cities were beginning to see similar uprisings. The far-right militias, emboldened by the government's tacit support, were growing more powerful by the day. The country was now effectively divided between the government, the far-right, and the Muslim militias, with no clear path to reconciliation.

Across the continent, millions of people were fleeing the violence, seeking refuge in countries that were still relatively stable. But even those nations—places like Spain and Italy—were beginning to see the strain. The influx of refugees, combined with rising nationalist movements, threatened to destabilize the entire region.

THE FRACTURED CONTINENT

For Malik, Yasmine, and Amir, the future was uncertain. They had each made their choices, and now they were caught in the storm that was tearing Europe apart. The war had consumed their lives, and there was no telling when—or if—it would end.

As the new year approached, the flames of conflict continued to spread, consuming everything in their path. Europe was burning, and there was no one left to put out the fire.

Chapter 12: Crumbling Alliances

Berlin, Germany – Early 2027

Berlin, now just a ghost of its former grandeur, had ceased to be a city for the living. The streets that once bustled with life were now either abandoned or filled with roving militias and government soldiers, each fighting a battle neither could win. Malik had never thought it could get worse than the early days of 2026, but 2027 proved him wrong. The city was collapsing from the inside, not just from external assaults but from the breakdown of its own inhabitants.

The alliance between Karim's faction and the other Muslim enclaves in Berlin was beginning to fracture. Resources were too scarce, and old rivalries, once held in check by the common goal of survival, were beginning to resurface. Karim had tried to keep his group united, but the internal pressures were mounting. Some fighters believed that they should surrender, while others, driven by revenge and desperation, wanted to launch increasingly aggressive attacks on both the government and the far-right.

"Malik, we have to hit them before they hit us," Karim said during a meeting with his senior commanders. His eyes burned with the same fire that had kept him going for so long, but Malik noticed something different—a weariness, an edge that hadn't been there before. The war was taking its toll on him, as it was on everyone.

Malik shook his head. "What's left to take, Karim? We're out of food. We're out of medicine. Half of our fighters are injured, and the rest are too exhausted to hold the line. If we push now, we'll only be weakening ourselves for the next attack."

Karim slammed his fist on the table, the sound reverberating through the underground bunker where they now held their meetings. "We push now because if we don't, they'll come for us. The government is on its last legs, and the far-right is growing stronger every day. If we don't act, they will, and when they do, we'll be wiped out."

Malik wanted to argue, to tell Karim that he was fighting a losing battle. But there was nothing left to say. They were all trapped, driven by forces beyond their control. The city, the war, the cause—it had consumed them, and now it was only a matter of how long they could last.

Outside, the sounds of distant gunfire echoed through the ruined streets. Berlin was no longer a place for families, for children, for the future. It was a battleground, a city locked in perpetual war, where survival was measured not in victories, but in days.

Paris, France – Early 2027

In Paris, the air was thick with tension. The French government, barely holding onto power, had implemented martial law across the country. But martial law did little to stop the rising tide of violence. The military could not be everywhere, and in the spaces, it couldn't reach, militias—both far-right and Islamist—had taken control. The banlieues, long marginalized and neglected, had become fortresses, cut off from the rest of the city, places where the government dared not enter.

Yasmine had spent months planning Amina's rescue. It was a suicide mission, she knew that, but she couldn't leave her closest ally to die at the hands of the government. The French military had announced that Amina and other key insurgent leaders would be executed as an example to those who dared resist the state's authority. For Yasmine, it wasn't just about loyalty—it was about the cause, about not letting the government crush their movement with impunity.

The plan was simple but risky. Yasmine and a small team of fighters would infiltrate the military compound where Amina was being held and break her out before the execution could take place. They knew the compound was heavily guarded, but the chaos in the city gave them a slim window of opportunity.

As they made their way through the crumbling streets of Paris, Yasmine felt the weight of the war bearing down on her. The city she loved was gone, replaced by a wasteland of bombed-out buildings and shattered lives. She had once fought for justice, for equality, but now it seemed like the only thing left was survival. The ideals they had once stood for had been buried under the rubble.

When they reached the military compound, the plan quickly went awry. The guards were more numerous and better armed than they had anticipated.

A firefight erupted, and Yasmine found herself pinned down behind a wall of debris, bullets whizzing past her head. Her team had managed to breach the outer defences, but it was clear that they wouldn't make it much further.

As Yasmine reloaded her weapon, she caught a glimpse of one of her comrades being hit by a stray bullet. She gritted her teeth, her mind racing as she tried to figure out their next move. There was no way they could reach Amina now—the mission was a failure.

"Yasmine, we have to fall back!" one of her fighters shouted over the din of gunfire.

Yasmine hesitated for a moment, her heart sinking as she realized there was no saving Amina. With a heavy heart, she signalled for her team to retreat. As they fled into the night, Yasmine couldn't shake the feeling that they had lost more than just the battle—they had lost the soul of their movement.

London, United Kingdom – Early 2027

East London had become a war zone. The government's lockdown had turned the area into a ghetto, a place where Muslim militias held sway, and the rest of the city watched from a distance. Supplies were scarce, and the population was dwindling as people either fled or succumbed to the violence. Amir had thought things couldn't get worse, but they had.

The government's most recent assault had pushed Zayn's militia to the brink. They were running out of weapons, and morale was at an all-time low. Far-right groups, emboldened by their success in other parts of the country, were now openly attacking East London, attempting to force their way into the Muslim stronghold.

Amir stood on a rooftop, surveying the crumbling landscape below. Fires burned in the distance, a constant reminder of the chaos that now defined their lives. Zayn's plan to take the government checkpoint had failed miserably. They had been outgunned and outmanoeuvred, and many of their fighters had been killed in the assault. The defeat had shaken Zayn's confidence, but it had also made him more determined.

"We need reinforcements," Zayn said, pacing back and forth in their makeshift command center. "If we don't get more fighters, we're done for."

Amir sighed. "Reinforcements from where, Zayn? Everyone is either dead or fighting their own battles. We're on our own."

Zayn stopped pacing and turned to face Amir; his eyes filled with a manic energy. "We're not done yet. I've been in contact with some of the other groups in Birmingham and Manchester. They're willing to send support, but we need to give them a reason. We need a victory, something to rally behind."

Amir shook his head. "Zayn, we don't have the numbers. We don't have the resources. We're barely holding on here."

Zayn's face hardened. "We don't have a choice, Amir. It's fight or die."

Amir knew Zayn was right, but he couldn't help but feel that they were fighting a losing battle. The government had too much power, too many resources, and the far-right was growing stronger by the day. But what choice did they have? This was their home, their community, and they couldn't just walk away.

As the sun set over the shattered skyline of London, Amir steeled himself for the battles to come. The war wasn't over—not yet—but the path ahead was darker than ever.

The New Face of Europe – Early 2027

The European continent had become a patchwork of war zones, failed states, and refugee camps. Germany, once the engine of the European Union, had fractured beyond repair. Berlin had become a battleground for various militias, each vying for control of what little remained of the city. The central government had collapsed, and far-right groups were now in control of much of the country. Immigrant enclaves, like the one Karim and Malik were defending, had become isolated pockets of resistance, surrounded by hostile forces on all sides.

France was no better. The government's brutal crackdown on the insurgency had only intensified the violence, and Paris was now a city divided between military-controlled zones and insurgent-held territories. The once vibrant culture of the city had been replaced by fear and uncertainty. Yasmine and her comrades were fighting a losing battle, trying to hold onto a cause that was slipping through their fingers.

In the United Kingdom, Nathan Hawke's government had lost control of large swathes of the country. Far-right militias were now openly challenging the government's authority, and the Muslim militias, like Zayn's, were fighting for survival in the ghettos of cities like London and Birmingham. The country was on the verge of collapse, torn apart by the very divisions it had tried to suppress for so long.

As Europe crumbled, the rest of the world watched in horror. The dream of a unified, peaceful Europe was gone, replaced by a nightmare of war and division. The continent, once a beacon of democracy and prosperity, had become a battlefield, where the only certainty was more violence.

The war that had started with the migrant crisis was no longer about refugees or integration. It was now a fight for survival, a struggle for control of a continent that was tearing itself apart. The religious, cultural, and political divisions that had simmered for decades had finally boiled over, and there was no turning back.

For Malik, Yasmine, Amir, and the countless others caught in the crossfire, the future was uncertain. But one thing was clear: Europe would never be the same again. The war had changed everything, and the old world was gone. What would emerge from the ashes was anyone's guess.

Chapter 13: The Collapse of Nations

Berlin, Germany – Spring 2027

By the spring of 2027, Berlin's collapse was all but complete. The German government, weakened and overwhelmed, had lost control of most major cities. The rural areas, once thought to be refuges, were either under siege or had become havens for various militias—both far-right extremists and immigrant groups. The remnants of the German army were stretched thin, struggling to protect vital infrastructure and what was left of the civilian population.

Malik stood in the middle of the ruined city, staring at what used to be Alexanderplatz. The iconic Berlin TV Tower still rose above the city, but now it was a symbol of survival amid chaos. Its steel frame had survived bombings and street fighting, a lonely sentinel in a city tearing itself apart.

After months of conflict, Karim's militia had managed to seize control of several blocks around the tower, turning it into their headquarters. But holding territory in a collapsing city was an ever-shifting game of survival, with resources dwindling and alliances fragile.

"Malik, the food drop didn't make it through," one of the younger fighters reported, his face pale with fear and exhaustion. "The convoy was ambushed by a far-right group near Tempelhof. We lost contact after the first explosion."

Malik closed his eyes for a moment, taking a deep breath to calm himself. This was the third supply run they had lost in two weeks. With each defeat, their chances of survival grew slimmer.

"I'll go with the next team," he said finally, though he knew the risk. "We can't afford to lose another convoy. And we can't keep losing people. We need to find another way to get food, medicine—anything."

The young fighter nodded, but Malik could see the doubt in his eyes. The war had drained everyone. Those who had once fought with conviction now fought out of desperation, clinging to life in a city that had forgotten what peace felt like.

Paris, France – Spring 2027

Paris was burning. Not in the figurative sense—actual fires dotted the skyline, their smoke blending with the dark clouds that hung over the city. The French government, weakened and overwhelmed, had lost its grip. Even with the military enforcing martial law, entire districts of Paris were no longer under their control. The insurgents held firm in their territories, and the banlieues had become fortresses.

Yasmine crouched behind a makeshift barricade in what was once a bustling neighbourhood, her breath shallow as the sounds of battle raged around her. The French military had launched yet another raid on the insurgent-held areas, hoping to break the resistance once and for all. But Yasmine knew they were only prolonging the inevitable. The country was broken.

Her thoughts were consumed by Amina. She had failed her, and now Yasmine carried the weight of that failure every day. Despite their efforts, they had been unable to stop her execution. The government had made a spectacle of it, broadcasting it to send a message to anyone else who dared rise against them.

But instead of breaking the resistance, Amina's death had become a rallying cry. The insurgency had grown fiercer, and Paris had become the epicentre of the war that was tearing France apart.

"We need to fall back," one of the fighters shouted over the gunfire. "They're bringing in tanks."

Yasmine knew they couldn't hold the position much longer. The government forces were better equipped, and the insurgents were running out of ammunition. But something inside her rebelled at the thought of retreating again.

"We'll give them hell," she replied, loading her rifle. "But we can't die here. Not today."

With a quick signal, the fighters began to pull back, retreating through the labyrinth of alleyways and crumbling buildings that had become their battlefield. Yasmine's heart pounded as they fled, her mind racing with thoughts of what would come next. Paris was on the brink of total collapse, and there was no safe haven left.

London, United Kingdom – Spring 2027

London, like the rest of Europe, was a city divided. East London had become a battleground, locked in a deadly standoff between the Muslim militias, government forces, and the far-right militias that prowled the outskirts, waiting for an opportunity to strike. Zayn's militia, once hopeful of survival, was now on the verge of collapse.

Amir had lost count of the days since the last major battle. They had barely survived the government's most recent assault, and now, holed up in what was left of a once-bustling neighbourhood, Amir could feel the despair in the air. Zayn had become increasingly erratic, driven more by hatred than strategy, and Amir knew it was only a matter of time before everything fell apart.

The far-right groups were getting bolder, attacking in broad daylight, and the government was using these attacks as justification for even harsher crackdowns. Caught in the middle, Amir felt trapped, fighting in a war he no longer believed in.

He looked around at the faces of his comrades, young men and women who had joined the fight out of desperation, hope, or a sense of duty. Now, they were gaunt, their eyes hollow from sleepless nights and constant fear.

"We can't keep fighting like this," Amir said one evening, as he and Zayn met to discuss their next move. "We're outnumbered, outgunned, and we've lost too many already. We need to find another way."

Zayn glared at him, his face twisted in anger. "What are you suggesting, Amir? Surrender? After everything we've sacrificed?"

Amir sighed. "I'm saying that if we don't stop, we'll all be dead. We've lost, Zayn. We need to find a way to negotiate, to get civilians out of here before it's too late."

Zayn shook his head violently. "There's no negotiating with them. They want us gone—dead. The only way we survive is by fighting. If we stop now, it will all have been for nothing."

Amir stared at his old friend, the fire in Zayn's eyes now indistinguishable from madness. He wanted to argue, to make Zayn see reason, but he knew it was futile. Zayn was committed to the fight, no matter the cost.

And the cost was becoming unbearable.

Brussels, Belgium – Spring 2027

In Brussels, the heart of what was once the European Union, the halls of power were eerily silent. The EU had officially dissolved months earlier, and Belgium was now in a state of chaos. The country, already fragile due to its linguistic and cultural divisions, had fractured completely. Brussels, once the political capital of Europe, had become a battleground.

Nationalist groups, both far right and secessionist, clashed with immigrant enclaves and what was left of the Belgian government forces. The conflict in Brussels was a microcosm of the larger war engulfing Europe—a war defined not just by religion, but by nationalism, xenophobia, and the failure of the old political order.

The collapse of the European Union had shocked the world, but it had been a long time coming. Years of economic stagnation, political infighting, and the inability to deal with the migrant crisis had eroded the foundations of the EU. When the violence in Germany and France reached its peak, the other member states had been unable to respond. The dream of a united Europe had died in the flames of civil war.

For Malik, Yasmine, Amir, and the countless others caught in the crossfire, Brussels was now just another casualty of a continent that had torn itself apart. The streets were lined with barricades, and the city's landmarks, once symbols of unity, were now battlegrounds.

The Fragmenting World Order – Spring 2027

The collapse of Europe was not contained to the continent. The rest of the world had watched in horror as the European Union fell apart, and now the repercussions were being felt globally. Refugee flows had overwhelmed neighbouring countries, sparking unrest in places that had once been considered stable. The political and economic impact of Europe's disintegration was rippling across the globe, threatening to destabilize other regions.

In North America, the United States and Canada were struggling to contain the wave of European refugees flooding their shores. The political divisions that had plagued the U.S. for years were deepening, with isolationist voices growing louder. The refugee crisis, combined with the economic fallout from Europe's collapse, had pushed the country to the brink of a political crisis of its own.

In the Middle East, the chaos in Europe had emboldened extremist groups, who now saw an opportunity to expand their influence. The vacuum left by Europe's disintegration had created new fronts in an already complex web of conflicts.

The global order, which had relied on Europe as a pillar of stability, was beginning to crumble. The world was entering a new era—one defined by uncertainty, violence, and a shifting balance of power.

The Uncertain Future

As the war in Europe raged on, the future remained unclear. Cities like Berlin, Paris, and London were now battlefields, their once-vibrant cultures destroyed by conflict. The people who had once dreamed of peace and unity were now caught in a fight for survival, their lives defined by the violence that had consumed their countries.

Malik, Yasmine, and Amir had each chosen their paths, but they were all part of the same tragic story—one of a continent that had failed to reconcile its past with its present. The war that had begun with the migrant crisis had spiralled into something far greater, a conflict that was reshaping the world.

The Long Summer of 2027
Berlin, Germany – Summer 2027

As summer settled over Berlin, the heat only worsened the suffocating atmosphere of a city already on its knees. The stench of decay clung to the air, and the streets remained eerily quiet except for the occasional bursts of gunfire and the rumble of military vehicles. Food was nearly impossible to find, and any supply drops were met with fierce battles between desperate militias and far-right extremists.

Malik's convoy mission, which was supposed to bring in essential supplies, had ended in failure. The ambush had decimated their group, and fewer than half had returned. Now Malik found himself in the crumbling remnants of their base, tending to injured fighters with little more than scraps of gauze and expired antibiotics.

Karim had grown more isolated, retreating into his role as a commander who would rather die fighting than surrender to what he saw as inevitable destruction. His once-inspiring speeches had become bitter tirades against the government and their enemies, and Malik feared that Karim was leading them all toward disaster.

"Do you think we can make it?" Malik asked Sanaa, one of the few remaining fighters he still trusted.

Sanaa sat across from him, wiping blood from her face with a dirty cloth. She looked at Malik with tired eyes, her face hardened by months of warfare.

"We're already gone, Malik," she said softly. "The question is how much longer we can hold on before they wipe us out."

Malik said nothing. Sanaa was right, of course. Berlin was a shell, and their cause, though just in its origins, had turned into a brutal fight for survival that had lost all meaning. The few civilians left in the city were barely holding on. Those who could had fled long ago, leaving behind the elderly, the sick, and the hopeless.

Outside, the city burned under the scorching summer sun, and Malik knew their time was running out.

Paris, France – Summer 2027

In Paris, the situation had grown even more dire. The once-glorious city had become a battleground for control, with the government and insurgents locked in a vicious cycle of raids, counterraids, and street warfare. The banlieues remained under insurgent control, but the rest of the city was divided, and both sides were weary from constant fighting.

Yasmine had barely slept in days. Every night brought more gunfire, more explosions, and more bloodshed. The streets were lined with barricades and makeshift checkpoints, and the French military's presence was suffocating. The insurgents had managed to keep their strongholds intact, but at a heavy price—casualties were mounting, and morale was fading.

She sat with a small group of fighters in an abandoned café, maps of the city spread out across the table. They were planning their next move—a desperate attempt to seize a nearby police station and secure weapons and medical supplies. But Yasmine's mind was elsewhere. Amina's death haunted her, and the cause she had once believed in seemed like a distant memory.

"Yasmine, we can't keep doing this," one of her comrades said, voicing what they were all thinking. "The city's falling apart. The people are suffering. We've lost so many already—what's left to fight for?"

Yasmine looked around at the faces of those who had fought by her side, faces etched with exhaustion and despair. She had no easy answers.

"We fight because there's no other choice," she said, though her voice lacked the conviction it once had. "We fight because if we don't, they'll destroy everything we've fought for."

But even as she spoke the words, Yasmine knew that the line between resistance and survival had blurred beyond recognition. The ideals they had once stood for had been consumed by the violence that now defined their lives. The dream of a free, just France had been reduced to ashes, and all that remained was the struggle to stay alive.

London, United Kingdom – Summer 2027

London, too, was on the edge of collapse. East London had become a no-man's land, a battleground where government forces, far-right militias, and Muslim enclaves clashed on a daily basis. The government's attempts to regain control of the city had only made things worse, as every assault brought more death and destruction.

Amir had grown disillusioned with Zayn's leadership. What had once been a movement to protect their community had turned into a desperate and chaotic fight for survival, and Zayn's increasingly erratic decisions were leading them down a dark path.

One evening, after yet another failed raid on a government checkpoint, Amir confronted Zayn in their makeshift base—a dilapidated apartment building that had been repurposed as a headquarters.

"We can't keep doing this, Zayn," Amir said, his voice tense. "We're running out of fighters, we're running out of weapons, and we're running out of hope. We need to find another way before we all get killed."

Zayn, gaunt and sleepless, glared at him. "There is no other way, Amir. We either fight, or we die. Do you think they'll show us mercy if we surrender? Do you think the far-right thugs prowling the streets will let us live in peace?"

Amir clenched his fists. "This isn't about survival anymore, Zayn. This is madness. You're leading us into a slaughter, and you know it."

Zayn's eyes burned with fury. "If you want to leave, then leave. But I'm not giving up. Not now. Not after everything we've been through."

Amir didn't respond. Instead, he turned and walked out, the weight of the war crushing his spirit. He knew Zayn was lost—lost to the violence, to the hatred, to the endless cycle of revenge. And Amir couldn't follow him any longer.

Brussels, Belgium – Summer 2027

The once-great city of Brussels had descended into chaos. The European Union had crumbled, its institutions abandoned, its leaders either dead, in hiding, or desperately clinging to what little power they still had. The collapse of the EU had been swift and brutal, and Brussels, the heart of Europe, had become a battlefield.

Nationalist militias roamed the streets, clashing with immigrant enclaves and what remained of the Belgian government forces. The ideals of European unity and cooperation had been buried beneath the rubble of civil war, replaced by the stark realities of division, hatred, and survival.

The collapse of Brussels had sent shockwaves throughout Europe and beyond. The fall of the EU had shattered the global political order, and the repercussions were being felt in every corner of the world. Refugees from Europe were flooding into neighbouring regions, sparking new conflicts and crises. The world was watching in horror as the continent descended into darkness.

The Long Summer

By the summer of 2027, Europe had become unrecognizable. The war that had begun with the migrant crisis had spiralled into something far greater—a conflict that had reshaped the entire continent. National governments had collapsed, cities lay in ruins, and millions of people were displaced, fleeing the violence that consumed their homes.

The old world was gone. The dream of a united, peaceful Europe had died in the fires of war, and what would emerge from the ashes was still uncertain. For the people still trapped in the cities, fighting for survival in the ruins of civilization, the only certainty was that the war was far from over.

Malik, Yasmine, and Amir, like so many others, had been swept up in a conflict they could not control. They had lost friends, allies, and loved ones. They had fought for causes that had become hollow, and they had seen the world they knew crumble around them.

As the long summer stretched on, the war showed no signs of ending. And for those who remained, the future seemed darker than ever.

But even in the darkness, there were whispers of something new. Of new alliances forming in the shadows, of people rising from the ruins to rebuild what had been lost. It was too soon to tell what would come next, but one thing was clear: the world had changed, and there was no going back.

Chapter 14: Crossroads

As the summer heat gave way to the chill of autumn, Berlin was no closer to peace. The once-proud capital, now reduced to a smouldering ruin of fractured ideologies, had become a symbol of Europe's fall from grace. What was once a city of history, culture, and unity had turned into a contested wasteland, where survival itself was a victory.

Malik had spent the last few months wandering the ruined streets of Berlin, watching as his beloved city fell apart, piece by piece. The fighter in him, once filled with purpose and conviction, now felt hollow. His body bore the scars of battle, but his soul ached from the war that had consumed everyone he loved.

He moved carefully through the bombed-out streets, his eyes scanning every corner for signs of movement. The far-right militias had become more aggressive in recent weeks, launching coordinated attacks on immigrant communities, claiming to "reclaim" the country for its native people. Meanwhile, the Muslim insurgent groups retaliated with their own brand of violence, pushing further into territory once held by government forces.

The government, or what was left of it, had retreated from the chaos. Berlin was now under martial law, but even the soldiers looked exhausted, their morale shattered. The city was in a state of paralysis—too broken to function, yet too stubborn to surrender.

Sanaa, still by Malik's side, had become the only constant in his life. Together, they had formed a small group of survivors, loyalists to neither the government nor the insurgents. They operated in the shadows, focused on finding food, water, and shelter rather than fighting a war that seemed never-ending.

One evening, as the sun set behind the skeletal remains of the Brandenburg Gate, Sanaa approached Malik. Her face was gaunt, her eyes hollow, but there was still a spark of defiance in her voice.

"Malik," she said quietly, "we can't stay here forever. The city is dying. We need to think about what comes next."

Malik turned to face her; his own exhaustion mirrored in her eyes. "What comes next? There is nothing left for us, Sanaa. We've lost everything."

She shook her head. "That's not true. We still have our lives, and that's more than most can say. We need to leave Berlin. Maybe we can find somewhere safer, somewhere we can start again."

"Start again?" Malik asked bitterly. "And where do you think that place is? Europe is burning, Sanaa. There's no safe haven anymore."

Sanaa placed a hand on his arm, her voice soft but firm. "We can't give up. Not yet. We've survived this long, haven't we?"

Malik looked into her eyes, seeing the hope she clung to despite everything. He wanted to believe her, but the weight of the war bore down on him, crushing his spirit. Still, if there was any chance of finding a way out, of starting over, he owed it to Sanaa to try.

"Fine," Malik said finally. "But we don't leave without the others. We're not abandoning anyone."

Sanaa nodded, her resolve strengthening. "Agreed. We leave together, or not at all."

As they walked back toward the makeshift hideout where their group had been staying, Malik couldn't shake the feeling that this decision—whether to stay and fight or flee and survive—was the real crossroads. They were all caught between a dying city and an uncertain future, and the choices they made in the coming days would determine not only their fate but the fate of Europe itself.

Paris, France – Autumn 2027

The streets of Paris had not seen peace in months. The once-beautiful city had become a battleground, a twisted mirror of its former glory. Burnt-out cars littered the boulevards, and barricades blocked major intersections, turning every street corner into a potential war zone.

Yasmine stood at the edge of one such barricade, her hands trembling as she watched her comrades prepare for another assault. The banlieues had been under siege for weeks, with French government forces trying to retake control of the insurgent-held areas. Each skirmish brought more bloodshed, more loss, but there was no end in sight.

"Are you ready?" a voice behind her asked.

Yasmine turned to see Imran, one of the few fighters she still trusted. His face was lined with exhaustion, his clothes covered in the dirt and grime of battle. He had become a brother to her in this war, a constant companion in the fight for survival.

"As ready as I'll ever be," Yasmine replied, her voice hollow.

Imran glanced at the makeshift barricade, then back at Yasmine. "You don't have to do this, you know. You've done more than your share. Maybe it's time to walk away."

"Walk away to where?" Yasmine asked, her voice filled with bitterness. "There's nowhere to go. This city is my home. I'm not leaving it."

Imran sighed. "Home doesn't exist anymore. Paris isn't the city we knew."

"I know," Yasmine admitted. "But what else do we have? If we leave, we lose everything."

"You mean if we stay, we lose everything," Imran corrected. "Look around you, Yasmine. This war is never going to end. Not in any way that leaves us standing."

She stared at him, the weight of his words sinking in. Deep down, she knew he was right. The cause they had fought for had been consumed by hatred, fear, and revenge. There was no going back to what they had before. But leaving felt like giving up, like letting the war take everything from her.

"I'm not ready to give up," Yasmine said quietly. "Not yet."

Imran looked at her for a long moment before nodding. "Then let's finish this. But after today, we need to think about what's next. Because if we keep fighting like this, there won't be anyone left to remember what we were fighting for."

London, United Kingdom – Autumn 2027

In London, the fog of war had settled over the city like a shroud. The skyline, once filled with iconic landmarks, was now punctuated by plumes of smoke and the distant sound of gunfire. The streets of East London, once bustling with life, were now battle-scarred and abandoned.

Amir sat in the remnants of a small flat, its windows shattered, and its walls covered in graffiti. He was alone, separated from his comrades after a government raid had torn through their ranks. Zayn had been captured—or worse—and Amir had barely escaped with his life.

For days, he had wandered the streets, avoiding both government forces and the far-right militias that patrolled the city. His mind raced with questions, doubts, and regrets. Had it all been for nothing? The movement they had built to protect their community had become something darker, something Amir could no longer recognize.

He thought about his parents, his siblings, the people he had lost. They had fled here for safety, for a new beginning. And now London had become a prison, a place where hope had died long before the war had reached its peak.

As he sat in the cold, Amir heard footsteps outside. His heart raced as he pressed himself against the wall, gripping the small knife he carried. But the footsteps were slow and deliberate, not the hurried steps of a soldier or militia member.

The door creaked open, and a figure stepped inside.

"Amir?"

He recognized the voice immediately. It was Hana, a woman he had fought alongside in the early days of the insurgency. Her face was gaunt, her clothes torn and bloodstained, but there was a fire in her eyes.

"Hana," Amir whispered, standing up slowly. "I thought you were dead."

"I thought you were, too," she replied, a faint smile touching her lips. "But here we are. Still breathing."

They stood in silence for a moment, taking in the sight of each other. Amir could see the pain in her eyes, the weight of everything they had endured. And yet, despite it all, there was still hope in her gaze.

"We need to get out of here," Hana said. "I've found a group. They're planning to leave the city, head north. There's a safe haven up there, away from all of this."

Amir hesitated. "A safe haven? Do you really believe that?"

"It's all we have left," Hana said. "And if we stay here, we die. You know that as well as I do."

Amir looked out the shattered window at the desolate streets of London. He knew Hana was right. The city was lost, and if he stayed, he would be too.

"Alright," he said finally. "Let's go."

BRYSON MINE

As they left the flat and made their way through the ruins of London, Amir couldn't shake the feeling that he was leaving more than just a city behind. He was leaving behind the last remnants of a life he had once known—a life that had been swallowed by the war.

Chapter 15: The Exodus

The Road North – Late Autumn 2027

The journey north was fraught with danger. Malik and Sanaa's small group, joined by a few other survivors, moved cautiously through the ruined countryside of Germany. They avoided main roads and towns, knowing that both government forces and insurgent groups were likely to be watching. They travelled under cover of darkness, their movements slow and deliberate, always aware that one wrong step could lead to disaster.

The landscape they passed through was haunting. Fields once filled with crops now lay fallow, burned to ash or overgrown with weeds. Villages had been abandoned; their homes reduced to rubble. Occasionally, they would come across other survivors—people who had lost everything and were fleeing just like them. Some were willing to share their meagre supplies, while others were too afraid to trust anyone.

One night, as they camped in the remains of an old farmhouse, Malik sat with Sanaa by a small fire. The others were asleep or keeping watch, their faces gaunt and exhausted.

"Do you think we'll make it?" Sanaa asked quietly.

Malik stared into the flames, his mind heavy with doubt. "I don't know. But we don't have a choice. We have to try."

Sanaa was silent for a moment before speaking again. "Do you ever think about what comes next? After this? If we make it out of Germany, what then?"

Malik sighed. "I don't know, Sanaa. I used to have a plan, a purpose. But now... now I'm just trying to survive."

Sanaa looked at him, her eyes filled with a quiet determination. "Surviving is enough for now. We can figure out the rest later."

Malik nodded, though he wasn't sure he believed it. The war had taken so much from him—his family, his friends, his city. What was left to fight for? What future could they hope for when everything around them was crumbling?

But as he sat there with Sanaa, surrounded by the ruins of the world they had known, he realized that maybe survival was enough. Maybe that was all anyone could hope for in a world like this.

Calais, France – Late Autumn 2027

Yasmine and Imran stood on the shores of Calais, staring out at the English Channel. The small boat that would take them across to England rocked gently in the waves, a fragile vessel in the face of the vast sea.

They had made it this far, escaping the chaos of Paris and the war-torn French countryside. But the journey had not been easy. Along the way, they had lost comrades—people who had fought and bled beside them. Some had been killed in skirmishes with government forces, while others had simply disappeared, swallowed by the night and the violence that surrounded them.

"We've come this far," Imran said quietly. "There's no turning back now."

Yasmine nodded, her heart heavy with the weight of everything they had lost. She thought of the people they had left behind, the lives they had fought to protect. But there was no going back. France was lost, and if they stayed, they would be too.

"Let's go," Yasmine said, her voice steady despite the fear that gripped her.

As they boarded the small boat, Yasmine couldn't help but think about what awaited them on the other side of the channel. England was no safe haven. The war had reached its shores as well, and London was burning just as Paris had. But it was a new start—a chance to rebuild, to find something worth fighting for again.

The boat set off into the choppy waters of the channel, carrying Yasmine, Imran, and the few survivors who had made it this far. Behind them, France faded into the distance, a land consumed by war and despair.

Ahead lay the unknown.

London, United Kingdom – Winter 2027

Amir and Hana's journey north had been slow and treacherous, but they had finally reached the outskirts of London. The city had become a fortress, with government forces and militias fighting for control of every street. But there were pockets of resistance—small groups of survivors who had managed to carve out a life amid the chaos.

They had heard rumours of a safe haven in the north, a place where the war had not yet reached. It was a long shot, but it was all they had left.

As they moved through the ruins of East London, Amir couldn't shake the feeling that they were being watched. The streets were eerily quiet, the only sounds the distant echo of gunfire and the occasional shout of a patrol.

"We need to keep moving," Hana whispered, her eyes scanning the darkened alleyways.

Amir nodded, his hand resting on the knife tucked into his belt. They had learned the hard way that trust was a luxury they couldn't afford. Everyone was a potential threat, and one wrong move could mean the end.

As they made their way through the rubble-strewn streets, Amir's thoughts drifted to the future. Could there really be a safe haven? Or was it just another false hope in a world that had lost its way?

He didn't know. But as long as there was a chance, however slim, he would keep moving forward.

Because the alternative was death.

Chapter 16: The Breaking Point

Berlin, Germany – Winter 2028

Berlin had reached its breaking point. The city, once the heart of Europe, had been reduced to a battleground of ideologies, torn apart by war and hatred. The government had lost control, and the far-right militias had seized large swathes of the city, declaring it a "liberated" zone. The Muslim insurgents, entrenched in their own territories, fought back with increasing ferocity.

Malik and his group had made it as far as the outskirts of the city, but their journey had been fraught with danger. They had lost members along the way—friends who had been with them since the beginning. Each loss weighed heavily on Malik's heart, but there was no time to grieve. They had to keep moving.

As they approached the edge of the city, Malik stopped, looking back at the skyline of Berlin. The once-familiar landmarks were now nothing more than silhouettes against a backdrop of smoke and fire.

"Are we really doing this?" Sanaa asked quietly, standing beside him.

"We don't have a choice," Malik replied, his voice heavy with resignation. "If we stay, we die."

Sanaa nodded, though her face was etched with uncertainty. "And if we leave?"

Malik didn't answer. There was no way to know what awaited them beyond the city limits. But he knew that staying in Berlin was no longer an option.

The group moved forward, leaving behind the city that had been their home, their battleground, and their prison. They were heading into the unknown, but for the first time in a long time, there was a glimmer of hope—a chance to escape the madness that had consumed them.

But as they walked away from Berlin, Malik couldn't shake the feeling that the war wasn't over. It had simply moved on, spreading its tendrils to new places, new people.

And wherever it went, it would leave destruction in its wake.

London, United Kingdom – Winter 2028

Amir and Hana had made it to the north of England, but the journey had taken its toll. They were tired, hungry, and broken in ways they hadn't been before. The safe haven they had heard so much about was nothing more than a few scattered camps, filled with refugees and survivors of the war.

There was no safety here, no peace. The war had followed them, creeping into every corner of the country. The far-right militias had spread north, and government forces were struggling to maintain control. The conflict that had started in the cities was now spilling over into the countryside, and there was no end in sight.

As they sat around a small fire, surrounded by other survivors, Amir looked at Hana, his heart heavy with the weight of everything they had lost.

"Is this it?" Amir asked quietly. "Is this what we were fighting for?"

Hana didn't answer right away. She stared into the flames; her face illuminated by the flickering light.

"I don't know," she said finally. "But we're still here. And that has to mean something."

Amir nodded, though he wasn't sure what it meant anymore. The war had taken everything from them, and the future was as uncertain as ever.

But as long as they were still breathing, there was a chance—a chance to rebuild, to find some semblance of peace in a world that had been shattered.

And that was all they had left.

Paris, France – Winter 2028

Yasmine and Imran had made it across the English Channel, but their journey was far from over. London, once their destination, was now a city under siege, and the war had spread to every corner of the country.

As they moved through the refugee camps scattered across the countryside, Yasmine couldn't help but feel a sense of despair. The war had followed them, and there was no escape. The safe haven they had hoped for was nothing more than a temporary reprieve from the violence that consumed their lives.

"We can't stay here," Imran said quietly, his eyes scanning the camp. "This isn't what we were fighting for."

Yasmine nodded, though her heart ached with the weight of everything they had lost. She thought of Paris, the city they had fought to protect, now a distant memory. She thought of the people they had left behind, the lives that had been destroyed by the war.

But as long as they were still alive, there was hope—a hope that one day, they might find a place where the war could no longer reach them.

And so, they moved on, leaving behind the remnants of the world they had known, searching for a future that was still uncertain.

Because in a world torn apart by war, hope was all they had left.

Chapter 17: Tipping Point

Brussels, Belgium – Early Spring 2028

The rain fell steadily on the cobblestone streets of Brussels, turning the city into a maze of slick, wet pavement and shimmering lights. The European Parliament building, once a symbol of unity and democratic ideals, stood like a fortress amidst the chaos. Its grand architecture now seemed an ironic relic of a different era—one where hope still reigned over fear. Inside its walls, the last vestiges of Europe's fractured leadership clung to power.

Elena Moreau sat in a dimly lit conference room, her hands trembling as she went over the latest reports. The information pouring in from across the continent painted a picture of Europe on the brink. Armed clashes between far-right militias and Muslim insurgents had escalated into full-scale battles in cities like Berlin, Paris, and Rome. The governments were barely holding onto control in the major cities, and in some regions, the rule of law had collapsed altogether. Refugee camps had become makeshift war zones, caught in the crossfire of religious and ideological warfare.

Elena, now the acting President of the European Commission after her predecessor resigned in disgrace, was among the few trying to steer the sinking ship. At 42, she had risen through the ranks of the EU as a moderate voice, advocating for dialogue and compromise. But compromise seemed like a distant memory now. The divisions ran too deep, and no one on either side was willing to back down.

"Madame President?" A voice interrupted her thoughts. It was Anwar Khaled, her chief advisor on international affairs, who had been with her since the early days of the crisis. Anwar, a refugee from Syria who had become a key political figure in Belgium, had been a staunch advocate for Europe's openness to migrants. But even he looked defeated, his usual calm demeanour cracked by the growing uncertainty.

"What is it, Anwar?" Elena asked, looking up from the endless stream of reports.

"More unrest in Germany. We've received confirmation that the far-right militias in Bavaria have declared the region independent from the federal government. They've aligned themselves with several other separatist movements across Europe," Anwar explained, his voice grim. "And it's not just them. Muslim insurgent forces in the south of France have taken full control of Marseille. They've declared it a 'city of refuge' for Muslims across Europe."

Elena's stomach twisted. "How did we let it come to this?" she murmured, more to herself than to Anwar. She had known this was coming. Everyone had. But knowing and witnessing it happen were two entirely different things.

"We didn't stop it because we couldn't," Anwar said, his voice barely above a whisper. "We thought we had more time."

Elena pushed back her chair and stood up, pacing the length of the room. The rain outside had intensified, pounding against the windows as if echoing her growing sense of dread.

"Have we heard from the UK?" she asked.

Anwar hesitated. "Nothing concrete. The situation there is chaotic. The government is struggling to maintain order in London. Reports suggest that northern England is practically lawless now, with militias controlling entire towns."

Elena closed her eyes, fighting the urge to scream. The UK had been one of their strongest allies in the early days of the migrant crisis. Now, it seemed, they were barely holding it together themselves. The dream of a unified Europe was unravelling before her eyes.

"We need to call an emergency summit," Elena said finally, her voice hardening. "We need all the heads of state here in Brussels. We can't keep pretending this is a series of isolated conflicts. This is Europe tearing itself apart."

Anwar nodded. "I'll make the arrangements. But you know as well as I do that getting them all to agree on anything will be... difficult."

"Difficult or not, it's our only option," Elena replied. "If we don't act now, there won't be an EU left to save."

Marseille, France – Early Spring 2028

The city of Marseille had become unrecognizable. The Mediterranean breeze that once carried the scent of sea salt and fresh fish now blew through streets littered with debris and bullet-ridden buildings. The port, once bustling with trade, was under the control of the insurgents, its waters now used to smuggle weapons and supplies from the Middle East and North Africa.

Youssef, one of the key commanders of the insurgent forces, stood on the balcony of a commandeered government building, looking out over the city he now ruled. For months, he and his fighters had been engaged in a brutal struggle for control of southern France, and now they had finally secured a stronghold. Marseille had fallen, and with it, a symbolic victory for the Muslim insurgency.

The French government had abandoned the city weeks ago, focusing their limited military resources on defending Paris and other northern regions. The insurgents had moved in swiftly, taking control of critical infrastructure and establishing their own form of governance. For Youssef, it was a personal triumph—his own family had fled Syria during the early days of the migrant crisis, and now he had risen to lead a revolution in Europe itself.

But victory came at a cost.

Youssef's lieutenant, a young man named Tariq, approached him on the balcony, his expression tense. "We've received word from the outskirts of the city," he said. "The French government is planning a counteroffensive. They've mobilized troops and armoured vehicles. They'll be here within days."

Youssef didn't flinch. He had been expecting this. The French would never let Marseille go without a fight.

"Let them come," Youssef said, his voice calm. "We've prepared for this. The city is fortified, and we have enough fighters to hold them off."

Tariq shifted uneasily. "But what about supplies? Ammunition? If they lay siege to the city, we might not have enough to last."

Youssef turned to face him, his eyes hard. "We'll find a way. We always do."

Tariq nodded, though his expression remained uncertain. "And what about the civilians? The ones who didn't leave when we took over. They're caught in the middle of this."

"Civilians?" Youssef scoffed. "They had their chance to leave. This is a war, Tariq. And in war, there are always casualties."

Tariq hesitated, as if about to say something more, but he held his tongue. He had learned long ago that questioning Youssef's decisions could be dangerous.

As Tariq left the balcony, Youssef looked out over the city once more. Marseille was his now, and he would defend it with everything he had. But deep down, he knew that the fight was far from over. The French government wouldn't stop at Marseille. And as the war spread, more cities, more lives, would be consumed by the flames.

London, United Kingdom – Early Spring 2028

London had become a city of fortresses. Makeshift barricades, barbed wire, and sandbags lined the streets, dividing the capital into zones controlled by various factions. The government still held the central districts, but the outer boroughs had fallen to militias, gangs, and insurgents.

Amir and Hana had found temporary refuge in one of the last functioning hospitals in East London. The building was overcrowded, its hallways filled with the injured and the dying. Doctors worked around the clock, tending to victims of bombings, shootings, and disease. Supplies were scarce, and the air was thick with the stench of blood and decay.

Amir sat by Hana's side, watching as a nurse bandaged her arm. She had been wounded during their escape from northern England, a close call with a militia patrol. The wound wasn't life-threatening, but it was enough to slow them down.

"We can't stay here," Amir said quietly, his voice tinged with frustration. "This city is falling apart. It's only a matter of time before the fighting reaches us again."

Hana winced as the nurse tightened the bandage. "Where do you suggest we go, Amir? There's nowhere left. The north is no better. We saw what it was like."

Amir clenched his fists, the feeling of helplessness gnawing at him. They had been running for so long—first from the war in Syria, then from the chaos that had consumed Europe. Every time they thought they had found a place of safety, the violence followed.

"I don't know," Amir admitted. "But we can't just sit here and wait to die."

Hana looked at him, her eyes filled with a mixture of pain and exhaustion. "And what if we're running toward our death, too? What if there is no escape?"

Amir opened his mouth to respond, but the words caught in his throat. He didn't have an answer. All he knew was that staying in London felt like waiting for the inevitable.

Before he could say anything more, the sound of distant explosions echoed through the city, shaking the walls of the hospital. People around them panicked, some running for cover while others simply huddled in fear.

"It's getting closer," Hana whispered, her voice barely audible over the chaos.

Amir stood up, his mind racing. They couldn't wait any longer. If they stayed here, they would be caught in the crossfire.

"We're leaving tonight," Amir said, his voice firm. "I don't care where we go, but we can't stay here."

Hana didn't argue. She knew he was right.

As the hospital staff worked frantically to tend to the new wave of injured flooding in, Amir and Hana quietly gathered what little supplies they had left. They would slip away under the cover of darkness, heading into the unknown once again.

Because in a world torn apart by war, there was no such thing as a safe haven.

Chapter 18: The Long Night

Brussels, Belgium – Early Summer 2028

The air in Brussels was thick with tension. The emergency summit that Elena Moreau had hastily called was set to begin, with the remaining leaders of Europe converging on the battered city. Armed convoys crisscrossed the streets, transporting heads of state and their entourages to the fortified compound where the meeting was to take place. This was no longer a diplomatic affair, not in the traditional sense. This was a war council.

Inside the European Parliament building, security was tighter than ever. Soldiers patrolled the halls, their expressions grim, as the spectre of violence loomed over the city. With so many powerful figures in one place, the threat of an attack was high, and no one was taking chances. The fragile alliances holding Europe together were fraying, and any misstep could set off a chain reaction of violence.

Elena sat at the head of a long table in the main chamber, waiting for the final delegates to arrive. Her face was pale, her hands gripping the arms of her chair tightly. She had spent the last few days in near-constant meetings, trying to rally what little political support she had left. But it was a losing battle. Every country had its own problems, its own survival to consider.

Anwar Khaled, her chief advisor, stood beside her, flipping through a thick dossier of reports. He looked exhausted, dark circles under his eyes from too many sleepless nights. The weight of Europe's survival rested on their shoulders, and it was starting to show.

"They're not going to listen," Anwar muttered, not looking up from his notes.

"They have to," Elena replied, her voice firmer than she felt inside. "There's no other option. If we don't unite, we fall."

Anwar gave her a sceptical look. "That's the rational argument, sure. But rationality went out the window years ago. Now it's about power, survival, and control."

Elena opened her mouth to respond but was interrupted as the doors swung open. The last of the leaders had arrived. Angela Berkovich, the embattled Chancellor of Germany, swept into the room, flanked by her security detail. Behind her was Emmanuel Lassalle, the French President, his face haggard and drawn, looking like a man on the verge of collapse.

"We're all here," Elena announced, rising to greet them. "Let's begin."

Marseille, France – Early Summer 2028

The sun beat down on the smouldering ruins of Marseille as Youssef surveyed the aftermath of the French government's failed counteroffensive. The insurgents had repelled the attack, but not without cost. The streets were littered with the bodies of both soldiers and civilians, victims of the relentless artillery strikes that had pounded the city for days. The stench of death hung in the air, and the once-bustling port was now a graveyard of twisted metal and shattered concrete.

Youssef's men moved quickly through the wreckage, salvaging what they could from the remains of the French army's abandoned vehicles. Ammunition, weapons, medical supplies—everything was in short supply, and every scrap mattered. His fighters were exhausted, but they couldn't afford to rest. Not yet. The government would be back, and the next attack might not be so easy to repel.

Tariq approached, his face streaked with grime and sweat. "We've secured most of the supplies, but it's not enough to last. We're going to need reinforcements."

Youssef nodded, his mind racing. "Send word to our contacts in North Africa. We need more fighters and more weapons. Marseille is our stronghold now, and we're not losing it."

Tariq hesitated, glancing around at the ruined city. "What about the civilians? The ones still here?"

Youssef frowned, his patience wearing thin. "What about them?"

"They're caught in the middle of this, Youssef. If we don't protect them, we risk losing their support."

Youssef's expression hardened. "This isn't about winning hearts and minds anymore, Tariq. This is about survival. If they're in the way, they need to move. And if they won't... then that's their choice."

Tariq didn't argue, though the tension between them was palpable. He had been with Youssef since the early days of the insurgency, but as the war dragged on, their visions for the future seemed to be diverging. Tariq still held onto the belief that they were fighting for something bigger than themselves—for a new world where the oppressed could rise up and take control of their own destinies. But Youssef... Youssef had become something else. Hardened. Ruthless. Focused only on the next battle, the next victory.

"Just make sure we're ready for the next assault," Youssef said, turning away from his lieutenant. "We can't afford any mistakes."

Tariq watched him go, a sinking feeling settling in his gut. This war was consuming them all, turning ideals into ashes.

Berlin, Germany – Early Summer 2028

Berlin had become a war zone. The fighting between the far-right militias and Muslim insurgents had torn the city apart, turning its streets into battlegrounds and its buildings into fortresses. Malik and his small group of survivors had managed to evade capture for weeks, hiding in the bombed-out ruins of what was once the city's industrial district. But they were running out of options.

The sound of gunfire echoed in the distance as Malik crouched behind a crumbling wall, his heart pounding in his chest. He glanced over at Sanaa, who was kneeling beside him, clutching a rifle. Her face was streaked with dirt, her eyes wide with fear.

"We can't stay here much longer," Malik whispered. "We need to move."

Sanaa nodded, though she didn't look convinced. "Where? Everywhere is crawling with militias."

Malik scanned the horizon, his mind racing. They had been trying to make their way out of Berlin for days, but every route was blocked by roadblocks, patrols, or firefights. The city was a labyrinth of danger, and the walls were closing in.

"There's a train station a few blocks from here," Malik said, his voice low. "If we can make it there, we might be able to hop on one of the freight trains heading west. It's risky, but it's our best shot."

Sanaa swallowed hard. "And if we get caught?"

Malik didn't answer. They both knew what would happen if they were caught by the militias. The far-right groups that now controlled large parts of the city had little mercy for people like them. They had seen what happened to the others—the public executions, the beatings, the disappearances.

"We won't get caught," Malik said, more to reassure himself than Sanaa. "We just have to move fast."

As they prepared to leave their hiding place, a sudden explosion rocked the street behind them. Malik instinctively ducked, pulling Sanaa down with him. The blast sent a shower of debris into the air, and the sound of shouting filled the air.

"They're getting closer," Sanaa said, her voice shaking.

Malik gritted his teeth. They were running out of time.

"Let's go," he said, pulling Sanaa to her feet. "We need to move now."

They darted from their hiding spot, staying low as they weaved through the rubble-strewn streets. Every step felt like a gamble, every corner a potential ambush. The sound of gunfire grew louder as they neared the train station, and Malik's heart raced with every passing second.

As they rounded the final corner, the station came into view—a hulking, abandoned structure with shattered windows and crumbling walls. It looked like a ghost of its former self, but it was their only chance.

"We're almost there," Malik whispered, his voice tight with adrenaline.

But as they approached the entrance, a figure stepped out of the shadows—a man in military gear, his rifle trained on them.

"Stop right there," the man barked.

Malik froze, his blood running cold. Sanaa gasped, her hand tightening around her rifle.

The man's eyes narrowed as he approached, his finger hovering over the trigger. "You're not going anywhere."

London, United Kingdom – Early Summer 2028

Amir and Hana had been moving through the ruins of London for days, evading patrols and scavenging what little they could find. The city had become a patchwork of controlled zones, each one more dangerous than the last. The central government still held parts of Westminster and a few key locations, but much of the city had fallen to chaos.

As they made their way through the deserted streets of South London, Amir's thoughts kept drifting back to the people they had lost along the way. The friends who had fought beside them, the strangers they had met in refugee camps and war-torn villages. Some had died in the fighting, others had simply vanished, lost to the madness that had consumed Europe.

"We need to find shelter for the night," Hana said, her voice breaking through Amir's thoughts.

Amir nodded, scanning their surroundings. The sun was setting, and the shadows were growing longer. The nights were the most dangerous time—when the militias and gangs roamed the streets, looking for anyone unlucky enough to be caught outside.

"There's an old church a few blocks from here," Amir said. "It's been abandoned for a while, but it should be safe enough."

They moved quickly through the empty streets, their footsteps echoing in the silence. The city felt like a tomb, its once vibrant neighbourhoods now desolate and haunted. As they approached the church, Amir couldn't shake the feeling that they were being watched.

"Hurry," he urged, quickening his pace.

They reached the church just as darkness fell. The building was old and crumbling, but it was still standing. They slipped inside, closing the heavy wooden doors behind them.

For a moment, they were safe. But in a world where safety was fleeting, they both knew it wouldn't last long

Chapter 19: Fractured Alliances

Brussels, Belgium – Summer 2028

Elena Moreau sat at the head of the long conference table, the weight of Europe's survival pressing heavily on her shoulders. The room was packed with the continent's last-standing leaders, each one representing a nation teetering on the edge of collapse. The flags of the European Union, faded symbols of a unity that once seemed unshakable, hung on the walls as silent witnesses to the chaos that now gripped the continent.

Tension hummed in the air. They had gathered here, in the heart of Brussels, to find a solution—or at least, to buy themselves more time. But the faces around the table were a mix of desperation, fear, and thinly veiled animosity. The days when these nations had been able to put aside their differences for the sake of a common future were long gone. Now, it was every country for itself.

"I don't see how we can possibly continue down this road," Emmanuel Lassalle, the President of France, said, his voice sharp with exhaustion. He looked like a man who hadn't slept in days—dark circles beneath his eyes, his hands trembling slightly as he spoke. "Marseille is lost. We're fighting insurgents on our own soil, and my government is barely holding on. How can we possibly defend our borders and continue to support the rest of Europe?"

Across the table, Angela Berkovich, the Chancellor of Germany, gave a weary sigh. "You think Germany is in any better position, Lassalle? Bavaria has declared independence, and the militias there have more firepower than our army. Every day, more cities fall into chaos. And now, with the migrant insurgencies growing in strength, our own people are turning against us. We cannot win this war."

"This isn't just about winning a war," Elena interjected, her voice firm. She could feel the eyes of every leader in the room on her, judging her, doubting her. "This is about survival. If we don't stand together now, we are lost."

"Stand together?" Viktor Kovács, the Prime Minister of Hungary, scoffed. He leaned forward, his eyes burning with frustration. "We've tried that. And where has it gotten us? Flooded with refugees, overrun by insurgents, our cultures eroded. I warned all of you that this would happen. Hungary has fortified its borders. We are protecting our own. If the rest of you want to continue down this suicidal path, that's your choice. But Hungary will not be dragged down with you."

The room erupted into arguments. Leaders from Eastern Europe sided with Kovács, calling for stricter borders and withdrawal from any remaining EU initiatives. The Southern European countries, already devastated by the insurgencies and civil strife, begged for military aid and humanitarian assistance. The few remaining Western European nations tried to broker some semblance of compromise, but it was clear that no one was listening.

Elena felt the frustration rise in her chest. She had spent her entire career working to hold Europe together, to bridge the gaps between nations and foster cooperation. But now, sitting at this table, watching the leaders of Europe tear each other apart, she felt that dream slipping away.

"We don't have time for this," Elena said, raising her voice to cut through the chaos. "While we sit here and argue, the insurgents are gaining ground. Entire cities have fallen. There are reports of coordinated attacks across multiple countries. If we don't act now, we lose everything."

"And what do you suggest we do?" Lassalle asked, his voice dripping with sarcasm. "Send more troops we don't have? Issue more condemnations while the streets burn?"

"We need to establish safe zones," Elena replied, trying to keep her tone steady. "Places where civilians can be protected, where aid can be delivered, where we can regroup and reorganize. We need to find a way to communicate with the insurgents, to open channels for negotiation."

"You're talking about surrender," Berkovich said, her voice icy. "You want us to negotiate with the people who are tearing our countries apart?"

Elena shook her head. "I'm not talking about surrender. I'm talking about survival. If we continue to treat this as a traditional war, we will lose. We need to be smarter. We need to find a way to stop the bloodshed before it consumes everything."

Kovács stood up, his face twisted in disgust. "You can talk all you want about peace, Moreau. But you're naive. These people—these insurgents—do not want peace. They want domination. You cannot negotiate with people who see you as nothing more than an enemy to be destroyed."

"And what's your solution, Viktor?" Elena snapped, unable to hold back her frustration any longer. "Lock yourself behind your walls and hope the rest of Europe burns? Do you really think that will keep you safe?"

Kovács glared at her but said nothing. After a long, tense silence, he turned and stormed out of the room, slamming the door behind him.

For a moment, no one spoke. The leaders left in the room exchanged uneasy glances, their fear palpable.

"This is our reality now," Elena said, her voice quiet but determined. "We can either adapt to it, or we can fall. The choice is ours."

Marseille, France – Summer 2028

The streets of Marseille were a battleground once again. Youssef watched from a rooftop as his fighters exchanged gunfire with what was left of the French military. The city, once the crown jewel of the Mediterranean, had become a war zone, its streets filled with rubble and the echo of gunfire. The government forces were relentless, trying to retake the city, but Youssef's insurgents had fortified their positions. They had turned Marseille into a fortress, and they were ready for a long fight.

Tariq, Youssef's second-in-command, approached, his face grim. "The French are pulling back for now, but they'll be back with reinforcements. They're not going to let Marseille go easily."

Youssef nodded, not taking his eyes off the battlefield below. "Let them come. We'll hold the city. And when they come back, we'll be ready."

Tariq hesitated. "Youssef, the civilians... they're suffering. We can't keep using them as shields. We need to find a way to get them out of the city."

Youssef turned to face Tariq, his expression hard. "We need every advantage we can get. The civilians are staying. We can't afford to lose ground."

Tariq's jaw tightened, but he didn't argue. He had learned that Youssef's mind was set. This war had changed them all, and Youssef had become a man driven by a single purpose: victory at any cost.

As Tariq walked away, Youssef's phone buzzed in his pocket. He pulled it out and saw a message from their contacts in North Africa. More fighters were on their way. The insurgency was growing stronger every day, and soon, they would have enough men and weapons to expand their control beyond Marseille.

Youssef allowed himself a rare moment of satisfaction. The French government was crumbling, and with each passing day, their grip on the country weakened. Soon, it wouldn't just be Marseille. Soon, they would control all of southern France. And from there, they could spread their influence across Europe.

London, United Kingdom – Summer 2028

Amir and Hana moved through the darkened streets of London, their breaths shallow and their eyes darting around for any sign of danger. The city was a labyrinth of abandoned buildings, makeshift barricades, and roaming militias. The air was thick with the acrid smell of smoke, and the distant sound of gunfire echoed through the streets.

They had been on the run for weeks, trying to stay one step ahead of the chaos that had engulfed the city. The government's control over London had all but collapsed, and now, various factions fought for dominance. Amir had heard rumours that some parts of the city were being completely cut off, turned into no-man's land by the constant fighting.

"We can't keep running like this," Hana whispered as they ducked into the shadows of a narrow alleyway. Her voice trembled; exhaustion etched into her face. "We need to find somewhere safe."

"There's nowhere safe," Amir replied, scanning the street ahead. "Not anymore."

But even as he said the words, he knew they couldn't keep moving forever. The city was a death trap, and every day they stayed, their chances of survival dwindled.

"We'll head north," Amir said finally. "Maybe we can find shelter in one of the smaller towns. Away from the fighting."

Hana nodded, though the hope in her eyes had long since faded.

They moved quietly through the ruined city, slipping between the shadows like ghosts. Every step was a gamble, every sound a potential threat. But they had no choice. To stay still was to die.

As they made their way toward the edge of the city, Amir's thoughts drifted to the future—a future that seemed more uncertain with every passing day. Europe was falling apart, torn between insurgents, militias, and collapsing governments. There was no safety, no sanctuary.

And yet, deep down, Amir still clung to the faintest spark of hope. Because as long as they were alive, as long as they kept moving, there was still a chance—no matter how small—that they might survive this long night.

Chapter 20: Into the Abyss

Berlin, Germany – Late Summer 2028

The once-proud capital of Germany was now a shadow of its former self, a place where the past seemed like a distant memory. Berlin, the city that had once been the heart of Europe's greatest dreams and ambitions, had descended into an abyss. The clash between far-right militias and insurgent groups had turned the streets into a battlefield, and the people—those who had once called this city home—were little more than collateral damage.

Malik and Sanaa crouched behind the crumbling remains of an old government building, waiting for the right moment to make their move. The sky above them was a dull, ash-grey colour, a reminder of the constant artillery bombardments that had ravaged the city. The air was thick with smoke, and every breath tasted of decay.

"Are you sure this is the right way?" Sanaa asked, her voice barely audible above the distant sounds of gunfire.

Malik nodded, though his own confidence was wearing thin. "We have no choice. The train station is just a few blocks away. If we can make it there, we might have a chance to get out of this city."

Sanaa didn't look convinced, but she didn't argue. They had been on the run for weeks, darting from one hiding place to another, always one step ahead of the militias that controlled Berlin. The city had become a maze of checkpoints, roadblocks, and hostile territory, and every day felt like a new roll of the dice.

"Let's move," Malik whispered, glancing around the corner to make sure the coast was clear.

They crept through the debris-strewn streets, keeping low and moving as quickly as they could. The once vibrant avenues of Berlin were now eerily silent, save for the occasional crack of gunfire or the distant rumble of a tank. The landmarks that had once symbolized the city's resilience—the Brandenburg Gate, the Reichstag—were little more than ruins now, reminders of a world that no longer existed.

As they approached the train station, Malik's heart began to race. The station was one of the few places in the city that still saw some semblance of order, with government forces occasionally using it as a staging area for supplies and troop movements. But it was also a dangerous place, patrolled by militias and insurgent fighters alike, all vying for control.

"Stay close," Malik whispered, gripping Sanaa's hand as they moved through the broken entrance of the station.

The inside of the station was a stark contrast to the chaos outside. The platform was eerily quiet, and the few remaining trains were covered in dust and grime. Most of the trains had been looted or abandoned, but Malik had heard rumours that a few freight trains still operated, carrying supplies to the remaining government-controlled areas in western Germany.

They made their way toward the far end of the platform, where a small group of refugees huddled together, waiting for the next train. The fear in their eyes mirrored Malik's own, but there was also a glimmer of hope—a hope that, somehow, they might escape the nightmare that Berlin had become.

Suddenly, the sound of footsteps echoed through the station, and Malik froze. He glanced over his shoulder to see a group of armed men approaching—a militia patrol.

"Get down," Malik hissed, pulling Sanaa behind a pile of debris.

The militia fighters moved methodically through the station, their rifles at the ready. Malik's heart pounded in his chest as he held his breath, praying that they wouldn't be seen.

But then, one of the fighters stopped. His eyes scanned the area where Malik and Sanaa were hiding.

For a moment, it felt as though time had stopped. Malik's grip on Sanaa's hand tightened as he prepared for the worst.

But then, the fighter turned away, motioning to the others to move on.

Malik exhaled slowly, relief flooding through him. They had been lucky this time, but he knew their luck wouldn't last forever.

"We have to go," Malik whispered, pulling Sanaa to her feet.

They made their way to the edge of the platform, where an old freight train sat idling. The engine was still running, and a few of the doors were open. It wasn't much, but it was their only chance.

"Come on," Malik urged, climbing onto one of the cars.

Sanaa hesitated for a moment, glancing back at the station. "Do you think this will take us somewhere safe?"

Malik shook his head. "I don't know. But anywhere is better than here."

Together, they climbed into the freight car and closed the door behind them. The train jerked to life, slowly beginning to move. Malik leaned back against the wall of the car, exhaustion washing over him. For now, they were safe.

But as the train rumbled away from Berlin, Malik couldn't shake the feeling that they were simply trading one nightmare for another.

Chapter 21: The Fall of Paris

Paris, France – Late Summer 2028

Paris had always been a city of contradictions—a place where history and modernity collided, where beauty and brutality often existed side by side. But now, as the insurgency swept across France, the contradictions had given way to something darker. The City of Light had become a city of shadows, where hope was a distant memory and survival was the only goal.

Emmanuel Lassalle, the President of France, stood in the ruins of the Élysée Palace, staring out at the broken skyline of Paris. The city that had once symbolized the heart of French culture and identity was now little more than a war zone. Buildings had been reduced to rubble, and the streets were filled with barricades and makeshift checkpoints. Smoke rose in thick columns from the neighbourhoods that had fallen to the insurgents, and the sound of gunfire echoed through the air.

Lassalle's grip on the railing tightened as he watched his city burn. The insurgency had begun as a series of small, isolated attacks, but it had quickly grown into something far more dangerous. Now, entire regions of the country were under the control of insurgent groups, and the French military was struggling to hold the line.

A knock on the door pulled Lassalle from his thoughts. He turned to see his chief of staff, Jean-Luc Gauthier, standing in the doorway, his face grim.

"Mr. President," Gauthier said quietly, "we've received word from the southern command. Marseille has fallen."

Lassalle's heart sank. He had known that the situation in Marseille was dire, but hearing the confirmation still felt like a blow to the chest.

"How bad is it?" Lassalle asked, his voice hollow.

"Bad," Gauthier replied, stepping into the room. "The insurgents have taken control of the city. Our forces have been forced to retreat, and we've lost contact with several units. We're not sure how many casualties there are."

Lassalle turned back to the window, his mind racing. Marseille had been one of their last strongholds in the south, and now it was gone. The insurgents were tightening their grip on the country, and there seemed to be no way to stop them.

"We can't hold Paris," Lassalle said quietly, almost to himself. "Not for much longer."

Gauthier hesitated before speaking. "Mr. President, we need to consider evacuating the capital. If the insurgents take Paris—"

"They won't take Paris," Lassalle interrupted, his voice sharp. "Not while I'm still standing."

But even as he said the words, Lassalle knew they were little more than empty bravado. The truth was that the government was losing control. Every day, the insurgents grew bolder, and the military grew weaker. The people were turning against them, tired of the constant fighting and the endless promises of a victory that never came.

"We need to send a message," Lassalle said, turning to face Gauthier. "We need to show the insurgents—and the world—that we are still in control."

Gauthier nodded. "What do you propose?"

Lassalle's mind raced as he considered his options. They had tried diplomacy, but the insurgents had no interest in negotiating. They had tried military force, but their resources were stretched too thin. Now, there was only one option left.

"We need to launch a counteroffensive," Lassalle said. "We'll hit the insurgents hard, push them back, and retake control of the city."

Gauthier looked hesitant. "Sir, our forces are already spread thin. A counteroffensive would be risky, and if it fails—"

"It won't fail," Lassalle snapped. "We don't have a choice. If we don't act now, Paris will fall."

For a moment, Gauthier said nothing. Then, with a reluctant nod, he turned to leave. "I'll begin preparations."

As the door closed behind him, Lassalle turned back to the window. Outside, the city burned, and the weight of the world pressed down on his shoulders.

Paris had always been a city of contradictions. But now, it was on the brink of destruction.

Chapter 22: The Last Stand

Brussels, Belgium – Late Summer 2028

Elena Moreau stood in the command centre, staring at the large map of Europe displayed on the wall. The map was covered in red markers, each one representing a city or region that had fallen to the insurgency. The sheer scale of the devastation was overwhelming, and every day, the red markers seemed to spread further across the continent.

"We're running out of time," Anwar Khaled said, standing beside her. His voice was calm, but there was an undercurrent of urgency. "The insurgents are gaining ground faster than we anticipated. If we don't act soon, it will be too late."

Elena nodded, her eyes never leaving the map. She had known that the situation was bad, but seeing it laid out like this made it all the more real. The insurgents had already taken control of large swathes of southern Europe, and now, they were making their way north. If they continued at this pace, it wouldn't be long before Brussels—one of the last remaining strongholds of the European Union—was under siege.

"We need reinforcements," Elena said, her voice steady despite the weight of the situation. "We need more troops, more supplies, more everything."

Anwar shook his head. "We don't have any more to give. Every country is stretched to the breaking point. France is in chaos, Germany is collapsing, and the UK is barely holding on. We're on our own."

Elena closed her eyes for a moment, trying to push back the overwhelming sense of hopelessness that threatened to engulf her. She had always been a realist, but even she had never imagined that things would get this bad. The insurgency had spread like wildfire, and now, it seemed as though nothing could stop it.

"We can't just sit here and wait for them to come to us," Elena said, opening her eyes. "We need to take the fight to them. We need to launch a pre-emptive strike."

Anwar raised an eyebrow. "A pre-emptive strike? Against whom? The insurgents don't have a central command. They're scattered across half of Europe."

"I know," Elena replied, her mind racing. "But we can still hit their supply lines, disrupt their communications, slow them down. If we can buy ourselves some time, we might be able to regroup."

Anwar looked sceptical, but he didn't argue. "It's a long shot."

"It's all we have," Elena said. "If we wait any longer, we'll lose everything."

For a moment, neither of them spoke. The command centre was filled with the hum of activity—military officers moving between consoles, analysts poring over intelligence reports—but it all felt distant, as though the room were a world away from the war that was tearing Europe apart.

"We'll need to coordinate with what's left of the French and German forces," Elena said finally. "And we'll need to move quickly. The longer we wait, the more ground they gain."

Anwar nodded. "I'll get in touch with our contacts. We'll need to be careful, though. The insurgents have infiltrated a lot of our communication networks. We can't afford any leaks."

Elena glanced back at the map, her mind already working through the logistics of the operation. It was a long shot, but it was their only chance.

As Anwar left the room, Elena allowed herself a moment to breathe. The weight of leadership was heavier than she had ever imagined, and every decision felt like a gamble with the fate of Europe hanging in the balance. But there was no time for doubt, no time for hesitation.

The insurgents were coming. And Brussels would be the last stand.

Chapter 23: A Fractured Alliance

London, UK – Early Autumn 2028

The air in Westminster was heavy, not just with the lingering smell of burnt debris from the recent riots but with a palpable sense of dread that seemed to hang over every room. Parliament, once the bastion of British stability, now resembled a fortress under siege. Armed guards stood at every entrance, and the steady hum of helicopters overhead only served to heighten the tension inside the hallowed halls.

Prime Minister Geoffrey Price sat at the head of the table in the war room, his face etched with exhaustion. The chaos across Europe had reached Britain's shores with full force, and the government was stretched beyond its limits. Price had aged significantly in the past year—his once neatly combed hair now a dishevelled mess of grey, and the lines on his face more pronounced with each passing day.

"We're losing control of the North," one of the military commanders said, his voice strained. "The insurgent cells have taken over several towns in Manchester, Liverpool, and even Leeds. We've deployed what forces we can, but it's not enough."

Price stared down at the map of the UK, covered in red dots marking insurgent activity. The attacks had become coordinated, more organized than they'd ever imagined. What had once seemed like isolated uprisings had turned into a full-blown invasion of ideology, the very fabric of British society tearing apart at the seams.

"We can't keep this up," Price said, rubbing his temples. "We don't have the manpower. The economy is collapsing, and our allies in Europe are barely holding it together."

Defence Secretary Amina Khan, sitting to his right, nodded grimly. "We've received reports that France is on the verge of capitulating entirely, and Germany's internal conflict is spiralling out of control. Brussels is barely functioning as a command centre. They can't help us, and we can't afford to send any more resources."

The Prime Minister leaned back in his chair; the weight of his office heavier than ever. The once-powerful NATO alliance had crumbled under the pressure of internal strife, mass migration, and economic hardship. Countries that were supposed to stand shoulder to shoulder had turned inward, consumed by their own struggles.

"Is there any word from the Americans?" Price asked, though he already knew the answer.

Foreign Secretary Emily Thompson shook her head. "Washington has withdrawn most of its military presence from Europe, focusing on its own internal problems. The new administration has made it clear—they won't be sending troops to prop up a crumbling Europe."

Price slammed his fist down on the table in frustration. "Damn it, we're on our own then."

The silence in the room was deafening. The political unity that had once defined Britain's relationship with Europe was fractured beyond repair. And as the insurgents continued their march through the northern cities, it became clear that Britain was slowly sinking into the same abyss as its neighbours.

Amina spoke up after a moment, her tone measured. "There's one option we haven't explored yet."

The room turned to her, waiting for her to continue.

"Martial law."

A ripple of unease passed through the room. Even as things spiralled out of control, the thought of imposing martial law had been seen as a last resort, a line that no one wanted to cross. But now, as the insurgents continued to spread their influence and the government's authority slipped away, that line was drawing closer.

Price let out a long breath. "You're suggesting we turn the country into a military state?"

Amina met his gaze with steady resolve. "We need control, Geoffrey. The police are overwhelmed, our intelligence services are crippled, and the insurgents are growing bolder by the day. If we don't act decisively, we could lose this country."

The room fell silent once more as the gravity of her words sank in. Everyone knew the stakes—Britain's future was hanging by a thread, and they were running out of options.

Finally, Price nodded. "We'll draft the order for martial law. We don't have a choice."

Chapter 24: The Siege of Berlin

Berlin, Germany – Autumn 2028

The thunder of artillery echoed across the devastated streets of Berlin as Malik and Sanaa huddled inside a makeshift bunker, the cold, damp walls pressing in around them. The city had been under siege for months, and the relentless shelling from both insurgent and government forces had turned what was once a proud metropolis into a landscape of ruins and ash.

Sanaa sat against the wall; her arms wrapped around her knees. She hadn't slept in days, her body wracked with exhaustion, fear, and hunger. The food supplies they had scavenged were running dangerously low, and the water had long since turned stagnant. But more than anything, it was the constant barrage of violence that wore them down—there was no escape from the fighting, no respite from the war that had engulfed the city.

Malik paced the narrow room, glancing out the small window slit that provided a limited view of the street outside. Smoke and fire filled the skyline, and the occasional crack of gunfire cut through the distant explosions. It was hard to tell who controlled what part of the city anymore; the lines of battle shifted constantly, and allegiances were as fluid as the tides.

"We can't stay here much longer," Malik muttered, his voice low.

Sanaa looked up at him, her eyes dull with fatigue. "Where would we go? The entire city is a war zone."

"I don't know," Malik admitted, running a hand through his matted hair. "But we can't stay here. If the insurgents push further into this area, we'll be trapped."

Just then, a deafening explosion shook the bunker, causing dust and debris to rain down from the ceiling. Sanaa flinched, instinctively pressing herself closer to the wall.

"They're getting closer," Malik said, his voice tight with fear. "We need to move."

Sanaa hesitated for a moment, then nodded. They had no other choice. The bunker, once a refuge, had become a death trap.

Gathering what little belongings they had, Malik and Sanaa prepared to leave. Every step felt like a gamble, every breath a reminder that death could be waiting just around the corner. They had seen too many bodies in the streets, too many lives torn apart by the chaos that had consumed Berlin.

As they made their way out of the bunker and into the ruined streets, Malik scanned their surroundings. The once-bustling neighbourhoods of Berlin had been reduced to rubble, and the few remaining buildings stood like hollowed-out husks, their windows shattered, and walls scorched by fire.

They moved quickly and quietly, keeping to the shadows as best they could. The streets were eerily quiet, save for the occasional distant gunfire or explosion. The insurgents and government forces were locked in a brutal stalemate, neither side willing to give an inch of ground.

But as they made their way toward the northern part of the city, Malik began to sense that something was wrong. The silence felt too heavy, too ominous. He slowed his pace, motioning for Sanaa to do the same.

"We need to be careful," he whispered.

Sanaa nodded, her eyes scanning the wreckage around them.

Suddenly, the sound of footsteps echoed down a nearby alley, and Malik's heart leaped into his throat. He grabbed Sanaa's arm, pulling her into the cover of a nearby building. They pressed themselves against the wall, listening as the footsteps grew closer.

Malik peered around the corner, his breath catching in his chest. A group of insurgent fighters were making their way down the alley, their weapons drawn and their faces grim. Malik's stomach twisted with fear—there were too many of them to take on, and he knew they wouldn't hesitate to kill anyone they found.

He pulled back, motioning for Sanaa to stay quiet. They waited, holding their breath as the insurgents passed by. The tension in the air was suffocating, but after what felt like an eternity, the footsteps faded into the distance.

Malik exhaled slowly, his body trembling with relief. "We need to keep moving."

Sanaa nodded, her face pale with fear. Together, they slipped out of their hiding place and continued on their path through the ruined city, always staying one step ahead of the chaos that threatened to consume them.

Chapter 25: The Exodus

Rome, Italy – Autumn 2028

The sun was setting over Rome, casting an orange glow over the ancient city as thousands of refugees poured into the streets. The once-majestic city had become a waypoint for those fleeing the devastation in the north, and its streets were now filled with the displaced—men, women, and children who had lost everything to the insurgency and the ensuing chaos.

Francesco Rossi, an Italian politician who had risen to prominence in the years of turmoil, stood on the balcony of his office overlooking the Piazza del Popolo. Below him, the crowd surged forward, desperate for food, shelter, and safety. The humanitarian crisis was spiralling out of control, and the government was struggling to manage the influx of refugees.

"They keep coming," Francesco said quietly, his voice tinged with weariness.

Standing beside him was Maria, his long-time advisor and confidante. She had been with him since the beginning of the crisis, guiding him through the political minefield that Italy had become. Now, like everyone else, she was running on fumes, her once sharp mind dulled by the endless strain of managing the catastrophe.

"There's no end in sight," Maria replied. "Every day, more refugees arrive. And with the insurgents closing in on southern France, we're going to see even more."

Francesco nodded, his gaze distant. Italy had managed to avoid the worst of the conflict so far, but he knew it was only a matter of time before the fighting reached their borders. The insurgency was spreading like a wildfire, and no country in Europe was safe.

"Have we heard anything from Brussels?" Francesco asked, though he already knew the answer.

Maria shook her head. "Brussels is barely holding itself together. The EU is fractured, and there's no coordinated response to the crisis. Each country is fending for itself."

Francesco let out a long breath. The European Union, once the symbol of unity and cooperation, was now a hollow shell of its former self. The mass migration, economic collapse, and insurgency had torn the continent apart, and the cracks were only getting wider.

"We can't keep this up," Francesco said, his voice heavy. "Rome is bursting at the seams. We don't have the resources to take in everyone."

Maria nodded in agreement. "We need to make a decision. Either we close the borders, or we risk collapsing under the weight of it all."

Francesco turned to face her; his eyes filled with uncertainty. "And if we close the borders? What then? Do we turn our backs on the people who need us most?"

Maria didn't answer right away. The moral dilemma weighed heavily on both of them. Closing the borders would mean condemning thousands of people to suffer or die but leaving them open meant risking the collapse of Italy itself.

"There are no good choices left," Maria said finally. "Only difficult ones."

Francesco leaned against the railing, staring down at the sea of refugees below. The world had changed in ways he never could have imagined. The Europe he had grown up in—the Europe of peace, stability, and prosperity—was gone, replaced by a continent on the brink of collapse.

And now, as the sun set over Rome, he realized that the decisions he made in the coming days would shape the future not just of Italy, but of all of Europe.

Chapter 26: The Turning Point

Brussels, Belgium – Winter 2028

The bitter cold had set in early that year, blanketing the streets of Brussels in a layer of frost that made the city feel as lifeless as the conflict that surrounded it. Brussels, once the bustling heart of the European Union, had become a fortress. High walls, military checkpoints, and armed guards patrolled every entrance and exit. Yet the air was heavy with dread, for even within these fortified walls, there was no escaping the reality that the insurgency was closing in from every direction.

Elena Kostova stood at the edge of the Grand Place, staring out at the makeshift barracks and defence posts that had been erected in the city square. Soldiers moved through the streets with the mechanical efficiency of men and women who had long been pushed past the point of exhaustion. The cold wind bit at Elena's face, but she barely noticed it. Her mind was elsewhere, consumed by the reports she had just received from the front lines.

General Anwar Malik joined her a moment later, his expression as grim as hers. He held a tablet in his hands, the screen filled with maps and data from the most recent skirmishes. He didn't need to say anything; Elena could already read the defeat in his eyes.

"It's worse than we thought," Anwar said finally, his voice low. "The insurgents have cut off supply lines to the south. We've lost contact with several key units in France, and there's been no word from the German forces in days. We're effectively surrounded."

Elena's jaw clenched. She had known this day was coming, but hearing it confirmed was like a punch to the gut. Brussels was supposed to be their stronghold, their final line of defence against the insurgent tide. But now, even that seemed to be slipping away.

"What about reinforcements?" Elena asked, though she already knew the answer.

Anwar shook his head. "None. The UK is locked down under martial law, France is in chaos, and Germany is all but gone. We're alone."

For a moment, Elena let the weight of his words settle over her. She had dedicated her life to the European Union, believing that it was the key to peace and prosperity in Europe. But now, as the continent crumbled under the weight of war, she could feel that dream slipping through her fingers.

"We need to send a message to the insurgents," Elena said, her voice resolute. "We can't just sit here and wait for them to overwhelm us. We need to show them that Brussels won't fall."

Anwar frowned. "What do you have in mind?"

Elena turned to him, her eyes blazing with determination. "A counter-offensive. We take the fight to them. Hit their command centers, disrupt their supply lines, weaken their hold on the surrounding territories. If we can destabilize them, even for a short time, we might be able to buy ourselves some breathing room."

Anwar considered her words for a moment, then nodded slowly. "It's a risk. But at this point, I don't see any other option."

Elena's heart pounded in her chest. She knew it was a desperate plan, but desperation was all they had left. She couldn't sit back and watch Brussels fall like so many other cities had. If there was even a chance that they could turn the tide, she had to take it.

"We'll need to coordinate with what's left of the French and German resistance forces," Anwar said, already tapping out messages on his tablet. "If we can launch simultaneous strikes on key insurgent positions, we might be able to force them into a retreat."

Elena nodded, her mind racing through the logistics of the operation. It would be dangerous, and they would be risking everything. But she couldn't afford to think about failure now. Not when the fate of Brussels—and perhaps all of Europe—rested on their shoulders.

"I'll speak with the council," Elena said. "We need to move quickly."

Anwar gave her a grim nod and disappeared into the military command centre, leaving Elena alone in the icy wind. She glanced up at the towering Gothic spires of the Hôtel de Ville, which stood like a ghostly reminder of a different time—a time when Brussels had been a symbol of unity and strength. Now, it was a city under siege, its future uncertain.

Later that evening, Elena stood before the European Emergency Council, a small group of exhausted politicians and military leaders who had become the last remnants of EU governance. The room was dimly lit, the only sound the occasional rustling of papers as the council members reviewed the latest intelligence reports. Their faces were etched with fear, weariness, and frustration.

"We can't hold out much longer," said Andreas Vogel, a German diplomat who had once been one of the EU's most respected statesmen. Now, he looked like a shadow of his former self, his eyes sunken and his voice filled with defeat. "The insurgents are closing in on every side. If we don't get reinforcements soon, Brussels will fall."

Elena took a deep breath, steeling herself for what she was about to say. "There are no reinforcements coming," she began, her voice steady. "We're on our own. But that doesn't mean we're finished. I propose that we launch a counter-offensive. A coordinated strike on key insurgent positions around Brussels. If we can weaken them, we might be able to hold out long enough to regroup."

The room erupted into murmurs of disbelief and concern. Some of the council members exchanged anxious glances, while others looked outright sceptical. It was clear that many of them had already resigned themselves to the idea that Brussels would fall.

"That's madness," Vogel said, shaking his head. "We don't have the resources for an offensive. We should be focusing on evacuation plans, not throwing what little we have left into a futile battle."

Elena stood her ground, her eyes blazing with conviction. "If we retreat now, if we abandon Brussels, the insurgents will sweep across Europe unchecked. This city is more than just a strategic stronghold—it's a symbol. If we let it fall, we're telling the world that Europe is finished."

A heavy silence fell over the room as the weight of her words sank in. Everyone knew that Brussels was more than just a city—it was the last vestige of European unity, the heart of the EU. If it fell, the insurgency would have free reign across the continent.

Anwar, who had joined the meeting after finishing preparations for the offensive, spoke up. "We have the element of surprise on our side. The insurgents believe we're on the defensive, that we're too weak to launch an attack. If we strike now, we can catch them off guard."

For a long moment, the council members were silent, each of them weighing the risks and the potential consequences of such a bold move.

Finally, it was Vogel who spoke again, though his voice was softer now. "And if we fail?"

Elena met his gaze, her expression unwavering. "Then at least we go down fighting."

The room was quiet for several more moments before, one by one, the council members began to nod in agreement. It was a long shot, but at this point, it was their only shot.

In the days that followed, the preparations for the counter-offensive began in earnest. Every able-bodied soldier, every piece of equipment, and every ounce of remaining energy was poured into the operation. The plan was simple but audacious: a series of coordinated strikes on insurgent command centers and supply lines, designed to destabilize their forces and buy Brussels enough time to regroup.

As the final preparations were made, Elena stood on the rooftop of the EU Parliament building, looking out over the city that she had fought so hard to protect. The streets below were filled with soldiers and civilians alike, all of them united in a single purpose: survival.

The night was cold and quiet, the calm before the storm. But Elena knew that within hours, the city would be engulfed in violence once again. And though fear gnawed at her, she forced it down. There was no room for doubt now.

The future of Europe hung in the balance, and Brussels would be their turning point.

As the first light of dawn began to break over the horizon, Elena turned away from the view and made her way back inside. The time for planning was over.

The fight for Europe's soul had begun.

Chapter 27: The Battle for Brussels

Brussels, Belgium – Dawn, Winter 2028

The soft grey light of dawn was creeping over the rooftops of Brussels, casting long shadows over the war-torn city. The city that had once been the heart of Europe now lay in ruins—burnt-out vehicles lined the streets, buildings stood like broken teeth against the skyline, and the people, those still left, moved like ghosts through the remains. Today, however, would be different. Today, the city would fight back.

Elena Kostova stood with her back to the rising sun, watching the final preparations unfold. The air was cold and crisp, filled with the electric tension of the hours before a battle. She had given the order, and now it was too late to turn back. Every available soldier, every remaining piece of military hardware, every drop of resolve the city had left, had been mobilized for this offensive.

Around her, a small but determined force was gathering. Soldiers in full combat gear moved with purpose, their faces hardened by the months of conflict. Civilians who had chosen to stay were assisting with the final logistics—loading trucks with supplies, moving ammunition, and setting up makeshift medical stations for the inevitable casualties.

"Elena," a voice called from behind her.

She turned to see General Anwar Malik approaching, his face as stoic as always, though there was a hint of tension in his eyes. He stopped beside her, glancing over the men and women preparing to march into what could very well be their last stand.

"Everything is in place," he said. "The French resistance is ready to launch their assault on the insurgent supply lines to the south. The Germans—what's left of them—will hit from the east. We'll be coordinating the main strike from the west."

Elena nodded, feeling the weight of the moment settle onto her shoulders. This was it—the culmination of months of planning, of sacrifice, of loss. The counter-offensive was a desperate gamble, but it was their only hope to buy time and prevent Brussels from falling into the hands of the insurgents.

"Any word from the EU leadership?" Anwar asked, though he knew the answer.

Elena shook her head. "No. As far as they're concerned, Brussels is already lost. They're focusing on evacuation plans for whatever is left of the EU administration. They're writing us off."

Anwar's jaw tightened, but he didn't respond. The European Union, once a symbol of strength and unity, had fractured under the weight of the crisis. Now, those in power were focused solely on their own survival.

"We'll prove them wrong," Elena said, her voice steady. "We hold this city, and we send a message to the insurgents that Europe isn't finished."

Anwar nodded, though both of them knew the odds were against them. The insurgents had grown stronger with each passing month, their forces swelling as more and more disillusioned men and women joined their cause. They had the numbers, the momentum, and the ruthlessness to crush any resistance. But they didn't have the heart of Europe. Not yet.

"Is everything ready on your end?" Elena asked.

Anwar glanced at his tablet, scrolling through the final battle plans. "Yes. The strike teams are in position. We'll hit their command centers and supply routes simultaneously. It won't wipe them out, but it should create enough chaos to give us an opening."

Elena looked out over the ruined city once more. "We've faced impossible odds before," she said quietly, more to herself than to Anwar. "We've survived every time."

"This will be different," Anwar said after a moment. "This isn't just survival. This is war."

Insurgent Headquarters, Outside Brussels

Farther beyond the city limits, hidden deep within the forests that surrounded Brussels, Amir Saeed stood in the insurgent command centre, watching the drone footage of the city. The insurgents had the advantage—they had taken large parts of northern France, spread chaos through Germany, and weakened the UK to the point of collapse. Brussels was the last holdout of the old European order.

"Brussels will fall," Amir said to his lieutenant, a man named Hakim who had been with him since the early days of the uprising. "They're on the verge of collapse. It's only a matter of time before they surrender."

Hakim nodded, his dark eyes scanning the map of the city. "Our forces are ready to move in. Once we take the city, we'll control the political heart of Europe. There will be no one left to stop us."

Amir's lips curled into a smile. The insurgency had started with whispers, with small, isolated attacks. But now, it had grown into a movement that stretched across the continent. The old Europe was dying, and a new one was rising from its ashes—a Europe where the forgotten and the oppressed would finally have their say.

"Make sure the assault teams are ready," Amir ordered. "We move in by nightfall."

Brussels – 0600 Hours

The streets were eerily silent as Elena, Anwar, and their strike teams moved into position. The sun had barely risen, casting long shadows over the city. They had chosen dawn for the assault, hoping to catch the insurgents off guard while they were still organizing their forces. The element of surprise was their only real advantage.

The plan was simple but dangerous. They would hit key insurgent positions in the outskirts of the city—command centers, supply depots, and communication hubs. With any luck, the confusion would slow the insurgents long enough for the French and German resistance forces to launch their attacks from the south and east.

As they approached the first target—a repurposed government building now serving as a command centre for the insurgents—Elena's heart pounded in her chest. She could feel the weight of every decision she had made leading up to this moment. The lives of everyone in Brussels, of everyone fighting for the survival of Europe, depended on the success of this operation.

"Positions," Anwar whispered into his radio. The strike teams moved swiftly, taking cover behind the wreckage of cars and buildings. The insurgents had no idea they were coming.

Elena gave the signal. The first explosion ripped through the air as the strike team planted charges on the insurgent command centre's outer wall.

Flames erupted, and the ground shook beneath their feet. In an instant, the quiet morning was shattered by the sound of gunfire and chaos.

"Go, go, go!" Anwar shouted, leading the charge.

The strike teams poured into the insurgent stronghold, weapons at the ready. The insurgents, caught off guard by the sudden assault, scrambled to defend their position. The air was thick with smoke and the deafening roar of gunfire.

Elena moved with precision; her weapon trained on the insurgents as they emerged from the wreckage. She fired with cold efficiency, her training and instinct taking over. There was no room for fear, no room for hesitation. Every shot counted.

The battle raged on, the insurgents fighting back with ruthless determination. But Elena's strike teams had the advantage of surprise, and they pressed their attack with relentless force.

Amidst the chaos, Elena's radio crackled to life. "We've taken the depot!" came the voice of one of the strike team leaders. "Moving to the next position."

Elena felt a surge of hope. The plan was working. For the first time in months, it felt like they had the upper hand. But the battle was far from over.

"Hold your ground!" Anwar shouted as the insurgents regrouped, launching a counterattack. The fighting intensified, the streets of Brussels becoming a battlefield once again.

For hours, the battle raged on, both sides exchanging blow after blow. But as the day wore on, it became clear that the insurgents were losing their grip. The coordinated strikes on their command centers and supply lines were taking their toll. Confusion spread through their ranks, and their ability to launch a full-scale assault on the city began to falter.

By the time the sun was high in the sky, the insurgents were in full retreat, falling back to their strongholds outside the city. Elena stood amidst the wreckage, her body shaking with exhaustion but her spirit burning with determination. They had won the first battle, but the war was far from over.

Insurgent Headquarters

Amir watched the drone footage of the battle with a clenched jaw. The Brussels forces had launched a surprise attack, and his forces were reeling. This was not the easy victory he had anticipated.

"They've pushed us back," Hakim reported, his voice tense. "We need to regroup."

Amir nodded, his mind racing. This was a setback, but not the end. Brussels might have fought back, but the insurgency was far from finished. The city was weakened, its forces stretched thin. He would regroup, and next time, he would not underestimate them.

"We'll be ready," Amir said coldly. "Next time, they won't be so lucky."

As the sun began to set over Brussels, Elena stood at the edge of the battlefield, watching as her forces regrouped. The city was still standing—for now. But she knew this victory was only the beginning of a much longer and bloodier fight.

Europe's future was still uncertain, but for the first time in a long while, there was a glimmer of hope.

Chapter 28: The Shadow of Defeat

Insurgent Camp – Outside Brussels

Amir Saeed sat in the dim light of the command tent, his eyes scanning the detailed maps spread across the table. His usually calm demeanour was now strained, his mind racing with the weight of their recent defeat. The Brussels counter-offensive had taken them by surprise, shattering their plans to seize the city and throwing the insurgency into disarray. For months, they had believed victory was inevitable, that Europe's resistance was crumbling under the pressure of war and chaos. But Brussels had defied them.

Hakim stood nearby, silent but tense. He knew Amir was furious, but he also understood the gravity of their situation. The insurgency had grown rapidly over the past two years, pulling in disillusioned fighters from all over Europe and the Middle East. But with rapid expansion came disorganization, and the defeat in Brussels had exposed the cracks in their strategy.

"They were prepared for us," Hakim finally said, breaking the silence. "Their counter-offensive was coordinated. We didn't expect them to push back with such force."

Amir's eyes flickered toward him, but he said nothing. He continued studying the map, tracing the insurgent positions that surrounded Brussels. They still controlled large swathes of territory, but their grip was slipping. The coordinated attacks by Elena Kostova's forces had thrown them off balance, and now, they were scrambling to regain control.

"We underestimated them," Amir muttered, more to himself than to Hakim. "We thought Brussels would fall like the others, that their defences were crumbling. But they still have fight left in them."

Hakim nodded. "And their leadership—Kostova and that general—are proving to be more resourceful than we anticipated. They've rallied what's left of the European forces."

Amir sat back in his chair, staring up at the canvas ceiling of the tent. He had always prided himself on being able to see the bigger picture, to think beyond the immediate battles and strategize for the long game. But this defeat had shaken him. Brussels was meant to be a swift victory, a symbol of the insurgency's unstoppable rise. Instead, it had become a costly setback.

"We need to regroup," Amir said finally. "Reinforce our positions around the city, cut off their supply lines, and bleed them dry. We can't let them build on this momentum."

Hakim stepped forward, his voice quiet but firm. "I've already begun coordinating with our commanders in France and Germany. They're moving additional forces into position, but it will take time."

Amir nodded, though his mind was already racing ahead. Time was something they didn't have. With each day that Brussels held out, the resistance forces grew stronger, emboldened by their victory. They couldn't afford another failure.

"I want to strike back," Amir said, his voice low but filled with determination. "We need to remind them who's in control. We'll launch targeted raids on their command centers, take out their leadership. Without Kostova and Malik, their resistance will crumble."

Hakim frowned, a trace of hesitation in his eyes. "It's risky. If we push too hard, we could overextend ourselves. Our forces are spread thin, and the insurgency is still fragile. We can't afford another defeat."

Amir's gaze sharpened. "We can't afford to hesitate, either. If we let them regroup, they'll start taking back more of their territory. We need to be decisive. Hit them hard, and make sure they understand that Brussels is only delaying the inevitable."

Hakim said nothing, though his silence spoke volumes. He understood Amir's desire for revenge, for a decisive blow that would break the will of the resistance. But he also knew the cost of overreach. The insurgency had momentum, but it was not invincible. Another defeat could fracture their ranks and give the resistance a fighting chance.

Amir stood, pushing away from the table. His eyes blazed with cold intensity; a man driven by the certainty that his vision for Europe was still within reach. He had built the insurgency from the ground up, pulling together disparate factions and leveraging the growing unrest across the continent. He couldn't let one defeat derail everything they had worked for.

"Prepare the teams," he ordered. "We strike at dawn."

Brussels – Resistance Headquarters

Elena Kostova stood at the edge of a makeshift medical tent, watching as doctors and nurses moved between rows of wounded soldiers. The air was thick with the smell of antiseptic and blood, the quiet murmur of the injured punctuated by the occasional groan of pain. The victory they had secured in the battle for Brussels had come at a heavy price.

General Anwar Malik stood beside her; his arms crossed as he observed the scene. His face was drawn, his usual stoic demeanour showing cracks after the brutal battle. The insurgents had been pushed back, but their forces were still strong, and the threat of another attack loomed over the city like a dark cloud.

"We did what we had to," Elena said, her voice quiet. "But it doesn't feel like a victory."

Anwar nodded. "Because it's not over. Not even close."

The counter-offensive had been a success, but it was only a temporary reprieve. They had bought time, nothing more. Brussels was still under siege, cut off from most of its allies, and the insurgents were regrouping. Every day, new reports filtered in of skirmishes on the outskirts of the city, of insurgent forces gathering for what would likely be a renewed assault.

"We need to solidify our defences," Elena continued. "Reinforce our lines, make sure we're ready when they come back."

Anwar glanced at her; his expression unreadable. "We're running on fumes, Elena. Half of our forces are injured or dead, and our supplies are running dangerously low. We can't hold out like this forever."

Elena clenched her fists, frustration bubbling beneath the surface. She knew he was right. Brussels had held, but at a terrible cost. Their forces were depleted, and there was no guarantee that reinforcements would arrive in time for the next attack. The European Union was in shambles, and the international community had largely abandoned them to their fate.

"We have to," Elena said, her voice firm. "We don't have a choice."

Anwar didn't argue. They both knew the truth. Brussels was the last bastion of resistance in a continent that had already begun to fall. If the city fell, so would the hope of any coordinated defence against the insurgency. And yet, as the days dragged on, it was becoming increasingly clear that they were fighting a losing battle.

"How are the other fronts?" Elena asked, changing the subject.

Anwar frowned. "Not good. The French resistance is holding their ground, but barely. They're facing heavy losses. The Germans are scattered—most of their forces are in disarray after the fall of Berlin. And the UK... well, they've sealed themselves off under martial law. They won't be helping anyone."

Elena felt a cold knot form in her stomach. Europe had never felt so isolated, so fractured. The unity they had once prided themselves on was gone, replaced by a sense of every nation for itself. The dream of a united Europe was dead, buried under the rubble of war and conflict.

But there was no time to dwell on the past. They had a city to defend.

"We'll hold," Elena said, more to herself than to Anwar. "We have to."

The Council of Elders – Somewhere in the Alps

High in the remote mountains of the Alps, a secretive group known as the Council of Elders convened in a stone fortress, far from the prying eyes of the world. The Council was an ancient order, bound by tradition and secrecy, with ties to the highest echelons of European power. Though their influence had waned in recent years, they still held considerable sway over the fate of the continent.

The Council had been watching the events in Brussels closely. They had seen the rise of the insurgency, the fall of Europe's great cities, and the fracturing of the EU. Now, as the battle for Brussels raged on, the Council knew that the future of Europe hung in the balance.

"We cannot allow the insurgents to seize control," said an elderly man seated at the head of the table. His voice was gravelly, his face lined with age and wisdom. "If Brussels falls, Europe falls."

The other members of the Council nodded in agreement; their faces grim. They had spent decades in the shadows, pulling strings and shaping the course of history. But now, they were faced with a crisis unlike any they had ever encountered.

"The resistance is holding," said another member, a woman with sharp features and piercing blue eyes. "But they are on the brink of collapse. They need our help."

The elderly man considered her words carefully. The Council had always operated behind the scenes, influencing events from a distance. But now, the time for subtlety was over. If they wanted to save Europe, they would have to take direct action.

"Then we will act," the man said, his voice resolute. "We will send aid to Brussels. Whatever it takes, we will ensure that the city does not fall."

The Council's decision was made. The battle for Brussels was not yet lost—and with the Council's support, it might still be won.

Chapter 29: A Glimmer of Hope

Brussels – Early Spring, 2028

The cold, bitter winds of winter had finally begun to retreat, giving way to the hesitant warmth of early spring. Brussels, scarred by months of conflict, was slowly beginning to stir back to life. The streets were still filled with rubble, and the buildings that remained standing bore the marks of war—blasted facades and shattered windows—but there was something new in the air: a sense of resilience, however fragile.

Elena Kostova stood on the balcony of a makeshift command centre, overlooking the city. The headquarters had once been a government building, but now it was a patchwork of hastily repaired walls and fortified defences. The occasional crackle of gunfire in the distance served as a reminder that the insurgents were still out there, lurking on the edges of the city, waiting for their moment to strike again.

But for now, Brussels held.

Below her, soldiers were moving with purpose, reinforcing barricades, repairing vehicles, and training new recruits. Most of them were civilians who had taken up arms out of desperation, but after months of battle, they had become hardened fighters. Every day they survived was a testament to their determination.

Elena's mind was racing as she mentally calculated their remaining resources. Food and medical supplies were running low, and ammunition was becoming scarce. The black market provided some relief, but they couldn't rely on it for long. More troubling was the dwindling number of able-bodied fighters. Many were injured, and there were few replacements. It was only a matter of time before the insurgents, who were growing bolder by the day, launched their next assault.

She felt the weight of the responsibility on her shoulders. Brussels was the symbol of resistance against the insurgency, but it had become more than that. It was the last beacon of hope in a Europe that was falling apart. If the city fell, it wouldn't just be a military defeat—it would be the death of the idea that Europe could survive this storm.

Behind her, the door opened with a soft creak. General Anwar Malik stepped out onto the balcony, his face lined with exhaustion, though his eyes were sharp and focused. He had aged visibly in the past few months, the toll of the unrelenting fight wearing him down. But like the city, he endured.

"Any word from the Council?" Elena asked without turning around.

Anwar shook his head. "Nothing yet. But we've intercepted chatter. It sounds like they're preparing to send something—aid, weapons, maybe even soldiers. But we don't know how soon it will come, or if it will be enough."

Elena sighed, gripping the railing in front of her. "We can't rely on them. If the insurgents attack again before we're ready, all the help in the world won't save us."

Anwar stepped up beside her, his gaze following hers over the battered city. "We've made it this far. We'll make it further."

She didn't respond immediately, her thoughts drifting to the soldiers they had lost, the civilians who had died in the crossfire, the sacrifices made to hold onto this patch of land. "I'm not sure how much more we can take," she said quietly.

"We'll hold," Anwar replied firmly. "We have no other choice."

Elena turned to face him, her expression hardening. "You're right. We fight on."

The Council of Elders – En Route to Brussels

The convoy moved swiftly through the winding roads of the Alps, escorted by heavily armed vehicles. Inside one of the armoured cars, a small group of the Council of Elders sat in silence, their faces grim. They were on their way to Brussels, carrying with them the supplies and reinforcements that could tip the balance in the resistance's favour.

Lady Helena Weiss, the sharp-featured woman who had urged the Council to take action, sat at the head of the group, her mind racing as the convoy descended toward the lowlands. She had been one of the strongest advocates for sending aid to Brussels, convinced that the survival of the city was crucial to the future of Europe.

Beside her sat Lord Cedric Beaumont, an older man with a weathered face and a deep frown. He had been more cautious, sceptical of intervening so directly. The Council had always operated from the shadows, shaping events without revealing their hand. This was a bold move, one that could backfire if they failed.

"This is a gamble," Cedric muttered, his voice heavy with doubt. "We're exposing ourselves in a way we've never done before. If Brussels falls, it won't just be a defeat for the resistance—it will be the end of the Council's influence."

"We cannot afford to be cautious any longer," Helena replied firmly. "Brussels is the key. If it falls, Europe will follow. We must give them the tools they need to fight back."

Cedric didn't respond immediately, his gaze fixed on the passing landscape. "I hope you're right."

Insurgent Headquarters – Forests Outside Brussels

Amir Saeed paced the dimly lit room, his mind racing with anger and frustration. His forces had regrouped after the defeat in Brussels, but the loss still stung. It had been a severe blow to their momentum, and now the insurgents were faced with a critical choice—strike again while the city was still vulnerable or pull back and regroup further.

Hakim stood by the doorway, watching his leader with wary eyes. "We've received intelligence that the Council of Elders is sending reinforcements to Brussels," he said, breaking the tense silence.

Amir's pacing stopped abruptly, his eyes narrowing. "Reinforcements?"

Hakim nodded. "Supplies, weapons, possibly soldiers. They're determined to keep the city from falling."

Amir's anger flared. The Council of Elders had remained in the shadows for too long, manipulating events behind the scenes, and now they were stepping into the open. They were meddling in a war that, in Amir's mind, was already won.

"They think they can stop us with a few shipments of guns and soldiers?" Amir spat, his voice seething with contempt. "They underestimate us. They underestimate me."

Hakim hesitated, choosing his words carefully. "Brussels is still vulnerable, but with these reinforcements, it could tip the balance. We need to act quickly if we're going to take the city."

Amir's eyes darkened. "We will. But not yet."

Hakim frowned. "You're proposing we wait?"

Amir's voice was cold and calculating. "Let them bring their reinforcements. Let them think they have a chance. When they feel secure, when they think they're safe, we will strike. And this time, we will not hold back."

Hakim nodded, though he still felt a flicker of unease. The insurgents had underestimated the resistance before, and it had cost them dearly. He only hoped that Amir's plan wouldn't lead to another disaster.

Brussels – Evening

As night fell over the city, Elena stood on the rooftop of the command centre, her eyes scanning the horizon. She knew the insurgents were still out there, watching, waiting for their chance. The recent lull in fighting felt ominous, like the calm before a storm.

Below her, the lights of Brussels flickered weakly, the power grid barely holding on. Civilians and soldiers alike moved through the streets, going about their duties with weary determination. They had survived this long, but no one believed that the insurgents would stay quiet for much longer.

Anwar approached from behind, his footsteps soft on the rooftop. "You're still up here?"

Elena glanced at him and nodded. "Just thinking."

"About?"

"Everything," she replied. "This city, this fight, what's at stake. It feels like we're walking on a knife's edge."

Anwar joined her at the railing, staring out at the city below. "That's because we are."

For a moment, neither of them spoke, the weight of the situation pressing down on them. Then, a faint sound reached Elena's ears—a distant rumble, growing louder. Her eyes narrowed as she looked to the horizon.

"What is that?" she asked.

Anwar listened, his expression hardening. "Engines."

A moment later, the first headlights appeared on the road leading into the city. A convoy of armoured vehicles, accompanied by trucks carrying supplies, was making its way toward the gates. The Council's reinforcements had arrived.

Elena felt a surge of relief, tempered by the knowledge that this was only the beginning. The real battle was still to come.

As the convoy rolled into the city, she turned to Anwar. "This might just give us the edge we need."

He nodded, though his eyes remained cautious. "Let's hope so."

In the distance, Amir watched the convoy through a pair of binoculars, his jaw clenched. He had been right—the Council had sent reinforcements. But it didn't matter. Let them come, he thought. Let them bolster their defences. It would only make their eventual defeat all the more satisfying.

"We strike soon," he said quietly, handing the binoculars back to Hakim. "And this time, we'll crush them."

The shadow of defeat still hung over Brussels, but with the arrival of the Council's forces, there was a glimmer of hope. Whether that hope would be enough to withstand the coming storm, only time would tell.

Chapter 30: The Calm Before the Storm

Brussels – April 2028

Brussels, the city that had defied the odds for so long, stood on the brink of another cataclysmic clash. The arrival of the Council of Elders' convoy brought a mix of relief and trepidation to the battered city. With reinforcements and supplies, the weary resistance fighters gained a sense of hope, but it was clear to everyone that the lull in battle was only temporary. The insurgents were regrouping, watching, waiting. The next strike would be decisive, one way or another.

Elena Kostova was fully aware of this. She paced the war room late into the night, reviewing strategies and running over battle plans with her team. General Anwar Malik stood by her side, always a calm, steady presence. The reinforcements were valuable, but they wouldn't last long if the insurgents mounted a full-scale assault again. The key to victory, Elena knew, lay not just in brute force but in strategy.

"We have enough supplies to last a few weeks, maybe a month," Malik reported as he reviewed the latest inventory figures. "But if they hit us hard, especially with coordinated strikes, we'll be overwhelmed again."

Elena nodded grimly. "They'll come at us harder than before. Amir Saeed won't make the same mistakes twice. We can't let them dictate the terms this time. We have to control the battlefield."

Malik raised an eyebrow, intrigued. "What are you suggesting?"

Elena turned to him, her eyes sharp with determination. "We need to take the fight to them. Surprise them before they're ready to attack. Hit their supply lines, disrupt their coordination, and weaken their morale."

Malik considered this for a moment. It was risky. Their forces were stretched thin, and venturing out of the relative safety of Brussels could leave the city vulnerable. But if they could pull it off, it might buy them enough time to fortify their defences.

"We don't have many fighters to spare," Malik cautioned. "But you're right—we can't just sit here waiting for the hammer to fall."

Elena turned back to the map of the city and its surrounding areas, her finger tracing the roads and highways leading to the insurgent camps. "We send out small, fast-moving units—hit-and-run attacks. Sabotage their fuel depots, take out their communications. Keep them off balance."

Malik nodded, a grim smile tugging at the corner of his lips. "That's more like it. We'll need our best fighters for this. I'll make the preparations."

Insurgent Encampment – Forests Outside Brussels

Amir Saeed stared into the flickering flames of the campfire, deep in thought. Around him, the insurgent commanders discussed the next phase of their assault. The defeat in Brussels still weighed heavily on his mind, but it had not broken his resolve. If anything, it had steeled his determination to finish what they had started.

"We've gathered enough reinforcements," one of the commanders reported. "Our ranks are growing every day. Fighters from across Europe, North Africa, and the Middle East continue to join us. The Council's reinforcements won't be enough to stop us this time."

Amir nodded but remained silent. He knew their strength had grown, but the resistance had proven more resilient than expected. Elena Kostova and General Malik had defied him, and that humiliation lingered. He couldn't afford another failure, not now when victory was within his grasp.

"The Council is getting directly involved now," Hakim added, standing to Amir's right. "They're desperate to hold onto Brussels. If we can take the city, it'll be a massive blow to their morale—and to Europe's."

Amir's eyes flickered. "We'll take it. But not by brute force alone."

The commanders exchanged glances, unsure of what Amir meant. He had always been a ruthless tactician, willing to sacrifice anything for victory. But after the setback in Brussels, he had grown more methodical, colder in his calculations.

"We won't just attack the city this time," Amir continued, his voice calm but filled with menace. "We'll turn its own people against it. Sabotage their infrastructure from within, spread misinformation, and sow distrust between the civilians and the resistance. By the time we strike, they'll be tearing themselves apart."

Hakim frowned slightly. "That could take time. Do we have the resources for such a campaign?"

"We'll make time," Amir replied sharply. "We have cells inside the city. We'll activate them. We'll feed the people's fear, convince them that Kostova's leadership is failing, that the resistance can't protect them. And when the time is right, we'll move in for the kill."

It was a strategy that played to Amir's strengths—psychological warfare, manipulation, and fear. The insurgents had the manpower to mount a frontal assault, but Amir wanted more than just a military victory. He wanted to break Brussels' spirit, to make the resistance crumble from within.

Hakim nodded, though there was still a trace of doubt in his eyes. He had always respected Amir's brilliance as a leader, but this plan required precision and patience—two things that had been in short supply in this brutal, chaotic war.

"We'll start tonight," Amir ordered. "Spread rumours, sabotage their supplies. Make them question their leaders. And when they're at their weakest, we'll finish this."

Inside Brussels – The First Signs

By the time dawn broke over the city, Elena and Malik's teams were already preparing for their first hit-and-run strikes against the insurgents. But as the day wore on, strange reports began trickling in. Food deliveries had been delayed, water supplies were disrupted, and the streets were buzzing with rumours of corruption and betrayal within the resistance.

At first, Elena dismissed the rumours as part of the usual chaos that came with war. But as the disruptions continued, she couldn't ignore them. Civilians were growing restless, whispers of dissatisfaction were spreading, and even some of the resistance fighters seemed to be losing faith.

"What's happening?" Malik asked, frustration evident in his voice as he slammed a fist down on the table. "We've been fighting the insurgents for months, and now we're dealing with sabotage from inside?"

Elena's mind raced. She had heard of these tactics before—divide and conquer, erode trust from within. Amir Saeed wasn't just a military commander; he was a master of psychological warfare. He was trying to weaken them before launching his next attack.

"We have traitors in the city," Elena said quietly, her eyes narrowing. "Amir is playing a long game. He's turning our own people against us."

Malik swore under his breath. "How do we stop it?"

Elena clenched her fists. "We root them out. We find the cells he's planted here, and we neutralize them. And we need to get ahead of the rumours. We can't let the people lose faith in us."

But it was easier said than done. With the city already on edge, it wouldn't take much to tip the balance into chaos. Elena knew they were running out of time. They had to act quickly, before Amir's plan took full effect.

The Underground Movement

In the shadowy corners of Brussels, a network of insurgent sympathizers was already at work. They had blended into the civilian population months ago, living quietly as shopkeepers, drivers, and workers. But now, with Amir's orders in hand, they were beginning to act.

Sabotage was their weapon of choice—cutting water lines, tampering with food supplies, and spreading false rumours about Elena Kostova's leadership. Some infiltrated the resistance's communication lines, sending misinformation to the frontlines and disrupting crucial supply chains.

Their work was slow and methodical, but it was effective. Within days, the city began to feel the strain. Discontent simmered beneath the surface, and the once-united resistance started to show signs of fracture.

But it wasn't just the sabotage that did the damage—it was the fear. People were afraid that the insurgents had already infiltrated their city, that their neighbours or friends could be working against them. Trust eroded, and the sense of solidarity that had held Brussels together began to fray.

The War Room – Crisis Management

"Elena, it's spreading," Malik said, frustration and concern deepening the lines on his face. "We're losing control of the situation. People are scared, and they're starting to question our leadership."

Elena nodded, her mind racing. "We need to get ahead of this. Publicly address the rumours. Reassure the people that we're in control."

Malik shook his head. "They won't believe us if they think we're just covering up."

"We don't have another option," Elena replied sharply. "We either win back their trust, or we lose the city."

As the days wore on, Elena and her commanders fought two battles—one against the insurgents outside the city, and one against the growing unrest within. The sabotage continued, the rumours spread, and it became clear that the insurgents were not going to strike immediately. They were letting the city tear itself apart.

The storm was coming. And Elena knew it was only a matter of time before Amir Saeed made his final move.

The Calm Before the Attack

Amir stood on a ridge overlooking Brussels, his eyes fixed on the city in the distance. The reports from his infiltrators were promising—the resistance was beginning to fracture. The people were afraid, unsure of who to trust. It was exactly what he had hoped for.

"It's almost time," Hakim said, standing beside him.

Amir nodded slowly. ""Yes. Let them destroy themselves a little longer. Then we will strike."

The calm before the storm was almost unbearable, the tension thick in the air. Brussels had withstood so much already, but this—this slow, insidious unravelling from within—was something else entirely.

As the city braced for impact, neither side knew who would come out of the battle ahead victorious. All they knew was that everything was about to change

Chapter 31: Fissures in the Wall

Brussels – April 2028

The tension in Brussels had reached a breaking point. Though the skies over the city were clear, the mood on the ground was clouded by mistrust, fear, and uncertainty. The insurgents had succeeded in planting seeds of doubt among the civilian population, and those seeds were beginning to bear fruit. The steady erosion of morale within the resistance was more damaging than any military assault Amir Saeed could have launched.

Elena Kostova had spent days and nights trying to put out fires—both metaphorically and literally. Isolated skirmishes had broken out in some neighbourhoods, and looters were becoming more brazen as food shortages worsened. The once unbreakable unity of Brussels was beginning to crumble, and Elena knew that if she couldn't restore order soon, the city would collapse from within.

Inside the Council Chambers – Crisis Meeting

Elena and General Malik stood before the Council of Elders; their faces worn from exhaustion. Lady Helena Weiss, one of the most influential voices in the Council, looked at them with grave concern. Beside her, Lord Cedric Beaumont sat, his sharp eyes fixed on the map of the city displayed on the holographic projector. The rest of the Council members were equally tense, their once-neutral positions shifting as the crisis deepened.

"We're losing control," Elena admitted, her voice raw with frustration. "The insurgents' sabotage is working. We've tried to contain the damage, but they're inside the city, and they're tearing it apart from within."

Lady Helena's eyes flickered with understanding. "What's the situation with the civilian population?"

"Restless," General Malik answered. "There's widespread fear, and with food supplies running low, people are growing desperate. The insurgents have spread rumours that we can't protect them, and that's all it's taken to start turning some civilians against us."

Lord Cedric frowned. "We anticipated sabotage, but not on this scale. How extensive is the infiltration?"

Elena exchanged a glance with Malik before answering. "We don't know for sure. They're everywhere, hiding in plain sight—shopkeepers, delivery drivers, even some low-level resistance members. We've started identifying a few of their agents, but they're hard to track. Every time we stop one incident, another one flares up."

The Council members murmured among themselves. The threat was far more serious than they had imagined.

"What about your strategy to hit the insurgents outside the city?" Lady Helena asked. "Have you been able to disrupt their plans?"

Malik shook his head. "We've launched a few hit-and-run strikes, but nothing significant. Their camps are well-guarded, and they've tightened their defences. We're spread too thin inside the city to mount a full offensive."

The room fell silent for a moment. The gravity of the situation weighed heavily on everyone present.

"We cannot afford to lose Brussels," Lord Cedric said finally, his voice steady but filled with urgency. "If the city falls, the rest of Europe will follow."

Elena straightened her posture. "We're not giving up. But we need more than just reinforcements. We need to regain control of the narrative. If the people believe we can't protect them, we've already lost. We need to expose the insurgents' lies and remind the civilians why they're fighting."

"And how do you propose we do that?" asked Lady Helena, her eyes sharp with interest.

Elena took a deep breath. "We need to be transparent. We need to show them the truth. Hold public addresses, take the Council into the streets, let them see the damage caused by the insurgents' sabotage. Show them that we're still here, still fighting for them. But more than that, we need to rebuild trust."

Lord Cedric raised an eyebrow. "You're suggesting a PR campaign in the middle of a war?"

"I'm suggesting we fight them on every front," Elena replied. "This isn't just a military battle. It's psychological. We can't win if the people don't believe in us."

The Council members exchanged glances, weighing the risks of such a strategy. Finally, Lady Helena spoke. "It's a bold move, but it may be our only option. We'll support you, but you'll need to tread carefully. If we misstep, the insurgents will seize on it."

Elena nodded. "Understood. I'll make sure we get it right."

Amir's Plan in Motion

Amir Saeed sat in the heart of his camp, surrounded by his closest advisors. The reports from inside Brussels were exactly what he had hoped for. The resistance was floundering, and the people were starting to turn on Elena Kostova. It was only a matter of time before the city imploded.

"We've disrupted their food and water supplies," Hakim reported, a satisfied grin on his face. "The people are growing desperate. They don't trust Kostova anymore."

Amir leaned back in his chair, his dark eyes gleaming with satisfaction. "Good. Let them starve. Let them tear each other apart."

Hakim hesitated for a moment. "There have been rumours that the Council is planning a public address—an attempt to rally the civilians. They're trying to rebuild trust."

Amir's smile faded slightly, but he remained calm. "They're grasping at straws. It won't work."

Hakim frowned. "We've seen them pull off miracles before."

Amir's eyes narrowed. "Not this time. We'll step up our operations. Continue the sabotage but ramp up the attacks. Hit them where they're weakest. If they want to make a public spectacle, we'll turn it against them."

The Resistance's Gamble

Elena stood in the heart of the Grand Place, Brussels' central square, her eyes scanning the faces of the gathered crowd. It was a risk—a huge one. The insurgents could strike at any moment, and the tensions in the city were palpable. But she knew they couldn't wait any longer. The people needed to hear from their leaders. They needed to see that they were not abandoned.

Beside her stood General Malik, stoic and vigilant, along with Lady Helena Weiss and several other Council members. The square was heavily guarded, but the atmosphere was tense. The crowd was a mix of civilians, resistance fighters, and a few dissenters whose anger and frustration were barely concealed.

Elena stepped forward, taking the microphone. She wasn't used to speeches, but this wasn't about eloquence—it was about honesty.

"People of Brussels," she began, her voice echoing through the square. "We are at a crossroads. For months, we've fought side by side to defend this city, to protect our homes and our families. We've faced the insurgents head-on, and we've survived. But now, a new threat has emerged."

She paused, letting her words sink in. The crowd was silent, hanging on her every word.

"The insurgents have infiltrated our city," Elena continued, her voice steady. "They're trying to divide us, to make us turn on each other. They've spread lies, sabotage, and fear. But we are stronger than their deception. We are stronger because we stand together."

There was a murmur of agreement from the crowd, but it was mixed with doubt and fear. Elena could feel the tension rising.

"They want you to believe that we can't protect you," she said, her voice growing more urgent. "But look around. We're still here. We're still fighting. We haven't given up, and neither should you."

At that moment, Lady Helena stepped forward, her voice commanding as she addressed the crowd. "We know these are dark times. But I ask you—what is the alternative? Surrendering to the insurgents, to those who would destroy everything we've built? We cannot give in to fear. We must hold on to hope, to unity."

The crowd was listening, but Elena could still sense the unease. It wasn't enough. They needed more than words—they needed action.

Suddenly, there was a commotion at the edge of the square. A small group of insurgent sympathizers had gathered, shouting accusations of betrayal and corruption. Elena's heart raced as she saw the situation escalating. This was exactly what Amir had planned—chaos, division.

But before the dissenters could provoke a full-scale riot, Malik stepped forward, his voice booming across the square. "Enough! We will not let them turn us against each other! This is what they want—to see us divided, weak. We are better than that!"

The dissenters hesitated, their shouts fading as the rest of the crowd began to rally around Elena and Malik. It was a tenuous victory, but it was a victory, nonetheless.

The Insurgents' Response

Amir Saeed watched the live broadcast of the public address from the comfort of his camp. Elena's speech had been better received than he had anticipated, but it didn't matter. He had been prepared for this.

"They think they can turn the tide with a few speeches," Amir muttered, a cold smile on his lips. "Let them believe they're winning."

Hakim stepped forward, holding a tablet displaying the latest intel. "We've identified several key targets inside the city—supply depots, communication hubs, and a few resistance strongholds. We can hit them all at once."

Amir's smile widened. "Then let's remind them who's really in control."

As night fell over Brussels, the insurgents prepared to strike. The city's brief moment of unity would soon be shattered. The storm was coming, and this time, there would be no reprieve.

Chapter 32: The Night of Ashes

Brussels – April 2028

The night air in Brussels was thick with a tense silence that seemed to blanket the city. After the public address, Elena and her team were cautiously optimistic, but the atmosphere remained fragile. Though some civilians had rallied to the cause, the city was still on edge, waiting for the next blow.

Elena stood at the top of a government building, overlooking the square where only hours earlier she had tried to unite the people. Her heart was heavy with the burden of leadership, knowing that despite her best efforts, the insurgents still had the upper hand. She felt the weight of the city's survival on her shoulders more than ever before. The war was no longer just about territory or ideology—it was about hope, and whether it could survive the darkness that had engulfed Europe.

She was interrupted by General Malik, who stepped up behind her. His presence was as solid and reassuring as ever, but even he couldn't hide the exhaustion etched on his face.

"They bought us some time," Malik said, referring to the positive response from the public. "But we both know this isn't over."

Elena didn't turn to face him. She kept her eyes on the horizon, scanning the dark streets below. "No," she replied quietly. "It's just beginning."

Insurgent Encampment – Outside Brussels

Amir Saeed was in high spirits. His network inside Brussels had confirmed that Elena's speech had made a temporary impact, but it wouldn't last. He was playing a long game, one that required patience and precision. The insurgents' real strength lay not in the number of soldiers but in their ability to disrupt, demoralize, and destabilize. And tonight, they would make their next move.

Amir paced before his commanders; a map of Brussels spread out before them. "We hit them where they least expect it," he said, his voice cold and calculating. "Supply lines, water infrastructure, energy plants—everything that keeps that city functioning. We cripple them from within."

Hakim, his most trusted lieutenant, nodded. "We've positioned the cells in key locations. The attacks can happen simultaneously."

"Good," Amir replied. "Once we've sowed enough chaos, the civilians will lose what little faith they have left in Kostova and her resistance. They'll turn on her."

He paused, his gaze sweeping over his men. "And when they do, we strike."

Brussels – Midnight

Elena was just beginning to descend from the rooftop when the first explosion shook the city.

It was far off, a deep rumble that echoed through the night, followed by a flicker of flames that illuminated the distance. Then another explosion, this one closer. The ground beneath her feet trembled as the noise reverberated through the streets. She turned to Malik, who had already reached for his radio.

"Report!" Malik barked into the device, his voice tight with urgency.

The crackling response came through almost immediately. "Explosions near the south district. Another in the industrial zone. We're seeing fires in three separate locations."

Malik swore under his breath as Elena's mind raced. It had begun. The insurgents were making their move, striking at the heart of the city when they were least prepared.

"Call in the teams. We need to lock down critical points before they spread," Elena said, her voice calm despite the panic rising in her chest.

Malik was already ahead of her, issuing orders to deploy defence units to strategic locations. But Elena knew it wouldn't be enough. The insurgents were too coordinated, too precise in their attacks. They had planned this for months, waiting for the perfect moment to strike.

The city's alarm system blared to life, piercing the night with its high-pitched wail. The streets, once quiet, were now alive with movement as civilians fled their homes, unsure of where to go or who to trust. Fear spread faster than the fires.

The Resistance's Headquarters

Back at the headquarters, chaos reigned. Maps of the city were strewn across tables, with resistance members shouting orders and coordinating their response. The insurgents had attacked key points throughout

Brussels—the water supply station, the city's primary power grid, and several food storage depots. The city's infrastructure was falling apart, one piece at a time.

Elena burst through the doors, Malik close behind her, as the headquarters buzzed with frantic activity.

"What's the situation?" she demanded.

A young officer, barely out of his twenties, rushed up to her, eyes wide with panic. "It's bad, ma'am. We're seeing attacks in multiple sectors. Communications are down in parts of the city. We've lost contact with two of our patrols."

Elena gritted her teeth. "Have we identified the insurgent cells responsible?"

"Not yet," the officer replied. "They've spread out across the city. They're hitting us from all sides."

Elena turned to Malik, who was already poring over the map. "We need to secure the power plant and the water station first," she said. "If we lose those, the city will descend into chaos."

Malik nodded. "I'll send units immediately."

But as they coordinated their next move, another explosion rocked the building, this one much closer. Dust and debris fell from the ceiling, and for a moment, the entire room froze in shock.

Elena's radio crackled to life. "General! We're under attack! Insurgents are—" The voice cut off abruptly, followed by static.

She swore, grabbing the radio. "Who is this? Report!"

No response.

"They're here," Malik said grimly, his hand hovering near his sidearm.

Elena's mind raced. Amir Saeed wasn't just content with sabotage—he was launching a full-scale assault on Brussels. The city was burning, and they were running out of time to stop it.

The Battle for Control

As the night wore on, the insurgents pushed deeper into the city. The resistance, already stretched thin, fought valiantly to hold them back, but Amir's forces were relentless. Small firefights broke out in the streets, with resistance fighters battling insurgents in alleyways and abandoned buildings.

In the industrial zone, one of the city's largest warehouses erupted into flames as insurgents set fire to its contents—food and medical supplies desperately needed by the civilian population. Smoke billowed into the sky, casting an orange glow over the darkened streets.

Meanwhile, in the southern district, a group of insurgents had managed to breach one of the city's primary water facilities, planting explosives near the main pipelines. The resistance rushed to defuse the bombs, but it was a race against time.

Elena was at the centre of it all, coordinating the defence from the headquarters. She moved from one crisis to another, trying to plug the gaps in their defences and keep morale from crumbling. But it was clear that the insurgents had the upper hand. Every victory the resistance achieved was overshadowed by another loss.

Amir's Gambit

As dawn began to break over Brussels, Amir Saeed stood on the outskirts of the city, watching the chaos unfold through binoculars. His plan was working perfectly. The resistance was scrambling to respond to the multiple attacks, and the civilians were losing hope. Soon, they would turn on Elena Kostova and her leaders.

"Phase two begins now," Amir said to Hakim, lowering the binoculars. "We push into the heart of the city."

Hakim nodded and relayed the order. The insurgents, having sown enough chaos and destruction, were now preparing for their final push into Brussels. It was a calculated risk, but Amir knew that the resistance was at its breaking point. They wouldn't be able to hold the city much longer.

Amir's forces began moving out of their hidden positions, converging on Brussels like a tightening noose. The time for subtlety was over. Now, it was all-out war.

The Last Line

In the heart of Brussels, Elena and her team were preparing for the final stand. Reports were coming in from all over the city—explosions, fires, insurgent movements—but one message stood out among the chaos.

"They're coming," Malik said, his face grim as he relayed the latest intel. "Amir's forces are moving into the city. This is it."

Elena felt a chill run down her spine. She had known this moment was coming, but she had hoped they would have more time to prepare. Now, they were out of options.

"We hold the line," Elena said, her voice steady despite the fear gnawing at her insides. "Whatever it takes, we hold."

Malik nodded, his expression resolute. "To the end."

The Dawn of Destruction

As the first light of dawn bathed Brussels in a pale glow, the insurgents made their final push. The city, already weakened by sabotage and internal unrest, buckled under the weight of the assault.

Elena watched as the insurgents advanced, her heart pounding in her chest. The streets were filled with the sounds of gunfire, explosions, and the cries of the wounded. She knew this was their last chance to defend the city—if they failed, Brussels would fall, and with it, the last stronghold of resistance in Europe.

The battle had begun, and there would be no turning back.

Chapter 33: The Fall of Brussels

April 2028 – Dawn

Brussels was burning. From the highest points of the city, the view was apocalyptic—a thick blanket of smoke hung over the skyline, punctuated by the orange glow of fires raging in every district. The insurgents had launched their final assault, and the city was crumbling under the weight of the attack.

Elena Kostova stood in what was left of the command centre, the sound of explosions and gunfire echoing through the streets. Maps of the city were scattered across the tables, useless now as the insurgents had broken through nearly every defensive line. Reports of casualties streamed in by the minute, and the faces of the resistance fighters around her were etched with exhaustion and despair.

General Malik entered the room, his expression as grim as the situation. "It's worse than we thought. Amir's forces are overwhelming us on all fronts. We've lost contact with most of our forward positions, and the southern district has fallen."

Elena closed her eyes, taking a deep breath to steady herself. She had known this moment was coming, but facing it was harder than she had anticipated. "What about the civilians? Have we evacuated them from the high-risk zones?"

Malik shook his head. "We've managed to get some out, but many are still trapped in the northern district. The insurgents cut off our main evacuation routes."

A heavy silence settled over the room. They were running out of time, and they all knew it.

"We need to regroup," Elena said, her voice hard with resolve. "We can't let them take the city without a fight."

Malik hesitated, his eyes filled with a mixture of determination and sorrow. "There's another option, Elena. We could retreat—pull back to the outskirts and regroup for a counteroffensive. If we stay here, we might not have the strength to hold."

Elena clenched her fists. The thought of abandoning Brussels felt like betrayal, but she knew Malik was right. If they stayed and fought to the bitter end, they would lose everything.

"I'm not leaving this city," she said firmly. "We've fought too hard and too long to give up now. But we need to be smart about how we fight. Send the remaining civilians to the western sector. We'll use the underground tunnels to move them safely. After that, we focus on holding the city centre."

Malik nodded, his respect for Elena clear in his eyes. "I'll coordinate with the remaining units. We still have a few surprises left for Amir."

The Insurgents Push Forward

On the outskirts of Brussels, Amir Saeed stood with Hakim and his top commanders, surveying the burning city from a distance. They had breached the city's defences faster than anticipated, and the resistance was falling apart.

"They're scattering," Hakim reported, a note of satisfaction in his voice. "We've taken the southern district and most of the industrial zone. It won't be long before the rest of the city falls."

Amir nodded, his expression calm. "Good. Continue pressing the attack. I want every resistance stronghold taken by the end of the day."

Hakim grinned, eager to carry out the orders. But Amir raised a hand, stopping him. "Focus on securing the northern district first. That's where Kostova will be. We take her out, and the rest of the resistance will crumble."

Hakim's grin faded slightly, but he nodded. "Understood."

Amir watched as his forces surged forward, moving through the burning streets like a tidal wave. He had been patient, waiting for the perfect moment to strike, and now it was finally here. Brussels was his for the taking.

The Last Stand

As the sun rose higher in the sky, the resistance prepared for what they knew would be their final stand. In the northern district, Elena and Malik rallied the remaining fighters, setting up barricades and fortifications around the city centre. The resistance was vastly outnumbered, and many of the fighters were exhausted, but they were determined to hold the line.

"We can't let them reach the civilians," Elena said as she stood with Malik on the front lines. "No matter what happens, we hold this position."

Malik nodded, his eyes scanning the horizon for any sign of the advancing insurgents. "We'll make them pay for every inch they take."

As the minutes ticked by, the tension in the air grew unbearable. The sounds of battle echoed from all around them, and the distant rumble of explosions shook the ground beneath their feet.

Suddenly, a scout ran up to them, his face pale with fear. "They're coming," he gasped. "Thousands of them. They're almost here."

Elena's heart raced, but she forced herself to stay calm. "Get everyone in position. We hold this line."

The resistance fighters scrambled to their posts, their weapons at the ready. Elena and Malik stood at the front, knowing that this was it—the final battle for Brussels.

The Battle Begins

The first wave of insurgents appeared over the horizon like a dark cloud, their numbers overwhelming. They moved swiftly through the streets, pouring into the city centre with brutal efficiency. Gunfire erupted as the resistance opened fire, but it was clear from the start that they were outmatched.

Elena fought alongside her soldiers, firing her rifle at the advancing enemy. The insurgents pressed forward relentlessly, and soon the battle devolved into hand-to-hand combat as they closed in on the resistance lines.

Amidst the chaos, Elena caught sight of Malik fighting off several insurgents with his bare hands. He was a force of nature, his sheer will and determination keeping him on his feet even as the odds stacked against him.

"Elena!" Malik shouted over the din of battle. "We need to fall back! We're losing too many!"

But Elena shook her head, her eyes blazing with defiance. "No! We hold!"

The insurgents continued to push forward, their numbers seeming endless. The resistance was being pushed back, inch by inch, as the insurgents overwhelmed their defences. Elena fought with everything she had, but it was clear that they were losing ground.

As the battle raged on, Elena's radio crackled to life. "Commander! We've received word—Amir Saeed is in the northern district. He's coming for you."

Elena's blood ran cold. Amir Saeed, the mastermind behind the insurgency, was here. The man who had orchestrated the downfall of Europe, who had driven the continent to the brink of collapse—he was coming for her.

She knew what that meant. If Amir killed her, it would be a devastating blow to the resistance. Without her, the last vestiges of organized resistance would crumble, and Brussels would fall completely under insurgent control.

The Showdown

Amir Saeed moved through the battlefield with calculated precision, his eyes scanning the carnage for any sign of Elena Kostova. He had come to finish what he had started. His forces had torn the city apart, and now he would take out its heart.

He spotted her through the smoke and flames, standing defiantly in the midst of the battle. She was covered in blood and dirt, but she was still fighting, still refusing to give in.

A cold smile crossed Amir's face. It was time to end this.

He made his way toward her, cutting down anyone who stood in his path. Elena saw him coming, and their eyes locked across the battlefield.

Time seemed to slow as they moved toward each other, the chaos of the battle fading into the background. This was the moment everything had been leading up to—the final confrontation between the leader of the resistance and the man who had orchestrated its destruction.

Elena raised her weapon, but Amir was faster. He knocked the gun from her hands and lunged at her, his blade flashing in the sunlight. She barely had time to react, dodging his first strike and countering with a punch to his ribs.

They fought fiercely, their movements a blur of violence and desperation. Elena was skilled, but Amir was stronger, and it quickly became clear that she was outmatched.

Amir caught her by the throat, slamming her against a crumbling wall. "You've lost," he hissed, his eyes burning with hatred. "Brussels is mine."

Elena struggled against his grip, but she refused to show fear. "You may take the city," she spat, her voice hoarse. "But you'll never break the people."

Amir's grip tightened. "We'll see about that."

Just as he was about to strike the final blow, a gunshot rang out. Amir froze, his eyes widening in shock. He stumbled back, clutching his side where blood was rapidly soaking through his clothes.

Malik stood behind him, his gun smoking. "Not today."

Amir fell to his knees, his face twisted in pain. He glared at Elena; his voice weak but filled with venom. "This isn't over."

Elena staggered to her feet, breathing heavily. She looked down at Amir, her face grim. "Yes, it is."

With one final shot, she ended his life.

Aftermath

The battle for Brussels ended with Amir Saeed's death, but the city was in ruins. The insurgents, leaderless and disorganized, began to retreat, but the damage had been done. The resistance had won the battle, but the cost had been staggering.

Elena stood in the rubble of what was once a thriving city, her heart heavy with grief. Brussels had survived, but at what price?

As the remaining resistance fighters began to rebuild, Elena knew that the war was far from over. Amir's death was a victory, but the insurgency had taken root in Europe, and it would take more than one battle to reclaim the continent.

Chapter 34: Rebuilding from the Ashes

May 2028 – Two Weeks After the Fall

The sun rose over Brussels, casting long shadows over the smouldering ruins of what was once Europe's political heart. The city was still. Silence, for the first time in days, enveloped the streets—no gunfire, no explosions, no desperate screams for help. The insurgents had retreated, and the war-torn survivors were left to pick up the pieces.

Elena Kostova stood in the remains of what had once been the city's government district. Around her, debris lay in heaps, shattered glass and broken concrete littering the streets. The once majestic buildings of the European Union lay in ruins, a haunting reminder of the power that once flowed through the continent's veins. Now, all of it was gone, reduced to dust and ash.

Her face, etched with fatigue and loss, reflected the weight of the war that still hung over her. The victory over Amir Saeed had come at a tremendous cost. The insurgency had been broken, but not defeated. His death had left a power vacuum, one that could quickly descend into further chaos if not carefully managed.

"Commander?" a voice called from behind her.

Elena turned to see General Malik approaching. His uniform was tattered, and his face bore fresh scars from the recent battle. Yet, despite the wear and tear, there was a glimmer of hope in his eyes.

"The first supply convoys have arrived," he reported, his voice rough but steady. "Medical teams are setting up field hospitals, and the engineers are beginning to assess the damage to the infrastructure. We've also started organizing the civilian evacuation of the most unstable zones."

Elena nodded, grateful for the good news, though her heart still felt heavy with the enormity of the task ahead. "How are the people holding up?"

Malik sighed. "They're shaken, scared. But some are starting to return to their homes, what's left of them. There's... resilience here, but it's fragile. They need leadership, Elena. Now more than ever."

Elena looked out over the broken city, thinking of all the lives that had been lost, all the sacrifices that had been made. She knew Malik was right.

The war was far from over. The insurgency was still embedded in Europe, and without proper direction, it could rear its head again at any moment.

But first, Brussels needed to heal.

The Healing Begins

In the days that followed, the scale of the devastation became clearer. Entire neighbourhoods were razed to the ground. Hospitals were overflowing with the wounded and the dying. The city's infrastructure was in tatters. Water supplies had been poisoned, the power grid was a shadow of what it once was, and food was scarce.

The international community, once fractured by internal conflicts, slowly began to turn its gaze back toward Europe. Aid convoys started arriving from allied nations, bringing much-needed supplies, but the scale of the disaster overwhelmed them. Brussels had been one of the last bastions of hope for Europe, and its fall had sent shockwaves across the continent.

Elena spent her days coordinating relief efforts, attending meetings with what remained of the city's government and resistance leadership. The immediate priority was stabilizing the region and preventing further collapse. But as the days turned into weeks, the question of the future loomed larger.

"What happens now?" asked Sophia, a young civilian leader who had taken on a prominent role in helping organize the survivors. She had been instrumental in evacuating civilians during the battle and had gained the respect of many in the resistance.

Elena and Sophia stood in a makeshift camp where civilians were gathering, trying to rebuild their lives. Children played among the rubble, oblivious to the weight of the world around them, while adults worked tirelessly to set up tents and distribute food.

"We rebuild," Elena said softly, though even as she spoke the words, she knew it would take more than just rebuilding structures. Trust had to be rebuilt. Communities needed to be brought together. And, above all, peace had to be secured in a world that had been shattered by war.

Sophia's eyes searched Elena's face. "And the insurgents? Amir may be dead, but his movement is far from defeated. There are whispers of new leaders rising to take his place."

Elena met her gaze with a quiet intensity. "We deal with them. But first, we need to secure Brussels. If we lose this city, we lose everything."

Power Struggles and New Alliances

As Brussels began to recover, political factions across Europe started to reemerge from the shadows. The power vacuum left by Amir's death had created a dangerous new dynamic. New leaders, both within the insurgency and among the European resistance, were jockeying for control. In the chaos of war, alliances shifted rapidly, and loyalty was a rare commodity.

Elena found herself at the centre of this new political landscape. Her victory over Amir Saeed had earned her the respect of many, but it had also made her a target. Some saw her as a threat to their power, others as the only hope for unity.

One of the most prominent figures to emerge in this new political struggle was Jean-Luc Arnaud, a former diplomat turned military strategist. Arnaud had led several successful campaigns in southern France against insurgent forces and had garnered a significant following among the southern resistance. He was charismatic, intelligent, and fiercely determined to see Europe restored.

But he was also ruthless.

"Elena," Arnaud said one evening, as they sat in a dimly lit room discussing the future of the resistance, "we need to be realistic about what comes next. The insurgents are weakened, but they are far from defeated. We can't afford to show weakness now. We need to take the fight to them, root them out, and crush them before they have a chance to regroup."

Elena studied him, sensing the ambition behind his words. Arnaud was a skilled tactician, but his approach worried her. He was focused on military victory, but Elena knew that a purely military solution would never be enough.

"We can't just focus on war, Jean-Luc," she replied. "If we don't start rebuilding the trust of the people, if we don't offer them hope, the insurgents will always have a foothold. We need more than just weapons—we need to give people a reason to believe in a future beyond this conflict."

Arnaud leaned forward, his eyes sharp. "Hope won't stop bullets, Elena. If we don't eliminate the threat completely, all your rebuilding will be for nothing."

The tension between them was palpable. Arnaud represented one faction of the resistance—those who believed that total military dominance was the only way forward. Elena, on the other hand, represented another vision: one where reconciliation and rebuilding went hand in hand with the fight for survival.

The question was, which vision would prevail?

The Rise of New Leaders

Meanwhile, on the other side of the conflict, new insurgent leaders were beginning to emerge. Without Amir Saeed's centralized leadership, the insurgency had fractured into smaller, more localized factions. But in the shadows, whispers of a new figurehead began to circulate—a mysterious leader known only as "The Architect."

No one knew who The Architect was or where they had come from, but their influence was growing rapidly. They had begun to unify the fractured insurgent cells across Europe, using Amir's death as a rallying cry for renewed jihad against the European governments. Their tactics were different, more strategic and less overt than Amir's brutal assaults. The Architect was playing a long game, and it was clear that they had learned from Amir's mistakes.

In the ruins of a war-torn continent, both sides were preparing for the next phase of the conflict. Elena Kostova and her allies were racing against time to rebuild a broken Europe, while The Architect and the remnants of the insurgency were gathering strength, waiting for the right moment to strike again.

The Fragile Peace

As the weeks passed, a fragile peace settled over Brussels. The city, though ravaged by war, was slowly coming back to life. Civilians returned to their homes, and makeshift markets sprang up in the streets. The resistance, battered but not broken, continued to patrol the city, watching for any signs of insurgent activity.

But Elena knew that the peace would not last. The war was far from over, and the next battle was already on the horizon.

She stood at the edge of the city one evening, watching as the sun set over the ruins. Malik joined her, his presence a quiet comfort.

"It's not over is it?" he asked softly, though he already knew the answer.

Elena shook her head. "No. This is just the beginning."

As the light faded and the shadows of night began to creep across the city, Elena felt the weight of the future pressing down on her. The war had taken so much from them, but there was still hope. There had to be.

And as long as there was hope, there was something worth fighting for

Chapter 35: The Shadow of The Architect

June 2028 – The Rising Threat

Brussels was still in ruins, but life, in its most basic form, had begun to return. The survivors were resilient, as Elena Kostova had predicted. Markets had opened in makeshift tents, and families huddled together in abandoned buildings, trying to find some semblance of normalcy. But beneath the surface, tensions simmered. The destruction of the city had left deep wounds, and with Amir Saeed's death, the insurgency had fragmented into smaller, dangerous factions.

Yet, something far more troubling loomed on the horizon. A new insurgent leader—someone even more cunning than Amir—had begun to rise through the ranks of the scattered cells. They called themselves **The Architect**. While Amir had been charismatic and ruthless, The Architect was invisible, shrouded in mystery and methodical in approach. This shadowy figure had not yet made any public appearances, but their presence was felt everywhere. The insurgent cells, which had been weakened after Amir's death, were now slowly coalescing, and it was The Architect who was pulling the strings.

Elena Kostova had heard the whispers. They had reached her through intercepted communications and through survivors fleeing areas recently overrun by insurgent forces. Whoever The Architect was, they weren't like Amir. They didn't rely on brute force alone. Instead, they focused on infiltrating governments, turning public sentiment against the resistance, and creating a narrative that the insurgents were the rightful rulers of a new Europe.

Elena paced in her temporary command centre—a former library repurposed into a military hub for the resistance. Maps were pinned to the walls, and the smell of coffee and stale air filled the room as her team sifted through reports of insurgent activity. She could feel the weight of the city's fate pressing down on her shoulders.

"We've received new intelligence on The Architect's movements," Malik announced, stepping into the room. He had barely rested in weeks, his eyes bloodshot, but his resolve remained unshaken. He tossed a folder onto the table, its contents spilling out—photos of new insurgent strongholds, intelligence reports, and snippets of intercepted communications.

Elena scanned the documents quickly. "They're rebuilding," she muttered under her breath. "Faster than we anticipated."

"They're more organized than before," Malik said, his tone grim. "The Architect isn't making the same mistakes as Amir. We've seen cells in France, Germany, and even southern England reorganizing under their leadership. It's like they knew exactly how to pick up the pieces after Amir's fall."

Elena frowned. "And the rumours?"

Malik nodded. "The Architect's influence is growing. There are whispers that they've already started making deals with former European politicians, people who've lost faith in the resistance. They're offering security and order in exchange for loyalty. If we don't act soon, we could lose entire regions to their control."

Elena clenched her fists. She had fought too hard and lost too many people to let the insurgency rebuild itself into a stronger force. But she knew rushing into action without a clear strategy could be disastrous. The Architect was playing a different game—a long-term one—and the resistance needed to adapt quickly.

"We need more information," Elena finally said, her voice steady. "If we can find out who The Architect is, we can disrupt their network before they gain too much ground."

Malik nodded. "We've sent agents to infiltrate their ranks. It'll take time, but if anyone can gather intel, it's our people."

Elena looked out the shattered windows of the library, the sun setting behind the charred remains of the skyline. Time was running out. Brussels may have survived the first wave, but the next battle was on the horizon, and this time, the enemy was more insidious.

The Insurgent Council

Far from Brussels, in the shadows of a remote compound somewhere in the Alps, the leadership of the insurgency had gathered. Around a long, dimly lit table sat men and women who had risen to power in the chaos following Amir Saeed's death. Each had their own agendas, their own vision for the future of Europe. But they were united under one banner: The Architect's vision of a new, unified caliphate across the continent.

The door at the far end of the room opened, and a figure entered, their face hidden behind a veil of shadows. The air in the room shifted, and every eye turned toward the newcomer. The Architect had arrived.

"Progress?" The Architect's voice was calm, controlled, but there was a sharp edge beneath it. The figure moved gracefully to the head of the table, taking a seat without any ceremony.

A man from the French cell, known only as Ibrahim, leaned forward. "We've successfully re-established control in the southern regions. The locals are... cooperative, for now. The remaining resistance pockets are weak, and we expect them to be neutralized within the month."

Another insurgent leader, a woman from the Balkans, spoke next. "We've begun infiltrating the resistance's supply lines in Germany. Disruptions are expected within weeks, possibly days. Their communications are vulnerable."

The Architect listened in silence, fingers steepled in front of their face. "And Brussels?" they finally asked, their voice low but commanding.

Ibrahim hesitated. "The resistance there remains strong under Kostova's leadership. She's... resilient. Her forces have held, despite the damage we inflicted. They are still a threat."

The Architect was silent for a long moment, contemplating the information. Then they spoke, their voice cold and decisive. "Kostova is a symbol. As long as she remains, the resistance will endure. It's time to remove her from the equation."

There was a murmur of agreement around the table, though some shifted uncomfortably at the prospect of targeting Elena directly. They all knew she was a formidable adversary, but The Architect's command was absolute.

"We will proceed carefully," The Architect continued. "I want her weakened first. Isolated. Let her see her city fall apart from within before we strike. Make sure she's vulnerable. Then we'll send our best to finish the job."

The room fell into a tense silence, and The Architect rose, leaving the room as quietly as they had entered.

Sabotage and Betrayal

Back in Brussels, Elena's efforts to stabilize the city were slowly gaining ground, but tensions were rising. The fractured infrastructure and ongoing food shortages left civilians on edge, and in some neighbourhoods, small insurgent cells had begun stirring up dissent. Some people, desperate for stability, were starting to question the resistance's ability to lead.

In the midst of this uncertainty, strange things began to happen. Supply convoys that had been critical to the city's recovery began to go missing. Key resistance leaders found themselves targeted by unknown assailants; their movements compromised. And, most concerning of all, whispers began to spread through the ranks of the resistance—rumours that someone on the inside was leaking information to the insurgents.

Elena and Malik held a meeting in their command centre late one evening, the air thick with unease.

"We've lost three supply lines in the past week," Malik said, pacing back and forth. "Every time we try to adjust our routes, the insurgents seem to know exactly where to strike. It's too precise. Someone's feeding them our plans."

Elena's face was set in a grim expression. "We have a traitor."

Malik stopped pacing and turned to face her. "We've already started investigating, but if someone inside our own ranks is working for The Architect, it won't be easy to root them out."

Elena nodded, her mind racing. She had always known that the insurgency would try to infiltrate their ranks, but this felt different. It wasn't just about gaining information—it was about destabilizing the resistance from within.

"We'll need to keep this quiet," she said, her voice firm. "If word gets out that there's a traitor, it could destroy what little morale we have left."

Malik agreed, though his expression was tense. "I'll put my best people on it. We'll find out who's responsible."

The Architect's Long Game

As the days passed, the situation in Brussels grew more precarious. The subtle sabotage orchestrated by The Architect was beginning to take its toll. People started to lose faith in the resistance's ability to protect them. Protests broke out in some of the more volatile districts, with civilians demanding answers and, in some cases, calling for new leadership.

Elena, exhausted from the endless stream of crises, began to feel the weight of isolation pressing down on her. She was doing everything in her power to keep the city together, but the cracks were widening. And all the while, The Architect watched from the shadows, waiting for the perfect moment to strike.

It wasn't just a battle for territory anymore—it was a battle for hearts and minds. And The Architect was proving to be a master of both.

As Elena stood on the balcony of the resistance's headquarters, looking out over the broken city, she couldn't shake the feeling that she was being watched. The Architect was out there, somewhere, pulling the strings. And as the sun dipped below the horizon, casting long shadows over the ruins of Brussels, Elena knew that the next phase of the war was about to begin.

Chapter 36: Shadows Within

June 2028 – Three Days Later

The tension in Brussels was palpable. The once vibrant, though wounded, spirit of the people had dimmed in the face of growing uncertainty. Sabotage, betrayal, and the rumours of The Architect's influence were beginning to unravel the delicate peace Elena had fought so hard to maintain.

Elena stood in front of a map spread out on the table in the war room. Her eyes scanned the positions of their remaining strongholds, noting the red marks that indicated the recent attacks. Brussels was still standing, but its survival was hanging by a thread.

Malik entered the room, his expression grim. "We've confirmed it," he said, tossing a folder onto the table. "There's a mole. We found evidence that information is being leaked directly to The Architect's insurgents."

Elena closed her eyes briefly, frustration boiling inside her. "How bad is it?"

Malik crossed his arms, looking as tired as she felt. "Bad. Whoever it is, they're high up enough to know our movements before we even finalize them. Supply lines, safe houses, even troop rotations—everything's been compromised. If we don't root them out soon, we're finished."

Elena leaned against the edge of the table, her mind racing. The insurgents had grown more audacious with each passing day, their strikes more precise. The resistance was crumbling from within, and the fear of betrayal was eating away at what little trust remained.

She had always known this war would be fought on more than one front. The insurgents didn't need to defeat the resistance in open combat if they could tear them apart from the inside. That was The Architect's strategy—a war of attrition, not of force.

"We need to keep this contained," Elena said, her voice steady but sharp. "If the rank-and-file learn there's a traitor among us, we'll lose more than just battles. We'll lose everything."

Malik nodded. "I've already started a discreet investigation. We're looking at a small group of individuals who've had access to sensitive information."

Elena's mind drifted to the men and women she had come to rely on. Most of them had been with the resistance since the early days, but she couldn't afford to trust anyone blindly now. The insurgents had proven capable of turning even the most loyal into their pawns.

"What about Sophia?" Elena asked, her voice dropping. The young civilian leader had quickly become one of the resistance's most vocal advocates. Her leadership had been invaluable during the aftermath of Amir Saeed's defeat, but recently she had been more distant, her focus on civilian matters pulling her away from the resistance's military operations.

Malik hesitated. "She's... been under some scrutiny. Her movements have been erratic lately, but she's clean, as far as we can tell. Still, she's been a bit unpredictable, especially with all the civilian unrest."

Elena's brow furrowed. She had grown to trust Sophia, but the insurgents were masters of deception. If someone was playing a long game, hiding in plain sight, it wouldn't be easy to detect.

"Keep an eye on her," Elena finally said, her tone reluctant. "But be discreet. I don't want to alienate anyone unless we have solid proof."

The Trap Tightens

Across the city, Sophia was meeting with a small group of civilians. They had gathered in an abandoned schoolhouse, its walls covered with faded murals and bullet holes. The room was cramped, the air heavy with the stench of sweat and desperation.

"We can't keep going like this," one of the civilians, a middle-aged man named Pieter, said angrily. "We're running out of food, supplies are disappearing, and the resistance is too focused on fighting the insurgents to care about us."

Sophia stood at the front of the room; her eyes filled with empathy. She had been working tirelessly to keep the civilian population organized, to offer them hope in the midst of chaos. But she knew the truth—things were getting worse, and fast.

"I understand your frustration," Sophia said, her voice calm but firm. "But the resistance is doing everything it can. We're stretched thin, and we're all suffering. The insurgents want us to turn against each other. We can't let them win."

Pieter's face twisted in anger. "Easy for you to say. You're part of the resistance's inner circle. You're not starving in the streets like the rest of us!"

Sophia felt a pang of guilt. Pieter wasn't wrong—she had access to food and shelter, things many civilians had been denied. But it wasn't out of greed or indifference; it was out of necessity. She needed to remain strong if she was going to help them.

"The insurgents are trying to undermine everything we've built," she said, her voice rising slightly. "We can't afford to let that happen. The resistance is our only hope."

The room fell silent, tension thick in the air. Pieter's glare softened slightly, but the resentment was still there, festering beneath the surface. Sophia could feel it spreading, infecting the hearts and minds of the people. If she couldn't find a way to unite them, The Architect would win without ever having to lift a weapon.

Malik's Investigation

Back at the resistance's headquarters, Malik was working late into the night, going through files and cross-referencing movements, communications, and supply logs. He was close—he could feel it. Whoever the mole was, they had been careful, but no one was perfect. There were always small mistakes.

He had narrowed it down to a handful of suspects, each of them with access to critical information. As he examined the logs again, his eye caught something unusual—an encrypted message sent from one of their secure channels to a location outside Brussels. The timing of the message coincided with one of the recent insurgent attacks.

His heart raced as he traced the communication back to its source.

It was from Sophia's terminal.

Malik sat back in his chair, his mind reeling. Could it be true? Could Sophia, the woman who had worked so hard to help the civilians, who had stood beside Elena in the aftermath of Amir's death, really be the traitor? It didn't make sense, but the evidence was there, staring him in the face.

He knew he had to bring this to Elena, but he also knew how close Elena and Sophia had become. It wouldn't be easy to convince her without solid proof.

Malik stood up, gathering the files. There was no time to waste. If Sophia was truly working with The Architect, they needed to act before more lives were lost.

The Confrontation

The next morning, Elena was in the command centre when Malik entered, his face a mask of grim determination. He handed her the files without a word.

Elena's eyes flickered over the documents, her expression hardening as she read through the details. She paused when she saw Sophia's name.

"Malik, this can't be right," she said, her voice tight. "Sophia has been with us since the beginning. She's risked her life for this city."

Malik shook his head. "I didn't want to believe it either, but the evidence is there. She's been sending encrypted messages to insurgent cells outside the city. Every time she moves, the insurgents seem to know exactly where to strike. It's too much of a coincidence."

Elena slammed the folder shut, her mind racing. She trusted Malik, but the thought of Sophia being a traitor was almost unbearable. How could she have been so blind?

"I want to confront her," Elena said, her voice low and resolute. "But we do it quietly. No one else can know until, we're sure."

Malik nodded, his jaw set. "Agreed. We need to handle this carefully."

The Architect's Gambit

As night fell over Brussels, Sophia sat alone in her small apartment, staring at the encrypted communicator hidden beneath a loose floorboard. She hadn't used it in days, but its presence weighed heavily on her conscience.

She had made a choice; one she wasn't sure she could live with. The Architect had approached her months ago, offering her something the resistance had never given security for the civilians. A promise that if she worked with them, the insurgents would spare the innocents caught in the crossfire.

Sophia had been torn between her loyalty to Elena and her desire to protect the people she had sworn to help. In the end, she had made a deal with the devil.

And now, the walls were closing in.

As she contemplated her next move, a soft knock came at the door. Sophia's heart skipped a beat. She stood, her hands trembling as she walked toward the door. When she opened it, Elena and Malik stood in the doorway, their expressions unreadable.

"We need to talk," Elena said, her voice cold.

Sophia swallowed hard, knowing that the reckoning had finally arrived.

A Choice Between Friends

The room was silent as Elena and Sophia faced each other, the weight of their shared history pressing down on them like a heavy fog. Malik stood nearby, watching with wary eyes, ready to intervene if things escalated.

"Sophia," Elena began, her voice carefully controlled, "we've intercepted communications. Messages sent from your terminal to insurgent forces. I need to know the truth."

Sophia's heart raced. She had been prepared for this moment, but now that it had arrived, she felt a deep sense of dread. Her throat tightened as she struggled to find the words.

"I didn't... I didn't want to betray you, Elena," she whispered, tears welling in her eyes. "I did what I thought was right."

Elena's face hardened. "Right? You've been feeding information to The Architect's forces. How is that right?"

Sophia took a deep breath, trying to steady herself. "The Architect promised to spare the civilians. They said if I helped them, they wouldn't target the innocent. I couldn't just stand by and watch people die. Not after everything we've been through."

Elena's jaw tightened; her fists clenched at her sides. "And what about the lives lost because of your betrayal? The soldiers who died in those attacks? The supply lines destroyed. How many more will suffer because of your choices?"

Sophia's tears spilled over, her voice breaking. "I didn't know it would go this far. I thought... I thought I could control it."

Elena's anger flared. "Control? You were never in control, Sophia. The Architect used you, just like they've used everyone else. You've put us all at risk, and now we're barely holding on."

For a long moment, the room was silent. The weight of the betrayal hung heavy in the air. Malik watched the exchange, his eyes flickering between the two women.

Sophia wiped her tears, her voice barely above a whisper. "I'm sorry, Elena. I never wanted this."

Elena stared at her friend, the woman she had trusted, fought besides, and depended on. A part of her wanted to forgive, to believe that Sophia had acted out of desperation, but the stakes were too high. Too much had been lost.

"Elena," Malik said quietly, stepping forward, "we need to make a decision."

Elena took a deep breath, her mind swirling with the weight of her responsibilities. She knew what had to be done.

"We can't afford any more mistakes," she said, her voice cold and final. "Sophia, you're under arrest for treason against the resistance."

Sophia's face crumpled, but she didn't resist. She knew her fate had been sealed the moment she made her deal with The Architect.

As Malik led her away, Elena stood in the dimly lit room, the burden of leadership pressing down on her shoulders like never before.

In the distance, the city of Brussels continued to burn.

Chapter 37: Rising Tempests

July 2028 – The Calm Before the Storm

The aftermath of Sophia's arrest rippled through the resistance like a shockwave. Whispers of betrayal and doubt swept across Brussels, where soldiers and civilians alike were questioning who they could trust. The once-united front that had held back The Architect's insurgents was cracking, and the fractures were deepening by the day.

Elena stood in her private quarters, staring out the window at the battered city below. She could hear the distant rumble of conflict, the occasional blast of artillery echoing through the streets. It had been a week since Sophia's arrest, and the guilt weighed on her like a stone around her neck. Elena had done what she had to for the sake of the resistance, but a part of her still couldn't believe Sophia had been capable of such betrayal.

A knock at the door pulled her from her thoughts.

"Come in," she called, her voice lacking its usual edge.

Malik entered, his face grim as always, though his eyes were softer. He had stood by Elena's side through every difficult decision, but this one had left a visible scar on both of them.

"Elena, we've received word," he said, holding up a worn envelope. "The message came through one of our remaining secure channels. It's from Paris."

Elena's heart skipped a beat. Paris had been under siege for months, their communications sporadic at best. The city had become a symbol of the resistance's resilience, and many believed that as long as Paris held, there was still hope. But Elena knew better. Paris, like Brussels, was teetering on the edge of collapse.

"What does it say?" she asked, her voice low and tense.

Malik handed her the letter, and as Elena unfolded it, her eyes scanned the hastily scrawled text.

The situation in Paris is critical. The insurgents have taken most of the northern districts, and food supplies are dwindling. We are requesting immediate aid, but we fear time is running out. If we do not receive support within the next ten days, Paris will fall.

Elena's stomach twisted. She had anticipated this day would come, but not so soon. The resistance was stretched too thin, and they had barely enough resources to defend Brussels, let alone send reinforcements to Paris.

"We can't help them," she said quietly, her voice laced with bitterness.

Malik nodded; his expression pained. "I know. But if Paris falls, it will be a devastating blow to the resistance's morale. We're losing ground, Elena. Every day, the insurgents grow stronger, and we grow weaker."

Elena clenched her fists, frustration bubbling beneath the surface. The Architect's plan had been methodical, tearing the resistance apart piece by piece, sowing chaos and distrust wherever they could. And now, with Sophia's betrayal still fresh in everyone's minds, the foundation of their cause was crumbling faster than ever.

"Do we have any word from London?" Elena asked, though she already knew the answer.

Malik shook his head. "Nothing. The last we heard; they were dealing with their own internal issues. Political infighting, lack of resources. It's a mess over there."

Elena exhaled slowly, trying to keep her emotions in check. London had once been a stronghold for the resistance, but as the crisis deepened, the cracks within the United Kingdom's leadership had grown. Old rivalries, ethnic tensions, and the strain of endless conflict had taken their toll.

The truth was the resistance was running out of allies.

The Power Struggle

Far to the west, in the heart of Germany, Chancellor Anneliese Baumann sat in her office, staring at a similar letter. It was a formal request for assistance from the resistance in Brussels, detailing their dire situation and their need for reinforcements.

But unlike Elena, Baumann's expression was cold and calculating as she read the message. She had long since come to terms with the reality that Germany could not afford to prop up the resistance much longer. The insurgents had made significant inroads into the country, and public opinion was rapidly shifting.

The German government had managed to maintain relative stability for longer than many of its European counterparts, but the cost had been high. Nationalist movements were on the rise, fuelled by economic hardship, fear of the Muslim insurgents, and frustration with the EU's inability to control the migrant crisis. There was a growing faction within Baumann's own government that wanted to withdraw from the EU entirely, to close the borders and adopt a more isolationist stance.

As much as it pained her, Baumann knew that Brussels was no longer her priority.

"The resistance is losing," she muttered to herself, her fingers tightening around the letter. "And we're losing with them."

She stood up, walking to the large window that overlooked the Berlin skyline. The city had suffered its own share of attacks, though it was nothing compared to what Paris or Brussels had endured. Still, the tension in the streets was palpable. Protests had become a regular occurrence, with both nationalist and pro-resistance factions clashing violently on a near-weekly basis.

Baumann knew she couldn't hold this fragile coalition together much longer. The people were demanding action, and soon, she would have to make a choice—one that would determine the future of Germany, and perhaps Europe as a whole.

The Architect's Message

In a dimly lit bunker somewhere outside Brussels, The Architect sat before a large screen, their fingers steepled as they watched the unfolding chaos. Their plan was proceeding almost perfectly. The resistance was fractured, and with Sophia's betrayal, they had managed to plant the seeds of distrust that would further erode the unity of their enemies.

A figure entered the room, their face obscured by shadows. "The mole has been taken into custody," the figure said, their voice low and formal. "But the damage has been done."

The Architect nodded slowly. "Good. The time for subtlety is ending. Soon, we will strike the final blow."

The figure hesitated for a moment. "Do you think the resistance will hold? They still have strongholds in Brussels and London?"

"They will hold for now," The Architect replied, their voice calm and measured. "But they are running out of time and resources. Every day, their people grow more desperate. Desperation breeds mistakes."

"And what of Paris?"

The Architect smiled faintly, though there was no warmth in the gesture. "Paris is already lost. The Chancellor in Germany will make sure of that."

The figure nodded and left the room, leaving The Architect alone with their thoughts. They had spent years planning this, positioning their pieces across Europe, and now it was all coming together. The resistance was bleeding out, and soon, there would be nothing left but ruins.

But The Architect wasn't content to simply let their enemies destroy themselves. No, they wanted to ensure that when the resistance finally crumbled, it would do so in a way that left Europe forever changed.

A new order was coming, and The Architect would be the one to usher it in.

A Desperate Plea

Back in Brussels, Elena sat with her head in her hands, the weight of leadership pressing down on her like a crushing force. Malik stood nearby, watching her with concern.

"We have to make a decision soon," Malik said quietly. "Paris won't last much longer without our help."

Elena lifted her head, her eyes filled with exhaustion. "And if we send reinforcements, Brussels will fall. We don't have the manpower to defend both."

Malik didn't respond. He didn't have to. They both knew the truth.

Elena sighed heavily, leaning back in her chair. "We've been fighting for so long, Malik. I don't know how much longer we can keep this up."

Malik stepped forward, placing a hand on her shoulder. "We'll keep fighting as long as we have to. For the people. For everyone who's depending on us."

Elena nodded, though the fire in her heart was flickering, weakened by the endless struggle. She didn't know how much longer she could bear the weight of it all. But she knew one thing for certain.

They couldn't afford to give up. Not yet.

THE FRACTURED CONTINENT

The storm was coming, and they would have to weather it, or be swept away forever.

Chapter 38: The Siege of Paris

August 2028 – The city on the Brink

Paris had always been a symbol of culture, art, and resilience, but now it was a warzone, on the brink of collapse. Once filled with life, the streets were now deserted, debris and smouldering wreckage littering the landscape. Black smoke billowed from the northern districts, where The Architect's forces had entrenched themselves, choking the city inch by inch.

Marie Dupont, one of the few remaining resistance commanders still fighting in the city, stood on the rooftop of a bombed-out building in the 11th arrondissement, surveying the ruined skyline. The Eiffel Tower loomed in the distance, barely visible through the smoke, a haunting reminder of what they were fighting for.

Her face was streaked with dirt and sweat, her once-bright eyes now dulled by months of sleepless nights and battle-hardened resolve. She had been in Paris since the beginning, leading one of the smaller resistance cells that had been defending the city's eastern flank. Now, she was one of the few left standing.

"Commander Dupont," a voice called from behind her.

Marie turned to see Jean-Luc, one of her most trusted lieutenants, rushing up the stairs. He was a young man, barely twenty, but the war had aged him beyond his years. His uniform was tattered, his body thin from hunger, yet his eyes still held a spark of determination.

"They've breached the outer barricades in Belleville," Jean-Luc said, his voice tight with urgency. "Our forces are falling back. We're losing ground, fast."

Marie clenched her jaw, her mind racing. Belleville had been one of the few districts still holding out, a stronghold for the resistance. If they lost it, the insurgents would gain a direct route into the heart of the city. It was a critical blow.

"How many men do we have left?" she asked, knowing the answer would not be good.

"Fewer than fifty," Jean-Luc replied grimly. "Most are injured. We're running out of ammo, food, and medical supplies."

Marie stared out at the burning city, feeling the weight of every decision pressing down on her. She had known for weeks that Paris was slipping away from them, but she had refused to abandon it. This city had survived revolutions, invasions, and world wars. Surely, they could find a way to survive this too.

But the truth was harder to ignore now. The resistance was crumbling, and with each passing day, The Architect's forces were tightening their grip.

"We can't hold Belleville," she said quietly, turning back to Jean-Luc. "Tell the men to fall back to the Marais. We'll set up a new defensive line there."

Jean-Luc nodded, though the disappointment was clear in his eyes. "Understood."

He turned to leave, but before he could descend the stairs, Marie stopped him. "Jean-Luc, if it comes down to it, we need to prepare for evacuation. We can't let The Architect capture us. Do you understand?"

Jean-Luc hesitated, then nodded solemnly. "Yes, Commander."

As he disappeared down the stairwell, Marie felt a sinking feeling in her chest. She had always been a fighter, someone who believed in never giving up, no matter the odds. But now, standing on the brink of defeat, she realized that sometimes, survival meant knowing when to retreat.

The Battle for Belleville

In the crumbling streets of Belleville, the battle was raging. Resistance fighters huddled behind makeshift barricades; their rifles clutched in trembling hands. They fired sporadically at the advancing insurgents, but their numbers were too few, their weapons too inadequate to hold off the relentless assault.

Explosions rocked the ground, sending dust and debris into the air. Cries of pain and desperation echoed through the narrow streets as men and women, many of them civilians who had taken up arms, tried to defend their home.

But it was a losing battle. The Architect's forces were well-organized, equipped with superior firepower and technology. Drones buzzed overhead, surveying the battlefield and directing artillery strikes with deadly precision.

The insurgents moved methodically, using the city's architecture to their advantage, flanking resistance positions and cutting off escape routes.

In a small alleyway, hidden behind a pile of rubble, Louis, a veteran resistance fighter, crouched with his back against the wall, reloading his rifle. His hands were shaking, not from fear, but from exhaustion. He hadn't slept in days, and the constant fighting had taken a toll on his body.

Beside him, Amélie, a young woman who had joined the resistance only a few months ago, was nursing a wounded leg. She had been hit by shrapnel earlier in the battle, and though the bleeding had stopped, she could barely stand.

"We're not going to make it out of here, are we?" she asked, her voice weak but steady.

Louis glanced at her, his eyes filled with a mixture of sorrow and determination. "We'll make it," he said, though he didn't fully believe his own words. "We just have to hold on a little longer. Reinforcements are coming."

But they both knew the truth. Reinforcements weren't coming. Paris was on its own.

Political Manoeuvring

While Paris burned, the halls of power in Berlin were filled with hushed conversations and secret meetings. Chancellor Anneliese Baumann sat at the head of a large conference table, surrounded by her advisors, each of them offering their opinions on the worsening situation.

"The resistance is finished," said Karl, the Minister of Defence, his tone blunt. "We've been monitoring their communications, and they don't have the resources to hold out much longer. Paris will fall within the next few days."

"And what about Brussels?" Baumann asked, her voice calm but tense.

"Brussels is holding, for now," Karl replied. "But they're stretched thin. If Paris falls, the morale across the resistance will plummet. The Architect's forces will likely turn their full attention to Brussels next."

Baumann tapped her fingers on the table, her mind racing. She had been walking a delicate line for months, trying to balance Germany's interests with the wider crisis unfolding across Europe. The insurgency had grown more powerful than anyone had anticipated, and the EU's ability to respond was crippled by internal divisions and infighting.

"The question," Baumann said slowly, "is whether we should intervene directly. We have the military capability to turn the tide in Paris, but doing so would be a major escalation. It would bring us into direct conflict with The Architect's forces."

Her advisors exchanged uneasy glances. None of them wanted to admit it, but they knew the risks involved in such a move.

"If we don't act now," said Markus, the Foreign Minister, "we risk losing Europe altogether. The insurgency is spreading, and if we allow Paris to fall, it will embolden The Architect to strike at other cities."

Baumann leaned back in her chair, deep in thought. She had always been a pragmatist, someone who weighed every decision carefully, but now, she was being forced to consider a bold and dangerous course of action.

"Prepare the military," she said after a long pause. "But keep it quiet for now. I want to see how the situation develops over the next 48 hours. If Paris is on the verge of collapse, we'll intervene. But until then, we hold back."

Her advisors nodded, though none of them seemed particularly reassured. The fate of Europe was hanging in the balance, and every decision they made could tip the scales.

The Final Stand

As night fell over Paris, the resistance fighters in Belleville made their final stand. The streets were eerily quiet now, the sounds of battle replaced by an oppressive silence. The insurgents had pulled back temporarily, likely regrouping for a final push.

Marie Dupont stood at the new defensive line in the Marais, her eyes scanning the darkness for any sign of movement. She knew this would be their last stand. If they couldn't hold this position, the city would be lost.

"Commander," Jean-Luc said, approaching her. "The men are ready. What are your orders?"

Marie glanced at him, then at the tired, battered fighters around her. Many of them were too injured to continue, but they stood with weapons in hand, ready to fight to the end.

"We hold the line," she said quietly. "No matter what."

As the first explosions lit up the night sky, Marie took a deep breath, steeling herself for the battle to come. The insurgents were coming, and this time, there would be no retreat.

Paris, the city of light, was about to be plunged into darkness.

Chapter 39: The Fall of Paris

August 2028 – The Darkness Descends

The night sky over Paris was illuminated by flashes of gunfire and artillery explosions. What had once been a city of beauty and romance was now a war-torn landscape of rubble and devastation. Fires raged in the northern districts, casting an eerie orange glow across the city, and the streets were choked with the acrid smell of smoke and death.

Marie Dupont stood at the front of the resistance's last line of defence, her body tense and ready. The insurgents had pulled back for only a few hours, giving the resistance a brief reprieve. But Marie knew this was only the calm before the storm. The Architect's forces were preparing for the final assault, and when they came, there would be no mercy.

Beside her, Jean-Luc loaded his rifle, his expression grim but determined. "Commander, how long do you think we can hold out?"

Marie shook her head, her voice low. "Not long. We're out of ammo, out of food. We've already lost Belleville. It's only a matter of time."

Jean-Luc nodded; his jaw clenched. "Then we make it count."

The remaining fighters in the Marais were a mixture of seasoned resistance soldiers and desperate civilians who had taken up arms. Many of them were injured, their faces pale and gaunt from hunger and exhaustion. But they stood ready, knowing that this was their last stand.

"Everyone to your positions!" Marie called out, her voice strong despite the despair gnawing at her insides.

As the fighters scrambled to reinforce their barricades, Marie's thoughts drifted to the people of Paris. The civilians who had been caught in the crossfire, the families who had lost everything. She had fought for them, for the soul of this city, for so long. But now, she feared it was all in vain.

The sound of approaching vehicles broke her from her thoughts. In the distance, she could hear the rumble of armoured trucks and the steady march of boots on the ground. The Architect's forces were on the move.

"They're coming," Jean-Luc said, his voice tense. "We need to get ready."

Marie gripped her rifle tighter, her heart pounding in her chest. She had fought in countless battles, but this one felt different. This one felt final.

"Hold the line," she said, her voice steady. "We can't let them through."

The First Wave

The insurgents struck with brutal efficiency. Explosions rocked the barricades, sending chunks of concrete and metal flying through the air. Resistance fighters fired back desperately, but they were hopelessly outgunned. The Architect's forces moved with precision, using drones to pinpoint resistance positions and coordinating their attacks with deadly accuracy.

Marie crouched behind a pile of rubble; her rifle pressed to her shoulder. She fired at an approaching group of insurgents, dropping one of them, but more kept coming. It was like trying to hold back a tidal wave with a spoon.

"Jean-Luc, fall back!" she shouted, her voice barely audible over the roar of battle.

Jean-Luc and a handful of fighters retreated to the second line of defence, but even that was crumbling under the onslaught. The insurgents had brought in tanks, their heavy guns blasting through the resistance's fortifications like they were paper.

"We can't hold this position much longer!" one of the fighters yelled, his face smeared with blood and dirt.

Marie knew he was right. They were being overwhelmed, and the line was collapsing. She could feel the weight of defeat pressing down on her, but she refused to give in.

"Keep fighting!" she shouted, even as the ground shook beneath her feet.

But deep down, she knew it was over.

Desperate Measures

As the situation deteriorated, Marie realized they had one last option. It was a desperate move, one that would likely cost them everything. But if they were going to go down, they would do so on their own terms.

"Jean-Luc!" she called, motioning for him to come closer. "We need to fall back to the command centre. We have to activate the demolition charges."

Jean-Luc's eyes widened in shock. "The demolition charges? But that will destroy half of the Marais!"

Marie nodded grimly. "I know. But if we don't do it, they'll overrun the entire city. We can't let The Architect take Paris."

For a moment, Jean-Luc hesitated, torn between the desire to fight and the harsh reality of their situation. But then he nodded, his face hardening with resolve. "Alright. I'll get the men ready to fall back."

As Jean-Luc moved to rally the remaining fighters, Marie turned her gaze toward the command centre. It was hidden beneath an old building near the Seine, filled with explosives rigged to detonate if the resistance was on the verge of losing the city. The plan had always been a last resort—a way to deny The Architect total control over Paris. And now, it was their only option.

The Architect's Final Push

As the resistance fighters retreated to the command centre, The Architect's forces advanced with terrifying speed. Armoured vehicles rolled through the streets, their cannons firing indiscriminately into buildings and barricades. Drones hovered overhead, scanning the retreating fighters and transmitting their locations to ground troops.

In the command bunker, Marie stood over the control panel, her hands shaking slightly as she input the final code. The explosives were wired to key points throughout the Marais, designed to create a chain reaction that would bring down entire city blocks.

"It's ready," she said quietly, her voice barely audible over the sounds of battle outside.

Jean-Luc stood beside her, his face pale but resolute. "Do we wait for the others?"

Marie shook her head. "There's no time. We have to do it now."

She reached for the switch, her fingers trembling. Once she flipped it, there would be no turning back. The Marais would be destroyed, and with it, any hope of holding Paris.

But they couldn't let The Architect win.

Taking a deep breath, Marie flipped the switch.

The Destruction of the Marais

The ground trembled as the first explosion tore through the streets. Fire and smoke erupted from the buildings, and within seconds, the entire district was consumed in a series of deafening blasts. The resistance fighters still trapped outside were caught in the inferno, their cries of pain lost in the roar of destruction.

Marie and Jean-Luc watched in silence as the Marais crumbled around them. The command bunker was shaking violently, the walls cracking under the force of the detonations.

"We did it," Jean-Luc said, his voice hollow.

But Marie didn't feel victorious. She felt hollow, like a part of her had been destroyed along with the city. Paris had been her home, her life. And now it was gone.

The Architect's Response

In their hidden bunker, far from the chaos of the battle, The Architect watched the destruction unfold on a series of monitors. Their expression was unreadable, but there was a flicker of something in their eyes—disappointment, perhaps, or maybe frustration.

"They destroyed the Marais," one of their subordinates reported, his voice tense. "They're trying to deny us the city."

The Architect nodded slowly. "It was expected. The resistance is nothing if not predictable."

The subordinate hesitated for a moment. "Do we press the attack?"

The Architect smiled faintly, a cold and calculated expression. "No. Let them have their moment. Paris is already ours. We've broken them. All that remains is to sweep away the ashes."

The End of an Era

As dawn broke over the shattered remains of Paris, Marie and the surviving resistance fighters emerged from the rubble of the command bunker. The city was unrecognizable. The Marais, once a vibrant district filled with life, was now a smoking wasteland. Bodies lay strewn in the streets, and the few buildings still standing were on the verge of collapse.

Marie stared at the devastation, her heart heavy with grief. They had won a hollow victory. The city had been saved from The Architect, but at what cost?

"We did what we had to," Jean-Luc said quietly, standing beside her.

Marie nodded, though she didn't truly believe it. Paris had fallen, and with it, a part of her soul. The resistance was in tatters, and the future of Europe was more uncertain than ever.

But even in the face of overwhelming loss, Marie knew one thing: the fight wasn't over. The Architect might have taken Paris, but the resistance would continue. They would regroup, rebuild, and strike back.

Because as long as there were people willing to fight, there was still hope.

And hope, fragile though it was, was all they had left.

Chapter 40: The Escape from Paris

September 2028 – Retreat in the Night

The streets of Paris were silent now, save for the occasional crackle of flames and the distant rumble of The Architect's forces securing their new territory. The fall of the Marais had been catastrophic, and what remained of the resistance was scattered, broken, and in hiding. The once-proud city was now nothing more than a tomb for its people, its culture, and its dreams.

Marie Dupont, her body battered and her spirit weary, crouched in the shadows of an alleyway near the Seine. Her heart raced, and every breath felt heavy with smoke and ash. In the distance, the Eiffel Tower stood tall, though it now resembled a skeleton against the burning sky. The fires had spread throughout the northern districts, casting a flickering, hellish glow over the city.

Beside her, Jean-Luc crouched, his face gaunt and streaked with dirt. His once-sharp eyes were dull with exhaustion, but still, they gleamed with determination. He, like Marie, had seen too much death in the last few weeks, and both knew that this was likely the last time they would ever set foot in Paris.

"They're close," Jean-Luc whispered, his voice barely audible over the crackling of flames. "We don't have much time."

Marie nodded, her eyes scanning the shadows for any sign of movement. The resistance had been all but wiped out during the final assault on the Marais. Most of their comrades were dead or captured, and those who had survived had been forced to scatter into the ruins. She and Jean-Luc had managed to slip away in the chaos, but now, there was no clear way out of the city.

"We head for the river," Marie whispered back. "There's a boat waiting near Île Saint-Louis. If we can make it there, we might have a chance."

Jean-Luc nodded, but both knew the risks. The Architect's patrols had been tightening their grip on the city, searching for any remaining resistance fighters. The Seine was heavily guarded, and the chances of slipping past unnoticed were slim. But staying in Paris was a death sentence. They had to escape.

Ghosts in the City

The pair moved silently through the ruins, sticking to the shadows and avoiding the main roads. Paris, once a bustling metropolis of lights and laughter, was now a ghost town. Broken glass crunched underfoot as they slipped past the remains of cafés, boutiques, and art galleries. The air was thick with the smell of burning wood, scorched stone, and death.

As they neared the riverbank, Marie paused, motioning for Jean-Luc to stop. Ahead, a patrol of insurgents moved through the streets, their flashlights sweeping the ground like predators hunting in the night. The sound of their boots echoed ominously in the stillness.

Marie held her breath, pressing herself against the wall of a nearby building. Jean-Luc did the same, his grip tightening on his rifle. They could hear the insurgents' voices now, speaking in hushed tones as they discussed their search for any remaining resistance fighters.

For a moment, Marie thought they might have gone unnoticed. But then, one of the insurgents stopped, his flashlight sweeping dangerously close to where they were hiding.

"Did you hear that?" one of the men asked, his voice suspicious.

Marie's heart pounded in her chest. If they were spotted now, there would be no escape. Her hand tightened on her rifle, ready to fire if necessary. But she knew that opening fire would only bring more of The Architect's forces down on them.

The insurgent took a step closer, his flashlight shining directly on the spot where Marie and Jean-Luc crouched. Just as it seemed all was lost, a distant explosion echoed from the other side of the city. The sound drew the attention of the entire patrol, and the men quickly turned to investigate.

"Must be another resistance hideout," one of the insurgents muttered. "Let's check it out."

With that, the patrol moved on, leaving the alleyway in silence once again. Marie let out a quiet sigh of relief, her heart still pounding in her ears.

"That was too close," Jean-Luc whispered, his voice shaky.

Marie nodded, her body still tense. "Let's move. We don't have much time."

The Seine: Path to Freedom or Death?

The riverbank was eerily quiet as they approached the Seine. The water, usually shimmering with the reflection of Paris's lights, was dark and foreboding. The iconic bridges that once connected the city's districts now stood like skeletal remains; their once-beautiful structures scarred by war.

Marie scanned the area, searching for the small boat that had been arranged by the resistance to aid in their escape. It had been hidden beneath the Pont Marie bridge, one of the few areas still unguarded.

"There," she whispered, pointing to a shadowy figure moving beneath the bridge.

A small boat was docked in the shadows, and a figure stood beside it, signalling them to approach. It was François, an old fisherman who had risked everything to help the resistance escape the city. His face was gaunt, his clothes tattered, but he had survived—just like they had.

"Marie! Jean-Luc!" François called softly; his voice filled with relief. "Quickly, before they see you."

They hurried down to the water's edge, their hearts racing as they climbed into the small boat. François immediately began untying the ropes, casting nervous glances toward the riverbank.

"We've got to move fast," he muttered, his hands trembling as he worked. "They've been patrolling the river all night."

Marie glanced around, her senses on high alert. The night was still, but she knew that danger lurked just beyond the darkness. If they were spotted on the river, they would be sitting ducks.

"We'll head downstream," François said, his voice low. "There's a safehouse outside the city where you can lay low for a while. After that, it's up to you."

Marie nodded; her eyes focused on the horizon. They had escaped the city, but the war was far from over.

The Architect's Hunt

As they drifted silently down the Seine, the sounds of Paris slowly faded behind them. The ruins of the city loomed in the distance, disappearing into the darkness like a fading memory. But Marie's mind was still in Paris, with the comrades they had lost, and the fight that was far from over.

"The Architect won't stop," Jean-Luc said quietly, his voice breaking the silence. "Even if we escape, they'll keep coming. They won't rest until every city falls."

Marie nodded, her eyes hardening. "I know. But we have to regroup. There's still a chance we can turn this around."

Jean-Luc looked at her, his eyes filled with exhaustion. "How? Paris is gone. The resistance is scattered. What hope do we have left?"

Marie didn't have an answer. The fall of Paris had been a devastating blow, not just for the resistance, but for all of Europe. The Architect's forces were growing stronger by the day, and every victory they won brought them closer to total domination.

But even in the face of overwhelming odds, Marie refused to give up. "There's always hope," she said, her voice steady. "As long as we're alive, we can still fight."

Jean-Luc nodded, though doubt still lingered in his eyes. The fight ahead was daunting, but they had no other choice. They had to continue, for the sake of those who had fallen, and for the future of Europe.

A New Chapter

By the time they reached the outskirts of Paris, the first light of dawn was beginning to break over the horizon. The small boat pulled into a secluded cove, and François guided them to shore.

"This is where I leave you," François said, his voice tinged with sadness. "The safehouse is a few kilometres to the east. You'll be safe there for a while."

Marie and Jean-Luc climbed out of the boat, their bodies aching from the long night. They were bruised, battered, and broken, but they were still alive.

"Thank you," Marie said, gripping François's hand tightly. "We wouldn't have made it without you."

François smiled weakly, though his eyes were filled with sorrow. "I only hope it wasn't in vain."

As François disappeared into the early morning mist, Marie and Jean-Luc set off toward the safehouse, their footsteps heavy with the weight of all they had lost. The road ahead was uncertain, and the future of the resistance was more precarious than ever. But they would keep moving, keep fighting.

For now, they had escaped Paris. But the war was far from over.

Chapter 41: Gathering the Remnants

September 2028 – The Safehouse

The safehouse was a crumbling stone cottage nestled deep within the forests east of Paris, a relic of another time. Moss-covered walls and wild overgrowth surrounded it, making it nearly invisible from the outside. To the casual observer, it appeared abandoned, but for the handful of resistance fighters left, it was now a sanctuary.

Marie and Jean-Luc reached the safehouse just as the sun fully crested the horizon, bathing the forest in a soft, golden glow. The beauty of the morning was lost on them. Their bodies ached from exhaustion, and their minds were still gripped by the trauma of Paris's fall.

Inside the cottage, the air was thick with the smell of damp wood and dust. A single lantern flickered weakly on the table, casting long shadows across the room. There were already a few survivors inside—men and women with hollow eyes and gaunt faces, all of them haunted by the horrors they had witnessed.

One of them, a young woman with dark hair pulled into a tight braid, stood up as Marie and Jean-Luc entered. Her name was Nadia, a former intelligence officer who had been instrumental in organizing the resistance's underground networks.

"Marie, Jean-Luc," Nadia greeted them, her voice tight with concern. "You made it. We weren't sure if anyone else would."

Marie forced a tired smile. "Barely. We got out just before The Architect's forces sealed off the city."

Nadia nodded grimly. "We've lost contact with most of our cells. Paris is gone. The rest of France... we don't know how much longer it'll hold."

Marie's heart sank. She had known things were bad, but hearing it spoken aloud made the reality even harder to bear. Paris had been the heart of the resistance, the city they had fought so hard to defend. Now, it was in ruins, and the resistance was scattered, leaderless.

Jean-Luc slumped into a chair, his hands shaking as he tried to steady himself. "What's the plan? Do we even have one?"

Nadia's expression hardened. "We're regrouping. There are still pockets of resistance in other parts of Europe, but we're cut off. The Architect has been tightening their control, and their forces are spreading faster than we anticipated."

Marie exchanged a glance with Jean-Luc. The fall of Paris had been a devastating blow, but there was no time to mourn. They had to keep moving, keep fighting.

"How many of us are left?" Marie asked.

Nadia hesitated, then glanced around the room. "A dozen, maybe. We've had reports of survivors trickling in from other districts, but it's hard to know for sure. The Architect's drones are everywhere."

Marie clenched her fists, her mind racing. They needed to reorganize, but with so few fighters and no clear plan, the situation seemed hopeless. And yet, giving up wasn't an option.

"We need to rebuild," Marie said, her voice firm. "We may be scattered now, but there are still people willing to fight. We have to find them, bring them together."

Nadia nodded. "That's easier said than done. We're isolated, and communication has been nearly impossible since The Architect took over the networks. But there's one thing working in our favor."

Marie raised an eyebrow. "What's that?"

"The Architect is overextending," Nadia replied. "They've conquered cities, but they don't control the people. Not yet. There are whispers of discontent, even among their ranks. If we can exploit that—if we can sow chaos from within—we might still have a chance."

A New Plan

In the days that followed, the safehouse became the headquarters for what remained of the resistance in France. They were few in number, but they were resourceful. They scavenged for supplies in the nearby villages, avoiding patrols and drone sweeps, and slowly began piecing together a new plan.

Marie took on the role of leader, though it was not a title she had sought. She had always been a fighter, someone who led from the front lines. But now, with so few of them left, she realized that leadership was as much about strategy as it was about action.

"We need to find the others," Marie said one evening as they gathered around a rough map of Europe spread out on the table. The flickering lantern cast shifting shadows across the map, highlighting the areas already under The Architect's control.

"There are resistance cells in Germany, Spain, and the UK," Nadia pointed out, tracing the borders with her finger. "But we've lost contact with most of them. If we can get word to them, we might be able to coordinate an offensive."

Jean-Luc shook his head, his brow furrowed in frustration. "How do we even get past the checkpoints? They're watching every border, every road. The moment we try to cross, we're dead."

Marie leaned over the map, her eyes scanning the terrain. "There's always a way. The old smuggling routes across the Pyrenees might still be operational, and there's a resistance stronghold in the Alps. If we can make contact there, we'll have a better shot at reaching the others."

"But how do we get through France without being caught?" another fighter, a grizzled man named Alain, asked. "The Architect's forces are everywhere."

"We move in small groups," Marie said, her voice steady. "We split up, use the forest and the mountains for cover. We make sure we're unpredictable. If we stay together, we'll be easy targets."

The room fell into a tense silence. The risks were immense, but there was no other option. If they didn't make contact with the other resistance cells soon, The Architect's hold over Europe would become unbreakable.

"We'll have to take down their drones," Jean-Luc said quietly. "If we don't, they'll track us."

Marie nodded. "We'll need to disable the drone network. That's our first priority. Without the drones, they'll be blind."

The First Mission: Sabotage

A week later, the first mission was ready. It was a simple but dangerous task: infiltrate one of The Architect's drone control centers on the outskirts of Paris and disable the network that monitored the surrounding areas. If successful, it would buy the resistance time to move undetected.

Marie, Jean-Luc, and a small team of fighters prepared for the mission in the dead of night. Their faces were grim, their movements quiet as they gathered their gear. Each of them knew the risks—if they were caught, there would be no rescue.

"This is it," Marie said as she adjusted her rifle and strapped a small pack of explosives to her back. "We disable the drones, and then we make our move. Everyone knows their role?"

The team nodded, their faces tense but resolute.

Jean-Luc stood beside her, his hand resting on his rifle. "We'll get in, plant the charges, and get out. Quick and clean."

Marie took a deep breath, feeling the familiar surge of adrenaline. This was what she had trained for, what she had fought for. The fall of Paris had been a devastating blow, but it hadn't broken her. Not yet.

As they moved out into the night, the forest around them was eerily quiet. The stars above were hidden by clouds, and the only sound was the soft rustle of leaves beneath their feet. Each step brought them closer to the drone control centre—and closer to the heart of The Architect's power.

The Infiltration

The drone control centre was a heavily fortified complex built into the side of a hill, surrounded by high walls and patrolled by armed guards. Drones hovered above the compound, their red lights blinking ominously in the dark.

Marie crouched in the underbrush, her eyes scanning the perimeter. "There's a gap in the patrol to the north," she whispered to Jean-Luc. "We move when the drones pass overhead."

The team waited, their breaths shallow, as the drones circled above. When the red lights moved out of sight, they darted forward, keeping low to the ground. They reached the wall, and Marie quickly scaled it, her fingers gripping the rough stone. One by one, the team followed.

Once inside, they moved silently through the shadows, avoiding the guards and security cameras. The control centre loomed ahead, a squat, bunker-like building that pulsed with the hum of machinery.

"We're almost there," Jean-Luc whispered. "You ready?"

Marie nodded, her heart pounding in her chest. They had come too far to fail now.

They approached the control centre's entrance, and Marie planted the first of the explosives on the door's locking mechanism. With a soft click, the charge detonated, and the door slid open.

Inside, the air was cool and sterile, the walls lined with rows of computer terminals. A handful of technicians sat at their stations, monitoring the drone feeds.

"Go!" Marie hissed, and the team moved swiftly, subduing the technicians before they could raise the alarm.

Jean-Luc planted the second set of charges near the central control panel. "We've got two minutes before this place blows," he said, his voice tight.

They turned to leave, but just as they reached the door, an alarm blared, echoing through the compound.

"We've been made!" Alain shouted. "Move!"

The team sprinted for the exit, the sound of boots and shouts growing louder behind them. Marie's heart raced as they scaled the wall once again, adrenaline pumping through her veins.

Behind them, the control centre exploded in a massive fireball, lighting up the night sky. The drones, their signals cut off, fell from the air, crashing to the ground like metal.

Chapter 42: Echoes of Resistance

October 2028 – Europe in Flames

The explosion had rippled through the night, its fiery glow lighting up the skies for miles. The resistance team made their way back to the safehouse, their breaths heavy and their bodies spent, but their mission a success. The drone network was down in the area around Paris, giving them a vital window of opportunity.

Marie and Jean-Luc had led their team out just in time. They'd lost Alain in the escape—an ambush on the outskirts had caught them off guard—but the charges had blown, and the drone control centre was reduced to rubble. The Architect's eyes in the sky were blind, for now.

Back at the safehouse, they gathered in the dimly lit room around a small table, their bodies still aching from the mission. Nadia was already waiting for them, her arms crossed, her face lined with exhaustion.

"Did you do it?" Nadia asked, her voice tight with anticipation.

Marie nodded, sliding into a chair and letting out a long breath. "It's done. The drones are down. We've got a few days, maybe a week before they can get the system back up."

A murmur of relief went through the room. It was a small victory, but in a war where every inch was hard fought, it felt monumental.

Jean-Luc sat down heavily next to her, rubbing his tired eyes. "What's next?"

Nadia hesitated, then unfolded a map on the table. The map was old and tattered, but the resistance had marked it with critical points: safehouses, supply caches, and known positions of The Architect's forces.

"Now that we've knocked out their drones, we have a chance to move some of our people across the border," Nadia explained, pointing to the Pyrenees. "We've made contact with a resistance group in Spain. If we can get to them, we can start coordinating efforts across the continent. The resistance is fractured, but if we unite..."

Marie leaned forward, studying the map. "How do we get there?"

Nadia's finger traced a line southward. "There's an old smuggling route through the mountains. It's dangerous, but it's our best shot. The Architect's forces are concentrated on the major roads, but they don't know the mountains like we do."

"Mountains," Jean-Luc muttered, shaking his head. "It'll be a hell of a trek."

"We don't have a choice," Marie said, her voice firm. "If we don't start organizing with the others, we're dead. The resistance won't survive much longer as splintered groups."

Nadia nodded. "It's decided, then. We move tomorrow night. Gather your gear, get some rest. We've got a long road ahead."

Through the Pyrenees

The mountains loomed ahead of them like a dark, jagged wall. The Pyrenees had always been a natural barrier, separating Spain from France, but now they were a lifeline for the resistance fighters trying to escape The Architect's tightening grip.

Marie led the group, her eyes scanning the rocky terrain ahead as they made their way up the narrow trails. The air was cold, and the wind howled through the valleys, carrying with it the distant sounds of gunfire and conflict. Every step was a struggle, the thin mountain air making it difficult to breathe, but they pressed on. They had no choice.

The group was small—just a handful of fighters who had survived the fall of Paris, including Jean-Luc, Nadia, and a few others who had joined them at the safehouse. Each of them carried what little gear they had, but the weight of the journey was more than just physical. The burden of what they'd left behind in Paris hung heavy in the air.

The path was treacherous. Loose rocks slid underfoot, and the narrow ledges offered little room for error. But the resistance fighters moved with determination. They knew what was at stake. If they could make it to Spain, they could regroup, rebuild, and perhaps even strike back at The Architect's forces.

As they reached a high plateau, Marie stopped, gazing out at the distant peaks. The sun was setting, casting a warm orange glow over the mountains, but there was no beauty in the scene for her. All she saw was the struggle ahead.

"We need to rest here for the night," she said, turning to the group. "We'll push through the pass tomorrow."

Jean-Luc nodded, dropping his pack with a grunt. "Good idea. We're running on fumes."

The group settled in for the night, making camp in the shadow of a large rock formation that offered some protection from the wind. A small fire was lit, and they huddled around it, the heat providing some comfort against the biting cold.

Nadia sat beside Marie; her face illuminated by the flickering flames. "Do you think we'll make it?"

Marie didn't answer immediately. The truth was, she didn't know. The mountains were dangerous enough, but if they were caught by The Architect's patrols, they wouldn't stand a chance.

"We have to," Marie said finally. "We don't have any other option."

Nadia nodded, though her eyes were filled with doubt. "What if the resistance in Spain has already fallen? What if we're walking into a trap?"

Marie's jaw tightened. "Then we'll deal with that when we get there. But right now, we have to believe there's still hope."

Jean-Luc, overhearing the conversation, chimed in. "Hope's all we've got left, isn't it?"

The fire crackled as the group fell into silence, each of them lost in their own thoughts. The war had taken so much from them already, and the future was uncertain. But as long as they kept moving, kept fighting, there was a chance—however small—that they could still turn the tide.

The Architect's Shadow

As they crossed into Spain, the landscape shifted from the jagged peaks of the Pyrenees to rolling hills and dense forests. But even as they descended, the tension in the group remained. The Architect's forces were never far behind.

For days, they moved cautiously, staying off the main roads and avoiding populated areas. They passed through small villages where the war had left its mark—burned-out buildings, abandoned homes, and the occasional group of refugees fleeing the conflict. The Architect's reach extended here, too, though not as strongly as in France.

It wasn't until they reached a secluded valley deep within the Basque country that they finally made contact with the local resistance. A small group of fighters greeted them, their weapons at the ready, but their eyes weary from years of battle.

"You must be the French resistance," one of the men said, stepping forward. He was tall and lean, with a scar running down the side of his face. "We've been waiting for you."

Marie nodded, her eyes scanning the group. "We heard you were still fighting here. We need to coordinate."

The man, who introduced himself as Javier, gestured for them to follow. "Come with us. There's someone you need to meet."

They followed Javier through the valley to a hidden base built into the side of a mountain. Inside, the air was cool, and the walls were lined with weapons, maps, and communication equipment. It was a far cry from the crumbling safehouse they had left behind in France.

At the centre of the base, a large table was spread with maps of Europe, marked with strategic points and battle plans. And standing at the head of the table was a woman—tall, with silver hair tied back in a braid, and eyes that burned with determination.

"This is Isabella," Javier said. "She's been leading the resistance in Spain."

Isabella turned to them, her expression hard. "Welcome," she said, her voice low but commanding. "I've been waiting to meet the remnants of Paris."

Marie stepped forward, meeting Isabella's gaze. "We've lost a lot," she said, her voice steady. "But we're still here. And we're ready to fight."

Isabella nodded, her eyes scanning the group. "Good. Because the war isn't over yet. In fact, it's only just beginning."

She leaned over the map, pointing to key locations across Europe. "The Architect may have taken Paris, but they're spreading themselves thin. We've got a window—a chance to strike back. But it won't last long."

Marie studied the map, her mind racing. This was it. The moment they had been waiting for. A chance to turn the tide, to rebuild the resistance and strike back at The Architect's forces.

"We're ready," Marie said, her voice firm. "What's the plan?"

Isabella smiled grimly. "We hit them where it hurts."

Chapter 43: The Plan to Strike

November 2028 – The Hidden Base

The resistance base in the mountains was a fortress of sorts, a hidden stronghold carved into the rock over years of careful planning. The Spanish resistance had been fighting longer than most, using the natural landscape to their advantage. Now, as Marie and the remnants of her team stood in the heart of it, they realized they were not alone in this fight after all.

Marie, Jean-Luc, Nadia, and a few others gathered around the large table in the center of the base's war room. Maps of Europe were spread across its surface, marked with strategic locations, supply routes, and enemy strongholds. The room buzzed with quiet intensity as other fighters moved in and out, preparing for the next phase of their operations.

Isabella, the leader of the Spanish resistance, stood at the head of the table. Her silver hair gleamed in the dim light, and her sharp eyes scanned the maps with the precision of a seasoned commander.

"We've been monitoring The Architect's movements closely," Isabella said, her voice low but filled with authority. "Their forces are spread thin across Europe, but they're focusing their resources on key strongholds—major cities, supply hubs, and communication centers."

She pointed to a cluster of marked locations on the map, each representing a stronghold under The Architect's control. Madrid, Berlin, and London were circled in red, with other smaller cities marked as secondary targets.

"Our advantage," Isabella continued, "is that they've overextended themselves. They control the cities, but not the countryside. And while their drones and patrols keep them informed, they can't be everywhere at once. That's where we strike."

Marie leaned forward; her brow furrowed. "What's the target?"

Isabella's finger moved to a location on the map that hadn't been marked before: a small town near the French-Spanish border. "This is where it starts. There's a communications outpost here, one of The Architect's major relay points. It's how they coordinate drone strikes and troop movements across southwestern Europe. If we can take it out, we'll cripple their ability to track us and respond to our movements."

Nadia glanced at the map, then back at Isabella. "Taking out one relay won't stop them. They have others."

Isabella nodded. "True, but it will buy us time. And more importantly, it will show other resistance cells that The Architect isn't invincible. Right now, morale is low across Europe. People are afraid, hiding in the shadows. We need to give them something to rally behind."

Marie felt the weight of the moment settle on her shoulders. This wasn't just another mission. It was a symbol, a spark to ignite the fire of rebellion across the continent.

Jean-Luc crossed his arms, his face grim. "How heavily defended is this outpost?"

"Very," Isabella admitted. "They've got automated defences, patrols, and drones monitoring the area. It won't be easy, but we've been preparing for this for months. We've gathered intel, we know their patrol routes, and we've identified weak points in their defences. If we hit hard and fast, we can take it."

There was a tense silence in the room as everyone processed the enormity of the task ahead. The Architect's forces had crushed rebellions across Europe, stamping out resistance with ruthless efficiency. But now, with the drones temporarily down and the element of surprise on their side, they had a slim chance to strike a blow that could turn the tide.

Marie broke the silence, her voice steady. "What's the plan?"

Isabella leaned over the map, outlining the details. "We'll split into three teams. The first will create a diversion at the southern edge of the outpost, drawing their forces away. The second team will move in from the east and disable their automated defences. Once the defences are down, the third team—led by you, Marie—will infiltrate the outpost and plant charges on the main relay tower."

Marie nodded, already visualizing the operation in her mind. It was risky, but it was their best shot. If they could pull it off, it would be a significant blow to The Architect's communications network.

Jean-Luc's eyes narrowed as he studied the map. "And what happens if we get pinned down? There's no backup coming."

Isabella met his gaze, her expression hard. "We fight our way out. There's no other option."

The Night Before the Attack

The mood in the base was tense as the fighters prepared for the mission. Weapons were cleaned, gear was packed, and final preparations were made in the quiet hours before dawn. Marie walked through the dimly lit corridors, checking in on her team, making sure everyone was ready.

She found Jean-Luc sitting alone in a small room, his rifle laid out on the table in front of him. He was staring at it, lost in thought.

"You, okay?" Marie asked, leaning against the doorframe.

Jean-Luc looked up; his eyes tired but determined. "As ready as I'll ever be."

Marie nodded, stepping inside. "This isn't like Paris. We know what we're up against this time."

"Yeah," Jean-Luc muttered, picking up his rifle and inspecting the scope. "But that doesn't make it any easier. We're walking into the lion's den."

Marie sat down across from him, her expression serious. "We've done it before. We'll do it again."

Jean-Luc smiled faintly, though the worry never left his eyes. "You really believe that?"

"I have to," Marie said, her voice soft but firm. "If we don't, then what are we fighting for?"

There was a long silence between them, broken only by the distant sounds of fighters preparing for the mission. Finally, Jean-Luc stood, slinging his rifle over his shoulder. "Let's make sure this one counts, then."

The Assault Begins

The night was cold and dark as the resistance fighters moved through the dense forest surrounding the outpost. The moon was hidden behind thick clouds, casting the landscape in shadow. Marie led her team through the trees, her heart pounding in her chest. Every step was calculated, every sound scrutinized.

Ahead of them, the faint glow of the outpost's perimeter lights appeared through the trees. The structure was heavily fortified, surrounded by tall fences topped with barbed wire and patrolled by armed guards. Automated turrets were positioned at key points along the perimeter, scanning for any signs of intruders.

Marie signalled for her team to stop and crouched behind a large tree, surveying the scene. They were in position. Now, they just had to wait for the diversion.

On cue, a series of explosions erupted at the southern edge of the outpost. Fire and smoke filled the sky, and alarms blared as the guards scrambled to respond. The diversion team had done their job.

"Let's move," Marie whispered, leading her team toward the eastern side of the outpost. They moved quickly but quietly, staying low to the ground as they approached the fence.

Nadia, who had taken on the role of demolitions expert, pulled out a small device and attached it to the fence. There was a soft click, followed by a quiet hum as the device short-circuited the electric grid. The fence's power went down, and they slipped through the gap.

Inside the perimeter, they moved with purpose, avoiding patrols and keeping to the shadows. The outpost's defences were focused on the southern diversion, giving them the cover they needed to reach the automated turrets.

Jean-Luc and Nadia worked quickly to disable the turrets, hacking into their systems and shutting them down one by one. The outpost was still oblivious to their presence.

"We're in," Marie whispered into her radio. "Proceeding to the relay tower."

With the defences down, they moved deeper into the outpost, heading toward the towering structure in the center. The relay tower was massive, its antennas reaching high into the sky, transmitting data across The Architect's entire network.

As they reached the base of the tower, Marie felt a surge of adrenaline. This was it. They were so close.

"Plant the charges," she ordered.

Nadia and Jean-Luc moved quickly, attaching explosives to the tower's support beams. The plan was to take out the tower in one massive blast, crippling the outpost's communications and sending a message to the rest of Europe.

Just as the last charge was placed, a shout echoed through the night. A guard had spotted them.

"Go! Now!" Marie yelled.

They sprinted toward the perimeter, gunfire erupting behind them. The guards had realized what was happening, and chaos broke out as the resistance fighters made their escape.

As they reached the edge of the forest, Marie turned back one last time, her finger hovering over the detonator.

With a deep breath, she pressed the button.

The explosion was deafening. The relay tower collapsed in a shower of sparks and debris, and the outpost was consumed by fire.

Marie didn't stop to watch. They had done what they came to do, but the war was far from over. As the flames rose behind them, she knew they had just taken the first step in a long, bloody fight.

But for the first time in months, there was hope.

Chapter 43: The Fall of Madrid

December 2028 – Madrid, Spain

Madrid had always been a symbol of resistance, a city that refused to break under the weight of The Architect's regime. But now, as the first rays of dawn pierced the horizon, the capital lay under siege. The Architect's forces had made their final push into the heart of the city, and the battle for control had reached a critical juncture.

Marie and her team had arrived in Madrid two days ago, their bodies weary from the trek through the mountains and the destruction of the relay outpost. But there had been no time for rest. Madrid's resistance fighters were on the brink, and their arrival had been met with desperate relief. The situation in the city was dire.

Now, as Marie stood on the rooftop of a crumbling building overlooking the city, she could see the full scale of the battle unfolding below. Smoke rose in thick plumes from various parts of the city, and the sound of gunfire and explosions echoed through the streets. The Architect's forces had broken through the outer defences and were pushing deeper into the urban core.

"We're losing ground," Jean-Luc said, stepping up beside her. His face was smeared with dirt and exhaustion, but his eyes remained sharp. "The Architect's troops are everywhere. The resistance is barely holding on."

Marie nodded; her gaze fixed on the distant flashes of light where the fighting was fiercest. She could feel the weight of the city's fate pressing down on her, but there was no time for doubt. Madrid was their last major foothold in Spain, and if it fell, the resistance across the entire country would collapse.

"We need to regroup," Marie said, her voice steady despite the chaos around them. "If we lose the city center, it's over."

Jean-Luc wiped the sweat from his brow, grimacing. "Easier said than done. Most of the resistance fighters are pinned down in the southern districts. We've lost contact with several key groups. We're stretched too thin."

Marie clenched her jaw, her mind racing. The plan had been to consolidate their forces and make a stand in the central districts, using the narrow streets and fortified buildings to their advantage. But The Architect's forces had moved faster than expected, and the resistance had been caught off guard.

She turned to Jean-Luc, determination hardening her features. "We need to hit them where it hurts. Their supply lines. If we can disrupt their reinforcements and cut off their supplies, we might buy ourselves enough time to regroup."

Jean-Luc raised an eyebrow. "You're talking about a suicide mission. Their supply lines are heavily guarded."

"I know," Marie said, her voice firm. "But if we don't do something drastic, Madrid will fall. And if Madrid falls..."

Jean-Luc didn't need to hear the rest. He knew what was at stake.

The Plan

The resistance fighters gathered in a makeshift command center deep within the city, a former underground parking garage that had been converted into a war room. The air was thick with tension as Marie outlined the plan.

"We're going to hit The Architect's supply convoy," she said, her voice echoing off the concrete walls. "It's coming in from the north, carrying weapons, ammunition, and reinforcements. If we can destroy it, we'll slow their advance and give our people a chance to regroup."

Nadia stood beside her, arms crossed, her face set in a grim expression. "We'll need to move fast. The convoy is heavily protected, and they'll be expecting resistance."

Marie nodded. "We'll split into two teams. Team A will create a diversion, drawing their attention away from the convoy route. Team B, led by Jean-Luc and me, will ambush the convoy and take out their vehicles."

The room was silent as the fighters absorbed the plan. It was risky—dangerous even—but they had no other options. Madrid was on the verge of collapse, and this was their last chance to turn the tide.

Jean-Luc stepped forward, his eyes scanning the group. "We don't have much time. The convoy is scheduled to arrive within the next few hours. We move now."

The fighters quickly dispersed, gathering their weapons and supplies. There was a sense of finality in the air, a grim understanding that this mission might be their last. But they were resistance fighters, and they would fight until the end.

The Ambush

The streets of northern Madrid were eerily quiet as Marie and her team moved into position. The city had been a battlefield for weeks, and the scars of war were everywhere—burned-out buildings, shattered windows, and crumbling walls. But now, as the sun began to set, there was an uneasy stillness in the air, broken only by the distant sounds of gunfire from the southern districts.

Marie crouched behind a pile of debris, her rifle at the ready. Beside her, Jean-Luc was checking his equipment, his face set in a grim expression. The rest of the team was spread out along the street, hidden in the shadows, waiting for the convoy to arrive.

"They're coming," Nadia's voice crackled over the radio.

Marie's heart pounded in her chest as she peered through the scope of her rifle. In the distance, she could see the faint outline of the convoy—three armoured trucks, escorted by a squad of soldiers on foot and two heavily armed vehicles.

"Wait for my signal," Marie whispered into her radio. The plan was to let the convoy move deeper into the ambush zone before striking. Timing was everything.

The convoy rolled closer, the sound of its engines growing louder as it approached. The soldiers moved in formation, their weapons at the ready, scanning the streets for any signs of resistance.

"Now!" Marie shouted.

The street erupted in a hail of gunfire and explosions. The first truck in the convoy was hit by an anti-tank rocket, sending it skidding to a halt in a ball of fire. The soldiers scrambled for cover as the resistance fighters opened fire from their hidden positions.

Jean-Luc was already on the move, sprinting toward the second truck with a grenade in hand. He tossed it under the vehicle, diving behind a pile of rubble as the explosion tore through the air.

Marie fired her rifle, taking out two soldiers who had broken away from the convoy. The ambush was chaotic, but it was working. The convoy was in disarray, and the resistance fighters were pressing their advantage.

"Keep pushing!" Marie shouted; her voice barely audible over the cacophony of battle.

The resistance fighters moved in, overwhelming the remaining soldiers and disabling the last of the trucks. Within minutes, the convoy had been destroyed, and the street was littered with the wreckage of burning vehicles and fallen soldiers.

But the victory came at a cost. Several resistance fighters lay wounded or dead, and the sounds of reinforcements approaching from the north echoed through the streets.

"We need to move," Jean-Luc said, his voice tight with urgency. "More of them are coming."

Marie nodded, her heart heavy with the losses they had suffered. But the mission had been a success. They had struck a critical blow to The Architect's supply lines, and for the first time in days, the resistance had a chance to regroup.

"Let's go," she said, leading the survivors back toward the city center.

The Last Stand

The news of the convoy's destruction spread quickly through the resistance ranks. It was a small victory, but it gave them hope—hope that they could still fight, still resist, even in the face of overwhelming odds.

For the next few days, the battle for Madrid raged on, with the resistance fighters making their last stand in the heart of the city. They fought with everything they had, using the narrow streets and alleyways to their advantage, setting traps and ambushes for The Architect's forces.

But the enemy was relentless. Despite the loss of their supply convoy, The Architect's troops pressed forward, their superior numbers and firepower slowly grinding down the resistance.

Marie found herself in the thick of the fighting, her rifle never leaving her hands. She moved from one battle to the next, rallying the fighters, coordinating attacks, and holding the line as long as she could. Jean-Luc and Nadia were always by her side, their faces grim but determined.

But it was clear that the situation was becoming untenable. The resistance was running out of ammunition, out of fighters, out of time.

"We can't hold them off much longer," Nadia said, her voice hoarse from shouting orders. "We need to retreat."

Marie looked around at the shattered remains of the city, her heart heavy with the weight of the decision. Madrid had been their last stand, their final bastion of hope. But now, it was clear that the city was lost.

"We retreat," Marie said finally, her voice barely audible over the sounds of battle. "We live to fight another day."

As the resistance fighters retreated from Madrid, the city burned behind them, consumed by the fires of war. The fall of Madrid marked the end of an era, but for Marie and her comrades, the fight was far from over.

There would be other battles, other cities, other moments of resistance. And as long as they kept fighting, The Architect's reign would never be absolute.

But as they disappeared into the night, Marie couldn't shake the feeling that the cost of the war was growing too high—and that the final battle was approaching faster than any of them could anticipate.

Chapter 44: Shattered Alliances

January 2029 – Berlin, Germany

The New Year had arrived with little fanfare in Berlin. The city's grand monuments, once symbols of unity and European progress, now stood as relics of a fractured Europe, their stones cracked by the weight of an ongoing war. The battle for Madrid had sent shockwaves through the continent. As the resistance retreated from Spain, it became clear that the tides of war were changing—what had once been a political conflict was now evolving into a full-scale collapse of European stability.

In Berlin, the heart of The Architect's power, political alliances were shifting, and the unease among the European governments was palpable. Leaders who had once believed in containing the unrest were now finding their countries engulfed in violence, and dissent simmered beneath the surface in capitals across Europe. In the halls of the German government, those tensions were beginning to boil over.

The Berlin Conference

Marie arrived in Berlin under a veil of secrecy. The resistance needed to regroup, and more importantly, they needed allies. The Spanish resistance had been driven underground, and the French resistance was on the verge of collapse. Now, Marie and her inner circle had travelled to Berlin to meet with a faction of the German government—one that was still sympathetic to their cause.

The conference room in the underground bunker was sterile and cold, a stark contrast to the chaos unfolding above. Berlin was quiet, but the streets were lined with soldiers, and drones patrolled the skies, ever vigilant. The German capital had been fortified into a fortress, but even the strongest walls couldn't contain the growing unrest within.

Marie stood at the head of a long, polished table, flanked by Jean-Luc, Nadia, and several other key resistance leaders. Across from them sat a group of German politicians and military officials, their faces tense with anticipation. They were led by Franz Keller, a high-ranking member of the German Bundestag who had been working in secret to undermine The Architect's regime from within.

Keller, a tall man with greying hair and sharp eyes, cleared his throat and spoke first. "The fall of Madrid was a devastating blow. The Architect's forces are advancing faster than we anticipated, and Europe's resistance movements are crumbling."

Marie nodded. "We know. But Madrid was not a total loss. We disrupted their supply lines and weakened their hold in Spain. What we need now is unity. We cannot fight this war in isolation. The resistance movements across Europe must come together."

Keller leaned forward, his fingers drumming against the table. "That's easier said than done. The Architect has sown division across Europe. Our governments are paralyzed by fear, and there's little trust left between nations. Even within Germany, there are those who support The Architect's vision of order—of control. Many believe this war will only end with total submission."

Marie's eyes hardened. "That's exactly what they want us to believe. The Architect has created chaos to justify their rule, but if we unite, we can stop them."

Nadia spoke up, her voice calm but firm. "We need resources—funding, weapons, intelligence. We know there are factions within your military that still resist The Architect's influence. If we can secure their support, we can launch a coordinated counteroffensive."

Keller exchanged glances with the other officials at the table. "There are still loyalists within the military, but their numbers are dwindling. The majority have either fallen in line or been purged. And those who remain are hesitant to act without a clear plan of victory."

Jean-Luc, who had remained silent until now, leaned in. "We have a plan. We strike at The Architect's heart—Berlin. We take out their leadership, disrupt their command structure. Without The Architect's top commanders, their forces will be thrown into disarray."

There was a murmur of concern among the German officials. Keller frowned, his brow furrowed in thought. "An assassination? You're talking about a coup."

"A coup is what this war needs," Marie said bluntly. "The people of Europe are waiting for a spark—something to show them that The

Architect's regime is not invincible. If we can take Berlin, if we can topple their leadership, the rest of Europe will follow."

Keller leaned back in his chair, exhaling slowly. "And what happens if you fail? If we back you, if we throw everything we have behind this plan and it fails, Germany will be the next Madrid. The Architect's forces will tear us apart."

Marie didn't flinch. "If we fail, then Europe will fall regardless. The Architect's grip is tightening every day. But if we act now, if we strike hard and fast, we have a chance. A small chance, but it's better than waiting for our cities to burn."

The room fell silent, the weight of Marie's words sinking in. It was a gamble, a high stakes move that could either turn the tide of the war or doom them all. But Keller and his allies knew that they were running out of options. The Architect was consolidating power, and every day that passed without action brought them closer to total domination.

Finally, Keller spoke. "We'll consider your proposal. But understand this—if we commit to this, there's no turning back. Berlin will become the epicenter of this war, and the world will be watching."

Marie nodded, her expression resolute. "We understand."

Fissures in the Resistance

As the meeting adjourned, Marie and her team retreated to a secure room deep within the bunker. The tension was palpable, and though the German officials had not given a final answer, Marie knew they were leaning toward supporting the plan. It was their only shot at turning the tide.

But not everyone in the resistance was on board.

"I don't like this," Nadia said as she paced the room, her arms crossed. "We're putting everything on the line for a coup in Berlin. If this goes wrong, we lose everything. We've seen how The Architect's forces react to even the smallest sign of rebellion. This will bring the full weight of their military down on us."

Jean-Luc, seated at a small table, rubbed his temples. "We don't have much of a choice, Nadia. Every resistance cell across Europe is on the verge of collapse. If we don't act soon, The Architect will crush us one by one."

Nadia stopped pacing, her eyes flashing with frustration. "And what about the rest of Europe? What about France, Spain, Italy? We're focusing all our efforts on Berlin, but what happens when The Architect retaliates? We're leaving entire countries vulnerable."

Marie stepped forward, her voice calm but firm. "I know it's a risk. But if we can take out their leadership, we'll buy time for the other resistance movements to regroup. This isn't just about Berlin—it's about sending a message to the rest of Europe. We're not fighting alone."

Nadia shook her head, her voice tight. "I just hope you're right, Marie. Because if we fail, there won't be anything left to fight for."

The Plot Thickens

Unbeknownst to the resistance, Berlin was not as secure as it appeared. Inside the halls of The Architect's headquarters, there was growing discontent among the leadership. Factionalism had begun to take root, and even among the inner circle, there were those who believed The Architect's brutal methods were sowing the seeds of their own downfall.

In the shadows of the regime, a secret network of military officers and bureaucrats had begun to plot their own coup. Their goal was not to overthrow The Architect's system entirely, but to seize power and steer the regime in a new direction—one that would maintain control but with less violence and oppression.

These internal fractures presented a unique opportunity for the resistance, but they also introduced new risks. If the resistance unknowingly allied themselves with one faction of The Architect's regime, they could find themselves trapped in a web of betrayal and deceit.

As Marie and her team prepared for their next move, they had no idea how deep the conspiracy ran. Berlin was a city on the edge, and in the coming days, the balance of power would shift in ways no one could predict.

A Decision Made

Back in the German command center, Franz Keller met with his closest advisors late into the night. The decision weighed heavily on him—throwing their support behind the resistance would mean committing to a full-scale rebellion. But it was becoming clear that they were running out of time.

"We back them," Keller finally said, his voice heavy with resolve. "We have no choice."

The decision had been made. The coup was in motion, and the fate of Europe now rested on the resistance's ability to strike at the heart of The Architect's regime.

The final battle for Berlin was about to begin.

Chapter 45: The Architects' Fortress

January 2029 – Berlin, Germany

Berlin had always been a city of stark contrasts—where history met modernity, and past divisions lingered beneath its sleek, urban facade. In 2029, it had transformed into a dark citadel, the center of The Architect's expanding control over Europe. The skyline was punctuated by watchtowers, surveillance drones patrolled the skies, and the once vibrant streets were now ruled by a palpable atmosphere of fear. The resistance had dubbed it "The Fortress," and for good reason. Every move, every breath was watched.

For the first time in months, Marie stood just beyond the outer walls of this imposing city, her breath rising in clouds of condensation against the biting cold. She wore a long black coat that concealed a small arsenal of weapons, her nerves steel against the growing tension in the air. Around her, Nadia, Jean-Luc, and a small team of resistance fighters were waiting for the signal to begin their infiltration. The mission was clear: eliminate The Architect, and bring the regime to its knees. But in the depths of Berlin, nothing would be as straightforward as it seemed.

Tensions Rising

Inside the heart of the city, The Architect's forces were mobilizing for something far larger than a mere show of power. The recent uprisings in Madrid and the brewing unrest across France had spurred The Architect into action. Reports of small-scale insurrections were coming in from across Europe, each a symptom of the resistance's growing momentum. But now, in Berlin, The Architect's inner circle was aware of an even more immediate threat—an assault on their stronghold was imminent.

In a dimly lit command center, deep beneath the streets of the city, General Heinrich Drach sat at a long table surrounded by the regime's highest-ranking officials. His face, deeply lined and hardened by years of service, betrayed no emotion. To his right was Petra Lang, the intelligence chief who had built the most effective surveillance network Europe had ever known.

"We've intercepted communication between resistance groups in Germany and France," Lang said, her voice cold and matter of fact. "They're planning something big. This isn't a series of random attacks anymore. They've consolidated, and they're preparing to strike here."

Drach's eyes narrowed as he leaned forward, placing his hands flat on the table. "How close are they?"

Lang exchanged a glance with one of her aides, who stepped forward to place a report in front of Drach. "Closer than we'd like," she replied. "They've already infiltrated the outskirts. Our surveillance teams have picked up suspicious activity in sectors three and five. We believe their goal is an assassination—an attempt to take out The Architect and destabilize the regime."

A murmur spread through the room. Even within the elite command, the presence of The Architect was a mystery. Few had ever met the enigmatic leader face-to-face. They worked in shadow, with whispers of their true identity spreading like myths through the ranks.

General Drach, however, knew better than to underestimate the resistance. He had risen to power by crushing uprisings and silencing dissidents with ruthless efficiency. But now, in the face of this growing rebellion, he sensed that the war was about to change.

"Double the security around the inner sanctum," Drach ordered. "And tighten control of the outer sectors. Nothing gets in or out without my approval."

Lang nodded, already sending out orders to her operatives. "What about the loyalists within the military?" she asked. "There are whispers of discontent. We may need to root them out before the resistance makes their move."

Drach's expression darkened. He had long suspected that not all of his forces were loyal to The Architect's vision. But for now, the most pressing concern was the threat looming outside the city's gates. "We'll deal with them later," he said, rising to his feet. "For now, our focus is on eliminating the resistance before they strike."

Infiltration

Back on the outskirts, Marie and her team received the signal they'd been waiting for. Their informant inside the German government—Franz Keller—had confirmed that a weak point in the northern section of the wall would be unguarded for a brief window. This was their chance to infiltrate the city and get close to The Architect's command center. The risks were high, but the opportunity was one they couldn't afford to pass up.

Marie pulled her hood up and signalled to her team. "This is it," she said quietly, her breath fogging in the cold air. "We stick to the plan. Once inside, we head straight for the inner sanctum. No detours."

Nadia, standing close by, gave a firm nod. "We're ready."

Jean-Luc adjusted the strap of his rifle and moved to Marie's side. "Once we're in, getting out might be the bigger challenge."

"We'll cross that bridge when we get to it," Marie replied. "First, we take down The Architect."

The team moved silently toward the northern gate, navigating the dark streets with precision. They had trained for months for this moment, learning every inch of Berlin's layout, memorizing the patterns of the surveillance drones, and preparing for the inevitable firefight. But as they approached the city's heavily fortified wall, Marie couldn't shake the feeling that something was off.

They reached the designated breach point—a section of the wall where an old maintenance tunnel had been repurposed into a hidden entrance. Keller had assured them that the guard rotation would leave this area momentarily exposed, but as they arrived, the tunnel was eerily silent.

Jean-Luc crouched down, inspecting the entrance. "It looks clear," he whispered.

Marie frowned. "Too clear."

Before she could give the order to advance, a sudden flash of light blinded the team. Searchlights from above swung down, illuminating their position, and the unmistakable sound of footsteps echoed through the tunnel.

"It's a trap!" Nadia shouted, diving behind cover as gunfire erupted from all sides.

Marie cursed under her breath, drawing her weapon and firing at the advancing soldiers. They had been exposed, and now they were outnumbered, pinned down in the narrow tunnel with nowhere to retreat.

"Fall back!" Jean-Luc shouted, his voice barely audible over the chaos.

But there was no time. The soldiers were closing in fast, and the team was running out of options.

The Betrayal

Inside the command center, General Drach watched the ambush unfold on a large screen. The resistance had been played perfectly, led into a trap they hadn't seen coming. Beside him, Petra Lang smirked in satisfaction.

"They thought they could infiltrate our city," Lang said, her voice dripping with disdain. "Fools."

Drach didn't share her amusement. He knew the resistance would fight to the bitter end, and this skirmish was only the beginning. But for now, the ambush had given them a much-needed advantage. The resistance's strongest fighters were trapped in the northern tunnel, and if they were eliminated here, the rebellion would be crippled.

Lang's voice cut through his thoughts. "We've intercepted more communications. It seems Keller's involvement goes deeper than we thought. He's been feeding the resistance information for months."

Drach's eyes narrowed. "Deal with him," he ordered, his voice ice-cold. "Make sure he doesn't live long enough to see the consequences of his betrayal."

As Lang turned to leave, Drach stared at the screen, watching as the resistance fighters continued to fight against overwhelming odds. For now, they were cornered. But Drach knew that as long as their leader remained alive, the rebellion would not die.

"The Architect must be protected at all costs," he murmured to himself. "The resistance will not stop until they've torn this regime apart."

A Desperate Escape

In the tunnel, Marie and her team were fighting for their lives. Nadia had been hit, a deep gash running across her shoulder, but she continued firing, her face twisted in pain and fury. Jean-Luc was at her side, providing cover as Marie scanned the area for an escape route.

"We can't hold them off forever!" Nadia shouted, gritting her teeth as she reloaded her weapon.

Marie's mind raced. They had been outmanoeuvred, but there had to be a way out. As she scanned the tunnel, her eyes fell on a small service hatch near the far wall. It was risky, but it might be their only chance.

"Over there!" she called out, pointing toward the hatch. "It's our only way out!"

Jean-Luc nodded, grabbing Nadia's arm and pulling her toward the hatch as bullets ricocheted off the walls around them. Marie and the remaining fighters laid down cover fire, buying precious seconds as they scrambled toward the escape route.

With a final burst of effort, they reached the hatch and forced it open. One by one, the team slipped through, disappearing into the darkness beyond.

As the sounds of gunfire faded behind them, Marie's heart pounded in her chest. They had escaped the ambush, but Berlin was still a labyrinth of danger—and now, The Architect knew they were coming.

The mission had changed. Now, it wasn't just about taking down The Architect. It was about survival.

And as the team disappeared into the shadows of the city, Marie knew the real battle for Berlin had only just begun.

Chapter 46: A City in Turmoil

January 2029 – Berlin, Germany

The sounds of distant explosions and sporadic gunfire echoed through Berlin's desolate streets. The once-proud capital of Germany, now the stronghold of The Architect's regime, was a city on the edge of war. Tensions simmered as the population lived in fear of both the oppressive government and the growing resistance. Civilian life, as it had been, was a memory, replaced by the harsh reality of curfews, military patrols, and constant surveillance.

Marie and her team had barely escaped the ambush, their breaths ragged, and their nerves frayed. As they emerged from the service hatch, they found themselves in a narrow alleyway, the darkness their only ally. The sounds of drones patrolling overhead were a constant reminder that they were being hunted. They had lost several members of their team in the firefight, and now, with Nadia injured and the city locked down, their mission to assassinate The Architect seemed even more impossible than before.

The Underground Resistance

In the depths of Berlin, hidden beneath layers of old subway tunnels and abandoned infrastructure, the remnants of the local resistance gathered. This underground network had grown in recent months as more civilians turned against The Architect's regime, but it was fragmented, its leadership divided on how best to fight back. Some called for more coordinated attacks, while others feared provoking the full wrath of The Architect's military.

Sitting around a dimly lit table, an eclectic group of resistance leaders discussed their next move. Most of them had lived in Berlin their entire lives, witnessing the gradual erosion of their freedoms. Now, they were determined to reclaim their city, but with the recent influx of refugees and the brutal crackdown by the regime, hope was in short supply.

"We can't keep fighting like this," said Gregor, a former journalist turned resistance commander. His voice was hoarse from months of shouting orders and rallying the scattered fighters. "Every attack we make, they hit back ten times harder. We lose more people, and the citizens are too afraid to support us openly."

Across the table, Hana, a younger but equally hardened resistance member, shook her head. "We have to keep fighting. If we don't, The Architect will crush any hope we have left. The people are scared, yes, but they're also desperate. We just need a victory—something to show them that we can win."

An uneasy silence fell over the group. They all knew what was at stake. The resistance was running out of time, and if they didn't act soon, The Architect's forces would root them out completely.

It was at that moment that Marie and her team arrived, slipping quietly into the underground hideout. Their presence brought an immediate shift in the room's energy. Despite the toll of their escape, Marie's reputation as a fierce leader had preceded her. The Berlin resistance leaders knew that if anyone could strike at The Architect, it was her.

"We were expecting you," Gregor said, standing to greet Marie. "But not like this. What happened?"

Marie looked around the room, assessing the tired, battle-worn faces of the resistance leaders. She knew they had been fighting this war for far longer than she had, but the ambush had been a blow to morale.

"We were compromised," Marie said, her voice steady despite the weight of their failure. "Someone in the regime knew we were coming. We lost good people in that tunnel, and now the entire city is on high alert."

Hana crossed her arms, her expression sceptical. "So, what now? Do we give up? Go underground and wait for the next opportunity?"

"No," Marie said firmly. "We keep fighting. We may have been outmanoeuvred, but we're not out of the fight yet. The Architect's regime is crumbling under its own weight. We need to hit them harder—make it clear that their time is running out."

The Architect's Next Move

Meanwhile, in the opulent confines of The Architect's inner sanctum, preparations were being made for the next phase of their plan. The elite of The Architect's command met in a lavish, high-tech conference room, where holographic maps of Europe displayed the regime's growing influence. The war was not just being fought in the streets—it was a battle for control of entire nations.

General Heinrich Drach stood at the head of the table; his steely eyes fixed on the map of Berlin. The failed ambush had rattled him, but he was not one to let setbacks weaken his resolve. He knew that the resistance was growing more daring, and though their numbers were small, their actions had begun to inspire more people to rise against the regime.

Petra Lang, the intelligence chief, was seated next to him, her sharp gaze unwavering. She had been monitoring the resistance's movements for months, trying to anticipate their next move.

"The resistance fighters that escaped are still in the city," Lang said, her voice clipped and precise. "They're likely regrouping with local insurgents. We can use this to our advantage."

Drach crossed his arms, his expression hard. "What are you suggesting?"

Lang leaned forward, her fingers tapping the table rhythmically. "We let them believe they've escaped. We let them think they have the upper hand. In the meantime, we track their every move. When they strike, we'll be ready."

Drach considered her plan, nodding slowly. "And The Architect?"

Lang hesitated. Even among the highest ranks of the regime, The Architect remained an enigmatic figure—seen only by a few, their presence looming over every decision made in the command structure. The Architect's influence was absolute, but their absence from public view had led to rumours and speculation.

"The Architect has given us the green light to proceed with full mobilization," Lang said after a moment. "Berlin is our priority now. If we crush the resistance here, the rest of Europe will fall in line."

Drach's lips twisted into a grim smile. "Then we'll give them what they want. Let them come for us. We'll be waiting."

Plotting the Next Strike

Back in the resistance's underground hideout, Marie and her team poured over maps of Berlin, trying to identify weak points in The Architect's defences. The failed infiltration had rattled them, but it had also given them valuable intelligence on how the regime operated within the city.

"The northern sector is too heavily fortified," Nadia said, wincing as she adjusted the bandage on her shoulder. "We won't make it far if we try that route again."

Gregor nodded in agreement. "And the central district is crawling with soldiers. Every major government building is surrounded by checkpoints and drone surveillance."

Marie stared at the map, deep in thought. They needed to find a way to get close to The Architect without alerting the entire city. But Berlin was a fortress—every inch of it was designed to keep them out.

"What about the tunnels?" Hana suggested, her finger tracing the old subway lines that crisscrossed beneath the city. "We used them to move supplies before the regime cracked down. Some of the older sections haven't been patrolled in months."

"It's risky," Jean-Luc said, shaking his head. "If they know we're coming, we could get trapped down there. But it might be our best shot."

Marie considered their options. The tunnels were dangerous, but they offered a way into the heart of the city without being detected. And if they could avoid the regime's patrols, they might be able to get close enough to strike at The Architect's command center.

"Let's do it," Marie said finally, her voice resolute. "We move through the tunnels and hit them where they least expect it."

The Final Countdown

As night fell over Berlin, the city was eerily quiet. The streets were deserted, save for the occasional patrol of heavily armed soldiers. Drones hummed overhead, scanning for any signs of resistance activity. But below the surface, in the forgotten depths of the subway tunnels, Marie and her team were on the move.

Their footsteps echoed through the dark, damp passageways as they navigated the maze of tunnels, their weapons at the ready. The air was thick with tension, each step bringing them closer to the heart of The Architect's regime—and to the moment of reckoning.

"We're almost there," Nadia whispered, her voice barely audible above the sound of dripping water. "Another hundred meters and we'll reach the service tunnel that leads to the command center."

Marie nodded, her senses on high alert. They were close—so close. But something felt off. The silence was oppressive, too perfect, as if they were being lured into a trap.

And then, as they rounded the corner, the tunnel ahead of them lit up with blinding floodlights.

"Ambush!" Jean-Luc shouted, diving for cover as a hail of gunfire erupted from all directions.

Marie barely had time to react as bullets ricocheted off the walls around them. The regime had been waiting for them. They had known all along.

As the resistance fighters scrambled to defend themselves, Marie's mind raced. This was it—the moment they had been preparing for. But the odds were stacked against them.

And as the battle raged in the depths of Berlin's underground, Marie knew that the fight for Europe's future was about to reach its most critical point yet.

Chapter 47: The Battle in the Depths

January 2029 – Berlin, Germany

The air in the tunnel was thick with smoke, dust, and the deafening roar of gunfire. Marie felt the vibration of each shot pounding in her chest as she crouched behind a rusted steel support beam. The narrow space amplified the chaos, every sound bouncing off the stone walls and reverberating around them like a death knell.

Marie's mind raced. This was supposed to have been their way in—an unexpected route beneath Berlin, avoiding the heavily fortified streets above. But The Architect's forces had been ready, and now, her team was caught in a fight for survival.

"Nadia! On my six!" Marie shouted over the din of bullets.

Nadia, despite the blood soaking her bandages, was already moving. She rolled out from behind a concrete column, firing a burst of rounds that sent two regime soldiers sprawling. She dove for cover again, her face set in grim determination. There was no time to stop and take stock of their losses. They had to keep moving or die where they stood.

Jean-Luc fired at the overhead lights, plunging the tunnel into flickering darkness. The strobe effect provided fleeting moments of shadow, offering the team brief cover to reposition.

"Fall back! Regroup at the maintenance shaft!" Jean-Luc barked as he reloaded his rifle.

Marie knew it was their only chance. If they stayed in the narrow passageway, they would be overwhelmed by the sheer number of regime forces. The Architect's soldiers were highly trained, and they had night vision, superior firepower, and, most of all, the advantage of preparation.

Marie signalled to the rest of the team and sprinted toward the maintenance shaft. Her heart pounded in rhythm with her footsteps as her boots splashed through pools of filthy water. Jean-Luc was at her side, his face streaked with dirt and sweat, a glint of determination in his eyes.

As they reached the shaft, Nadia let out a grunt of pain and stumbled, her hand pressed to her side. Jean-Luc pulled her up, his voice urgent but steady. "We're not losing you here. Keep moving!"

Marie scanned the area ahead. The maintenance shaft led to a series of smaller, less-mapped tunnels that crisscrossed beneath Berlin. If they could navigate through them, they might be able to slip away from the immediate danger. But there was no telling how deep the enemy's net had spread.

She motioned for the team to follow. "Let's go! Now!"

The Pursuit

Inside the tunnel, the clatter of gunfire subsided for a brief moment as the resistance fighters disappeared into the shadows of the maintenance shaft. But the respite was short-lived. The pursuing soldiers regrouped, their boots pounding in unison as they charged after their prey.

"Don't let them escape!" barked a regime lieutenant, his voice mechanical through his helmet's comms system. His orders were clear: eliminate the insurgents at all costs.

The Architect's forces were relentless, their discipline and training evident in every coordinated movement. They knew the tunnels just as well as Marie and her team did—perhaps even better, thanks to the regime's surveillance network. Drones were already being deployed to cut off the resistance's escape routes, while reinforcements were being diverted to strategic exits.

Marie's breath came in ragged gasps as she led her team deeper into the underground labyrinth. The air grew stale, thick with the smell of mildew and decay. The oppressive weight of the city above pressed down on them, a reminder that the entire regime's apparatus was working against them.

Nadia limped beside her, her face pale but determined. Jean-Luc brought up the rear, covering their escape with calculated bursts of gunfire to keep the enemy at bay.

"This isn't working!" Nadia hissed through gritted teeth. "They're everywhere. We'll be trapped in here like rats if we don't change course."

Marie's mind raced as she considered their options. They had to make a move, and fast, but where? The regime had already anticipated their path. To outmanoeuvre them, they'd need to find a route the enemy wouldn't expect.

And then it hit her.

"The old sewer lines," Marie said suddenly, her voice hoarse. "They're off the grid. No patrols, no surveillance. The regime stopped using them years ago."

Jean-Luc gave her a wary look. "You want us to go deeper?"

"It's our only chance. If we stay in the main tunnels, we're dead."

Jean-Luc nodded grimly. "Lead the way."

The Descent

The team made their way to a rusted, circular grate embedded in the floor. With a grunt of effort, Jean-Luc pried it open, revealing a narrow, ancient shaft that dropped down into pitch-black darkness. A foul smell wafted up from below, but no one hesitated. One by one, they descended into the forgotten depths of Berlin.

The sewer system was a relic of a bygone era, a maze of winding tunnels that stretched beneath the city like veins. The stench of stagnant water and rotting waste hung in the air, but the oppressive silence that greeted them was a small mercy. Here, at least for the moment, they were free from the relentless pursuit of the regime.

Marie turned on her flashlight, the narrow beam cutting through the darkness. The walls were slick with grime, and the ground was uneven, but they pressed forward, their footsteps muffled by the filth that lined the floor.

Nadia struggled to keep up, her wound slowing her down, but she refused to stop. "We have to make this count," she muttered. "We can't keep running forever."

Marie didn't respond. She knew the truth of Nadia's words. Every step they took brought them closer to their objective, but also closer to the inevitable confrontation with The Architect's forces. The regime wouldn't rest until they were dead.

"We'll find a way out," Marie said, though she wasn't sure if she was trying to convince her team or herself. "We always do."

The Architect's Plan

High above, in the sprawling government complex that dominated Berlin's skyline, The Architect watched the situation unfold in real-time. Seated in a private chamber filled with holographic displays, The Architect observed the resistance's every move through the city's surveillance network.

Though they had lost contact with Marie and her team when they descended into the sewers, the regime's forces were already closing in on other resistance cells scattered throughout Berlin.

Beside The Architect stood General Heinrich Drach, his posture rigid as he awaited his leader's next order.

"They'll come for us," Drach said. "Even if they slip through this net, they'll try again. It's only a matter of time before they strike at the heart."

The Architect remained silent, gazing at the flickering screens. Their face, as always, was hidden in shadow, their identity a closely guarded secret known only to a select few.

"They're desperate," The Architect said finally, their voice calm, almost indifferent. "And desperation breeds recklessness. Let them come."

Drach inclined his head in agreement. "And when they do?"

The Architect turned to him, their eyes unreadable. "We'll be ready."

Closing In

Back in the sewers, Marie's team pressed on, their pace quickening as they moved through the maze of tunnels. They could hear the distant sound of regime forces above, the clatter of boots and the hum of drones patrolling the surface. But for now, they were out of sight, if not out of danger.

Marie paused at a junction, consulting the map she had memorized. The sewers led to an old water treatment facility near the outskirts of the city. If they could reach it, they might be able to slip past the regime's perimeter and regroup with the rest of the resistance.

But time was running out. The longer they stayed underground, the more likely the regime would find them.

Suddenly, Jean-Luc held up a hand, signalling for the group to stop. Marie froze, listening intently. At first, she heard nothing, but then, faintly, came the sound of voices—voices that weren't theirs.

"They've found us," Nadia whispered, her voice tight with fear.

Marie's heart raced. They were being hunted, cornered in the depths of the city. She glanced at Jean-Luc, who gave her a grim nod.

"We'll make our stand here," he said quietly, raising his weapon.

Marie swallowed hard. The fight was coming to them, whether they were ready or not. But this time, they wouldn't be running.

With a steely resolve, she drew her own weapon and prepared for the inevitable clash. The regime had thrown everything at them, but they were still standing. And as long as they were alive, the fight for Berlin—and for Europe—was far from over.

The resistance wasn't finished yet.

Chapter 48: The Inevitable Clash

January 2029 – Berlin, Germany

The sewer tunnel was suffocating, filled with the musty stench of stagnant water, decay, and the acrid scent of impending violence. Marie crouched low, her back pressed against the cold, wet wall. Every muscle in her body was tense, her mind hyper-focused on the distant footsteps echoing through the tunnel. The regime's soldiers were closing in, methodically sweeping the underground labyrinth.

Jean-Luc moved beside her, his rifle at the ready, eyes scanning the shadows. Nadia, despite her injuries, was stationed further back, her weapon trained on the entrance to the junction. The entire team was poised for the inevitable clash.

"Hold your fire until they're in range," Marie whispered, her voice barely audible above the drip of water from the ceiling. "We can't afford to waste ammunition."

The tunnel around them was eerily silent, save for the rhythmic drip of moisture that echoed like a ticking clock counting down to the confrontation. The light from their flashlights barely pierced the darkness, casting long shadows on the damp, narrow walls. Time seemed to stretch, every second laden with the weight of anticipation.

They had chosen this junction because it offered a semblance of tactical advantage. The narrow tunnel would force the regime soldiers to approach single file, limiting their ability to overwhelm Marie's team with sheer numbers. But even with this advantage, the odds were stacked heavily against them.

In the distance, the footsteps grew louder. Marie tensed, signalling with a flick of her hand for her team to get into position. There were at least a dozen soldiers, maybe more, advancing slowly but deliberately through the sewers. They were trained, disciplined, and heavily armed—the elite forces of The Architect's regime.

Marie's breath was shallow, her heart pounding in her chest as she peered around the corner. Her vision flickered between the narrow beams of light and the encroaching shadows. She knew this wasn't just a skirmish; it was a fight for survival, and more than that, it was a symbol of their rebellion. If they fell here, Berlin might never rise again.

The first regime soldier appeared at the far end of the tunnel, a silhouette backlit by the dim emergency lights still flickering above. Marie counted three, then five, then seven. Their black armour blended with the shadows, their movements efficient and predatory. They advanced in silence, weapons drawn, sweeping the area for any sign of movement.

"Wait," Marie mouthed, raising her hand to still the team's nerves. They needed patience. Surprise was their only advantage.

The soldiers moved closer, unaware of the resistance fighters lying in wait. The tension was unbearable, a coiled spring ready to snap. Marie's finger hovered over the trigger of her rifle. She could feel the weight of every second, knowing that once the battle began, there would be no turning back.

As the first soldier crossed an invisible threshold in the tunnel, Marie squeezed the trigger.

The shot rang out like thunder in the confined space, a crack that reverberated through the sewer, shattering the silence. The lead soldier crumpled to the ground before he had a chance to react. A split second later, the tunnel erupted into chaos.

Gunfire blazed in both directions, the muzzle flashes illuminating the dark space in erratic bursts. Marie ducked back behind the corner as bullets ricocheted off the walls, sending sparks flying. Jean-Luc was already firing, his shots precise, each one finding its mark with lethal accuracy.

Nadia, her face pale but focused, let out a short burst of fire from her side of the tunnel, taking down another soldier who had tried to flank them. The regime's forces, though caught off guard, responded with brutal efficiency. They quickly formed a line, returning fire with a hailstorm of bullets that forced the resistance fighters to retreat further into the junction.

"We're pinned down!" Jean-Luc shouted over the noise, his voice strained with the effort of maintaining their defensive position.

Marie gritted her teeth. She knew they couldn't hold this position for long. The regime soldiers were better equipped, better trained, and they had the numbers on their side. But retreat wasn't an option. Not here. Not now.

"We hold them as long as we can," Marie barked, her voice filled with resolve. "Then we move to the secondary exit."

Nadia gave her a grim nod, her face etched with pain but still resolute. "Got it. We're not going down without a fight."

The regime forces pressed forward, their advance relentless. The sound of their boots splashing through the shallow water was drowned out by the continuous roar of gunfire. Marie popped up from behind cover, firing a few more rounds before ducking back as bullets tore into the concrete where her head had been moments before.

"They're coming in hard!" Nadia called out, her voice barely audible over the cacophony.

Jean-Luc was already moving, tossing a flashbang down the tunnel. The device exploded in a burst of brilliant light, momentarily blinding the soldiers. It bought them a few precious seconds, but not enough.

Marie's mind raced as she tried to calculate their next move. The regime forces were too close now, and there was no time for a full retreat. She needed something to tip the scales—something that could disrupt the enemy's advance long enough for her team to regroup.

"We need to collapse the tunnel!" she shouted suddenly, her voice carrying an urgency that cut through the chaos.

Jean-Luc glanced at her, a mix of surprise and understanding in his eyes. "You sure? There's no coming back from that."

Marie didn't hesitate. "Do it. It's our only chance."

Without another word, Jean-Luc pulled a small, shaped charge from his pack. He quickly rigged it to the support beam closest to their position, his hands moving with practiced speed. The sound of gunfire continued to echo through the tunnel, but now, every shot felt like a countdown to their escape.

"Hurry!" Nadia urged, her voice tight with pain.

"Almost there," Jean-Luc muttered, his focus unbroken. "Just a few more seconds..."

Marie's heart pounded in her chest as she kept her rifle trained on the approaching soldiers. The regime forces were advancing again, their helmets gleaming in the dim light. Another few meters, and they'd be within range to overwhelm the resistance completely.

"Now!" Marie shouted.

Jean-Luc hit the detonator.

The explosion rocked the tunnel, a deafening blast that sent shockwaves through the underground labyrinth. The ceiling above them groaned and buckled, and for a moment, it seemed as though the entire tunnel might collapse. Dust and debris rained down, filling the air with a choking cloud of concrete and dirt.

Marie grabbed Nadia, pulling her to her feet as the tunnel began to cave in. Jean-Luc was already sprinting toward the secondary exit, the rest of the team following close behind.

Behind them, the regime soldiers were caught in the collapse, their shouts of alarm drowned out by the sound of falling rubble. The narrow passageway they had fought so hard to hold was now buried beneath tons of debris, sealing the soldiers inside.

Marie didn't look back. There was no time to savour the small victory. They had bought themselves a few minutes—maybe more—but the fight wasn't over. The regime would be back, and when they came, they would come with everything they had.

As they reached the secondary tunnel, Marie could hear the distant hum of drones and the faint clatter of more soldiers moving through the sewers. The Architect's forces were relentless, and this was just one skirmish in a much larger war.

But as Marie led her team deeper into the dark, winding tunnels beneath Berlin, she knew one thing for certain: they weren't beaten yet.

The resistance was still alive, and as long as they had breath in their lungs and fire in their hearts, they would keep fighting.

Chapter 49: The Rising Storm

February 2029 – Paris, France

The winter sun hung low over Paris, casting long shadows across the city's streets. It was a cold, gray morning, with clouds thickening overhead, threatening snow. The once-bustling city was now tense, its people caught in the tightening grip of fear and uncertainty. Protests had turned to riots, and riots had escalated into armed skirmishes. France, like much of Europe, was on the brink of civil war.

The Avenue des Champs-Élysées, normally filled with tourists and shoppers, was eerily quiet. Barricades lined the famous boulevard, and armed police patrolled in groups, their eyes scanning every passerby with suspicion. The cracks in the French Republic were widening by the day, and even the most hopeful optimists struggled to imagine a peaceful solution.

Aurelien Marchand watched the scene unfold from a rooftop near Place de la Concorde. His sniper rifle rested on its bipod, the scope trained on the crowds below. His target was a government official due to arrive at a press conference that afternoon. The assassination had been ordered by one of the more radical factions of the resistance, a desperate move to strike at the heart of the regime's propaganda machine.

"We have twenty minutes before the motorcade arrives," a voice crackled through his earpiece.

Aurelien didn't respond. He was focused, his finger hovering near the trigger. The streets below were a battlefield in waiting. Protesters clashed with police at almost every turn, and the tension was so thick it seemed to permeate the air itself. France had always been a country of revolutionaries, but this time, the divisions ran deeper than ever before—Muslims and Christians, migrants and natives, the government and the people. It was a fight for identity, for survival, and for control of a nation teetering on the edge.

As he lay on the rooftop, Aurelien's mind drifted back to the beginning, to when the first waves of migrants had arrived in France from the Middle East and North Africa. He remembered the promises of integration, the speeches of unity, and the belief that multiculturalism would strengthen the nation. But those promises had been hollow, the speeches empty, and the unity had never truly materialized. Instead, ghettos had formed, tensions had risen, and resentment had festered in the underbelly of French society.

Aurelien had once believed in those promises too. He had been an idealist, a young student at the Sorbonne, full of hope for a future where diversity could be a strength rather than a source of division. But as the years passed and the divisions grew more pronounced, his hope had turned to anger. He had watched as his country became a battleground, and now, he was part of the fight to reclaim it.

The sound of an approaching helicopter snapped him back to the present. Aurelien's pulse quickened as he adjusted his scope. The motorcade was approaching, moving slowly through the heavily guarded streets. In the backseat of the lead vehicle was François Duvall, the French Minister of Defence and a key architect of the government's response to the growing unrest. Duvall had been one of the loudest voices calling for harsher crackdowns on protestors, and he had supported the controversial decision to deploy the military in the suburbs—areas now considered war zones.

"This is it," Aurelien whispered to himself. He inhaled deeply, his finger tightening on the trigger.

The Plan Unfolds

As Aurelien prepared to take the shot, the streets below continued to shift and roil with activity. Hundreds of protestors had gathered near the Arc de Triomphe, their chants echoing through the cold morning air. A mix of banners waved in the air—some calling for peace, others demanding revolution. Among the crowd, one figure stood out. Amira, a local activist and community leader, was doing her best to calm the protestors. She had been a voice for dialogue and peace, but even she was beginning to lose faith that words could stop the storm that was coming.

"Amira, you need to get out of here," her friend Malik urged, pulling at her sleeve. "It's going to get ugly. The police aren't going to hold back this time."

"I can't leave," she said, her voice firm. "Not now. If we abandon this protest, what does that say to everyone who still believes in non-violence?"

Malik shook his head. "No one's listening anymore. You saw what happened last week in Marseille. The army opened fire. People died, Amira. You need to be smart about this."

Amira glanced at the armoured police vehicles lining the boulevard, her chest tightening with fear. She knew Malik was right. The country had passed the point of peaceful protests long ago. Still, she refused to give up hope.

Suddenly, a loud explosion rocked the street, sending a shockwave through the crowd. Panic erupted as people scrambled to find cover, screams filling the air. Amira and Malik ducked behind a makeshift barricade, their hearts racing.

"God, what was that?" Malik gasped.

Amira peered over the barricade and saw a plume of black smoke rising from the direction of the motorcade. Police were already rushing toward the scene, weapons drawn, while the protesters scattered in every direction.

"Something's happening near Duvall," Amira whispered, her voice tight with anxiety.

The Missed Shot

Aurelien had been seconds away from pulling the trigger when the explosion had gone off. The sudden blast had thrown him off balance, causing his shot to go wide. He cursed under his breath, quickly readjusting his position. The motorcade was now in chaos. One of the escort vehicles had been hit by what appeared to be an improvised explosive device, and the entire convoy was grinding to a halt.

Through his scope, Aurelien could see Duvall's car. The windows were bulletproof, but he had a clear shot at the engine block. If he couldn't take out Duvall, he could at least disable the car and force the minister out into the open.

He took a deep breath, steadying himself, and fired.

The bullet hit its mark, puncturing the engine and sending a plume of steam billowing into the air. Aurelien smiled grimly as he watched the driver scramble out of the car, panic written across his face. Duvall was still inside, but not for long.

As police officers rushed to the scene, Aurelien knew he had to act quickly. He grabbed his rifle and began disassembling it, packing it into the slim black case he always carried. His exit plan was already in motion, but the timing was crucial. He had to disappear before the police locked down the area.

As he slipped through a back entrance and down a narrow staircase into the depths of the building, Aurelien's thoughts raced. This wasn't just about Duvall. The attack on the motorcade was part of a broader strategy, one that would send a message to the regime: The people of France were not afraid to strike at the heart of power.

The Wider Conflict

Across Europe, the situation was deteriorating at an alarming rate. Germany was facing similar unrest in its cities, with clashes between right-wing nationalists and Muslim migrants erupting into street battles. The United Kingdom, struggling to maintain control of its own restive population, had declared martial law in certain areas of London, where tensions had boiled over into open conflict.

The European Union, once a symbol of unity and cooperation, was fracturing under the weight of its internal divisions. Countries were closing their borders, suspending trade agreements, and blaming each other for the escalating chaos. Brussels, the heart of the EU, was struggling to maintain any semblance of order, with member states openly defying the bloc's directives.

For The Architect, watching from the shadows, it was all going according to plan. Every violent confrontation, every act of rebellion, pushed Europe closer to collapse. And when the old order fell, a new one would rise from the ashes—one that The Architect would control.

In a secure location far from the streets of Paris, The Architect received word of the attack on Duvall's motorcade. They smiled beneath the mask they always wore, their eyes cold and calculating.

"Let them fight," The Architect whispered to no one in particular. "Soon, they'll come begging for our solution."

As the storm continued to rise across Europe, it was clear that the conflict was no longer just about religion or migration. It had become a battle for the very soul of the continent. And in that battle, no one was safe.

BRYSON MINE

Back on the streets of Paris, as Aurelien melted into the crowd and Amira braced herself for what was to come, the winds of revolution were blowing. The rising storm would consume them all—one way or another.

Chapter 50: The Fall of Brussels

March 2029 – Brussels, Belgium

The headquarters of the European Union was an imposing structure, built to symbolize the unity and strength of Europe. But now, the grand building in Brussels felt more like a fortress under siege. The air was thick with tension, and the streets surrounding the EU complex were deserted, save for the military checkpoints and barbed wire fencing that had become a common sight in recent months.

Inside the building, the situation was equally dire. The European Union, once the embodiment of cooperation and peace across the continent, was unravelling. The constant waves of protests, violence, and escalating nationalistic rhetoric had broken the fragile bonds between member states. Many countries had already begun distancing themselves from the bloc, leaving Brussels to contend with an ever-growing crisis of legitimacy.

At the center of it all was Council President Erik Schmidt, who sat behind a large oak desk in the heart of the EU headquarters. His face was etched with exhaustion, the weight of the collapsing union pressing down on him. His once-proud idealism had given way to grim pragmatism as he struggled to hold the remnants of the EU together.

His advisor, Claudia Lefèvre, stood by the window, looking out at the grim scene below. The streets of Brussels, usually teeming with politicians, tourists, and bureaucrats, were eerily quiet. Military trucks patrolled the avenues, and a state of emergency had been declared weeks ago.

"They're coming, Erik," Claudia said softly, her voice tinged with resignation. "Germany and France have already shut their borders. The UK is effectively in lockdown. We're running out of options."

Schmidt didn't respond at first. He rubbed his temples, trying to alleviate the pounding headache that had become his constant companion in recent months.

"I know," he finally replied, his voice hoarse. "But we can't let them destroy everything we've built. We can't let Europe fall into chaos. If we don't act, the entire continent will become a warzone."

Claudia turned to face him, her expression serious. "It already is, Erik. We've lost control of the situation. The member states are doing whatever they want, and there's nothing we can do to stop it. The EU is powerless."

Schmidt knew she was right. The European Union had lost its ability to enforce its own rules. The open borders policy, once the cornerstone of European unity, had been abandoned. Member states were acting unilaterally, prioritizing their national interests over the collective good. The trust that had once bound them together had eroded completely.

A soft knock at the door interrupted their conversation. An aide entered, his face pale and nervous.

"Mr. President, we have a situation," the aide stammered. "The protest outside... it's turned violent. They've broken through the barricades."

Schmidt's heart sank. Another riot, another breach of security. It was becoming a daily occurrence. He nodded grimly and stood, pulling on his jacket. "I'll address it," he said, his tone resolute.

Claudia shot him a worried look. "Be careful, Erik. This isn't like the other protests. These people are armed. They're not just here to demonstrate—they're here to overthrow the EU."

Schmidt gave her a tight smile. "I know. But we can't back down now. If we show fear, it's over."

The Streets of Brussels

Outside, chaos reigned. Thousands of protesters had gathered in the city, their ranks swelled by disillusioned citizens from across Europe. The banners they carried were no longer just slogans calling for reform or change—they were demands for revolution. Nationalist groups, religious extremists, and militant factions had united in their shared hatred of the EU, blaming the institution for the collapse of order, the economic downturn, and the influx of migrants that had changed the face of Europe.

Among the crowd, a man named Jörg Bauer marched with grim determination. He was a former German soldier, disillusioned by the government's handling of the crisis and furious at what he saw as the betrayal of Europe's heritage. He had joined one of the far-right militias that had sprung up across the continent, groups dedicated to taking back control from the "globalist elite" in Brussels.

"We take the building today," Jörg shouted to his comrades, his voice barely audible over the roar of the crowd. "This is the day we end the EU and reclaim our nations!"

His words were met with cheers and chants of "Europa für die Europäer!" (Europe for Europeans). The mood in the crowd was electric, charged with anger and a desire for vengeance. They had come prepared—not with mere placards and chants, but with weapons. Rifles, Molotov cocktails, and makeshift explosives were in the hands of many of the rioters, their intentions clear.

As they pushed past the final barricade, the EU's security forces responded with tear gas and rubber bullets, but it was too late. The mob was too large, too determined. They surged forward, overwhelming the police, who were outnumbered and outgunned.

Jörg led the charge, smashing through the glass doors of the EU headquarters with a sledgehammer. The sound of shattering glass echoed through the street, a symbolic blow to the institution that had once prided itself on stability and unity.

Inside the Storm

Erik Schmidt stood in front of a television screen, watching in horror as the protesters stormed the building. His security detail was already urging him to evacuate, but he remained rooted to the spot, unable to believe that it had come to this. The European Union, the dream of unity that had once seemed so inevitable, was collapsing before his eyes.

"They've breached the building, sir," one of the guards said urgently. "We need to leave—now."

Schmidt nodded, finally shaken from his stupor. He grabbed his coat and followed the security team down a series of back hallways, his mind racing. How had it come to this? How had Europe descended into such chaos so quickly? He had always believed that the European Union could weather any storm, but this... this was something else entirely. This was the death of a dream.

As they made their way through the winding corridors, the sounds of the mob grew louder. Shouts, gunfire, and the crash of breaking furniture filled the air. Schmidt's heart pounded in his chest as he realized that they might not make it out in time.

Suddenly, the lights flickered, and the building's alarm system blared to life. The mob had reached the inner sanctum of the EU headquarters. There would be no more time to deliberate or plan. The fall of Brussels was happening in real time.

Claudia was already at the emergency exit, her face pale but calm. "We have to get to the safehouse," she said, pulling Schmidt by the arm. "It's the only way."

Just as they reached the exit, a loud explosion rocked the building, sending debris raining down from the ceiling. The shockwave knocked Schmidt off his feet, and for a moment, everything went black.

The Aftermath

When Schmidt came to, the scene around him was one of utter devastation. Smoke filled the air, and the once-grand hallways of the EU headquarters were now a battlefield, littered with debris and the bodies of the fallen. In the distance, he could hear the faint sound of sirens, but it was clear that the battle for Brussels had already been lost.

Claudia was beside him, helping him to his feet. Her face was streaked with dirt and blood, but her eyes were sharp. "We have to move, Erik. There's no time."

They stumbled out into the cold night air, the streets of Brussels now ablaze with fires and gunfire. The EU's downfall was unfolding around them, and Schmidt knew there was no way to salvage it. The European Union was over. The dream had died in the flames of revolution.

As they disappeared into the shadows, Schmidt realized that Europe would never be the same again. The storm that had been brewing for years had finally broken, and the continent was now in the grip of forces far beyond anyone's control.

The fall of Brussels marked the end of an era—and the beginning of a new, darker chapter in European history.

Chapter 51: The Ashes of Rome

April 2029 – Rome, Italy

The Colosseum, one of the most iconic symbols of Western civilization, stood silhouetted against the blood-red sky of a dying empire. Smoke billowed from the city below, rising from buildings set ablaze by rioters and revolutionaries. The Eternal City, once a symbol of Europe's grandeur, had descended into chaos. Rome was burning—again.

Father Alessandro sat in the quiet of the Vatican, deep in thought. His simple black cassock contrasted sharply with the opulence of the room, but he found no comfort in the riches of the Church. The world outside was collapsing, and the Vatican had been rendered powerless, trapped in its own historical inertia. What could prayers do in the face of such violence?

Since the migration crisis had worsened, Italy had become a battleground between various factions. On one side were nationalist forces calling for the expulsion of migrants, most of whom were Muslim refugees from Africa and the Middle East. On the other side were those who defended the refugees' rights, citing Italy's humanitarian obligations. The center could not hold.

But now, the fighting was no longer ideological. It had become religious, and the streets of Rome had turned into killing fields. Armed Christian militias, many radicalized in response to what they saw as the "Islamization" of their country, clashed violently with Muslim groups defending their communities. It was no longer just a political struggle; it was a holy war, and the Vatican was caught in the middle of it.

A Broken Alliance

Cardinal Vincenzo Rossi, one of the most powerful figures in the Vatican, entered the room and sat across from Father Alessandro. His face was grave, his eyes shadowed by the weight of recent events.

"Father," he began in a low voice, "Rome is lost."

Alessandro sighed. "I know."

"The Italian government is crumbling, and the police have no control. We've been receiving messages from across the country—towns falling to militia groups, Muslims retaliating in self-defence, and Christian extremists committing atrocities in the name of preserving Italy. We are witnessing the fall of our civilization."

Alessandro leaned back in his chair, his mind heavy with the gravity of the situation. "What of the Church? Are we not supposed to guide the people in times of crisis?"

Rossi shook his head slowly. "The people aren't listening anymore, Alessandro. Our influence is fading. Many of the Christian militias reject the Vatican's authority. They see us as too soft, too accommodating of the refugees. They call us traitors. They even talk of storming the Vatican to purge it of 'liberal' clergy."

The younger priest looked out the window at the streets below. He could hear distant gunfire, the sound of glass shattering, and the chants of mobs. The violence was growing closer every day. Rome was no longer the safe haven it once was. The Vatican's high walls, once enough to protect its secrets, now felt like a prison, trapping them in a city under siege.

"Then what do we do?" Alessandro asked, his voice filled with despair. "We can't just abandon Rome. We are the Church. We must be a beacon of hope."

Rossi stood, his expression firm but resigned. "The Church has survived many trials—wars, schisms, revolutions. We will survive this. But right now, we must prioritize survival over ideology. If we stay here, we will be consumed by the fire that is sweeping through the city."

Alessandro rose to follow Rossi, his heart heavy. "Where will we go?"

"To the north. The Swiss Guard is preparing to evacuate the Pope and key members of the Curia. We'll regroup in safer territory, away from Rome. It may be the only chance we have to preserve the Church in these dark times."

The Streets of Rome

Across the city, Luca Feretti crouched behind a burned-out car, clutching a makeshift rifle. He had never intended to become a soldier, but now he found himself fighting in the streets of his own hometown. He was part of a militia group called La Croce Italiana, one of the many Christian paramilitary organizations that had sprung up in recent months.

Luca was not an extremist by nature. In fact, he had spent most of his life indifferent to politics and religion. But when the violence had begun—when his neighbourhood had been overrun by gangs, when friends and family had been killed in clashes with Muslim groups—he had felt he had no choice. The country he knew was vanishing before his eyes, and he couldn't just stand by and watch it burn.

"Ready, Luca?" his friend Marco whispered beside him, eyes scanning the street ahead.

"Yeah," Luca replied, gripping the rifle tighter. He could hear the footsteps of their enemies approaching. A group of Muslim men had been spotted a few blocks away, and the militia had been ordered to engage. It was a cycle that had become all too familiar: retaliation for retaliation, vengeance for vengeance. No one could remember what had started the latest flare-up of violence, and no one seemed to care anymore. All that mattered was survival.

Suddenly, the group of men emerged from an alleyway. Luca could see the fear and anger in their eyes, a mirror of his own. They were young, barely older than teenagers, carrying an assortment of weapons—knives, bats, and even a few handguns. This wasn't a professional army; it was a war fought by the desperate and the disenfranchised.

Marco fired first, his rifle cracking through the cold evening air. Chaos erupted. The Muslim men scrambled for cover, and the battle was on. Luca's heart pounded in his chest as he took aim and fired. He saw one of the men collapse to the ground, blood pooling beneath him. Another ran in the opposite direction, disappearing into the maze of narrow streets that made up the neighbourhood.

It was over as quickly as it had begun. The bodies of the fallen lay scattered on the street, and the silence that followed was deafening.

"We should move," Marco said, pulling Luca by the arm. "They'll be back with reinforcements."

Luca nodded, but his feet felt like they were rooted to the ground. He stared at the body of the young man he had shot, a boy no older than 20. Was this what he had become? A killer? He had always told himself he was defending his country, his people, but in that moment, all he could see was the futility of it all. How many more would have to die before the bloodshed ended?

The Vatican's Last Stand

Back at the Vatican, the preparations for evacuation were nearing completion. The Pope, his face pale and weary, sat in the back of a heavily armoured vehicle, flanked by members of the Swiss Guard. It was a far cry from the papal processions of old. This was not a pilgrimage, but a retreat.

As the convoy moved through the streets of Rome, Cardinal Rossi remained silent, watching as the flames consumed the city. They passed through neighbourhoods that had once been bustling with life, now reduced to ruins by the relentless violence. Rossi knew that the Vatican's withdrawal would be seen as an admission of defeat by many. The Church had failed to protect its people. It had failed to provide the moral leadership needed to guide Europe through its darkest hour.

As they crossed the Tiber River and headed north, leaving the burning city behind, a profound sense of loss settled over Rossi. Rome, the heart of the Catholic world, was falling. But more than that, the ideals that had once sustained Europe were crumbling too.

The flames that licked the skies above Rome were not just consuming buildings—they were consuming the very soul of Europe. The old world was dying, and in its place, a new and uncertain future was being born.

A New World

Luca and Marco continued their retreat through the ruined streets, their thoughts heavy with the weight of what they had done. The violence in Rome was spreading like wildfire, and they both knew that their fight was just beginning. The city had become a battlefield, a place where there were no winners, only survivors.

As they reached the outskirts of the city, Luca stopped to catch his breath. He looked back at the skyline, now dominated by smoke and fire, and wondered how it had all come to this. What had happened to the Italy he once knew?

The answer, he realized, no longer mattered. The world was changing, and he would have to change with it. He couldn't afford to think about the past anymore. All that mattered now was surviving the storm that was engulfing the world.

And so, with a heavy heart and bloodstained hands, Luca turned his back on the city of Rome and walked into the night.

THE FRACTURED CONTINENT

Europe was burning, and the ashes of Rome were just the beginning.

Chapter 52: The Siege of Berlin

May 2029 – Berlin, Germany

The city of Berlin had always been a symbol of resilience. It had survived war, division, and reunification. But now, in 2029, it was a city under siege—not by an external enemy, but by the turmoil festering within its own borders. The migrant crisis, once seen as a temporary challenge, had turned into a full-blown catastrophe, one that threatened to tear the fabric of Europe apart.

The once-vibrant capital of Germany had become a flashpoint of conflict. Its streets were no longer filled with the hum of tourists and businesspeople but with the sound of gunfire, explosions, and the constant whirr of military helicopters overhead. Berlin had become the epicenter of the battle between nationalist militias and migrant communities, with the German government caught in the crossfire, losing control of the situation.

Inside the Reichstag

Chancellor Lena Kaufmann stood at the window of her office in the Reichstag, watching the dark smoke rising from the eastern part of the city. The skyline, once a proud display of modernity, was now scarred by the fires of revolution. Riots and skirmishes had broken out across Berlin, with both sides—radical nationalist factions and Muslim communities—claiming vengeance for the violence inflicted upon them. The German government had deployed the military, but even they were struggling to contain the anarchy.

Kaufmann rubbed her temples, feeling the weight of the nation's future pressing down on her shoulders. Germany, like much of Europe, was facing a moment of reckoning. Years of political indecision, infighting, and rising tensions had culminated in this—an implosion that seemed unstoppable. Her ministers were divided, the parliament paralyzed, and the streets of her capital had become a battlefield.

"Chancellor, we need to make a decision," said General Helmut Weber, the head of the German Armed Forces, standing just behind her. He was a tall, stern man, his gray uniform crisp and imposing. His face showed no emotion, but his voice carried the gravity of the situation.

"What's the latest from the ground?" Kaufmann asked, still staring at the smoke on the horizon.

"We've lost control of large sections of East Berlin. The militias are better organized than we anticipated, and the migrant communities are fighting back with unprecedented force. They've started arming themselves. It's no longer just protests or riots—it's urban warfare. Our forces are being stretched too thin to contain it."

Kaufmann nodded; her lips pressed into a thin line. She had always prided herself on being a rational leader, but now, reason seemed useless in the face of such chaos.

"Have you considered martial law?" Weber asked bluntly, though he knew the question was loaded.

Kaufmann turned to face him, her eyes tired but determined. "It's been discussed, but imposing martial law could escalate things further. We could provoke a nationwide insurrection. We're already dangerously close to civil war."

"Chancellor," Weber pressed, "the situation is deteriorating rapidly. The longer we wait, the less control we'll have. If we don't act decisively, Berlin will fall. And if Berlin falls, so does Germany."

The weight of his words hung in the air. Kaufmann knew he was right, but the consequences of declaring martial law terrified her. It would be an admission that the government had failed, that democracy had crumbled under the pressure of this crisis.

A knock at the door interrupted the tense silence. Kaufmann's chief of staff, Ingrid Müller, entered the room, her face pale. She held a tablet in her hands, the screen flashing with urgent news.

"Chancellor," Müller said, her voice tight with anxiety. "The Brandenburg Gate... it's been bombed."

Kaufmann's eyes widened in horror. The Brandenburg Gate was one of Germany's most iconic landmarks, a symbol of unity and peace. To attack it was an assault not just on Berlin, but on the heart of the nation itself.

"How bad is it?" Kaufmann asked, though she already knew the answer.

"Bad," Müller replied. "The east side is completely destroyed. Casualties are still being counted, but early reports suggest dozens dead, many more injured. We believe the attack was carried out by a nationalist group calling themselves 'Die Reiniger'—the Cleansers."

Kaufmann's heart sank. Die Reiniger had emerged in the last year, a far-right paramilitary group dedicated to "purifying" Germany of all foreign influences. They had gained a large following, tapping into the fear and anger of those who believed that Germany's migrant policies had destroyed the country.

"Weber," Kaufmann said quietly, "begin preparations for martial law."

The general nodded solemnly and left the room to carry out her orders.

The Outskirts of Berlin

On the outskirts of Berlin, in a district filled with migrant communities, a different kind of battle was brewing. Tariq Al-Mansour, a Syrian refugee who had arrived in Germany five years earlier, was now a commander of one of the many Muslim defence groups that had sprung up across the city. What had once been peaceful demonstrations for equal rights and protection had turned into a fight for survival.

Tariq had never imagined this when he fled the war in Syria. He had come to Germany seeking peace, a new life for his wife and two young children. But the world he had found here was not the one he had dreamed of. The hatred, the fear, the violence—it had followed him across continents.

Now, his neighbourhood was a warzone. The mosques had become fortresses, the schools turned into barracks. Tariq's group, calling themselves the Defenders of Al-Quds, had armed themselves with whatever they could find—hunting rifles, Molotov cocktails, and makeshift explosives. They had no choice. The nationalist militias were relentless, and the government was doing nothing to protect them.

"This isn't what I wanted," Tariq muttered to his second-in-command, Hakim, as they crouched behind a barricade of overturned cars. "I didn't come to Europe to fight another war."

Hakim nodded grimly. "None of us did. But here we are."

Tariq watched as the sun began to set over the city, casting an orange glow over the chaos. He knew that nightfall would bring more violence. The nationalists liked to strike under the cover of darkness, and his people were running out of supplies and energy.

"I don't know how much longer we can hold out," Tariq admitted, wiping the sweat from his brow. "Our numbers are dwindling, and the militias are better armed. If the government doesn't intervene soon, we'll be overrun."

Hakim looked at him with a mixture of frustration and resignation. "The government? They're too busy trying to save themselves. We're on our own."

The reality of Hakim's words hit Tariq like a punch to the gut. He had always believed that Germany, with its history of human rights and democracy, would protect him and his family. But now, that belief was crumbling. The country that had once opened its doors to refugees was being torn apart by the very divisions they had sought to escape.

The Breaking Point

As night fell, the violence escalated. The streets of Berlin became a battlefield, with nationalist militias and migrant defence groups locked in brutal combat. Fires burned through entire neighbourhoods, the flames licking at the sky as the city tore itself apart.

In the midst of the chaos, the German military struggled to regain control. Soldiers patrolled the streets, enforcing the newly declared martial law, but even they were overwhelmed by the scale of the violence. The military checkpoints became targets for both sides—nationalists who saw them as traitors, and migrants who viewed them as oppressors.

Chancellor Kaufmann watched the reports flood in from the military command center beneath the Reichstag. She had hoped that martial law would restore order, but it was becoming clear that the situation was beyond anyone's control. The lines between enemy and ally had blurred, and the violence was feeding on itself.

"Chancellor," General Weber said, standing beside her, "we may need to consider a full evacuation of the government."

Kaufmann's eyes widened. "Evacuate? You mean abandon Berlin?"

"I mean save what's left of our leadership before it's too late," Weber replied grimly. "Berlin is falling. If we stay here, we could lose the entire government. We need to regroup, possibly in Munich or Frankfurt."

Kaufmann stared at the map of Berlin, her heart heavy with the weight of the decision. If they abandoned Berlin, it would be a signal to the rest of

Germany—and to Europe—that the capital was lost. It would mean that the government had failed to protect its people.

But as the hours passed and the violence grew worse, it became clear that there was no other option.

"Prepare the evacuation," she said quietly, her voice barely above a whisper. "We'll leave at dawn."

A City in Ruins

By morning, Berlin was unrecognizable. Smoke rose from the ruins of buildings, and the streets were littered with debris and the bodies of the fallen. The Brandenburg Gate, now a symbol of the city's destruction, stood in the distance, partially collapsed.

Tariq and his group had survived the night, but barely. The nationalist militias had launched a full-scale assault, and the Defenders of Al-Quds had fought valiantly, but their losses were heavy. Tariq looked around at the survivors, many of them wounded, all of them exhausted.

"This can't go on," he muttered to Hakim as they surveyed the devastation. "We're fighting a losing battle."

Hakim nodded, his face grim. "So is everyone else."

As the first rays of sunlight broke through the thick clouds of smoke, the city of Berlin stood on the edge of complete collapse. The war that had begun with whispers of discontent had become an inferno that threatened to consume not just the city, but the entire country.

And as the government prepared to flee, the people of Berlin were left to face the fire alone.

Chapter 53: The Exodus

June 2029 – The Road to Munich

Berlin was behind them now, a broken city consumed by chaos. The convoy of armoured vehicles, helicopters, and unmarked vans wound its way south through the highways of Germany. Chancellor Lena Kaufmann sat in the back of an armoured SUV, the weight of her nation's collapse pressing heavily on her chest. Every few minutes, her eyes darted to the windows, as if expecting to see the fires of revolution creeping up behind them, chasing them down the autobahn.

"We're nearly halfway," said General Weber from the front seat, glancing at a tablet that showed their position on the map. "We should reach Munich by dusk, assuming the roads stay clear."

"Assuming," Kaufmann repeated, the word filled with bitter doubt. She had learned to trust nothing in these last few months. The Germany she had known her entire life was gone, replaced by a war-torn land where every town, every road, every face could belong to either friend or foe. The exodus from Berlin was not just a retreat—it was an acknowledgment of failure.

Beside her, Ingrid Müller, her chief of staff, shuffled through a thick file of documents, phone lines still ringing with the fallout from the government's retreat. The media, international leaders, and even her own ministers were clamouring for answers. But what could she say? How could she explain the total collapse of one of the most powerful nations in Europe without sounding like she had failed?

"We've lost control of Saxony," Müller said, her voice low. "Die Reiniger has taken Dresden. They're claiming it as their new capital."

Kaufmann felt her breath catch in her throat. Dresden, once one of the cultural gems of Germany, now claimed by a far-right paramilitary group bent on purging the country of anyone who didn't fit their twisted idea of purity. It was the first real blow since they'd left Berlin.

"We've also got reports that Bavaria is seeing a huge influx of refugees," Müller continued, barely looking up. "Migrants from the north and east are flooding Munich and the surrounding areas. The local authorities are overwhelmed."

Kaufmann closed her eyes, feeling the walls close in on her. There was no sanctuary, no place untouched by this disaster. Munich was supposed to be their safe haven, but now it was drowning in the same chaos that had engulfed Berlin.

Munich – The Last Stronghold

By the time the convoy arrived in Munich, dusk had settled over the city. The once-pristine capital of Bavaria was a shadow of its former self. Roads were clogged with makeshift barricades, military checkpoints, and crowds of people—some civilians, some militia fighters, all looking for answers that would never come.

The convoy rolled through the city, escorted by soldiers who scanned the crowds with wary eyes. Everywhere, signs of desperation were evident. People gathered in clusters, holding banners that called for peace, for justice, for help that would never arrive.

Kaufmann gazed out at the streets as the SUV made its way toward the government complex that would serve as their new headquarters. The faces she saw were haunted—refugees, Germans, children, and the elderly—all caught in the same maelstrom of uncertainty. These were her people, and yet she had failed them.

The government complex was a fortress, ringed with barbed wire, sandbags, and heavily armed guards. As the convoy entered, Kaufmann could see helicopters circling overhead, a constant reminder of the precariousness of their position.

Inside, the remaining ministers, military officials, and senior advisors waited in a tense, dimly lit war room. Maps of Germany were spread across the walls, marked with red dots indicating hotspots of violence and unrest. The largest cluster, unsurprisingly, cantered around Berlin, but new flare-ups were now popping up across Bavaria, Saxony, and even the western provinces.

"Chancellor," said Defence Minister Markus Reuter as she entered, "we've received intel suggesting that Die Reiniger is planning a coordinated strike against Munich. They know we're here."

Kaufmann rubbed her temples, trying to think through the fog of exhaustion and despair. "How long do we have?"

"Days, maybe less," Reuter replied. "We've fortified the city, but if they strike in force, we're looking at another Berlin."

"Another Berlin," Kaufmann muttered. The thought was unbearable. Munich had to hold—it was their last refuge. But with the nationalists gaining ground, the military stretched thin, and the migrant crisis worsening by the day, the odds were stacked against them.

General Weber entered the room, his face as grim as ever. "Chancellor, we need to make a decision regarding the incoming refugees. The local authorities can't handle the influx, and tensions are rising. The migrant communities are arming themselves, fearing attacks from both the militias and local residents."

Kaufmann slumped into a chair, the enormity of the situation crashing down on her. Everywhere she looked, there was fire. Every choice seemed like the wrong one. She was supposed to be leading this nation, but now she felt like she was just trying to survive from one moment to the next.

"We can't close the borders to our own people," she said, though the words felt hollow. "But we also can't let this city become another battlefield."

"Then what do we do?" Müller asked, her voice quiet but firm. "We're running out of time."

Kaufmann closed her eyes and took a deep breath. "We have to negotiate. There has to be someone within Die Reiniger who's willing to talk."

Weber snorted, a rare display of emotion from the stoic general. "Negotiate? With those terrorists? Chancellor, they don't want to negotiate—they want to wipe out anyone who doesn't fit into their vision of a pure Germany."

"Maybe," Kaufmann replied, "but if we don't at least try, we'll be condemning this city to war. We can't let Munich fall like Berlin."

There was silence in the room, the weight of her words settling over them like a shroud. No one had a better answer. There were no good choices left, only the least terrible ones.

Tariq's Dilemma

Meanwhile, on the outskirts of Munich, the situation in the migrant communities was reaching a boiling point. Tariq Al-Mansour and his group of Defenders of Al-Quds had managed to flee the devastation of Berlin, but now they found themselves in a city that was just as dangerous. The refugee camps outside Munich were bursting at the seams, with people from all over Germany seeking safety in numbers.

Tariq stood with Hakim in the middle of a crowded camp, watching as families huddled together around makeshift fires. The air was thick with tension—everyone knew that the peace was fragile. Every night, there were rumours of nationalist attacks, and every night, more people armed themselves with whatever they could find.

"We can't stay here much longer," Hakim muttered, scanning the camp with wary eyes. "This place is a powder keg. One spark, and it'll blow."

Tariq nodded, though he didn't know what other options they had. The roads were dangerous, and Munich was already overflowing with refugees. He had heard rumours that the government was preparing to negotiate with the nationalists, but he didn't trust them. After Berlin, he trusted no one but his own people.

"We need to find a way into the city," Tariq said finally. "We need to speak with the government, see if there's any chance of a real solution."

Hakim raised an eyebrow. "You think they'll listen to us? They couldn't even protect us in Berlin."

"Maybe not," Tariq replied, "but if we don't try, this will just keep happening. There has to be a way out of this—before the whole country goes up in flames."

The Countdown Begins

Back in the government complex, the mood was no less tense. Chancellor Kaufmann had sent out feelers to the leadership of Die Reiniger, but so far, there had been no response. Time was running out, and every hour brought new reports of violence and unrest.

As the sun set over Munich, casting long shadows across the city, Kaufmann stood at a window, staring out at the distant mountains. She had never felt more helpless. The city was on the brink of disaster, and her options were dwindling. She had spent her entire career fighting for a better Germany, but now she feared that the country she loved was beyond saving.

"Chancellor," Müller said softly, entering the room, "we've just received word. Die Reiniger has issued a statement."

Kaufmann turned slowly, her heart pounding in her chest. "And?"

Müller handed her a piece of paper, her face pale. "They've rejected any talks. They say there will be no negotiations."

Kaufmann's hands trembled as she read the words. The message was clear: Die Reiniger was coming for Munich, and they would not stop until the city was theirs.

She crumpled the paper in her hand, her mind racing. This was it—the final countdown. The siege of Munich was about to begin, and with it, the last hope for peace in Germany.

As the city braced for war, Kaufmann knew that the next few days would decide the fate of the nation.

Chapter 54: The Siege of Munich

July 2029 – Dawn of the Assault

The morning of the siege began like any other summer day in Bavaria, with a pale blue sky stretching above Munich, dotted by soft clouds that seemed out of place in a city bracing for war. Yet, below the serene sky, Munich was a fortress on the brink of collapse. The streets were eerily quiet, save for the sounds of distant gunfire and the occasional thump of helicopter blades circling above. The air was thick with tension, and an uneasy calm hung over the city, as if everyone was holding their breath for what was to come.

Chancellor Kaufmann stood in the war room; her eyes glued to the massive digital map on the wall. Red markers denoted areas where Die Reiniger had established control, encircling the city like a tightening noose. Munich, once the heart of Bavarian culture and life, had become the last refuge of the federal government—and its last battleground.

"How long until they breach the outer defences?" she asked, her voice hoarse from exhaustion.

General Weber, his face as hard as granite, stood beside her. "Their main forces are just outside the city limits. I'd say we have until sunset before they launch a full assault. We've reinforced the barricades, but we're heavily outnumbered. If they bring in artillery or air support, it'll be over quickly."

Kaufmann bit her lip. "And the refugees?"

Weber glanced at her, his expression unreadable. "We've done what we can to protect them. But the camps outside the city are vulnerable. If Die Reiniger decides to target them, we won't be able to hold them off for long."

The Chancellor's heart sank. She knew what that meant thousands of civilians, mostly migrants, trapped between the advancing nationalist forces and a city on the verge of destruction. They were caught in the crossfire of a war they had no part in starting, but they would pay the highest price.

"Get the helicopters ready for evacuation," she ordered. "We need to get as many people out as we can before the fighting starts."

"Evacuation where?" Weber asked, his tone carrying an edge of scepticism. "There's nowhere left to go, Chancellor. Berlin is gone, Hamburg is under siege, and the borders are closed. Even if we could get them out of the city, where would they go?"

Kaufmann didn't have an answer. Every escape route had been cut off. Europe had closed its doors. Even neighbouring countries like Poland, Switzerland, and Austria had fortified their borders, unwilling to accept any more refugees or risk importing the chaos that had consumed Germany.

But she couldn't give up. Not yet.

"We'll find somewhere," she said, though the words felt hollow.

Weber didn't press the issue, but the silence that followed was filled with grim understanding. Time was running out, and everyone knew it.

Tariq's Resolve

On the outskirts of the city, in one of the sprawling refugee camps, Tariq Al-Mansour paced restlessly. The air was electric with anxiety as rumours of the impending siege spread like wildfire. Families huddled together in tents, some praying, others staring blankly at the horizon, as if waiting for the apocalypse to arrive. And for many, that's exactly what this felt like—the end of everything.

Hakim approached, his face tense. "We need to make a decision, brother. We can't stay here when the fighting starts."

Tariq nodded. He had known this moment was coming, but the reality of it was still difficult to face. "Where would we go?"

Hakim glanced toward the city. "We could try to make it into Munich, but it's dangerous. The government is barely holding on, and the nationalist militias are closing in from all sides. But if we stay here..."

He didn't need to finish the sentence. They both knew that staying in the camp was a death sentence. Die Reiniger had made it clear—they viewed the migrants and refugees as enemies, intruders who needed to be purged. When the siege began, the camps would be among the first targets.

Tariq looked around at the people in the camp. Men, women, children—people who had fled the violence of the Middle East and North Africa only to find themselves trapped in a new war in Europe. They had come seeking safety, but there was none to be found.

"We'll take as many people as we can into the city," Tariq said finally. "At least there, we have a chance."

Hakim's eyes narrowed. "You think the Germans will welcome us with open arms? They're barely holding it together themselves. We'll be walking into another warzone."

"Maybe," Tariq admitted. "But we can't stay here and wait to be slaughtered."

Hakim sighed, nodding in agreement. "You're right. I'll gather the others."

As Hakim moved off to organize the group, Tariq felt a heavy weight settle on his shoulders. He had become a leader, not by choice but by necessity. Now, the lives of dozens—maybe hundreds—of people rested on his decisions. And with each passing hour, the pressure mounted.

The First Strike

By mid-afternoon, the first sounds of battle reached the heart of Munich. Distant explosions echoed through the city, followed by the sharp crackle of gunfire. In the war room, Kaufmann and her ministers watched as the red markers on the map began to move closer and closer to the city center.

"They've breached the first line of defence," Weber reported grimly. "Our forces are falling back to the second perimeter."

"How long can we hold them off?" Müller asked, her voice trembling slightly.

Weber shook his head. "Hours, maybe less. They're hitting us with everything they've got."

Kaufmann felt a cold sweat break out on her forehead. The siege had begun, and Munich was quickly becoming a battlefield.

Outside the government complex, the streets of Munich were in chaos. Tanks rumbled down the boulevards, soldiers moved from building to building, setting up defensive positions, while civilians hurried to find shelter wherever they could. Many had already fled the city in the days leading up to the siege, but for those who remained, there was nowhere left to run.

In the refugee camp, Tariq and his group were making their way toward the city gates. Dozens of people followed them—families carrying what little they had left, children clutching their parents' hands, faces pale with fear. Behind them, the distant sounds of the battle grew louder with each passing minute.

"We're almost there," Hakim said, pointing toward the gates of Munich, where soldiers were setting up a checkpoint.

But as they approached, a group of armed men appeared on the road ahead—members of Die Reiniger, their white armbands clearly visible even from a distance. They had cut off the road leading into the city, and they were heavily armed.

"Get down!" Tariq shouted, pushing the nearest group of refugees toward the ditch at the side of the road. Bullets whizzed past them as the nationalists opened fire, cutting through the air with deadly precision. Panic erupted in the group, and people scrambled for cover, some running back toward the camp, others dropping to the ground in terror.

Hakim returned fire, but he was outgunned and outnumbered. "We can't stay here!" he shouted. "We need to get out of the open!"

Tariq gritted his teeth, scanning the area for any possible escape route. But they were pinned down, caught between the nationalist fighters and the city walls. The very gates of Munich that had once promised safety now seemed like an unreachable dream.

"We're trapped," Hakim muttered, his voice laced with despair.

The Collapse

Back in the war room, the situation was deteriorating rapidly. Reports flooded in from all over the city—Die Reiniger had breached the second perimeter, and their forces were pushing deeper into Munich with every passing hour.

"Chancellor," General Weber said, his voice tight with urgency, "we need to consider evacuation. If we stay here, we'll be overrun."

Kaufmann looked at him, her face pale but determined. "And leave the city to them? Abandon the people?"

"There's nothing more we can do," Weber replied bluntly. "Our forces are outnumbered, and we're losing ground fast. If we don't leave now, we'll be trapped."

Kaufmann's eyes flicked to the map on the wall, where the red markers of the nationalist forces were closing in on the government complex. She had spent her entire career fighting for a united Germany, for a country that could rise above its divisions and build a better future. But now, in the face of this catastrophe, all her ideals seemed like distant dreams.

"Prepare the evacuation," she said quietly. "But I'm staying."

Weber and Müller both turned to her in shock. "Chancellor, you can't—"

"I'm not abandoning the people of Munich," Kaufmann interrupted, her voice firm. "If this city falls, I'll fall with it."

And so, as the siege of Munich raged on, the Chancellor of Germany made her final stand.

Outside the walls, Tariq and his group were still pinned down, fighting for survival as the battle for the soul of Germany reached its climax.

Chapter 55: The Fall of Munich

July 2029 – The Turning Point

The air was thick with smoke as dusk settled over Munich. Flames danced across the skyline, casting an eerie orange glow that reflected the city's collapse. Buildings that had once symbolized Bavarian heritage were now smouldering ruins. The hum of military vehicles, the sharp crack of gunfire, and the distant cries of the wounded were the only sounds cutting through the oppressive silence of a city under siege.

Inside the fortified war room, Chancellor Kaufmann stood before the map, watching as the red markers—the nationalist forces—continued their unrelenting advance. Despite the best efforts of the federal troops, Die Reiniger had broken through the final perimeter. It was only a matter of time before they reached the government complex.

The once-united Germany was fracturing before her eyes.

"Chancellor, they've breached the city center," General Weber reported, his voice gruff but tinged with the weariness of a man who had seen too much battle. "We're losing control of the northern districts. I recommend a full-scale retreat."

Kaufmann's eyes flickered to the general. Her face, usually composed, was etched with lines of fatigue. She hadn't slept in days, nor had she left the war room except for brief moments of respite. The city—her country—was falling apart around her, and she knew the time for retreat had long passed.

"Retreat where?" she asked softly, though the question was rhetorical. There was no safe haven left. Munich had been their last stronghold, and now it was burning.

Weber exchanged glances with his officers, then turned back to the Chancellor. "We've already evacuated most of the government officials, but there's still time for you. The helicopters are ready."

Kaufmann shook her head. "I'm not leaving this city."

"You'll be killed if you stay," Weber warned, his voice rising slightly. "Die Reiniger won't show mercy, especially to the head of the federal government. You're a symbol to them—a target."

The Chancellor's jaw clenched. "This city—these people—they've put their faith in me. If I abandon them now, I'm no better than those who created this mess in the first place. I made a choice to fight for a united Germany, and I will die with it if I have to."

Weber stared at her for a long moment before finally nodding. "Then we fight."

Kaufmann turned back to the map, her fingers trailing over the red encroaching zones. There was no longer any strategy to deploy, no last-minute solution that could turn the tide. This wasn't just a battle for Munich anymore; it was the final chapter in a long war that had fractured Europe.

Tariq's Desperate Gambit

At the southern gates of the city, Tariq and his group had narrowly escaped the nationalist ambush earlier in the day. The group of refugees he had taken under his wing huddled together, hidden in the rubble of a bombed-out church. Night was falling, and with it came a sense of growing dread.

"We can't stay here," Hakim said, crouching beside Tariq. His eyes darted to the shadows beyond their shelter. "The city is falling apart, and the nationalist patrols are getting closer. We need to find a way out."

Tariq nodded grimly. "But where do we go? The gates are sealed, and the roads are blocked. We're surrounded."

Hakim looked out at the crumbling city beyond the church walls. "Maybe we can get into the government complex. It's the most fortified place left in the city."

Tariq hesitated. The idea of seeking refuge with the very government that had failed to protect them seemed like a bitter irony. But they had no other options. The nationalists had already begun targeting the refugee camps outside the city, slaughtering anyone they deemed an enemy of their cause. Staying in the open meant certain death.

"Alright," Tariq agreed finally. "We'll head for the complex, but we need to move carefully. If we're caught..."

Hakim didn't need to hear the rest. The stakes were clear.

Gathering the group—a mix of families, elderly men, and frightened children—Tariq led them through the rubble-strewn streets of Munich. The city had become a labyrinth of destruction, with entire neighbourhoods reduced to ash and debris. Smoke billowed from collapsed buildings, and the distant sounds of gunfire echoed through the night, growing closer with each passing hour.

As they crept toward the government complex, Tariq's heart pounded in his chest. Every step felt like it could be their last.

The Siege Intensifies

By midnight, the battle for Munich had reached a fever pitch. Die Reiniger's forces had penetrated deep into the city, and their troops were closing in on the government complex from all directions. Federal soldiers, outnumbered and exhausted, fought valiantly to hold their ground, but it was a losing battle.

Inside the complex, Chancellor Kaufmann paced the war room. Reports of casualties and territory losses streamed in, each more dire than the last. The nationalists were now only a few blocks away.

"We need to secure the inner perimeter," Weber barked at his remaining officers. "No one gets in or out without our say."

But even as the general issued his orders, the sounds of fighting could be heard just beyond the walls. The war had come to the heart of the government.

"How long do we have?" Kaufmann asked, her voice low.

Weber looked at her, his face grim. "An hour, maybe less."

The Chancellor's hands clenched into fists. She had spent her life fighting for Germany—for the ideals of democracy, unity, and progress. But all of that was unravelling before her eyes, and she was powerless to stop it.

A sudden explosion rocked the building, sending a shower of dust and debris falling from the ceiling. Weber's officers scrambled, barking orders into their radios, but it was clear the end was near.

"We can still get you out of here, Chancellor," Weber urged, his voice tense. "There's a secret tunnel that leads out of the complex. It's our last chance."

Kaufmann shook her head. "I'm staying. I made my choice."

Weber stared at her for a moment, then nodded. "Then we'll defend this place to the last man."

Tariq's Last Stand

As Tariq and his group approached the government complex, the sounds of battle grew deafening. The air was filled with the stench of burning buildings and gunpowder. Federal soldiers had set up barricades outside the gates, their faces etched with the same grim determination that had carried them through the siege.

"Stay low," Tariq whispered to the group as they crouched behind a wall. "We need to make it past the barricades."

But before they could move, a group of Die Reiniger fighters appeared at the far end of the street. Their white armbands gleamed in the moonlight as they advanced toward the government complex, rifles raised.

"We're out of time," Hakim muttered.

Tariq's heart raced. If they didn't act now, they would be caught in the crossfire.

"Go!" he shouted, pushing the group toward the complex gates. "Run!"

The refugees bolted toward the barricades, but the nationalists opened fire. Bullets whizzed past them, striking the ground and sending up plumes of dust. Tariq grabbed a young boy who had fallen behind and dragged him forward, his legs burning with the effort.

Federal soldiers at the barricades saw them and waved them forward, covering their retreat with gunfire. Tariq and his group scrambled through the gates just as the nationalists reached the barricades.

Inside the complex, chaos reigned. Soldiers rushed to defend the inner walls, while government officials scrambled to evacuate the last remaining personnel. Tariq led his group to a corner of the courtyard, trying to catch his breath.

"We made it," Hakim panted, collapsing beside him.

But as Tariq looked around at the burning city and the soldiers preparing for their final stand, he realized the truth. They had made it this far, but the fight was far from over.

The nationalists were closing in, and the fall of Munich was imminent.

The End of an Era

In the war room, Chancellor Kaufmann stood before the map one last time. The red markers had reached the government complex. The siege of Munich was almost over.

She closed her eyes for a moment, allowing herself a brief moment of reflection. This wasn't how she had envisioned the end. She had hoped for peace, for unity—but all she had found was war and division.

As the sounds of gunfire echoed through the halls of the government building, Kaufmann opened her eyes and faced the reality of the situation. The fall of Munich wasn't just the fall of a city—it was the fall of an era. The Germany she had fought for was gone, replaced by a fractured and war-torn nation.

And now, as the final battle raged on, she knew that the fight for the future of Europe had only just begun.

Chapter 56: The Aftermath of Munich

August 2029 – A Broken City

The air in Munich was thick with the scent of burnt wood, smoke, and death. The once proud Bavarian city, the heart of Germany's historical identity, now lay in ruins. The fall of Munich marked a significant turning point in the European crisis—a final, symbolic collapse that reverberated across the continent.

In the wake of the battle, the streets were eerily quiet. The relentless sound of gunfire had ceased, replaced by the soft hum of drones surveying the wreckage, and the occasional groan of a building collapsing under the weight of its own destruction. Bodies, both civilian and military, lay scattered throughout the streets, unburied and ignored as survivors focused on the grim task of salvaging what little remained.

Tariq sat in the remnants of an old café, its windows shattered, its interior charred. He and the few survivors of his group were huddled together, waiting. Their faces were drawn, their eyes hollowed out by days of fear and exhaustion. The government complex had fallen, and the city had descended into chaos, leaving them with nowhere to go.

"How long are we going to stay here?" Hakim asked, his voice quiet. He had aged ten years in the past few days, the lines on his face deepening, his spirit worn down by the constant fight for survival.

"I don't know," Tariq replied, staring at the ruined street outside. "But we can't stay here forever. The nationalists have taken over the city."

Hakim clenched his jaw, his eyes flickering with anger. "And what happens to us when they find us? They'll kill us like they did to everyone else."

Tariq didn't have an answer. He had witnessed the brutality of Die Reiniger firsthand. The nationalist movement had promised to cleanse Germany, to rid it of outsiders and restore the country to its former glory, but all they had brought was death and destruction. Refugees like them were nothing more than enemies in their eyes.

"We need to move," Tariq said finally. "Maybe there's a way out of the city."

Hakim glanced at him sceptically. "And where will we go? Everywhere else is just as bad."

Tariq sighed, running a hand through his hair. He didn't know where to go, but staying meant certain death. The fight for Munich was over, and they had lost.

The Collapse of German Federal Authority

The fall of Munich marked the de facto collapse of federal authority in Germany. What remained of the government had fled the city in the final hours of the siege, leaving a power vacuum that Die Reiniger was quick to fill. Across the country, similar nationalist groups seized the moment to take control of their regions, proclaiming the death of the federal system and the birth of a new, fractured Germany.

In Berlin, the former seat of the German government, confusion reigned. Chancellor Kaufmann had perished in the final hours of the battle, a victim of the very conflict she had tried so hard to prevent. Her death sent shockwaves throughout the remaining federal institutions, and within days, the fragile threads that had held the government together snapped.

The nationalists wasted no time in declaring victory. In a public address, Leonhard Vogel, leader of Die Reiniger, proclaimed the establishment of the "Germanic Federation"—a loose coalition of nationalist states united by their desire to purge the country of foreign influence and restore what they considered the true German identity.

The message was clear: Germany, as it had existed, was no more.

International Repercussions

The fall of Munich and the collapse of the German federal government sent shockwaves through Europe. In France, President Delacroix called an emergency meeting of the European Union leadership to discuss the rapidly deteriorating situation, but it was clear that the EU's ability to control the crisis was waning. The union, already fractured by years of political infighting and nationalist uprisings, was now facing an existential threat.

The United Kingdom, having distanced itself from the crisis following its own struggles with the migrant situation, declared a state of emergency and closed its borders entirely. Prime Minister Thompson delivered a grim address to the nation, warning of the growing instability on the continent and vowing to protect the UK at all costs. The military was deployed along the southern coastline, and the government increased surveillance of Muslim communities, fearing a rise in extremist activity as tensions continued to escalate.

In the United States, the crisis in Europe dominated the news cycle. President Carter, under pressure from both political parties, debated whether to intervene. America had watched from afar as the crisis unfolded, but now, with Germany in chaos and Europe on the brink of war, the question of intervention loomed large. The administration was torn between the desire to stabilize the region and the fear of being dragged into another costly and endless conflict.

As Europe teetered on the edge of collapse, world leaders scrambled to find a solution. But it was becoming increasingly clear that the problems they faced—decades of political mismanagement, the failure to integrate migrant populations, and the rise of nationalism—were not problems that could be solved overnight.

Leonhard Vogel's Vision

In the heart of Munich, Leonhard Vogel stood on a makeshift stage in Marienplatz, flanked by nationalist soldiers in crisp white uniforms, their insignia glinting in the fading sunlight. Thousands of people gathered in the square, their faces a mix of hope, anger, and desperation. The city had been ravaged by war, but to Vogel's supporters, it represented a new beginning—a chance to rebuild Germany in their image.

Vogel was a commanding figure. His speeches had ignited the fires of nationalism across the country, and now, with Munich under his control, he was the undisputed leader of the new Germanic Federation. The crowd watched in silence as he stepped forward, his voice booming through the speakers set up around the square.

"Brothers and sisters," he began, "today marks the beginning of a new era. An era where we, the people of Germany, will no longer be dictated to by foreign powers, corrupt elites, or outsiders who do not belong."

Cheers erupted from the crowd, but Vogel raised a hand to quiet them.

"For too long, we have been made to feel ashamed of who we are. Our culture, our traditions, our very identity has been eroded by those who seek to turn us into something we are not. But no more. Today, we reclaim our birthright. Today, we build a Germany for Germans."

The cheers grew louder, reverberating off the broken walls of the surrounding buildings.

"We will not be intimidated by the weak and cowardly leaders of Europe. We will not be threatened by their armies or their sanctions. Germany is strong, and we will show the world that we are not afraid to fight for our future."

As Vogel spoke, Tariq watched from the shadows of a nearby building. His blood ran cold. This was the man who had led the destruction of Munich, the man who had unleashed Die Reiniger on the refugees, killing anyone who stood in his way.

Vogel's words echoed in Tariq's mind as he turned to Hakim, who had joined him at the edge of the crowd.

"We have to leave," Tariq whispered. "We can't stay here."

Hakim nodded, his face pale. "But where will we go?"

"I don't know," Tariq admitted, his heart heavy. "But we can't stay in Munich. This city isn't safe anymore."

Together, they slipped away from the crowd, blending into the shadows as Vogel continued his speech. As they made their way through the ruined streets, Tariq knew that the fight for survival was far from over. Munich had fallen, but the war was just beginning.

Chapter 57: The Exodus

August 2029 – The Road Out

Munich was no longer a city but a scar on the landscape. The destruction had reached every corner, transforming once-vibrant neighbourhoods into piles of rubble. Tariq, Hakim, and the remaining refugees trudged through the outskirts, each step feeling heavier than the last. The road ahead was uncertain, but they had no choice. Munich had become a death trap.

The streets were eerily quiet, the silence punctuated only by the distant rumbles of explosions or the faint crackle of fires still burning in the city's core. As they made their way through the ruined streets, Tariq kept a watchful eye on the surrounding buildings. Danger lurked around every corner, from nationalist patrols to desperate scavengers willing to kill for a loaf of bread.

"We need to find water," said Fatima, a mother carrying her young daughter, her voice weak with exhaustion. She had joined Tariq's group during the siege, fleeing the nationalist purge in her own neighbourhood.

Tariq nodded grimly. They had barely escaped with their lives, and while the chaos of Munich had momentarily shielded them, survival now meant facing new challenges. Dehydration, hunger, and the gnawing fear that Die Reiniger might still be hunting them weighed heavily on his mind.

"We'll stop soon," he promised. "Just a little further. We need to reach the forest before nightfall."

Hakim walked beside him, his face drawn with fatigue. He had been the voice of reason throughout the siege, but even he seemed unsure now. The forest on the outskirts of Munich represented their only hope—an escape route through the trees, away from the watchful eyes of Vogel's forces. But the forest also carried its own dangers, not least of which was the unknown.

"You think they'll follow us?" Hakim asked quietly, his eyes scanning the deserted street behind them.

Tariq shook his head. "I don't know. Maybe they're too busy celebrating their victory."

But neither of them believed it. Die Reiniger had been methodical in their purge of refugees, and Tariq knew they wouldn't stop until they had rooted out every last one.

The group trudged forward in silence, a sense of unease settling over them as they approached the edge of the city. Behind them, Munich smouldered, its skyline now marked by smoke and collapsed buildings. Ahead, the trees loomed like a dark, foreboding wall.

The Forest Refuge

By late afternoon, the group had reached the forest's edge. The cool shade of the trees offered some respite from the heat and the oppressive atmosphere of the city. Tariq and Hakim scouted ahead, weaving through the dense foliage as they searched for a suitable place to camp.

The forest was quiet, unnervingly so. Every rustle of leaves or snap of a twig put them on edge, as if the trees themselves were hiding enemies. But there was no choice. They couldn't remain in the open, not with Vogel's forces combing the city and its outskirts for any stragglers.

"This should do," Tariq said, finally stopping in a small clearing surrounded by thick undergrowth. "We'll rest here for the night."

Hakim surveyed the area, nodding in agreement. "It's hidden enough. We should be safe, at least for a few hours."

They returned to the group, who had collapsed at the edge of the forest in exhaustion. Fatima and her daughter, along with the others, settled into the clearing, grateful for a moment of rest. There was a palpable sense of relief among them, but it was tinged with fear—fear of what lay ahead, fear of what they had left behind.

"Do you think anyone made it out of the city?" Fatima asked, her voice trembling.

Tariq hesitated, unsure of how to respond. "I hope so," he said finally. "But we can't think about that now. We have to focus on getting ourselves out of this."

The group sat in silence, the weight of their situation settling over them like a heavy blanket. The forest provided shelter, but it was also a reminder of how far they had fallen. There was no plan, no destination. They were simply trying to survive.

The Hunt Begins

Nightfall brought new dangers. As darkness descended over the forest, Tariq couldn't shake the feeling that they were being watched. The distant sounds of the city had faded, replaced by the eerie silence of the woods, but the sensation of unseen eyes lingered.

"Do you hear that?" Hakim asked, his voice low. He had been keeping watch with Tariq while the others rested.

Tariq strained his ears, but heard nothing. "What?"

"I don't know," Hakim muttered, frowning. "It's too quiet. Like something's out there."

Tariq nodded, gripping the small knife he had scavenged from a fallen soldier. It was their only weapon, and it offered little comfort against the possibility of an armed patrol.

As the hours stretched on, Tariq's nerves began to fray. Every crack of a branch or rustle of leaves sent his heart racing. But it wasn't until just before dawn that his worst fears were confirmed.

A faint light flickered through the trees—flashlights. And the distant murmur of voices reached his ears. They weren't alone.

Tariq crouched beside Hakim, his breath catching in his throat. "They're coming."

Hakim cursed under his breath. "Die Reiniger?"

"Who else?"

The group had been careful, avoiding major roads and keeping to the shadows, but it hadn't been enough. Vogel's forces were relentless, determined to wipe out every last trace of resistance or refugee from the city.

"We have to move," Tariq whispered, glancing toward the others, who were still sleeping. "Now."

Hakim nodded, his face tense. "Wake them. Quietly."

One by one, Tariq and Hakim roused the others, their movements quick but cautious. Fatima clutched her daughter tightly, her eyes wide with fear as she realized what was happening.

"Are they here?" she whispered.

Tariq nodded grimly. "We don't have much time."

Without a word, the group began to slip through the trees, moving as silently as they could. The flashlights in the distance grew brighter, the voices louder. Die Reiniger was closing in.

Escape or Capture

The forest became a maze of shadows as the group fled, their footsteps barely audible on the soft forest floor. Tariq led the way, his heart pounding in his chest as he searched for a way out—any path that would take them deeper into the forest and away from their pursuers.

But it wasn't enough. The nationalists were too close, their searchlights sweeping through the trees like the gaze of a predator.

"They're gaining on us," Hakim hissed, glancing over his shoulder. "We can't outrun them."

Tariq knew he was right. Their group was too slow, weighed down by fatigue and fear. They had been running for days, and now, when they needed to move the fastest, their bodies were betraying them.

"We have to split up," Tariq said suddenly, his mind racing. "If we all stay together, they'll catch us. But if we spread out, some of us might make it."

Hakim stared at him in disbelief. "You're serious?"

Tariq nodded. "It's the only way."

The others had overheard and were already looking panicked. Fatima shook her head, clutching her daughter closer. "No, we can't split up! We won't survive!"

"We won't survive if we stay together, either," Tariq said firmly. "Listen to me. We split into groups, and we meet up again at dawn. If you find a safe place, wait there. But we have to do this now."

Hakim hesitated, then nodded. "Alright. But if we don't make it..."

Tariq gripped his shoulder. "We'll make it."

With a heavy heart, Tariq watched as the group split into smaller factions, each disappearing into the trees. He stayed behind, helping Fatima and her daughter as they struggled to move quickly. Hakim disappeared into the darkness, his figure soon swallowed by the forest.

For a moment, the silence returned, and Tariq dared to hope that they had slipped away unnoticed. But then the sound of a branch snapping nearby shattered that hope.

Flashlights appeared again, much closer this time. Tariq's heart leaped into his throat. They had been spotted.

Without thinking, he grabbed Fatima's hand and pulled her forward. "Run!"

The forest erupted into chaos as the nationalists gave chase, their shouts echoing through the trees. Tariq ran, his legs burning, his lungs screaming for air. But no matter how fast they moved, the lights grew closer.

And then, just as the trees began to thin, Tariq heard the unmistakable sound of gunfire

Chapter 58: Caught in the Crossfire

August 2029 – The Gunfire

The sharp crack of gunfire echoed through the forest, slicing through the dawn's eerie silence. Tariq's heart pounded in his chest as he ducked low, pulling Fatima and her daughter behind a thick cluster of trees. The once still forest had erupted into a frenzy, the calm shattered by the chaos of pursuit.

The beams of flashlights swept through the trees like searchlights on a battlefield, erratic but unrelenting, each beam representing the imminent danger of discovery. Tariq could feel the pulse of the earth beneath his feet, a mix of his own terror and the heavy footsteps of Die Reiniger's men closing in from behind.

"We can't outrun them forever," Hakim whispered, crouching beside Tariq. His face was smeared with dirt, his eyes wide with fear but still resolute. "We have to find another way."

Tariq nodded, his mind racing. They were outnumbered and outgunned, with nowhere to hide. The forest, once a place of refuge, had become a death trap. Every direction seemed blocked, the underbrush thick and suffocating. The only thing that kept them alive was the darkness and the terrain, but even that advantage was slipping away.

"We need to split up again," Tariq whispered, his voice barely audible over the rising panic in the group.

Fatima, holding her daughter close, looked at Tariq with desperate eyes. "No, we can't! We're stronger together—"

"We don't have a choice," Tariq interrupted, his voice firmer this time. "If we stay together, we're too easy to spot. We split up and meet at the river. It's our only chance."

Hakim glanced toward the direction of the approaching flashlights. "He's right. We can cover more ground and maybe confuse them long enough to slip away."

Fatima hesitated, her face tight with worry, but she eventually nodded, clutching her daughter's hand even tighter. "Alright," she whispered. "Just... please... don't leave us behind."

Tariq gave her a brief, reassuring nod before turning to Hakim. "You take the others and head east. I'll take Fatima and her daughter to the west. We'll meet at the river."

With a silent understanding, the group split once more, each pair or small cluster disappearing into the shadows. Tariq took Fatima's hand and led her westward, the thick undergrowth tugging at their legs, slowing their progress. Behind them, the sound of gunfire continued to crack the air, followed by the heavy crunch of boots through the foliage.

The Chase

As Tariq, Fatima, and her daughter pushed forward, the forest seemed to close in on them, the trees bending low as if to block their escape. The distant roar of the river gave Tariq a flicker of hope—it was their rendezvous point, and if they could reach it, they might be able to lose their pursuers in the fast-flowing waters.

Fatima stumbled, her foot catching on a root, and her daughter gasped in pain as they both fell to the ground. Tariq quickly knelt down, helping them up, his ears attuned to the sounds behind them. The flashlights were getting closer, and he could hear the occasional shout, the men barking orders in the distance.

"We're almost there," he whispered, though he wasn't sure if it was true. The river still felt too far away.

Fatima winced, her ankle twisted from the fall, but she pressed on without complaint. Her daughter, silent and wide-eyed, clung to her, too frightened to speak.

They moved as quickly as they could, but the pace was agonizingly slow. Every step felt like a betrayal of their need to hurry. Tariq's muscles burned, fatigue creeping in as the night wore on. Still, they pressed forward, the forest stretching endlessly ahead.

Then, suddenly, a flashlight beam swept across the trees just a few yards behind them.

"They're here!" Hakim's voice rang out from somewhere to the east, a sharp warning that sent a jolt of adrenaline through Tariq.

He turned and saw the dark silhouettes of nationalist soldiers moving through the trees, their rifles raised. Tariq's heart leapt into his throat. They were surrounded.

Without thinking, he grabbed Fatima's arm and pulled her into a thick grove of bushes, crouching low to the ground. The foliage provided some cover, but it wasn't enough to completely hide them.

"Stay low. Don't make a sound," Tariq whispered.

Fatima nodded, holding her daughter close, her entire body trembling.

The soldiers' footsteps grew louder, and Tariq could hear their voices now—sharp, barking commands in German. They were methodically sweeping the forest, closing in on anyone left behind. Tariq's breath hitched as one of the soldiers paused mere feet from their hiding spot, his flashlight sweeping across the bushes.

For a moment, it felt as though time stood still. Tariq could hear the soldier breathing, could see the faint glow of his cigarette as he stood there, scanning the area.

Please, don't see us, Tariq prayed silently.

The soldier moved on, his flashlight beam disappearing into the trees once again. But the danger hadn't passed. The gunfire in the distance intensified, and Tariq knew the others were still being hunted.

"We have to move," he whispered to Fatima. "Now."

They crept out of the bushes and continued westward, their movements cautious and deliberate. Every sound in the forest seemed magnified—the crunch of leaves underfoot, the snap of a twig. Tariq's nerves were frayed, his senses on high alert. He could feel the cold sweat dripping down his back, his hands shaking with fear.

The river

Finally, after what felt like hours, the roar of the river grew louder. The trees thinned, and the underbrush gave way to a rocky embankment. Tariq could see the water now, a dark, rushing torrent that offered both salvation and danger.

"We made it," Tariq breathed, though there was no time to celebrate.

Fatima stumbled to the edge of the river, clutching her daughter tightly. The little girl looked pale, her wide eyes reflecting the fear of the night's ordeal. Tariq quickly scanned the area, looking for any sign of Hakim or the others.

"They're not here yet," Fatima whispered, her voice tight with worry.

Tariq bit his lip. He had expected them to arrive by now, but there was no sign of movement in the trees. The only sound was the rushing water and the distant echo of gunfire.

"We'll wait for them," Tariq said, though uncertainty gnawed at him.

As the minutes ticked by, the unease grew. Tariq crouched by the riverbank, watching the dark waters swirl and crash against the rocks. His mind raced, trying to calculate their next move. If Hakim and the others didn't show up soon, they would have to cross the river on their own. But crossing the river was dangerous—the current was fast, and they risked being swept away.

Just as Tariq was about to suggest moving on, he heard footsteps approaching from the trees. His heart leapt—Hakim!

But the relief was short-lived.

Emerging from the shadows, a group of nationalist soldiers appeared, their flashlights flickering through the trees. They had found them.

Tariq froze, his mind racing. There was no time to run, no time to hide. The soldiers raised their rifles, their eyes locking onto Tariq, Fatima, and her daughter.

For a moment, everything seemed to slow down. Tariq could hear the pounding of his own heartbeat, feel the cold sweat trickling down his spine. He knew there was no escape. The soldiers had them trapped.

"Get down!" one of the soldiers barked in German, his rifle trained on Tariq.

Tariq raised his hands slowly, his heart hammering in his chest. He glanced at Fatima, who held her daughter tightly, tears streaming down her face. This was it. They were caught.

But just as the soldiers stepped closer, something unexpected happened.

A gunshot rang out from the trees. Then another. The soldiers whirled around, their attention momentarily diverted.

Tariq didn't hesitate. "Run!" he shouted, grabbing Fatima's arm and pulling her toward the river.

They sprinted toward the rushing water as chaos erupted behind them. More gunfire crackled through the air, and Tariq could hear the shouts of the soldiers as they returned fire. He didn't look back. There was no time.

With a final burst of adrenaline, Tariq plunged into the river, the cold water engulfing him as he fought against the powerful current. Fatima and her daughter followed, their terrified screams drowned out by the roar of the water.

They were swept downstream, the force of the river pulling them away from the gunfire and into the unknown.

To the Unknown

The current was relentless, dragging them along at breakneck speed. Tariq struggled to keep his head above water, his limbs flailing as he fought to stay afloat. Fatima and her daughter were close by, their screams mingling with the sound of rushing water.

"Hold on!" Tariq shouted, though his voice was barely audible over the roar of the river.

The water was icy cold, numbing his body as it pulled him downstream. His muscles burned with exhaustion, but he forced himself to keep going. They had escaped the soldiers, but now the river posed its own deadly challenge.

The night had been a blur of chaos, and now, as they were swept toward the unknown, Tariq could only hope that they would survive the river's wrath. But for now, they had escaped the immediate threat.

Where the river would take them, Tariq didn't know.

All that mattered was that they were still alive.

Chapter 59: The Divided Path

September 2029 – Uncertain Shores

The cold, rushing water had swallowed Tariq whole. He couldn't tell how long he had been submerged, but when he finally surfaced, gasping for air, he was alone. The roar of the river had quieted to a steady hum as it flowed beneath him, its currents now slower and less violent. The shore was rocky and jagged, but at least he was out of the immediate danger.

Panic surged through him as he looked around, his eyes desperately searching for any sign of Fatima or her daughter. They had been right behind him when they entered the water. Where were they?

"Fatima!" he shouted, his voice hoarse and barely audible over the river's current. There was no reply, only the eerie stillness of the dawn breaking around him. The forest had receded to distant shadows, the oppressive closeness of the trees giving way to a more open landscape. But it wasn't freedom. It was uncertainty.

Tariq pulled himself to the shore, his limbs trembling with exhaustion. The chill from the river had seeped deep into his bones, leaving him shaking uncontrollably. His clothes were drenched, clinging to his skin, making every movement feel like a battle. But he didn't stop. He couldn't afford to. He dragged himself up onto the rocky shore, every breath a painful reminder that he was still alive.

"Fatima..." he whispered again, his voice trailing off into the emptiness around him. He knew he had to find them, had to keep moving. The nationalist soldiers were still out there, and though the river had bought them time, it wouldn't stop the relentless pursuit.

With immense effort, Tariq staggered to his feet, his body weak but his resolve unbroken. His eyes scanned the riverbank, hoping for a sign of life—a splash, a voice, anything. But there was nothing.

His thoughts raced. The river had carried them all downstream, but with the strong current, they could have been separated by miles. He didn't have time to dwell on the fear that gripped him. He needed a plan. If Fatima and her daughter had survived, they would be looking for him, too.

A Glimpse of Hope

Tariq stumbled along the riverbank, his legs shaky but moving with purpose. As he walked, the terrain began to change, the harsh, rocky shore giving way to softer sand and patches of tall grass. The oppressive weight of the forest began to ease, and Tariq could see distant hills rising on the horizon. There was a faint path that ran along the river, barely visible through the overgrowth, but it was something—a direction, a guide.

He followed the path, his eyes scanning the river for any sign of life. The sun was beginning to rise, casting a pale orange glow over the landscape. He hadn't realized how long they had been in the water. Time seemed to slip away in moments of terror.

Then, in the distance, he spotted something—a figure, small and hunched over by the water's edge. His heart leapt into his throat as he broke into a run, his exhaustion momentarily forgotten.

"Fatima!" he shouted, his voice cracking with desperation.

The figure didn't move. As Tariq drew closer, he realized it wasn't Fatima. It was a man, his clothes soaked and torn, his face pale with fear. One of the refugees, like them.

The man looked up, startled by Tariq's approach. He was injured blood stained his shirt, and his arm hung limply at his side.

"Help... please..." the man rasped; his voice weak.

Tariq's heart sank. This wasn't who he had hoped to find, but he couldn't leave the man here to die.

"Hold on," Tariq said, kneeling beside him. "I'll help you."

The man groaned in pain as Tariq carefully examined his injury. It wasn't good—the wound was deep, likely from shrapnel or a stray bullet. But it wasn't immediately fatal. Tariq tore a piece of fabric from his own shirt and wrapped it tightly around the wound, doing his best to stop the bleeding.

"Where... where are the others?" the man asked, his voice trembling. "We got separated... in the water..."

Tariq shook his head. "I don't know. I'm looking for them too."

The man winced in pain, his eyes glazing over with fatigue. "I think... they're further downstream... I saw... a woman... and a little girl. They were heading toward the hills."

Tariq's heart raced. "Fatima? Where? How far?"

The man shook his head weakly. "I don't know... not far... I think..."

279

Tariq stood, his mind racing. Fatima and her daughter were alive. They had made it out of the water, and they were close.

"I'll help you," Tariq said to the man, pulling him to his feet. "But we have to move. We can't stay here."

The man nodded weakly, leaning heavily on Tariq as they began to walk. The path along the river was treacherous, but they pressed on, driven by the hope of finding Fatima and the fear of being caught by Die Reiniger's men.

A Gathering Storm

As they walked, Tariq's mind was filled with dread. The war between the nationalist militias and the refugees was escalating, and every day brought more violence, more death. The fragile peace that Europe had known for decades was unravelling, and now it seemed as though the entire continent was on the brink of collapse.

Tariq couldn't help but think of the countless warnings that had gone unheeded. Years of political tensions, religious divisions, and mass migration had finally boiled over into a full-blown conflict, and there was no turning back. The streets of Paris, Berlin, and London were battlegrounds now, with both sides unwilling to relent.

But it wasn't just Europe that was in turmoil. The entire world was watching, waiting to see how this conflict would unfold. Nations that had once prided themselves on their human rights and democratic values were now turning a blind eye to the atrocities being committed in their own backyards.

The fragile alliances between governments were crumbling, and the rise of nationalist parties had shifted the political landscape in ways that no one had anticipated. Even within the European Union, leaders were at odds, some calling for stronger borders and stricter immigration policies, while others pushed for diplomacy and humanitarian aid.

But it was too late for diplomacy. The streets were on fire, and the divide between Christian and Muslim communities had reached a breaking point. What had started as a migrant crisis had become a full-blown religious war.

Tariq could see the tension in every village they passed, every town they approached. The fear and hatred were palpable, simmering just below the surface. The local populations were divided—some sympathetic to the refugees, others ready to join the militias in driving them out.

And in the midst of it all, there were families like Tariq's—caught in the crossfire, trying to survive in a world that no longer made sense.

The Refuge

After what felt like hours of walking, they reached the outskirts of a small village nestled in the hills. Tariq's legs were heavy with exhaustion, but he pushed on, driven by the faint hope that Fatima was somewhere nearby.

The village was eerily quiet, its streets deserted, as if the inhabitants had fled or were hiding from the violence that was creeping closer every day. The houses were small and worn, their windows boarded up, their doors locked tight. It was a ghost town, a place that had been abandoned by the world.

But as they made their way through the narrow streets, Tariq saw movement—a small group of people huddled together by the village square. Refugees, like him.

Tariq's heart leapt as he spotted Fatima and her daughter among them. She was sitting on the ground, cradling her daughter in her arms, her face pale with fear but alive.

"Fatima!" Tariq called out, his voice breaking with relief.

She looked up, her eyes widening in disbelief. "Tariq!"

They ran toward each other, collapsing into a tearful embrace. Fatima held him tightly, her body shaking with sobs. "I thought... I thought we'd lost you," she whispered.

Tariq held her close, his own tears mixing with hers. "I'm here," he said softly. "We're still here."

For now, they were safe. But the storm that was brewing across Europe showed no sign of ending. The path ahead was uncertain, and the war was far from over.

Chapter 60: Unrest on the Horizon

October 2029 – Brussels, Belgium

The European Union headquarters in Brussels had never felt so tense. The vast glass façade of the building gleamed in the pale autumn light, but inside, the atmosphere was heavy, like a pressure cooker waiting to explode. Politicians, diplomats, and advisors moved quickly through the corridors, their conversations hushed but urgent. A storm was coming, and they all knew it.

The migrant crisis, once considered a manageable issue by Europe's bureaucrats, had spiralled into chaos. Far-right parties had surged in popularity, fuelled by fear, xenophobia, and nationalist fervour. Meanwhile, religious tensions between Muslims and Christians had reached a boiling point. The violence that had once been confined to isolated protests or skirmishes now consumed entire cities. The EU, once a beacon of unity, was now fracturing along political, religious, and cultural lines.

At the center of this storm sat Karl Hesse, the German chancellor. He was in his mid-fifties, a career politician with sharp features and a stern demeanour. He had risen to power on a platform of security and strength, promising to restore order to a Europe in chaos. But the events of the past few months had shaken even his confidence. He was seated at a large table in the EU Council chamber, surrounded by his European counterparts, each of them representing nations on the brink of their own internal collapses.

"We cannot ignore what is happening any longer," Hesse said, his voice cutting through the murmur of conversations. "We are facing a civil war on our streets. If we do not act now, it will be too late."

To his left sat Marie DuPont, the French president, her face a mask of exhaustion. France had been hit particularly hard by the violence. Entire neighbourhoods in Paris had become no-go zones, with militias patrolling the streets and imposing their own brutal form of order. Her eyes were weary, but she nodded in agreement.

"We've tried diplomacy," DuPont said. "We've tried compromise. But the fact is, the division between the Muslim and Christian populations is too deep. No one is willing to listen anymore."

Across the table, Prime Minister Oliver Blake of the United Kingdom leaned forward. His tone was measured, but the worry in his voice was evident. "The question now is, how do we respond? If we clamp down too hard, we risk further radicalizing both sides. But if we don't act decisively, we're handing our countries over to chaos."

The leaders exchanged glances, knowing the weight of the decision before them. No one wanted to admit that they had lost control, but the signs were everywhere. Violent clashes were escalating daily, fuelled by extremist groups on both sides. In Germany, Die Reiniger had transformed from a fringe group into a powerful militia, their anti-Muslim rhetoric appealing to a growing number of citizens. In France, the situation was similar, with homegrown Islamist militias forming in response to the far-right threat. The UK, while somewhat insulated by geography, was not immune. London had seen its share of riots, and the rising tide of nationalism threatened to drown the country's famed multiculturalism.

"We need to be honest with ourselves," Blake said, his voice low. "The EU is breaking apart. The refugee crisis was the spark, but the fire is now out of control."

Hesse leaned back in his chair, his brow furrowed. "We've allowed this to go too far. The influx of migrants—young men, primarily—was a destabilizing force. We thought we could manage the cultural integration, but it's clear that the social fabric of Europe is tearing apart."

There was an uncomfortable silence around the table. The leaders all knew that the situation had reached a point of no return. The initial goodwill that had welcomed refugees fleeing from war-torn regions had evaporated, replaced by suspicion, fear, and hatred. The demographic shifts in cities like Berlin, Paris, and London had sparked a backlash from native populations, and the promises of assimilation had failed to materialize.

Hesse's voice grew steely as he continued. "We must take control. I propose a temporary suspension of the Schengen Agreement. We need border controls, we need curfews, and we need to stop the flow of people across Europe. Our citizens demand safety, and we cannot provide it in this current state."

Blake nodded grimly. "It will be controversial, but I think the people will support it. They're scared. They want action."

DuPont hesitated for a moment before speaking. "What about the religious conflict? We can close borders, but that won't solve the division between Muslims and Christians within our borders."

"The religious element is... complicated," Hesse admitted. "But we cannot allow extremists on either side to dictate the future of Europe. We need to address the underlying issues—economic disparity, lack of integration—but for now, we must restore order. That is our priority."

A young advisor standing by the door suddenly stepped forward, his expression urgent. "Chancellor, we've just received word from Berlin. There's been another attack."

Hesse's face darkened. "Where?"

"The Charlottenburg district. A suicide bomber targeted a Christian church. Early reports indicate at least thirty dead."

The room fell silent. Hesse closed his eyes for a moment, the weight of the news pressing down on him. This wasn't the first attack, and it wouldn't be the last. Each act of violence only fuelled the cycle of retaliation, pushing the continent closer to all-out war.

"We cannot wait any longer," Hesse said, standing abruptly. "I will not let Germany fall into civil war. We must act now."

DuPont rose as well, her expression resolute. "France stands with you, Karl. We'll take whatever measures are necessary to restore peace."

Blake followed suit, though there was a flicker of doubt in his eyes. "The UK will support you as well, though we must be careful. If we push too hard, we may make things worse."

Hesse nodded, his mind already racing ahead to the next steps. "We will need to coordinate our efforts. Military, intelligence, law enforcement—everything must be on the table. We need to send a clear message to these extremists that their reign of terror is over."

As the leaders began to leave the chamber, the weight of the decisions they had made pressed down on each of them. The path ahead was fraught with danger. No one could predict how the populations of Europe would react to the new measures, or whether the violence would truly subside. But one thing was clear: the Europe they had known was gone, and in its place was a continent on the brink of war.

The Streets of Berlin

Meanwhile, on the streets of Berlin, the tension was palpable. Armed police patrolled every corner, their presence a stark reminder of the fragile peace that hung by a thread. The city had become a battleground, with neighbourhoods divided along religious and cultural lines. Christian and Muslim communities no longer coexisted—they were in open conflict, each side blaming the other for the violence that had torn their lives apart.

In the Charlottenburg district, where the latest attack had occurred, a crowd had gathered. The air was thick with grief and anger as people stood outside the ruined church, their faces etched with disbelief. The once-beautiful building now lay in ruins, a gaping hole where the bomb had exploded.

A woman knelt by the remains of the church, her hands clasped in prayer. Her face was streaked with tears, her voice trembling as she whispered for peace. But there was no peace to be found in Berlin anymore. The city was a powder keg, and it was only a matter of time before it exploded.

The police presence did little to calm the tension. As night fell, the streets became more dangerous. Groups of young men—both Christian and Muslim—gathered in the alleyways, ready for a fight. The city was on edge, waiting for the next spark that would ignite the flames of war.

Tariq, now settled in a makeshift camp with Fatima and her daughter, watched the unfolding chaos from a distance. He knew that they were no longer safe, even here. The violence was spreading, and soon, it would reach them. There was no escaping it.

As he held Fatima close, his mind drifted to the future. What would become of Europe? Of his family? There were no answers, only the creeping realization that their survival now depended on choices that were being made in rooms far away from them. Choices that would shape the fate of millions.

And for Tariq, there was only one certainty: the worst was yet to come.

Chapter 61: Beneath the Surface

October 2029 – Berlin, Germany

Berlin had become a microcosm of Europe's escalating chaos. The vibrant, multicultural city once celebrated as a symbol of unity was now fractured. Streets that were once bustling with life had transformed into zones of contention. Christian and Muslim communities, pushed to the brink by political manipulation, violence, and fear, found themselves trapped in a bitter struggle for survival. The social fabric of the city was unravelling.

Tariq watched it all unfold from the cramped refugee camp on the outskirts of Berlin. The camp had grown dramatically in recent weeks, as more people fled the violence in the city center. It was no longer just a place of shelter; it was a melting pot of fear, resentment, and desperation. Tensions among the refugees were rising, mirroring the hostilities outside the camp's gates.

Tariq sat outside the small tent he shared with Fatima and her daughter, Layla. The air was heavy with smoke from nearby fires, and the faint sounds of distant gunshots echoed in the evening air. The camp's atmosphere had shifted from one of temporary refuge to a place of anxious uncertainty. People were no longer simply hiding from the violence; they were preparing for it to come crashing through the gates.

Fatima sat beside him, her face worn with exhaustion. She stroked Layla's hair, trying to calm her as the little girl stared blankly at the distant city skyline.

"We can't stay here much longer," Fatima said quietly, her voice thick with fear. "The camp isn't safe anymore. People are starting to turn on each other."

Tariq nodded grimly. He had sensed it too—the unease, the quick tempers, the arguments that could turn violent at any moment. Food was becoming scarce, and the makeshift security within the camp was crumbling. The international aid workers who had once offered a semblance of order were now overwhelmed. Fights over rations had broken out in recent days, and rumours of an impending raid by nationalist militias hung like a dark cloud over everyone.

"We'll have to move again," Tariq said, though he knew there was no real escape. "But where? There's nowhere left."

Fatima didn't answer. She knew the truth as well as he did. Every border was closing, and every safe haven was now a battlefield. The war that had started in isolated pockets across Europe was spreading, and Berlin was at its epicenter.

Tariq glanced around the camp. The faces of the people—men, women, and children from all walks of life—were etched with the same fear and uncertainty. Some had been here for months, others for only days. But all of them were trapped, waiting for a future that seemed more uncertain by the hour.

As the sun dipped below the horizon, casting a blood-red glow over the camp, Tariq heard a commotion at the gates. A group of new arrivals had appeared, their faces gaunt with exhaustion and terror. They had fled from the heart of the city, where the violence had reached new heights.

Tariq stood, making his way to the crowd that had gathered to greet the newcomers. He pushed through the mass of people, his heart pounding in his chest as he listened to the frantic conversations.

"They've burned another mosque," one man was saying, his voice trembling. "And the church on Karlstrasse... it's gone. They're tearing the city apart."

Another woman, clutching a small child, spoke through tears. "The militias... they're taking people. They're rounding up anyone they think is a threat—Muslims, Christians, it doesn't matter anymore."

Tariq's stomach churned. He had hoped that the violence would stay confined to certain parts of the city, that the authorities would regain control before it spilled into the outskirts. But now it seemed inevitable. The camps, the outskirts—nowhere was safe.

The Shadow of Extremism

As the new refugees were led into the camp, Tariq turned and saw a familiar figure in the distance: Hassan, one of the few men in the camp he had come to trust. Hassan was a calm, soft-spoken man in his thirties who had fled Syria with his family years ago, long before the current wave of conflict. He had become something of a leader among the refugees, helping to mediate disputes and offering advice to those who were new to the camp.

287

But tonight, Hassan's face was clouded with worry. He motioned for Tariq to follow him to the far edge of the camp, where the trees provided some cover from prying eyes.

"I've heard rumours," Hassan began, his voice low. "There's talk of a group—some of the younger men in the camp—they're planning something."

Tariq frowned. "Planning what?"

Hassan glanced over his shoulder, making sure no one was listening. "A retaliation. They've had enough of the militias attacking us, and they're planning to fight back. But it's not just self-defence—they want to strike first."

Tariq's heart sank. The idea of armed conflict spilling into the camp was his worst nightmare. "That's madness," he said, his voice barely a whisper. "If they attack, the militias will retaliate tenfold. This camp will be wiped out."

Hassan nodded, his expression grim. "I know. But they're young, angry, and scared. They've lost everything, and they think this is the only way to take control of their lives again."

Tariq felt a surge of frustration. He understood their anger, their desire for revenge, but he also knew the consequences. The cycle of violence would only escalate, and innocent people—people like Fatima and Layla—would be caught in the crossfire.

"We have to stop them," Tariq said, his mind racing. "We can't let them do this."

Hassan sighed, running a hand through his hair. "I've tried talking to them, but they're not listening. They're being egged on by a few extremists—men who've seen more war than peace. They're convincing the younger ones that this is their only chance to fight back, to show strength."

Tariq clenched his fists. The lines between right and wrong had blurred so much in this conflict that even the victims were becoming aggressors. The young men in the camp had grown up in war zones, had seen their homes destroyed and their families torn apart. Now, pushed to the brink, they were willing to risk everything in a desperate bid for control.

"Where are they?" Tariq asked. "I need to talk to them."

Hassan hesitated. "They're meeting tonight, near the old factory by the river. But I don't know if you'll be able to change their minds. They're too far gone."

Tariq shook his head. "I have to try."

A Dangerous Gambit

Later that night, Tariq made his way through the camp, careful to avoid drawing attention. Fatima was asleep in the tent, Layla curled up beside her. He hadn't told Fatima about what was happening—he didn't want to worry her more than she already was. But he knew that if the young men went through with their plan, it could spell disaster for all of them.

The path to the old factory was dark and deserted, the sounds of the camp fading into the distance as he walked. The air was cool, and a thick fog had settled over the river, making the abandoned building loom like a shadowy monster in the night.

As he approached the factory, he heard voices—muffled but urgent. Tariq crept closer, hiding behind a stack of rusted barrels as he listened to the conversation.

"They've been attacking us for weeks," one young man was saying. "We can't just sit here and do nothing. We have to hit them where it hurts."

Another voice, older and more grizzled, responded. "They think we're weak. But if we strike first, they'll know we're not afraid."

Tariq recognized the voice of the second man—Imran, a former soldier who had fled the Middle East after years of fighting in various conflicts. He was one of the extremists Hassan had warned him about, a man hardened by years of war who had no qualms about using violence to achieve his goals.

"We have to act now," Imran continued. "Before they come for us again."

Tariq took a deep breath, stepping out from behind the barrels. "This isn't the answer," he said, his voice firm but calm.

The group of men turned to face him, their expressions ranging from surprise to anger. Imran's eyes narrowed as he sized Tariq up.

"What are you doing here?" Imran growled. "This isn't your fight."

Tariq held his ground. "It's everyone's fight. But what you're planning—it will only make things worse. If you attack them, they'll retaliate, and more innocent people will die."

One of the younger men, barely in his twenties, stepped forward. "They've already killed innocent people. Our families, our friends. We can't just sit by and let them do it again."

Tariq looked at the young man, seeing the pain and anger in his eyes. "I know you've suffered. We've all suffered. But violence won't bring them back. It won't end this war—it will only fuel it."

Imran scoffed. "You sound like one of them—the cowards who hide behind their walls and let the rest of us bleed."

Tariq shook his head. "No. I'm just a man who wants to protect his family. And I know that if you go through with this, none of us will survive."

For a moment, there was silence. The young men glanced at each other, their resolve wavering. Imran, however, was not so easily swayed.

"This is war," Imran said coldly. "And in war, you don't wait for the enemy to strike first. You hit them hard, and you hit them fast."

Tariq met Imran's gaze, his voice steady. "But this isn't a war. Not yet. And if you go through with this, you'll be the ones who start it."

The group was silent again, the weight of Tariq's words hanging in the air. The younger men shifted uncomfortably, doubt creeping into their minds.

Finally, one of them spoke. "Maybe he's right," the young man said, his voice uncertain. "Maybe we should wait. See if things calm down."

Imran glared at the young man, his eyes burning with anger. "Cowards," he spat. "All of you."

But the momentum had shifted. One by one, the young men began to back away, their desire for revenge tempered by the realization that they were playing with fire.

Imran, seething with rage, turned on Tariq. "You've just signed your own death warrant."

Tariq didn't flinch. "Maybe. But at least I'll die knowing I didn't make things worse."

With that, Imran stormed off into the night, leaving Tariq and the remaining men standing in the shadow of the factory.

Tariq let out a long breath, relief washing over him. He had stopped the attack—for now. But he knew that this was only a temporary reprieve. The violence was far from over, and the fragile peace that remained could shatter at any moment.

As he made his way back to the camp, the weight of what lay ahead pressed heavily on his shoulders. The future was uncertain, and the choices he made now could determine not just his fate, but the fate of everyone he cared about.

And somewhere, in the distance, the drums of war continued to beat.

Chapter 62: The Gathering Storm

November 2029 – London, United Kingdom

The streets of London were eerily quiet as Abigail Thompson, now an influential MP, stood by the window of her office in Westminster. The usual hustle and bustle of the city had been replaced by an air of tension so thick that it was almost suffocating. The once vibrant metropolis was now under an uneasy calm, with police patrols visible on every street corner and military checkpoints scattered throughout the city.

The news had been relentless in recent weeks—protests erupting in cities across Europe, ethnic clashes turning violent, and governments teetering on the edge of collapse. What had started as isolated incidents of unrest in small towns and border regions had snowballed into full-blown crises, consuming capitals like Paris, Berlin, and even London itself. The refugee crisis that had ignited these tensions was now an unquenchable inferno of political turmoil, social unrest, and ideological conflict.

Abigail took a deep breath, her fingers tightening around the edge of the windowsill. She had been fighting this battle in Parliament for years, warning her fellow MPs that the escalating tensions between native European populations and the influx of predominantly Muslim refugees would lead to disaster if left unchecked. Few had listened. Now, as the country verged on the precipice of collapse, they were all scrambling to find solutions that should have been enacted long ago.

Her phone buzzed on the desk behind her. Without turning, she knew it was another message from the Home Office, or perhaps a news alert about more clashes in the streets. The pattern was always the same—another city was on the brink, another district had been cordoned off, and another hastily convened security meeting was needed.

The door creaked open, and Marcus, her longtime aide, stepped into the room. His face was pale, his usually calm demeanour replaced by visible anxiety.

"Abigail, we've just received word from Paris," he said, closing the door behind him. "There's been an attack on the National Assembly. A group of extremists stormed the building during a session. They're holding several MPs hostage."

Abigail turned, her eyes widening. "Extremists? Are we talking about—"

"Militant Islamists," Marcus confirmed, his voice tense. "It seems they've coordinated this with several other cells across Europe. We're getting reports of similar incidents in Madrid, Rome, and Brussels."

Abigail sank into her chair, the weight of the news settling heavily on her shoulders. This was it—the moment she had feared for so long. The fragile peace was breaking, and Europe was once again becoming a battleground.

"What are they demanding?" she asked, her voice barely above a whisper.

"Immediate recognition of an Islamic state in Europe," Marcus replied grimly. "They claim the governments have failed their people, and that only a new caliphate can bring order to the chaos."

Abigail felt a surge of anger rise within her. "A caliphate? In Europe? This is madness."

Marcus nodded in agreement, but the fear in his eyes was palpable. "Madness, yes. But it's spreading. These groups have been growing in the shadows for years, feeding on the anger and frustration of disenfranchised young men. The governments ignored the warning signs, and now..."

"Now it's too late," Abigail finished for him, her voice bitter.

For years, she had argued for integration policies that didn't just pay lip service to the concept of multiculturalism but actually addressed the deep-rooted issues facing these communities—poverty, lack of opportunity, cultural alienation. But every proposal she had made was either watered down or rejected entirely by those more concerned with their political careers than with preventing the collapse of society.

She stood up, her mind racing. "We need to act, and fast. Have you spoken to the Prime Minister?"

Marcus hesitated, glancing at the door. "He's in a meeting with the security council. They're discussing imposing martial law across the country. There's talk of suspending Parliament altogether until the crisis is under control."

Abigail shook her head in disbelief. "Martial law won't stop this. It will only inflame the situation. If we clamp down too hard, we'll push even more people toward extremism."

Marcus frowned. "What do you suggest, then? If we don't take drastic measures, we'll lose control."

"We've already lost control," Abigail said quietly. "But we can still salvage what's left if we're smart about it."

She walked over to her desk, picking up her phone and dialling a number she had hoped she wouldn't need to call. After a few rings, a familiar voice answered.

"Abigail," said David Bishop, her old mentor and former leader of the opposition. "I was wondering when you'd call."

"You've heard the news, I assume," Abigail said, not bothering with pleasantries.

"Of course," David replied. "It's all anyone's talking about. The world is falling apart, and we're on the verge of civil war."

Abigail closed her eyes, the weight of the moment pressing down on her. "We need to come together, David. All parties. The government can't handle this alone. We need a unified front to stop this from spiralling out of control."

There was a pause on the other end of the line. "You know as well as I do that unity is a pipe dream right now. The political divide is as deep as the religious one."

"I know," Abigail said. "But if we don't find a way to bridge that divide, there won't be anything left of this country by the time the dust settles. We have to try."

David sighed. "I'll see what I can do. But don't expect miracles. People are scared, and fear doesn't lead to rational decisions."

"I'm not expecting rationality," Abigail replied. "I'm expecting survival."

She hung up the phone, her mind already racing with plans. If there was one thing she had learned in her years of politics, it was that in times of crisis, people were desperate for leadership. They would follow anyone who seemed to have a plan, even if that plan was flawed.

But this was more than just political manoeuvring—this was about the survival of Europe as they knew it.

The Rising Tide

Across the city, in a small mosque nestled between two nondescript buildings in East London, Imam Yusuf stood before his congregation, addressing them in a voice that was both calm and commanding.

"We must not let fear and anger dictate our actions," he said, his eyes scanning the room. "The situation is dire, yes. But violence will only lead to more suffering. We must find a way to coexist, to bring peace back to our communities."

The crowd, made up of men and women from all walks of life, nodded solemnly. But the tension in the air was palpable. They had all seen the news, heard the rumours. Attacks were happening across Europe, and the fear of retaliation was spreading through the Muslim community like wildfire.

After the sermon, as the congregation slowly filtered out of the mosque, Yusuf was approached by a young man named Khalid. He had been a regular at the mosque for years, always respectful and quiet, but tonight there was a fire in his eyes that Yusuf hadn't seen before.

"Imam," Khalid began, his voice low. "I respect your call for peace, but how can we sit idly by while our brothers and sisters are being slaughtered? They're calling for jihad in France, in Spain. Maybe it's time we joined them."

Yusuf frowned, his heart heavy with concern. He had feared this moment would come—when the anger and frustration brewing within the younger generation would boil over into something dangerous.

"Khalid," Yusuf said gently, placing a hand on the young man's shoulder. "Jihad is not the answer. Islam teaches us to strive for peace, even in the face of adversity. Violence will only breed more violence."

Khalid shook his head, his jaw clenched. "But they're attacking us. They're burning mosques, killing innocent people. How can we just stand by?"

Yusuf sighed. "I understand your anger, but we must be wise in our actions. The extremists who are calling for violence—they do not represent Islam. They are using our faith as a weapon, and that is not the path we should follow."

Khalid's eyes flickered with doubt, but the anger still simmered beneath the surface. "And what if they come for us next? What if we're the ones being attacked?"

Yusuf's grip tightened on Khalid's shoulder. "Then we stand strong in our faith. We protect our families, our communities, but we do not become the very thing we are fighting against."

For a moment, Khalid seemed to waver, but the tension in his body remained. With a curt nod, he pulled away from Yusuf and walked out of the mosque, disappearing into the night.

Yusuf watched him go, a sinking feeling in his chest. The storm was coming, and he wasn't sure if his community was ready to weather it.

Chapter 63: The Breaking Point

December 2029 – Berlin, Germany

The sound of sirens echoed through the streets of Berlin as Sara Schneider pushed her way through the thick crowd gathered near the Brandenburg Gate. The air was thick with tension, the crisp December cold biting at her cheeks as she pulled her coat tighter. Armed police officers lined the barricades, standing at the ready, their faces obscured by riot helmets. It was an all-too-familiar scene these days—a gathering of angry protesters, met by the force of the state, as the city teetered on the edge of chaos.

Sara, a seasoned journalist, had covered unrest before, but the situation in Berlin was different. The clashes that had erupted in the last few weeks were more than just protests. They were the outward manifestation of something much darker—a society fractured along religious and cultural lines, with neither side willing to compromise. What had begun as a migrant crisis years ago had morphed into something far more dangerous, and the divisions in Germany had never been so deep.

She found a spot near the front of the crowd, her camera ready. Today's demonstration was supposed to be peaceful, at least according to the organizers, but Sara had seen how quickly peace could turn into violence. On one side of the street, a coalition of nationalist groups had gathered, waving German flags and carrying signs that read *"Deutschland zuerst" (Germany first) and *"Stoppt die Islamisierung Europas" (Stop the Islamization of Europe).* On the other side, a group of pro-refugee activists held banners proclaiming, *"No borders, no nations,"* while a smaller group of leftist activists chanted slogans calling for solidarity with the Muslim population.

Sara scanned the crowd, her eyes catching sight of a young man standing near the barricade, his face half-hidden by a scarf. His eyes were intense, filled with anger, and she recognized the look. This was not the face of someone attending a peaceful protest. She shifted her focus, snapping a few quick photos, when suddenly, a shout rang out from the far end of the square.

A young man on the nationalist side of the protest had broken through the barricade, charging toward the opposing group, his fist raised in anger. In an instant, chaos erupted. The crowd surged forward, clashing with the

297

police as the two sides collided in the middle of the square. Fists flew, bottles were thrown, and Sara found herself caught in the crush of bodies, her camera nearly knocked from her hands.

"Damn it," she muttered, trying to regain her balance as she backed away from the melee. But the violence spread quickly, the nationalist group pushing further into the crowd, their chants drowned out by the roar of the fight.

Sara's heart pounded as she ducked behind a nearby column, snapping photos as the scene devolved into a full-blown riot. Tear gas canisters were launched into the crowd, and the air filled with the acrid smell of smoke. She caught glimpses of police officers swinging batons, protesters hurling bricks, and the flash of camera lights from other journalists capturing the carnage.

She felt a tug on her arm and turned to see a familiar face. It was Jakob, a freelance photographer she had worked with before. His face was pale, his expression a mix of fear and disbelief.

"This is worse than last week," he shouted over the noise. "They've completely lost control."

Sara nodded, her mind racing. "We need to get closer. We have to document this."

Jakob hesitated for a moment before nodding in agreement. Together, they pushed their way toward the front, dodging debris and riot police as they moved. The crowd had scattered in every direction, but small pockets of fighting continued, with the police struggling to maintain order.

As they reached the front line, Sara raised her camera, focusing on a group of nationalist protesters who had cornered a young Muslim man against a wall. His face was bloodied, his eyes wide with fear as they taunted him, their voices dripping with hate.

Sara's finger hovered over the shutter button, but before she could take the shot, a figure barrelled through the crowd, tackling the attackers to the ground. It was a tall man in his thirties, dressed in jeans and a leather jacket, his fists swinging wildly as he fought off the group. For a moment, Sara was too stunned to move, her camera frozen in her hands.

Jakob grabbed her arm, pulling her back. "We need to go! This is getting out of hand!"

But Sara couldn't tear her eyes away from the scene unfolding in front of her. The man had managed to fend off the attackers, helping the young Muslim man to his feet before the two of them disappeared into the chaos.

"Who was that?" Sara asked, more to herself than to Jakob.

"No idea," Jakob replied, pulling her further away from the violence. "But we need to get out of here before we get caught in the middle of it."

Reluctantly, Sara followed him, her mind still racing. She had seen plenty of riots, plenty of clashes, but something about this felt different. The anger in the crowd was more than just political. It was primal, a deep-seated hatred that had been festering for years, and now, it was boiling over.

As they reached a safer distance, the police finally began to regain control of the square. The sound of sirens filled the air as more reinforcements arrived, and the fighting slowly began to subside. But the damage had been done. The once peaceful protest had turned into a battleground, and Sara knew that this was only the beginning.

Jakob lit a cigarette, exhaling a plume of smoke as he shook his head. "I've covered conflicts in the Middle East that looked more controlled than this."

Sara nodded, her thoughts elsewhere. The events of the day would dominate the headlines, but she knew that the real story wasn't just about what had happened in Berlin. It was about the slow unravelling of Europe itself. The nationalist movements were growing stronger, feeding on the fear of cultural loss, while the Muslim communities were becoming increasingly isolated and radicalized in response.

She pulled out her phone, scrolling through her contacts until she found the name she was looking for. David Müller, a political analyst she had interviewed several times over the years. He had been one of the few voices warning of the rising tide of extremism in Germany, and now, his predictions were coming true.

She typed out a quick message: **"David, we need to talk. Things are escalating faster than anyone expected."**

As she hit send, she couldn't shake the feeling that they were standing on the edge of something far worse than anyone was willing to admit.

The Political Fallout

In a sleek government building on the other side of the city, Chancellor Frieda Klein stared at the television screen in disbelief. The images of the riot played on an endless loop, showing the brutality of the clashes in stark detail. She had been briefed on the potential for violence at today's protest, but no one had predicted it would spiral out of control this quickly.

Her aide, Klaus, stood beside her, his face grim. "The situation is deteriorating, Chancellor. We've received reports of similar incidents in Hamburg and Munich. The nationalist groups are becoming more organized, and the Muslim communities are growing increasingly desperate. We're losing control."

Frieda leaned back in her chair, rubbing her temples as a headache began to form. "And the international response?"

"The French government has declared a state of emergency," Klaus replied. "They're deploying military forces to major cities. Spain and Italy are considering similar measures. The EU is calling for an emergency summit, but…"

"But no one has a solution," Frieda finished for him. "We've let this go on for too long. The divisions are too deep now."

Klaus nodded. "There are rumours that some EU member states are considering closing their borders entirely. If that happens…"

"If that happens, the EU is finished," Frieda said quietly. She had fought hard to keep Germany at the forefront of the European Union, but now, even she wasn't sure if it could survive the crisis.

"We need to act decisively," she said, her voice firm. "We need to show the people that we are still in control. Call for a national address tonight. I'll speak to the country directly."

Klaus nodded, already moving to carry out her orders. But as he left the room, Frieda couldn't shake the feeling that it might already be too late. The storm was coming, and she wasn't sure if anyone could stop it.

Chapter 64: A Nation Fractured

December 2029 – Paris, France

The streets of Paris were no longer the grand boulevards of romance and beauty. They had become battle lines, marked by shattered glass, overturned cars, and the lingering smoke from recent fires. The smell of tear gas clung to the air, and the sounds of sporadic gunfire echoed in the distance. What had once been the heartbeat of Europe's intellectual and cultural life was now a city in lockdown, teetering on the edge of collapse.

Jean-Luc Girard, an aging politician with over three decades of public service, stared out the window of his office in the Élysée Palace. His hands rested on the ornate desk in front of him, now cluttered with reports of violence, civil unrest, and government responses that seemed woefully inadequate. In all his years in politics, Jean-Luc had never seen anything like this.

Across from him sat President Sophie Duval, a woman known for her calm demeanour and steady leadership. But today, even she looked worn, her usual poise slipping beneath the weight of the decisions she had to make. Sophie's face was pale, and her eyes betrayed the stress she had been under for weeks.

"How did we get here, Jean-Luc?" Sophie asked, her voice barely above a whisper. "How did we let this happen to our country?"

Jean-Luc sighed, his mind racing as he considered the history that had led to this moment. France, like much of Europe, had been struggling with the aftereffects of the migrant crisis for years. What had started as a humanitarian issue had snowballed into a political and social crisis that no one had predicted. The waves of migrants from Africa and the Middle East had strained France's resources, and the failure to integrate these communities had created a breeding ground for resentment on both sides.

The far-right nationalist movements had been growing steadily, their rhetoric becoming more extreme with each election. And now, as unemployment soared, and as refugees and migrants continued to pour in, the lines between political ideology and violence had blurred.

"I don't know, Madame President," Jean-Luc finally said. "Perhaps we thought that France was immune to this kind of division. We were blind to the anger growing in the suburbs, and now that anger has found a voice."

Sophie's hands trembled slightly as she picked up one of the reports on her desk. "This is no longer about anger," she said, her voice growing steadier. "This is about survival. The National Assembly is under siege, and our cities are burning. We've declared a state of emergency, but the military can't be everywhere at once. If we don't find a way to de-escalate this situation, France will fall into civil war."

Jean-Luc could hear the weight of her words. France had been on the verge of collapse before, during the riots in 2005, and again during the Yellow Vest protests a few years ago. But this time, it felt different. This time, the country's very identity was at stake.

"There's only one option left," Sophie continued, her gaze hardening as she looked directly at Jean-Luc. "We have to negotiate with the leaders of the Islamist groups."

Jean-Luc's face darkened. "Negotiate? You can't be serious, Madame President. We can't negotiate with terrorists."

"They're not all terrorists," Sophie shot back. "Many of these people are just as desperate as the rest of the country. Their leaders have seized on their fear, using religion as a weapon to radicalize them. If we don't open a dialogue, we'll only push more of them into the arms of extremists."

Jean-Luc clenched his fists. "And what about the rest of the country? What about the people who are terrified that they're losing their France? If we sit down with these groups, we risk legitimizing their demands for an Islamic state. What message does that send to the millions of French citizens who are watching their neighbourhoods being overrun by violence?"

Sophie stood, her resolve hardening. "It's not about legitimizing their demands. It's about preventing more bloodshed. We are the government, Jean-Luc. We must be the ones to restore order, even if that means sitting across the table from those we despise."

Jean-Luc rose from his seat, his frustration boiling over. "This is a mistake, Sophie. We can't allow France to be divided. Negotiating with them is just the first step toward the end of the Republic."

Sophie turned to face him, her expression unreadable. "And what's the alternative? More troops in the streets? More violence? We're running out of time, Jean-Luc. We have to choose the lesser evil."

Jean-Luc stared at her for a long moment, weighing his options. He had spent his career defending the principles of the Republic—liberty, equality, fraternity. But those ideals were slipping away in the face of an increasingly divided nation. Perhaps Sophie was right. Perhaps the only way to save France was to make a deal with the very people threatening to tear it apart.

"I'll arrange the meetings," Jean-Luc said finally, his voice heavy with resignation. "But I don't like it."

Sophie nodded, understanding his reluctance. "None of us do."

A New Kind of Leader

Across the city, in the northern suburbs where the violence had been the most intense, a man named Farid El-Fahd stood in front of a group of young men gathered in a makeshift mosque. Farid was not a politician, nor was he a traditional religious leader. He was something far more dangerous—a charismatic figure who had risen to prominence as the voice of a disillusioned generation. To his followers, he was a revolutionary, a man who spoke to their anger and frustration with the French government and the systemic racism they had faced all their lives.

"The government talks about peace," Farid said, pacing in front of the group. "But they do not understand what peace means for us. They want us to bow to their laws, to assimilate into their culture. But we have our own culture, our own laws. We are Muslims first, and we will not be silent any longer."

The young men nodded in agreement, their eyes filled with the same anger that burned in Farid's. Most of them had grown up in the neglected banlieues, surrounded by poverty, crime, and unemployment. They had watched as their families struggled to make a life in a country that seemed to reject them at every turn.

"They call us terrorists," Farid continued, his voice rising. "But who are the real terrorists? The ones who bomb our countries, who invade our lands, who leave us with nothing but rubble and refugees? They expect us to forget that, to integrate into their society while they spit on us."

He paused, his eyes scanning the room. "No. We will not forget. We will not bow. If they want war, then we will give them war."

There was a murmur of approval from the crowd, but one of the older men, a former imam named Ibrahim, stood and raised his hand. "Farid, we must be careful. Violence will only lead to more violence. We must protect our community, yes, but we must also seek a way to live in peace."

Farid turned to him, his expression hardening. "Peace? You speak of peace when our people are being killed in the streets? When our mosques are being burned? What kind of peace are you talking about, Ibrahim?"

Ibrahim held his ground. "A peace that does not destroy us. If we continue down this path, we will become no better than those who oppress us. The Prophet, peace be upon him, taught us to strive for justice, but also for mercy."

Farid's eyes flashed with anger. "And what mercy have they shown us, Ibrahim? What justice have we received? I will not ask my brothers to lie down and accept their fate. We will fight, and we will win."

The room fell silent as Farid's words hung in the air. Ibrahim, seeing that he could not sway the younger man, simply bowed his head and sat down.

Farid turned back to the crowd, his voice softening. "I understand your fear. I understand your pain. But we cannot allow ourselves to be divided. This is our time, brothers. We will not be silenced. We will not be defeated."

As he spoke, Farid knew that the government would soon come knocking, seeking to negotiate. He had already heard rumours that the president was preparing to reach out to leaders like him. But Farid had no intention of making peace. He had seen too much, suffered too much, to believe in their promises.

No, he would not negotiate. He would use their desperation to his advantage, rallying more of the disenfranchised youth to his cause. The streets of Paris were his battlefield now, and he would not stop until his vision of a new order was realized.

The Darkening Horizon

In the coming days, negotiations between the French government and Islamist leaders would begin. But these talks, held behind closed doors, would only serve to further polarize the nation. Nationalist groups would decry the government's willingness to engage with those they saw as enemies of the Republic, while the Muslim population would see the talks as a sign of weakness from the state.

Farid, for his part, would use the negotiations as a platform to spread his message further, emboldening his followers and deepening the divide. As the new year approached, it became clear to everyone that France was no longer the country it had been. It was a nation fractured, with neither side willing to yield.

And as the violence continued to spread across Europe, it was only a matter of time before the breaking point was reached.

Chapter 65: The Fault Lines of Power

January 2030 – Berlin, Germany

The crisp winter air bit at Chancellor Heinrich Müller's face as he stood by the window in his office overlooking the Reichstag. The once pristine streets of Berlin, where peaceful protests and democratic debates had been the hallmark of Germany's modern history, now bore the scars of unrest. The shattered remnants of what had become a deeply divided country were visible in every city—migrant neighbourhoods walled off from the native German enclaves, the tension palpable at every intersection.

Chancellor Müller felt the weight of history on his shoulders. Germany, like France and the UK, had long prided itself on its ability to adapt, to bring together disparate communities under one banner. But over the past decade, that facade had cracked. Now, as the year 2030 dawned, Germany's fragile unity was threatening to break apart entirely.

A knock on the door interrupted his thoughts.

"Come in," Müller said, turning away from the window.

His chief of staff, Brigitta Schneider, entered briskly, a tablet in her hand. She was always efficient, always composed, but today there was something different in her demeanour. Her lips were drawn into a tight line, and her eyes betrayed a hint of unease.

"Chancellor, we've just received the latest intelligence briefings," Brigitta began, handing him the tablet. "The protests in Munich have escalated. What started as a peaceful demonstration in the Turkish immigrant community turned violent when far-right groups arrived. The police are overwhelmed, and the army is being called in."

Müller scanned the report quickly. He had been expecting this, but it didn't make the reality any easier to bear. Munich was just one of many cities on the brink. Leipzig, Frankfurt, even Berlin itself had seen clashes between migrant communities and far-right nationalists. The social fabric of Germany was unravelling.

"What are our options, Brigitta?" Müller asked, his voice heavy with exhaustion.

Brigitta hesitated for a moment, then met his gaze. "We need to make a decision on how to handle these uprisings. The cabinet is divided. Some are pushing for a harder line—more military presence, curfews, and stronger measures to curb both migrant violence and the nationalist protests. Others are advocating for immediate talks with the leaders of these migrant communities, hoping to broker some kind of truce."

Müller sighed and ran a hand through his greying hair. "Negotiations will be seen as a sign of weakness by the opposition. If we start talks, the AfD will use it to fuel their narrative that we're giving in to the Islamists."

"And if we don't negotiate," Brigitta added, "the violence will only escalate. The migrant communities feel abandoned. The far-right feels emboldened. It's a powder keg, Chancellor. Any wrong move could tip the country into open conflict."

Müller knew she was right. The far-right Alternative for Germany (AfD) party had capitalized on the growing fear and resentment within the native German population. They painted migrants as invaders, a threat to Germany's identity and security. And with each violent incident, their rhetoric gained more traction.

But the migrants weren't invaders. They were people fleeing wars, poverty, and persecution. Germany had welcomed them, prided itself on its humanitarian stance. Now, many of these same people found themselves trapped in ghettos, blamed for the country's problems, and facing violent backlash.

"Set up the negotiations," Müller said finally, his voice steely. "But quietly. We can't afford to broadcast this to the public, not yet."

Brigitta nodded. "I'll arrange it. But we need to be cautious. Some of the leaders we'll be negotiating with have ties to radical groups. The security risk is high."

"I understand," Müller replied. "But if we don't try, we'll be facing a civil war."

Unseen Forces

As Müller and his administration grappled with the immediate crisis, forces beyond Germany's borders were watching closely. In Ankara, Tehran, and Moscow, political strategists and intelligence agencies monitored the developments with keen interest. The unravelling of Europe's unity had long been predicted, and for some, encouraged.

In Turkey, President Abdullah Demir saw an opportunity. His government had quietly supported the Turkish diaspora in Germany for years, ensuring that their loyalty remained tied to their homeland, even as they lived and worked in Europe. Now, with Germany in chaos, Demir saw a chance to exert greater influence over the continent. He began making subtle overtures to migrant leaders in Germany, offering them protection and financial support in exchange for loyalty.

In Tehran, the Islamic Republic's leadership saw the growing unrest as a sign that Europe's secular, democratic order was crumbling under the weight of its own contradictions. Iran's Supreme Leader issued statements in support of Muslim communities across Europe, framing the struggle as a fight for religious freedom and dignity. Behind the scenes, Iran funnelled resources to groups willing to resist European governments, hoping to further destabilize the region.

But it was Moscow that played the most dangerous game. President Alexei Volkov had long sought to weaken the European Union, viewing it as an obstacle to Russia's ambitions. Russia's state-controlled media pushed narratives that deepened the divisions within Europe, portraying Muslim migrants as dangerous extremists and European governments as weak and incapable of protecting their citizens. Volkov's intelligence agencies spread disinformation on social media, fanning the flames of fear and distrust on both sides.

For Russia, a fractured Europe was a Europe that could no longer stand in the way of its geopolitical goals.

Shadows on the Horizon

Back in Germany, the fault lines of power were becoming more apparent by the day. In the Bundestag, political factions were tearing themselves apart over how to handle the crisis. The Social Democrats and Greens pushed for greater integration efforts, insisting that the key to stability lay in addressing the socioeconomic issues that had fuelled the unrest. They argued for expanded welfare programs, job training initiatives, and anti-discrimination measures.

The Christian Democrats, traditionally the centrist force in German politics, were split down the middle. Some agreed with the Social Democrats, while others, facing pressure from a growing nationalist base, called for stricter immigration controls and a heavier police presence in migrant neighbourhoods.

And then there was the AfD, the far-right party that had risen to prominence by exploiting the fears of ordinary Germans. They framed the crisis as a clash of civilizations—a fight between Western Christian values and Islamic radicalism. In every speech, every campaign ad, they painted migrants as a threat to German identity, to the safety of women and children, and to the future of the nation.

In the working-class neighbourhoods of Leipzig and Dresden, their message resonated. People who had once been proud of Germany's post-war democratic values were now questioning those same values. They watched as the country they loved descended into chaos, and they blamed the government for what they saw as its failure to protect them.

But even within the AfD, there were fractures. The party's more extreme elements called for direct action—vigilante groups had already begun to form, targeting migrant communities with violence and intimidation. Some AfD leaders tried to distance themselves from these groups, but their rhetoric had already lit the fire.

As Chancellor Müller prepared for the secret negotiations with migrant leaders, he knew that time was running out. The violence in the streets was only one part of the problem. The greater danger lay in the collapse of trust—trust between the government and its people, between native Germans and migrants, between Europe and the rest of the world.

As he looked out over Berlin, the city's landmarks bathed in the cold January light, Müller couldn't help but wonder if this was how it would all end. Not with a decisive victory for one side or the other, but with the slow, painful unravelling of everything Germany had built in the post-war era.

The warning signs had been there for years. Now, the reckoning had arrived

Chapter 66: The Brink of Collapse

February 2030 – London, United Kingdom

The air in Westminster was thick with tension, the usual buzz of political intrigue drowned out by the growing sense that the country was on the verge of something catastrophic. The Houses of Parliament, once a symbol of stability and order, now felt more like a fortress under siege. Protests raged outside, thousands of demonstrators from both sides—nationalists and migrant communities—clashing in the streets, while police forces, already stretched thin, struggled to maintain control.

Inside the prime minister's office at 10 Downing Street, Prime Minister Eleanor Cartwright sat across from her advisors, the weight of the situation pressing down on her shoulders. The conference table was littered with reports—police briefings, intelligence assessments, and the latest polling numbers. None of them brought any good news.

Cartwright had risen to power on a platform of unity, promising to heal the divisions that had plagued the country since the Brexit debacle. But now, just three years into her term, she faced a nation more fractured than ever. Mass migration, economic instability, and the rise of extremist groups had all converged into a perfect storm. The question wasn't whether the UK would survive—it was how much longer it could hold on.

Her Home Secretary, James Thompson, stood by the window, looking out at the growing crowd of protesters. His face was grim.

"It's getting worse by the day," Thompson said, not turning from the window. "The clashes in Birmingham and Manchester have escalated. The army's been called in, but it's only a matter of time before something snaps. We're running out of options, Prime Minister."

Cartwright rubbed her temples, trying to fend off the headache that had been building for days. "What's the latest from MI5?"

Thompson turned back to her, his voice low. "They've intercepted communications between some of the more radical elements within the Muslim Brotherhood and local cells here in London. There's chatter about coordinated attacks if the government doesn't meet their demands."

"Demands?" Cartwright scoffed, her frustration boiling over. "They want an Islamic state in the heart of the UK. How are we supposed to negotiate with that?"

Sitting to her right, Defence Secretary Sarah Jenson spoke up. "We can't. If we give in to any of their demands, we lose what's left of our authority. The far-right groups will see it as a complete capitulation. They're already mobilizing—some are openly calling for armed insurrection. The last thing we want is a full-scale civil war."

The term "civil war" hung in the air, unspoken until now but clearly on everyone's mind.

"What about community leaders?" Cartwright asked. "Is there anyone left we can talk to, anyone who can help calm things down before it gets worse?"

Thompson shook his head. "It's too late for that. The moderate voices have been drowned out by the extremists on both sides. The Muslim community feels abandoned, targeted by police raids and surveillance. And the nationalist groups—especially those in the north—are feeling betrayed by a government they believe is prioritizing migrants over native Britons."

Cartwright leaned back in her chair, feeling the weight of the impossible decisions ahead. She had tried to address the economic inequality that had fuelled much of the resentment among working-class communities, but it wasn't enough. Years of austerity measures and deindustrialization had gutted entire regions of the country. Meanwhile, the migrants arriving in droves from Africa and the Middle East were seen as a direct threat to the already dwindling resources.

The reality, however, was far more complex. Many migrants were refugees, fleeing war-torn nations, seeking safety and a better life for their families. But in the eyes of the British working class, they were competitors for jobs, housing, and healthcare. It had created a toxic environment, where suspicion and hatred thrived, fuelled by a media that thrived on sensationalism and fear-mongering.

"What's our next move?" Thompson asked, breaking the silence.

"We can't just keep sending in more police and soldiers," Cartwright said. "That will only escalate things further. But we can't sit by and let the streets burn."

Jenson leaned forward, her expression serious. "We need to take a stronger stance. If these radical groups are planning attacks, we need to pre-empt them. Target their leadership, dismantle their networks before they can act."

"That's exactly what they want," Cartwright countered. "If we crack down too hard, we'll only confirm their narrative that the government is at war with Islam. We need a different approach."

Thompson crossed his arms, clearly sceptical. "What do you have in mind?"

Cartwright looked around the table, weighing her words carefully. "What if we called for a national referendum on immigration? Give the people a chance to express their views, let them feel heard. It might diffuse some of the tension."

Jenson immediately shook her head. "You're playing with fire, Prime Minister. A referendum could easily spiral out of control. If the vote goes against the migrants, we'll be accused of legitimizing xenophobia. And if it goes the other way, the nationalists will claim the government is rigging the system to favour them."

Thompson nodded in agreement. "It's a gamble we can't afford. You've seen how volatile the situation is. Giving people a platform to air their grievances might just incite more violence."

Cartwright knew they were right. But she was running out of ideas. The country was teetering on the brink, and no one solution seemed adequate to stop it from falling into chaos. She needed time—time to stabilize the situation, time to calm both sides before things spiralled completely out of control.

"Then what do we do?" Cartwright asked, her voice laced with frustration. "We can't just sit here and wait for the country to tear itself apart."

Before anyone could respond, the door to the room swung open, and a young aide rushed in, breathless.

"Prime Minister, you need to see this," the aide said, handing over a tablet.

Cartwright took the device and saw a live feed from central London. The camera zoomed in on a massive crowd of protesters, pushing against police barricades. In the distance, a building was on fire. But what caught her attention was the banner being waved by a group of young men at the front of the crowd. It was black, with white Arabic script.

"The Islamic State," Cartwright whispered, recognizing the familiar symbol from years of Middle Eastern conflicts.

Thompson moved to stand behind her, his face darkening as he saw the flag. "It's started. They're making their move."

Cartwright's heart sank. She had known this day was coming, but seeing the black flag raised in the streets of London made it all the more real. The radicals weren't just demanding change—they were declaring war.

"We need to act now," Jenson said, her voice firm. "This is the signal we've been waiting for. If we don't respond immediately, we'll lose control of the city."

Cartwright's mind raced. They had prepared for this scenario, but now that it was here, the gravity of the situation felt overwhelming. The UK had faced terror attacks before, but this felt different. This was the opening shot in what could become an all-out insurgency.

"Mobilize the army," Cartwright ordered, her voice steady despite the panic rising in her chest. "Secure London, and get a message out to the public. We're declaring a state of emergency."

Thompson nodded and began issuing orders to his team. Jenson moved quickly to organize the military response.

As the room buzzed with activity, Cartwright stood motionless for a moment, staring at the black flag on the screen. This wasn't just a domestic crisis anymore. The war that had torn apart Syria, Iraq, and Afghanistan had come to the heart of the United Kingdom.

She took a deep breath and straightened her posture. There was no turning back now. The country was on the brink, and only decisive action could pull it back. But in her heart, she feared it was already too late.

A Nation in Flames

In the days that followed, London became a battleground. The government's swift response—deploying military forces to the streets—was met with immediate resistance. Clashes between the army and militant groups erupted across the city. Buildings burned, and entire neighbourhoods were locked down. The flag of the Islamic State was seen in other cities too—Birmingham, Manchester, and even as far north as Glasgow.

At the same time, far-right nationalist groups seized on the chaos, calling for an armed uprising to "defend the nation" from what they saw as an Islamic invasion. Vigilante attacks on mosques and migrant communities spiked overnight. The army, now stretched thin, struggled to maintain control as violence spread from the cities to rural areas.

The rest of Europe watched in horror as the United Kingdom descended into civil strife. Germany, France, and other nations facing similar tensions braced themselves, knowing that the flames of conflict could easily spread across borders.

For Prime Minister Eleanor Cartwright, the next few weeks would test her leadership in ways she had never imagined. The fate of the country—perhaps even the future of Europe—hung in the balance.

And as the fires raged, the world could only watch as the United Kingdom, once a beacon of stability, faced the most dangerous chapter in its history.

Chapter 67: The Breaking Point

March 2030 – Paris, France

The grey skies over Paris seemed to mirror the dark mood that had enveloped the city. What was once a bustling metropolis full of life and culture had become a place of barricades, burning cars, and shattered storefronts. Every night, the sounds of sirens and distant explosions filled the air, a testament to the violence that had gripped not only Paris but all of France.

President Louis Durand stood at the window of his office in the Élysée Palace, staring out at the empty streets below. Military checkpoints had been set up around the perimeter of the palace, with armed guards patrolling the grounds. It was a far cry from the days when tourists and locals alike would gather in front of the gates, taking photos and enjoying the atmosphere of one of the world's most iconic cities.

"Mr. President," a voice came from behind him, breaking the silence.

Durand turned to see Jean-Luc Bernier, his Minister of the Interior, standing in the doorway, looking grim. "It's getting worse," Bernier said, stepping inside. "The radicals have taken control of three more districts. Police forces are being overwhelmed. We're running out of time."

Durand nodded, but his expression remained impassive. "And the far-right?" he asked, knowing the answer already.

"They've begun patrolling the streets openly, particularly in Marseille, Toulouse, and Lyon," Bernier said. "They're calling themselves defenders of France. In reality, they're little more than vigilantes."

Durand clenched his jaw. He had spent his entire political career fighting for unity, for a France where everyone—regardless of race, religion, or background—could live together in harmony. Now, it seemed like that dream was crumbling before his eyes. The country was fracturing into pieces, each group retreating into its own camp, arming itself for the fight they all knew was coming.

"And what do you suggest we do, Jean-Luc?" Durand asked quietly. "Send in more troops? Declare martial law? It's already a war out there."

Bernier hesitated before answering. "We need to stop this before it escalates further. If we don't take decisive action now, the entire country will descend into chaos. We need to authorize the military to take control of the situation."

Durand shook his head. "The military won't fix this. They'll only make it worse. Look at London. Look at Berlin. Sending in the military didn't bring peace; it brought more violence. We need a different approach."

"What approach?" Bernier asked, frustration creeping into his voice. "Negotiation? Dialogue? These people don't want to talk, Mr. President. They want to win."

Durand walked over to his desk, his fingers tracing the edge of the wood as he thought. He knew Bernier was right in some ways. The radicals on both sides had become entrenched in their positions. The far-right nationalists, fuelled by hatred and fear of the migrants, had become more emboldened. And the disenfranchised Muslim youth, angered by years of systemic neglect and discrimination, were fighting back with equal ferocity.

But there had to be another way. Durand refused to believe that France—a country with a long history of resilience—could not find a path toward peace.

"Jean-Luc," Durand said slowly, turning to face his minister, "I want to try something different."

Bernier raised an eyebrow. "Different how?"

"We need to bring both sides to the table," Durand said. "I want to initiate a ceasefire, a real one. We need to start negotiations with representatives from both the nationalist groups and the Muslim leaders. There has to be some common ground."

"Negotiations?" Bernier repeated, his disbelief palpable. "With the people who are bombing our cities and shooting civilians? They'll never agree to it."

"They might," Durand countered, his voice hardening. "If we give them a reason to."

Bernier's expression shifted from disbelief to outright concern. "Mr. President, you're risking everything by even suggesting this. The nationalists will see it as weakness. The Muslim radicals won't care—they'll keep fighting. You'll be blamed for not taking action."

Durand knew Bernier was speaking from a place of genuine concern, but he couldn't shake the feeling that there was no other option. The violence had reached a tipping point, and if they didn't find a way to de-escalate, France would be lost.

"We have to try," Durand said softly. "If we don't, this country will burn."

The Shadow of Conflict

That night, Durand convened a special meeting of his inner circle. They debated the pros and cons of attempting to broker a ceasefire, with most of his advisors echoing Bernier's concerns. But Durand was resolute. He believed that if they could get both sides to agree to stop the violence, even temporarily, it would give them the breathing room they needed to find a more permanent solution.

The next morning, discreet messages were sent to both the far-right nationalist groups and the Muslim community leaders, proposing a ceasefire and inviting them to begin talks. It was a gamble, and Durand knew it. There was every chance that one—or both—sides would reject the offer outright.

Days passed with no response. The violence in the streets continued to escalate, and the media had begun openly speculating about how long Durand could hold on to power. His approval ratings, already low, had plummeted further as the public became increasingly frustrated with the government's inability to restore order.

Then, just as Durand was beginning to lose hope, a breakthrough came.

The leaders of both the nationalist movement and the Muslim community had agreed—reluctantly—to send representatives to a secret meeting. It wasn't much, but it was a start.

The Ceasefire Summit

The summit took place in a secluded estate outside Paris, far from the chaos of the capital. The security was tight, with armed guards patrolling the perimeter. Inside, the atmosphere was tense as the two sides sat across from each other at a long table, their faces filled with distrust and animosity.

On one side was Charles Lefevre, a charismatic and dangerous leader of the far-right Génération Identitaire. He was well-dressed and spoke with a confidence that belied his extremist views. Opposite him was Amine Khalil, a prominent figure in the Muslim community, known for his fiery speeches and his ability to galvanize disillusioned youth.

Durand sat at the head of the table, flanked by a few trusted advisors. His eyes moved from Lefevre to Khalil, gauging their reactions as he spoke.

"Thank you all for coming," Durand began. "I know this isn't easy. But we are at a crossroads. The violence in our cities is tearing this country apart, and if we don't act now, we may lose everything. I'm not here to place blame or to take sides. I'm here because I believe that there's still a way to pull this country back from the brink. But we need your help."

Lefevre was the first to speak, his voice cold and measured. "Help? Mr. President, with all due respect, we've been trying to help. We've been trying to protect France from the influx of migrants who refuse to assimilate, who bring with them violence and extremism."

Khalil's eyes narrowed. "Protecting France? By attacking our communities, burning our mosques, and harassing our families? That's not protection. That's terrorism."

Lefevre's jaw tightened. "We're defending ourselves. If your people weren't so quick to riot and burn every time something didn't go their way, we wouldn't have to."

Durand raised his hands, cutting off the exchange before it could spiral further. "This is exactly why we're here," he said firmly. "We need to stop the violence, on both sides. That's why I'm proposing a ceasefire. No more attacks, no more protests. We need time to work out a solution."

Lefevre scoffed. "And what solution would that be? Allowing them to take over our cities? To impose their Sharia law on the rest of us?"

Khalil shook his head, his voice low and controlled. "No one is trying to take over your cities. We want to live in peace, just like you. But we won't sit by while our communities are attacked and marginalized."

Durand could feel the tension in the room rising, but he pressed on. "We're not going to solve everything today. But we need to start somewhere. I'm asking you both to agree to a temporary ceasefire, to give us the space we need to negotiate."

The room fell silent, the weight of Durand's request hanging in the air. Both Lefevre and Khalil exchanged glances, their expressions unreadable.

Finally, Lefevre spoke. "A ceasefire? Fine. But make no mistake, Mr. President—this isn't over. We won't sit idly by while our country is destroyed."

Khalil nodded slowly. "We'll agree to a ceasefire. But know this: if our people continue to be targeted, we will defend ourselves."

Durand exhaled, feeling the tension ease just slightly. It was a fragile agreement, but it was a start. Whether it would be enough to save France remained to be seen.

The Calm Before the Storm

The ceasefire held for a few days, and for a brief moment, it seemed like the violence might actually subside. But beneath the surface, the hatred and mistrust were still there, festering, waiting for the right spark to ignite the flames once more.

S

Epilogue: A New Dawn or a Dark Horizon?
December 2035 – Brussels, Belgium

The cold wind whipped through the narrow streets of Brussels as dawn began to break over the European capital. The once-bustling square in front of the European Parliament stood eerily quiet, a sharp contrast to the scene that had unfolded here just a few months earlier. The glass windows of the towering building bore the scars of what had been the most violent protests in European history. Fires had raged through the city, and gunfire had echoed in the distance as the very foundations of the European Union were shaken to their core.

Mina Amara, now the first Muslim representative to sit on the EU Council, stood before the charred remains of the parliament building, her breath visible in the cold morning air. She had seen the rise and fall of so many political ideals, the clash of cultures, and the devastating aftermath of Europe's fractured unity. She had witnessed a continent that had once prided itself on its openness and tolerance descend into fear and division. And now, in the fragile calm that followed the storm, she wondered what would come next.

Her rise to power had been meteoric, propelled by the chaos and the demands of a growing Muslim constituency that sought representation and a voice in shaping the future of Europe. But her position was precarious, a symbol of hope to some and a target of resentment to others. She carried the weight of a generation's hopes and fears on her shoulders.

As she walked toward the makeshift memorials that had been set up by the families of those lost in the violence, Mina thought back to the early years—those days when the migrant crisis had first begun. Back then, no one had truly understood the full implications of the mass migrations from Africa and the Middle East. It had been seen as a humanitarian issue, a temporary problem that would be resolved with time and resources.

But time had only deepened the divisions.

The promises of integration had given way to disillusionment as both migrants and locals grew increasingly frustrated. Governments struggled to manage the influx, while extremist ideologies on both sides began to take hold. And in the end, it wasn't the people who had failed—it was the system. The dream of a united Europe, open and free, had been shattered by the weight of its own contradictions.

Now, as Mina stood in the center of that broken dream, she wondered whether it could ever be rebuilt.

The ceasefire in France had held, but only for a time. In the years that followed, the violence had spread across Europe, reaching into Germany, Italy, Spain, and even the UK. The tensions between Christian and Muslim communities had escalated into full-blown religious conflict, drawing comparisons to the wars that had torn apart the Balkans in the 1990s. Martial law had been declared in several cities, but it did little to quell the unrest.

In the end, it was the collapse of the European Union itself that marked the true turning point.

The Fall of the Union

In 2033, after years of internal strife and political gridlock, several member states had begun to break away from the EU. Nationalist leaders, emboldened by the chaos and the growing resentment toward Brussels, had called for referendums to leave the union. France was the first to go, followed quickly by Italy and Poland. With each departure, the EU's grip on the continent weakened, and by the end of 2034, the European Union as it had once been known was no more.

In its place was a fractured continent, divided not only by borders but by ideology and identity. The rise of the Muslim population across Europe had reshaped the political landscape, and with it came new alliances and power dynamics. In some countries, Muslim-majority areas had formed their own political movements, demanding greater autonomy and recognition of their rights. In others, far-right nationalist groups had seized control, declaring their nations Christian states and vowing to defend their heritage at all costs.

The balance of power had shifted, and Europe was now a patchwork of competing interests, each fighting for survival in an uncertain future.

A Fragile Peace

Mina's footsteps echoed in the empty square as she approached a group of children playing near the edge of the plaza. They were of different backgrounds—some with dark hair and olive skin, others fair with blue eyes—but they played together without a care in the world. It was a small reminder of the potential for unity, even in the most divided of times.

As she watched them, a figure approached her from the shadows. It was Omar, one of her closest advisors and a key figure in the Muslim political movement that had gained momentum across Europe in recent years. He wore a long coat, his hands tucked into his pockets as he stepped into the light.

"You're up early," he said, his voice low but warm.

"I couldn't sleep," Mina replied, her eyes still on the children. "I keep thinking about everything that's happened. Everything we've lost."

Omar nodded, his expression grave. "We've lost much, yes. But we've also gained something. We have a voice now. We have power."

"Power," Mina repeated, the word heavy on her tongue. "But at what cost? Europe is in ruins, Omar. We're standing on the ashes of what was once the greatest union in history."

He looked at her, his eyes searching hers. "What do you want, Mina? Do you want to turn back the clock? Go back to a time when we were ignored, marginalized, and oppressed? We fought for this. We earned it."

Mina sighed, turning away from the children. "I don't want to go back. But I don't want to move forward in a world like this either. We fought for equality, for recognition, but all we've done is replace one form of division with another. We're no closer to peace."

Omar's voice softened. "Peace doesn't come easily. We're in a new world now. A world where we get to decide what comes next. The old Europe is gone. We can build something better."

Mina looked at him, her heart heavy with the weight of responsibility. She had fought for this moment, had believed in the cause, but now, standing in the ruins of what once was, she wondered if they had truly won. The Europe they had inherited was not the one she had dreamed of. It was broken, divided, and scarred by years of conflict.

But it was also a blank slate.

Perhaps, as Omar had said, they had the chance to build something new. Something better. A Europe where all people, regardless of their religion, race, or background, could live together in peace. It was a lofty dream, and after everything she had seen, she wasn't sure if it was even possible.

But she had to try.

As the sun rose higher in the sky, casting a pale light over the city, Mina turned to Omar with a sense of resolve. "Let's start again," she said quietly. "Let's build a Europe that can finally live up to its promise."

Omar smiled faintly. "It won't be easy."

"I know," she replied. "But it's the only way forward."

Together, they stood in the shadow of the old world, ready to forge a new path. The future of Europe was uncertain, but it was theirs to shape. And perhaps, in time, they could find a way to heal the wounds of the past and create a new dawn for the continent they both loved.

The road ahead would be long and fraught with challenges, but for the first time in years, Mina felt a glimmer of hope.

And that was enough

Don't miss out!

Visit the website below and you can sign up to receive emails whenever Bryson Mine publishes a new book. There's no charge and no obligation.

https://books2read.com/r/B-A-DTOPC-MJHDF

BOOKS 2 READ

Connecting independent readers to independent writers.